CLutcH

I Am Just Junco
BOOK ONE

By J. A. Huss

CLutcH

I Am Just Junco
BOOK ONE
By J. A. Huss
Find me at
New Adult Addiction
Jahuss.com

Edited by RJ Locksley
Cover design by J. A. Huss

ISBN-13: 978-1-936413-49-2

Books by J.A. Huss
Clutch
Fledge
Flight
Range
The Magpie Bridge
Return
TRAGIC
MANIC
PANIC
SLACK
TAUT
BOMB
GUNS
COME
COME BACK

DEDICATION

To all the nerdy, geeky people who love this SF shit
as much as I do.

Chapter One

Picture yourself standing on the edge of a dock...
I shake my head.
Fuck that.
I'm standing on a dirt road barefoot, exhaust from the Goat swirling dust up my funeral dress, trying to make some sense of things.

The closed stop-gate in front of me signals the entrance to the Stag, but the antlered skull in the middle of the arm spawns a moment of pause. My eyes linger on the decorations only long enough to log them. Blood-red paint on the antlers, an old wooden arrow sticking out of one of the orbits, and a crown of acacia thorns draped around the tines.

A child's prank.

The cigar slips between my lips. I cup my hand to block the wind, touch the cigar to the striker, and suck in deeply as the end glows bright orange. They stink and they make me stink, but I don't care.

Today, I don't care about much.

I slam the Goat's door and walk towards the skull, then hear the tell-tale crack of a sonic boom and turn to squint at the sun as it loses its battle with the rotating earth. Peak City has been out of my sight line for hours but I know where it should be on the horizon. I find the contrail of a suborbital coming out of the north pointing back to my home.

Turning back to the gate, I watch as the wind picks up

the strip of wood hovering across the sorry excuse for a road and makes it dance. A stray magpie lands and rides the skull with a rhythm that reminds me of better days. It watches me, tilts its head to the side, and squawks, "Away!"

I flick the cigar and chase the magpie away.

There is nothing here to stop my progress into the Stag but since this is a forbidden zone in the Rural Republic, I pause before taking this final step into disobedience. Consequences tend to mean less with the loss of precious things, so they mean nothing to me now.

Reaching up, I release my long auburn hair from the tie and let it flap around my face as the wind tries to carry it across the grasslands.

If only the wind would carry me across the grasslands.

My cold toes scrunch into the dirt and I remember my funeral shoes are in the backseat, discarded hours ago. I walk over to the Goat and fish around until I pull together a pair of field boots and some black thermals. I hike the warm leggings up to my hips and then sit on the edge of my old Humvee and meticulously lace up each boot so they are snug, but not tight.

A sheathed hunting knife is in danger of dropping through the rusted-out floorboard and I rescue it, stashing it inside the boot. Then I slide my shotgun onto the front seat and drop my little pistol into the crap box along with other items one usually finds in a vehicle. The lid drops closed with a snap.

In the end I didn't need to waste all this time in front of the gate. It was never a question of if I would go. Only when. I climb back into the front seat, jam the Goat in gear and veer off the road, pressing up against the low-hanging branches of cottonwoods that have crept up from the dry riverbed. I brace myself as my vehicle bounces down into the ditch and then jolts back up. I gun it as the tires lose a little traction in the rain-softened earth, swing her around the ominous gate, and surge back onto the dirt track that still thinks it is a road.

On the other side I stop once more to check for Peak City in the distance, but all I see is the magpie, back on the skull, riding it out. I flip it off and gun the Goat again. We lurch forward, sputtering out a cloud of smoke that could get you hanged in some parts of the world.

But not here.

The Rural Republic might officially be part of the United Republics, but that's pretty much where it ends. Our national motto is quaint. *Simple Serves.* A reference to the throwback life we are supposed to be leading. But if you're not from around here and need help, (which is strictly theoretical, we're a closed campus, kids) the answer you get is disinterest. If you're lucky.

The drive out to Stag Camp is a stretch of open road, peppered with the occasional falling-down farmhouse or small herd of antelope. So I settle in, light another cigar, and slide the window down even though the warm November afternoon has given in to the cold November evening.

Nothing to do now but think about the job. My eyes track to the passenger seat, past the shotgun, and come to rest upon the thick envelope pressed into my hands as I left the funeral several hours ago. The label on the front is machine-printed, but it doesn't say Junco. It says Dale. Resident of one Stag Camp in the middle of nowhere.

I push the funeral from my thoughts and allow the dying light to seep out of my world a little at a time. The eye-shine peering back at me from the side of the road as I take a wide turn clues me in that twilight is gone. The two glowing dots are far enough apart to estimate size and my body gives up an involuntary shiver as I run down the short list. Nightdog or prairie lion. Either one would eat me alive.

If they could catch me.

The sky is filled with stars long before I spy the dark shadow of the landmark hill in the distance. It's a slow climb that turns into a nightmare halfway up, then a flat patch to gather some steam so you can push your vehicle to its limit and struggle up the final grade that will plunge you over the other side.

I watch the approaching ridge with some trepidation. Once over it, I'll be more in than out. A sigh escapes my lips and I push the Goat until her body shakes, getting ready for the ascent.

We hit the hill going about 110, but the steep initial grade checks us and we lose speed quick. I downshift, then again, and by the time the grade evens back out for several hundred feet we are barely skimming 60. I gun it so we can gain some momentum to get over the hump and catch a little air as we clear the summit.

The buck in the road never has a chance. The Goat slams into the animal midair and the tendons and bones snap loudly in the cold night. The lower half of the deer slips under the tires, creating a slick mess of tissue and blood on the road. The head flies straight at my face and the bloodied antlers crash into the glass.

I slam on the brakes and the head loses its hold on the window and flies off out of sight. I hit a patch of greasy mud left over from the last rain and slide sideways, towards the edge of what may be a cliff, or just a gently rolling embankment.

I quickly correct, not waiting to find out, only to discover I'm now sliding backwards. I swing the wheel around, body parts flipping out from under the tires, and hit the brakes again. The Goat and I slip sideways into the ditch and I use the bounce to straighten out the wheels. When she comes down hard we're moving forward into a sparse grove of pines.

I force my foot down on the brake one more time, sliding sideways in the softened mud, and barely manage to aim between two old-growth Ponderosas as the lower branches slap against the doors.

I steer as best I can, but when you're racing a five-thousand-pound vehicle through a small forest, you tend to run out of luck sooner rather than later. A deep ditch of water erosion plunges the Goat down, but she recovers and jerks back up. My head hits the steering wheel and I feel the blood slip down my face, then taste iron as it trickles into my mouth. The Goat's front tires find another ditch and I lurch forward, cracking my head on what's left of the driver's side windshield. Finally we slam into the thick twisted trunk of a cottonwood. I have a second or two to moan, and then it all goes black.

Picture yourself standing on the edge of a dock. In front of you is a mountain lake...

The blood seeps into my mouth and I cough, then spit out a coagulated hunk of something before opening my eyes.

Shit.

I listen for noises around me and panic sets in when I hear the sharp snap of a dry tree branch off to my right. My head rolls towards the noise, not quite controlled, and I wait a few more moments to let things clear up a bit. The pain in my shoulder is like fire and the blood is hot as it trickles down the side of my head.

In front of me is a stream, not a goddamn mountain lake.

Wait.

I shake my head.

A small stream of water has materialized in the river bed from the last rain and the sound of it makes my mouth dry up immediately. I move my head slightly, allowing a moan to escape, and let my right hand reach out for the water bottle on the seat.

Of course, it's not there.

I twist my body a little so I can make a more earnest search of the cab, then grab the steering wheel with my left hand to stabilize my movement.

"Fucking shit!"

That hurts.

The pain is pulled up into every synaptic center of my brain. The resulting vertigo almost makes me heave as a thousand birds take flight from the trees and the wingbeats flare up in my ears.

And then the whispers start.

The dark whisper of a flock of starlings too long in the company of men. There is nothing more creepy than human words coming out of a starling beak and the contents of my stomach experience another moment of protest until I can push them down.

I reach into the crap box with my right hand and pull out the pistol, aiming it through the broken glass of the window in front of me. The shot rings out and the recoil travels through my body like a standing wave. When it reaches my left shoulder I cry out. This time the starlings stay silent.

More tree branch snapping hauls me back to my current situation and my eyes dart around, alert for movement. I take a deep breath and let it out slowly, but that does nothing to stop whatever is moving out in the trees.

I shoot another round off and do a better job at damping down the recoil. This time I see a shadow of a great owl fly off in the distance. It must have been hunting in the trees.

I sit there for a little longer and then swing my legs across the gear stick, scoot over to the passenger side door and release the handle. Pure determination allows me to coerce my legs into standing and then I seize my water bottle off the floor and down it in large gulps.

A thorough shuffling through dirty field clothes leads to a belt. I position it across my body and slip my arm into the loop of leather to take the weight off my injury, then sling the shotgun over my good shoulder and grab my pack to begin my walk back up the hill to the road. Looking and listening for any sign of apex predators.

The road looks like it usually does when a large deer gets mowed over by a military vehicle, so I don't dwell on it and instead walk back up to the top of the hill and try to see if there are any lights in the distance.

The Rural Republic is a chancy place to be stranded on any given day, but being alone in the Stag is exceptionally bad luck. There are no vehicles on the road, nor will there be. No one knows where I am, so no one will come looking.

I look east and see nothing but grasslands and scrub. I look west and see the same shit. That pretty much sums up the extent of what's available in terms of assistance. It makes no difference which way I go, the stop-gate back in Council 5 and the Stag Camp proper are about equal distance from the spot where I stand. I will have to winch the Goat up and out of that ravine before any other decisions can be made.

The night isn't as black as it could be and for that I'm grateful. The moon has fully risen in the time it took me to free myself from the Goat and hitch up my arm, and while it isn't anything near full, neither is it a sliver of hopelessness. Walking outside of the boundaries of the road leads me to an almost flat patch of shortgrass. I find the Big Dipper and then Cassiopeia to ease the creeping feeling of aloneness, and lower myself down on the ground, resting my throbbing head back into the palm of my hand for just a few moments.

The sounds of nature come back.

And with them are the dark whispers of starlings. They haunt me as I drift off to sleep.

Picture yourself standing on the edge of a dock. In front of you is a mountain lake and behind you is a small cabin, pristine white curtains flowing in the breeze passing through the windows. Down below the water you can see the scales of brightly colored fish reflecting the sunlight...

... and then you are in a church, looking down on a meeting.

No, wait, that's not how it goes.

I'm a piece of stained glass high up in the window. I look down at my body and see that I'm naked, but that's not the disturbing thing. Instead of feet I have long raptor talons that host a variety of knives instead of claws. From my mouth come the whispers of the starlings and the gurgling in my throat causes me to scream and break free of the glass. It shatters down to the floor where people argue. The shards of blood-colored glass kill them as they slice through their backs and then I am flying high up in the air, looking down on the Stag. I know it's the Stag because of the tall perimeter wall and the guardhouse at the gate. I land near the guardhouse, still outside the camp, and my father exits in full uniform and puts his hand up to stop me. I need to get in, Daddy, I say—even though I haven't called him Daddy since my mother disappeared when I was six. He opens his mouth and starlings fly out, screaming their whispers in my ears, and then they attack me with their long thin beaks and their wings beat against my body. I fly away, circling the Stag Camp, and then I dive down, spiraling into the gushing wind. The camp explodes and I am thrown up into the sky as a constellation where Orion hunts me like the bull for time everlasting.

And then I am warm and the starlings are gone, but the whispers are still there, making me feel safe. They are soft now, not deep and evil, but soft. And I listen to them and I say OK.

Chapter Two

The warmth of the dream fades and I wake shivering as the sweat drips off my body. A movement catches my eye across the expanse of wild grass and I sit upright in an instant, ignoring the fire in my shoulder. I have the shotgun out, propped in the dent where my hip meets my stomach, and I brace my arm on my thigh as I level the barrel on the shadow in the distance as best I can. My finger slips onto the trigger and squeezes lightly as I prepare for the shot.

It's not a prairie lion because I can see the outstretched wings back-lit by starlight as it skulks across the field. And it's obviously not an owl because it's walking on two legs.

"I wouldn't do that if I were you," it says.

I squeeze the trigger and the recoil slams me into the ground, screaming in pain.

I'm back in the blur of agony once again and fuck is coming out of my mouth at regular intervals. The black shadow stands over me now, the dark wings fully outstretched and imposing.

"I told ya not to do that."

It's a male voice.

I pull away wincing, trying to sink down into the ground to avoid him as he leans into my personal space.

"That's really going to hurt now. You humans. It's always shoot first, ask questions later."

I find my voice and snort at him. "At least a human would know better than to sneak up on a girl stranded in the middle of nowhere with a shotgun."

The avian's hypnotic green eyes brighten as he smiles at me. "Ya have a point there, darlin'."

We have a semi-serious staring contest for a few seconds and then he reaches out to me. "Ya need a hand?"

I look him up and down from my unfortunate submissive situation. His wings are a lot more imposing than I figure they should be. I've seen images of avians here and there over the years, but not enough to be any kind of expert on them.

Sighing, I consider my options as he waits. I can either roll around on my knees and try to get up—or I can get up with some dignity left intact. I shrug and extend my good arm up to him. "Sure."

He takes it and I brace for the explosion of agony that will surely come from my shoulder, but he pulls me to my feet in a smooth, gentle manner. I manage to end upright with only a few squeaks of pain escaping my lips.

"That was unlucky, eh?"

"Unlucky? I almost shot you. I figure that's pretty fucking lucky myself."

"The accident, friend. An unlucky thing to hit that animal."

I grab my gun and ignore him as I hitch my pack up on my hip and shuffle through to check my ammo supply.

"Missing something?"

I give him a long once-over and he waits patiently for me to finish. "You do realize you're trespassing, right? *Aliens are not permitted in the RR under any circumstances.*"

"You'd be surprised," he says.

I swing the shotgun on the strap so it's out in front of me, brace it on my thigh to compensate for my injured shoulder, cycle the next round into the chamber, and then point it straight at his chest. I strain to prevent the wince that really wants to spread across my face. "Look, I don't know who you are, or why you're here, but as a Farm Family Representative of Council 3, I'm asking you to leave under Regulation V.1.b—*Aliens are not permitted in the Rural Republic under any circumstances.* I have the authority to shoot and if you doubt me, I apologize ahead of time for taking your life. You are hereby legally warned."

"Look, sweetheart—"

I squeeze back and the round blasts out of the chamber but he's high above me in the air as the shot passes into the trees. The leaves rustle and the birds are wild once again. The recoil pain isn't as bad from the standing position, but I feel the blood leaking out under the skin on my hip, creating a bruise. I push the pain down. "I've been shooting since I could walk, sweetheart, and I've had a really shitty day. Do not fuck with me."

He flies off over the trees about a dozen yards away and I can just barely make him out as he lands in the cover of the brush.

"Is that how ya treat someone who saves yer life? Shoot them?"

I snort. "Saved my life? I must have missed that one while I was sleeping."

"Except ya weren't sleeping, Junco. You were unconscious."

It isn't often that I get stunned into silence, but an alien knowing my name in the middle of nowhere can do it. "How the hell do you know my name?"

Silence from him now.

The glimmer of light that was previously there is gone, and so is he.

I take stock of the mountaintop meadow. *Where are*

you, where are you?

Silence.

I pivot on my heel, gun braced one-armed against my stomach to catch the recoil, and do a proper survey of the area. My good arm is tiring quick after all the adrenaline I've used up and it begins to shake. I force the bravado. "Guess you decided to take my—"

Then he is behind me, the gun is flying across the field, and he's twisted my bad shoulder just enough to make me scream out. His lips touch my cheek as he whispers, "Look, I'm not usually the type of person who abuses little girls, but you've shot at me two times now and I'm not going to stand for it. I'm here for the moment and yer just gonna to have to deal with it. Ya got it?"

He eases up on my shoulder and pushes me away from him.

I rub the flaming tissue and wince. "Did you just insult me?"

He tilts his head at me. "What? Me? Ya tried ta shoot me—twice!"

"I might be little, but the way you said it implied I'm insignificant. Which I assure you, I am not. And besides, you're the one who's trespassing, right? That's you." I point my finger up at him. "I have every right to tell you to leave, I'm a fucking representative of Council—"

"3, yeah, I heard ya the first time. Who gives a shit? I'm here. Get over it."

I stare at him in the dim moonlight and quite frankly, I don't care for what I see. "You're so fucking lucky I'm injured."

"Or what?"

"Why are you here?"

"Why are *you* here?"

"Oh my fucking God, are we in playschool or what?"

"I know where you were going."

I laugh. "The road only goes one place, alien. That's not a hard deduction."

"I know what you were gonna do, as well."

That's it, I'm done. I begin walking down the hill.

"Oi! Where're ya going?" he calls.

I ignore him as he trots a little to catch up. He keeps his distance to a few paces behind as I make my way to the road and then begin the descent down the slope back to the Goat. When I finally reach it I wiggle into the back seat of the cab and lie down, trying to even out my breathing before he gets there. My eyes close as I hear him climb into the front passenger seat.

"What are you doing?" he asks.

"I'm sleeping. Get the fuck out of my Goat." My good arm slides under the seat and I allow my finger to caress the high-powered rifle tucked away for emergencies. I can't shoot it, my shoulder would never tolerate that, but it gives me comfort to know it's there.

He doesn't get out. Instead he talks.

"I saw yer headlights coming in the darkness. I didn't think much about it really, but the accident had me concerned. Ya hit yer head pretty hard, there."

Yeah, thanks for the update.

"I'm sorry for twisting yer shoulder, OK?"

My anger leaves me as I listen to his hypnotic words. I struggle to keep my eyes closed but an overwhelming force urges me to look him in the face.

"Junco, I did save your life. Ya had a bad concussion. It was a mistake to fall asleep. I was just tryin' ta help when I brought ya out of it."

This revelation jolts me out of my trance and I fight to shake off my weariness to get this story straight. "Wait," I say as I painfully push my body back up into a half-sitting position. "What? You were touching me when I was sleeping?"

He squirms a little at my tone. "No, look, it wasn't like that. You weren't sleeping, you were unconscious—I just—wrapped ya in my wings so I could bring ya back up."

"You were touching me." It's a statement this time, not a question. "In my sleep."

"Look, I saved your life, for Christ's sake!"

"How dare you swear at me! Don't you realize—"

"I'm sorry, you're right." he looks away and blows out a breath. "I shouldn't have said that. I forgot you are a pious bunch out here."

"Get out!" I snarl. I feel the blood rush to my face and the adrenaline flood my muscles as I watch him extract himself from my vehicle, stopping only to release one of his wings from the floppy seat belt as he exits the Goat.

I let myself smile after he leaves. That pious bullshit works every time on strangers. And he even heard me cussing like a soldier up on the hill. But I'm glad he's gone. I don't remember reading anything about avians having glowing green eyes before. Creepy.

When I wake my crusted-closed eyelids are the least of my worries. I struggle to force them open once I realize the sun is up. My muscles have been welded into my current sleeping orientation and no matter how hard I fight against it, they reward me with an intense shooting pain in my left shoulder with the slightest of movements.

A delicious smell meanders into the cab from outside so I force a shift in position until I can prop myself up without contorting my face into a disfigured expression. I ease my head up just enough to peer out the window and see the avian poking a stick at a roasting bird over a small campfire.

He looks up at me and smiles.

Dammit. So much for stealth. I should be ashamed of myself.

"Hungry now?" His accent is something different than mine, but I can't place it. "Still not talking, eh? Well, I made breakfast," he points to the smoking fowl, "so that should buy me some goodwill."

I wrestle around frantically for a second, trying to find an extraction route that won't cause me to scream, but I can't see it.

"So, how long do ya *young ladies* typically pout out here in the wilds, then?" he calls. "Can ya give me an estimate?"

I struggle again, pulling on the seat belt that hangs limply behind the driver's seat to get some leverage, but the aging bracket attaching it to the headliner snaps off from my weight and I give up and lie back with a sigh.

He appears at the broken window on the passenger side. "I can't believe you slept back there in that tiny space." He laughs at me, and I have to admit, he's got a nice look to him, plus his green eyes are bright in the sunlight and they are no longer glowing, so the creep factor has been dialed down a bit.

His large black wings are tucked tight against his back and the tips cup over the top of his shoulders, so I can't see much of them. A few loose arcs of dark hair tumble off his forehead and fall around his eyes. He's wearing some kind of foreign get-up that might be the alien equivalent of black jeans and t-shirt, but they are cut to his specific body modifications and made out of some kind of heavy canvas. It has the look of light armor, something we might wear for war games. His skin is light, but not fair. Like fall has stolen most of the golden tan of summer away.

"That's nice. Short jokes. Very funny." My voice sounds as cranky as I feel.

He lets off a little laugh. "Need some help out?"

I scowl and try to think up another way. But I can't. "Yeah, sure. Just come around here to the other side of the Goat and get in so you can push me up a little." Then I add, "Please."

He smiles at my manners, which make his eyes twinkle a little. Not glow, but still. The creepiness is just under the surface.

The old door creaks as he opens it and I try to turn and look at him but the shoulder flares up at my attempt. I feel his hands reach under me to my good arm and I struggle not to laugh, but it bursts out anyway. I wriggle away from his touch before he pulls back in hesitation.

"Now, what the hell was that?"

"I'm ticklish, so kill me. You can't just slip your hands into someone's pits and not expect them to laugh."

"Can I push you up or not?"

"Yes, push. Just don't stick me in my pits."

He does push and I flail around like a turtle on its back for a few embarrassing seconds, then find myself upright and looking out the window facing the campfire. It smells wonderful.

"Whew, that's better," I say as I turn my whole body so I can see him properly. "Thanks, I really appreciate it." I even manage a smile, which in turn allows him to offer me one back.

"Would you like some help with that shoulder before ya eat?"

"What's that mean?" I ask, looking at him sideways.

"The wings, darlin'," he says, pointing a thumb towards his shoulders, "they heal, remember?"

Of course I remember but I'm not even remotely interested in letting him get a hold of me again, so I lie instead. "No, I'm fine. Really." And just to prove it I scoot over to the door and flip the handle with my good hand, then smile back at him as I push it open.

His hand goes to my good shoulder and stops me before I can make my hasty exit. "Relax, Junco. I can fix it. We aren't going to get far with ya like that, anyway."

"I don't know what you mean by we, but in case you haven't noticed my legs are just fine."

"Yeah, I see that. But we won't be walking out of here. That would take days."

I laugh a little and send him a crooked smile. "The Goat has a winch, so don't you worry about me."

"Sorry, darlin', you won't be winching anything if you don't let me take care of that shoulder."

My lips involuntarily form a snarl and my eyes narrow in anger. "What's with this darling bullshit? Stop calling me that."

He just smiles. "Fine, Junco. Come here, I'll fix the shoulder. Think of it as a gift."

"No." I move to get past him but his eyes catch mine and begin to glow. I'm drawn in and I can't stop looking at him.

"I said come here, Junco."

In my mind I say no. But my body is already wrapped up in his wings and my head begins to spin. I can hear him whisper in my ear, and his breath dances across my cheek.

"Does it feel good?" he asks.

"Mmmmhmmmm, yesss," I say, slurring my words a bit. The heat from his body exchanges between us and

19

my shoulder is sucking it up like a vacuum. My thoughts twist around in an incoherent mess as we sit, melded together. He stays that way for several minutes and my mind is carried away with the effects of his body.

Then I am high above looking down on the Stag. I see a few straggling antelope and watch the wind caress the grass as I begin to float away. "Stop, no flying."

In an instant the heat is gone and the avian has twisted me around to see my face. "What did you just say?"

My shoulder doesn't hurt anymore but my head is really fuzzy, like I'm drunk, so I don't even remember what I said.

He shakes me a little to jar my memory. "Junco? What are you talking about?"

I think hard and squint. "Flying? Did I say flying?"

"What about flying?"

"The Stag is burning," I say as I try to open my eyes.

I feel his chest collapse as he exhales. "What?"

"Just a dream," I say, forcing myself to concentrate. "It was just a dream. Didn't make any sense."

We sit there as I recover. He's still got his arms around me, but his wings never return to make their addictive cocoon of healing. I stay still as the world comes back to me a little at a time. Then our closeness gets weird and I push him off. He hops out and comes over to my side of the door to help me out.

"I'm starving. Can I have some of that?" I point over to the browned bird strung up over the coals.

"Help yourself, there's water too."

"Aren't you going to eat?" I ask. But he just walks away and busies himself with his pack.

"More for me then. And hey," I call out, "thanks, I guess. Shoulder really does feel better."

Chapter Three

He's leaning up against a twisted cottonwood trunk on the other side of the now-dead campfire and I'm gulping down the last of the filtered water from the stream just below us on the hill. "You do realize that you're in a lot of trouble for this," I say, pointing to his uneaten portion of grouse on the spit. "Prairie chickens aren't in season and strangers aren't allowed to hunt in the RR. And aliens are totally forbidden." I stick that in to remind him that he's still a trespasser.

He looks up just long enough to insult me with a dirty look and then goes back to his tech device, his black hair dropping down to cover his forehead and hide his eyes. Ever since I told him about my dream he is acting different and it makes me uneasy, so I talk.

A lot.

"You're a good cook though," I continue. "Not many people can pluck all the feathers out of such a small bird." He doesn't even look up this time.

The tech isn't anything I recognize, but that's not saying much since Farm Families aren't supposed to have much tech in their regular life. My father wasn't in any way obsessive or extreme in his adherence to the doctrine, plus we're military and that comes with certain privileges in the tech department, but I only had a few personal tech items as a kid. I wasn't allowed any communication devices and I wasn't allowed to have programmed learning. I had to read books and study the old-fashioned way.

"So, what do you have there? Some sort of phone or computer?" I ask.

He looks over and laughs. "A phone, eh? Earth must've entered the 22nd century while you were out planting corn or something." His head returns to the device in his hand.

"Mmmmhmmm. Yet another insult. That must be your default setting. And for your information we produce horses, not corn."

He looks up and lets out a deep sigh, shaking his head at me slightly, then holds up the thing in his hand to let me see it. "Sorry. It's a tracker."

I look at it intensely until I can make out a small map with some blinking lights. I'm almost afraid to ask but I do anyway. "What's it tracking?"

"Me, maybe? Not sure yet," he replies as he bows his head once more.

I let out a little "Oh," and then get up. "Well, thanks for breakfast and the healing stuff." I try to think of a word to call it so it doesn't sound like I'm being flippant or rude, but I can't find one. "I'm gonna get going now." I gather myself up and walk back over to the Goat where my shotgun is propped up against the mangled front end.

"Oh, and thanks for retrieving my shotgun," I say as I turn around to find him directly behind me, his wings slightly uplifted, like he's on the verge of something. I never even heard him move and the creepiness from last night is back out in full force. "Wow, you're quite quick and silent when you want to be."

"I think we should stick together, Junco. In fact I was thinking I can help get ya back to safety. Ya know, help ya get the Goat back up on the road. Even though yer healed, yer still pretty—" He hesitates.

"I'm pretty?" I ask.

He laughs a little and shakes his head, which pisses me off for some reason. "No, I was going to say pretty weak, ya know. From yesterday's crash. But then I wondered if ya would take that as an insult as well."

I roll my eyes and try to push past him to get the winch hooked up to a tree, but he leans his hands on either side of the Goat, essentially boxing me in. I shoot him a nasty look and he drops his hands to let me through.

"Thanks for all your help," I call back to him, "but I'm going to take it from here. And I won't report you, so don't worry about that. Just get hell out of the RR before anyone else sees you." I turn to see how he's taking the news but he's not there. When I turn back he's in front of me again.

He shakes his head at me.

I shake mine back and raise my eyebrows.

"You'll refuse my help?"

"Look," I huff, "you have those people tracking you and neither of us is supposed to be out here in the first place, so let's just cut our losses and move on. Separately."

He looks down to the tech that is still in his hand. "They can't see anything here. Some sort of shield."

"Right. That's called a defense system. The deeper you go into the Stag, the thicker the shields. So why don't you just fly over to the Mountain Republic where they probably can track you?"

He lifts the device to illustrate his point. "In case ya haven't figured it out yet, these people aren't my ride home."

"So why are they tracking you?"

His eyes twinkle and I know what's coming and push past him at a full run. He's on me before I can take more than half a dozen strides and pulls on my shirt until I slip in the mud and go down hard on my back.

"Stop!" I scream, but instead of stopping he pins my arms down and sits on top of me as I wriggle and kick. His legs twine around mine, essentially cutting off any thoughts of getting him off me that way. Then his eyes are glowing again and his lips are touching my cheek, whispering for me to settle and be calm.

To my surprise, I do settle. I can't help it. I realize too late that the soft words brushing past the sensitive skin on my cheek are controlling me. I can feel the sound waves trickling into my ear canal, making their way to the nerve pathways that control my muscles, and I bring my shoulders up to try and get his face away from me. His lips remain next to my ear and I am just about to fully give in when the tech device, forgotten and left on the ground during our struggle, sounds off an alarm. He loses his concentration and the words stop for half a moment, but that's all I need.

I take my opportunity and flip myself over so that I'm on my belly. This takes him by surprise and for a split-second he is off balance. I flip back around and use my right arm to knock him in the throat as my body turns. He goes reeling off of me and I'm up and running down into the little creek.

A boot goes flying just past my head, but I don't stop and wonder at this weird turn of events. I run as hard as I can, over the opposite bank, out of the small grove of cottonwoods, and into the tall flowing prairie grass. I'm short, so the leftover husks slap me in the face as I run, blurring my vision.

The wings descend and he's swooping down upon me. I look up to see talons where his boots were just a few minutes ago and they latch onto my shoulders, puncturing my skin and making me scream. His grip tightens and I fall. I roll in practiced regulation fashion and pop back up, booking it again without missing a beat.

One second I'm hauling ass towards the open prairie, the next he's on the ground in front of me and we're on a collision path. I plan my move and let him get to within a few strides of me and then I flip into the air and land on the other side of him. He misses a step and I take advantage of it, turn and deliver a hook kick to his jaw. His head snaps to the side and he stumbles over sideways a little.

I run hard for a few seconds and don't look back. Off in the distance I hear the roar of a hovercopter and a few seconds later I feel the effects of the prairie grass wind tunnel it creates from the blades, but still I push my way through the now wildly swaying grass until I come upon the alien again.

His lip is bleeding and his jaw is slightly red from my kick. I stop in my tracks, bent over and panting hard.

He's not even out of breath.

"I'm not the enemy, Junco," he screams above the roar, "and if you know what's good for ya, you'll run like hell because if those guys from the Mountain Republic get you, you'll end up in the same messed-up place as your father."

He flies off, disappearing in the tallgrass before I can even string together a sentence.

But his words stay with me. Dead like my father is not something I want to be so I follow his advice. I run until the MR soldiers blast me with a plasma bolt and I fall to the ground unconscious.

Picture yourself standing on the edge of a dock. In front of you is a mountain lake and behind you is a small cabin, pristine white curtains flowing in the breeze passing through the windows. Down below the water you can see the scales of brightly colored fish reflecting the sunlight and up above in the sky you see the eagles as they soar, free from terrestrial boundaries. The planks on the deck are warm under your feet and you're wearing a long thin white shirt, open in the front, that barely covers your body. The waves lap against the dock and you reach over and drag your fingers through the water. It folds against your wrist and smells like blood...

The blood on my bound wrists has hardened, making them itchy and painful at the same time. I take a deep breath in, wince, then cough as my lungs protest in earnest at the expansion.

"Plasma blast will do that to you." The voice originates a few paces off to my left and I open my eyes to take in the interior of a military plane. I manage to move my head just enough to log a look of concern on Aren's face.

... up above in the sky you see the eagles as they soar, free from terrestrial boundaries...

I mentally shake the image out of my mind and cough before I answer him. "I know"—the cough comes back up as I try to croak out some words, so I start again—"I know that. Asshole."

Aren lets out a prolonged sigh. "What do you want from me, Junco? I had my team set their rifles to stun. They wanted to fucking kill you—and even after I told them how small you were, they still had their rifles dialed up for fully armored tactical. I saved your ass."

I spit out some blood and take a moment to wonder what might be bleeding inside me to cause it, but my mind is blank. I drop it and turn in his general direction, wincing at the throb this simple change in perspective creates in my head. "What are you doing here? You cut and run from the Mountain Republic too? Or is treason something you reserve only for the Rural folks?"

He's bending down a few paces off, to stay eye level with me I guess, but my comment makes him stand. "You're such a fucking bitch, you know that?"

I nod and my coughing takes on a whole new level.

"Will you be rational? Or do I have to keep you bound?"

I don't answer, I just continue to cough, my chest searing in pain with every desperate inhalation of air.

He comes over, slits the bindings with a knife, and pulls me to my feet, then bends me over and whacks me on the back good and hard. Harder then he should, actually.

I take a large gasp of air, wince, and then spit more blood out towards his boots. "Fuck, Aren—mind the damn plasma burn, will ya?"

He stops and leaves me to it, then turns away as I straighten up. "We were sent to get you."

"Bullshit," I say, wiping the spit off my lips, "since when do we let MR soldiers in the Stag?"

"Since you went AWOL yesterday and were tracked to a certain alien who killed more than two dozen scientists out at the Camp. Not to mention a whole shitload of corporate executives from all over the United Republics for the past two years."

I don't react, except for a little cough that I can't tuck down, but internally I'm privately stunned. My dream comes back to me and I roll this new fact over in my mind. "So what's he got to do with me?" I look up at him now. He looks like shit. But I suppose he's thinking the same thing about me.

"You tell me and then we'll all know."

I shake my head, then take another second to catch my breath. "I wrecked my Goat, Aren. Hit a fucking tree and went unconscious. He was there and helped me out. That's it."

He walks away to the far end of the mini-drop plane so that he can stand on the edge of the ramp and look out across the tallgrass. I follow him over there, still trying to remember what it's like to breathe without the sting of residual plasma burns. When I get to the edge he grabs me by my arm and holds me so I can't go down the ramp.

"Try again, Junco," he says, exhaling a deep sigh. I look at him and see my best friend for just a moment. His face is one I know so well I could recognize it in the dark with just my fingertips. His blue eyes are still the same— deep and soulful. But they harden as I study him and then the old face is gone and it's just the asshole who left us to join the other team.

"They want to string you up for that last stunt you pulled."

I shake my head, not understanding, but he squeezes my arm a little tighter and I look back up in his eyes. "I gotta restrain you, Junco. We're still searching for him, so it'll be a while before I can take you home." He pulls me by the arm and we stomp down the ramp together, our boots clanking on the steel until we hit the grass.

Outside there is regulated bedlam as the base camp is established and I figure I was out for several hours by the look of their progress. A wiry little soldier barely out of his teens comes up as we exit and Aren hands me off to him without saying another word. The guy introduces himself as CP and tugs on my arm. I follow him to a recently fabbed bubble about the size of a small house. It's your typical on-the-fly covert-op motor pool. There are three prairie buggies parked inside and CP leads me over to one and then produces a first-aid kit, slaps some numbing antibacterial on my wrists, wraps them, and then thumbs the biometrics on the bracelet as he attaches it to my wrist and points to the passenger seat of the buggy.

"This is your guardhouse?" I let out a little laugh, then regret it when the coughing comes back. If he thinks being tethered to a prairie buggy is an inappropriate substitute for a regulation holding cell, he doesn't show it. Instead, he just points to the passenger seat again and scowls.

I get in and he attaches my new piece of jewelry to a matching tether connected to the roll bar above my head. "You're kidding me, right?"

He walks off and leaves me there.

The garage fab is not quite soundproof, but almost, and the outside world is reduced to muffled tones that are not even close to intelligible once the door slams behind him.

The bucket seats in the buggy are quite comfortable for military grade and I spend the next several minutes looking over what they have in here. Much of it is the same as what we have in our prairie buggies, but they have different aftermarket equipment.

I'm busy sifting through the contents of a case wedged between the driver and passenger seats when a blast of sound from outside disrupts my quiet world, making me turn.

"Find anything useful?"

I shrug. "I'm just passing time, Aren."

"You ready to tell me something?"

"Do I look like I'm fucking interested in chatting you up? Am I a prisoner of the MR, or what's going on here?"

He smiles. "I told you, we were sent to get you. You're being held under the direct orders of RR Command."

"Which is who exactly?"

His face turns away and I regret my outburst. It took me a little longer than usual, but I've finally crossed a line.

"Who are you these days?" He turns back towards me, his face a mixture of anger and disgust. "I heard you didn't even stay for his funeral. Just lit up in that deathtrap and left right in the middle of the ceremony."

"I stayed for most of the ceremony. Not that it has anything to do with this."

He laughs. "No? You tell me then, what the hell are you doing, Junco? What did you think you'd accomplish out there at Stag Camp?"

"I had a message to deliver."

"Yeah, like the bullshit you pulled last week?"

I shake my head. "What the hell—"

The garage doors roll up and soldiers file in, grabbing keys and jumping in the buggies. Aren walks over to CP and they whisper so I can't hear. Then CP comes over. "Gotta move now, Junco. They got a track on the alien's hiding place and they need all the buggies." I watch his thumb connect with the tether mechanism and it releases from the roll bar. "Jump out and come with me."

Aren barks orders at everyone as they fill the vehicles and he jumps into the buggy near me. "I'm gonna get your friend, Junco."

I shrug and answer back as I dutifully follow CP into another room. "Like I care."

Chapter Four

"You're chaining me to the head?"

"Sorry," CP says. "This is our most secure building. So. Nothing I can do."

At least the tether is long.

He spies me looking at it. "I gave you enough room to move around and—"

"And what?"

"Well, you know. You look like shit."

"Gee, thanks for the compliment." He shrugs and closes the door and I'm alone again.

I'm afraid to look in the mirror, so I use the facilities to prolong the agony, but that doesn't make the sight of my reflection any less shocking.

"Oh, my sweet Jeremiah!"

That face cannot belong to me. I have a giant gash that runs from my scalp and down to my right ear that has leaked blood all over one side of my hair, plastering it into a half helmet-like configuration.

Since I'm a prisoner locked in a bathroom I take advantage of what I have and fill the entire reserve water tank with the hand pump and gulp down long drinks of water. Then I stick my head into the basin and rinse as much of the blood out as I can.

When I'm done I look around and soak it all up, one square inch at a time.

And I smile.

The handle of the latrine isn't locked and opens when

I push it down. I expect CP, but I get another guy. Bigger. Meaner. He's looking out a small window in the door and speaks before turning around. "Who's sweet Jeremiah?" he asks.

"What?"

"You called his name, in there. A while back." He turns, waiting for my answer.

"It's no one. It's how RR people who prefer not to swear say holy shit or something to that effect. Hey, uh," I begin, trying out a smile on him, "I'd like to change into one of these clean jumpsuits hanging in here. Will you please remove the tether so I can slip my arm through the sleeve?" He shrugs and walks over towards me.

I ease back into the bathroom and grab the jumpsuit as he follows me in.

"Just so you know, I can't leave you in here untethered. So you're gonna have to change in front of me."

"Whatever." I slip out of my thermals then step into the jumpsuit and pull it up to my waist. "I'm pretty sure you've seen everything I've got. If you want to gape at me, go right ahead."

To my surprise he turns his head away.

"Honey, I'm damn sure I've never seen a naked avian before."

He says it like it's nothing. I stare at him hard, then shake my head. "You care to elaborate on that statement?"

He stares back. "Which part? The part about what kind of girls I've seen naked? Or the part where I break the news that you're a freak?"

"Is that a joke?"

"Do I look like I'm joking?"

He doesn't.

He's a big guy, not just in height, but also in muscle and weight. Easily a hundred and thirty pounds heavier than me. I play my card and strip off my dress, letting it hang off the tether, and stand there naked in front of him.

"There you go, take a good look." I even lift my hands up in the air and twirl around so he can see my back. "Not a wing in sight. Satisfied?"

He looks, long and hard even, but I can tell his only interest is in my nonexistent wings. "Put your damn clothes on, Junco."

"Oh, have we met before—?"

He grunts. "Cole."

"Cole. I don't recall your face. Are you an RR deserter as well?"

"You gonna change or what?"

"I'm ready to go. Just waiting on you." I shake the dress that's hanging off my tethered arm and smile. I'm not really the seductive type, so whether or not this even interests him is over my head. But I only need him to underestimate me, not be interested. This would never work on RR soldiers. They *all* know me and an RR guard would never even get this close to me, let alone fall for this bullshit I'm trying to pull right now.

But this guy? He looks a little dumb and if there's one thing I've learned about being small, it's that big guys like this don't even want to *think* about the possibility that I might kick their ass.

I watch as he bends down and my world slows down. In between these fractions my eyes dart around looking—

His thumb moves closer and closer to the release pad.

— for the long plumber's wrench propped up against water reservoir. I track his thumb and the second he releases the tether I grab the wrench and swing.

I laugh a little as he goes down, then reach over and use his thumb to release the other bracelet, slip my clothes back on, and slide the jumpsuit over them. I roll up the pants and poke my head through the bathroom door to see if anyone is outside.

Clear.

I twirl my hair up on top of my head and grab his cap, then rush over to the motor pool door. The window he was looking through wasn't built for short girls so I just open the door and walk through.

Into utter chaos.

I slide into the fray and walk like I've got somewhere to go as people rush around shouting orders, receiving orders, and generally doing everything soldiers do when *something's up*. I pick up a stray gas can as I walk and weigh my possibilities. I'm typically a quick decision maker but my pant legs are coming uncuffed, fucking up my concentration.

A thick bank of shrubs provides cover as I slip out my knife and begin hacking away at the length of extra fabric draping down my leg. I'm just about done when I spy CP walking with an RR officer.

That little traitor. Aren wasn't lying. They are here under RR orders. I briefly consider how uncomfortable I'd be if I had a joint mission with the army I walked out on and shiver a little.

CP turns to respond to something and I see that the RR officer has a gun to his head. He pushes CP forward and yells so loud I can pick out the words. "You tell your boss that he doesn't get the prize, and there better not be a damn thing wrong with her, soldier, or I'll have your brains splashed across this whole goddamn hillside."

Huh.

Nice to know at least someone cares.

I wait until they enter the motor pool and walk back out in the activity. I've got about ten seconds before they find Cole and sound an alarm so I dash into the trees and book it towards the river.

My ten seconds are absolutely up when it hits me. There is no ravine, no small trickle of a stream, and no Goat. I am on the wrong side of the road.

Shit.

There are only two choices, keep going out in the Stag alone with just my boot knife, or go back for the gun and make a run for it from there.

Off in the distance I hear the howling and make up my mind. I'd rather be caught and crucified than running in the tallgrass at night with no gun.

I walk down the hill until the activity breaks off, then make my way across the road, over to the stream, and begin the walk back up.

The little bit of chrome that's left on the bumper of my Goat twinkles at me like a Christmas star and I feel a sense of relief.

Until the screaming starts.

The first scream isn't even remotely human but I know exactly what's making it. The ones that follow are, and I can hear the savage pain he is inflicting on them. My stomach clenches for a moment and I almost pee my pants. I stand there for a little longer, indecisive, my eyes searching the trees and the black sky, then climb in the Goat and reach for the rifle.

My hand slips in under the back seat and comes back empty.

I just stare at my open palm, a little dumbfounded.

"Looking for this?" says the snarling voice in the darkness on the other side of the open front door. I push myself up and peer out. Cole has a look of death on his face as he holds up my rifle. Another blood-curdling scream erupts just off to the left of where we are and a plasma bolt lights up the air a fraction before the crackle of discharge catches up with it. The flash dances across Cole's face and his expression says he's not fucking around.

"Cole, look, I'm sor—"

He lunges into the back seat and I scramble away towards the passenger door. He forces his body over the middle console and begins to pull me back by my legs. I kick and scream. "Stop it!" One foot lands squarely on his head and he is still for a moment. I reach over and open the door and tumble out on the ground head-first. He flings himself after me through the cab faster than I could ever imagine a guy that size moving, landing on top of me.

"You bitch! I will fucking kill you!" Cole's fist is raised high, ready to plunge down onto my face, when the talons appear out of nowhere.

I scream as the head is snatched from the body. He falls forward and the hot sticky blood shoots out from his decapitated neck and drenches everything around me. I scramble backwards, push him off, get to my feet, and turn to run when the avian appears.

"Get away from me, goddammit!" I run the other direction but he takes flight. I look back at the bear-sized claws reaching down to grab me when a plasma bolt hits him in the chest. He screams so loud I have to stop and hold my ears to dampen down the pain, and then I hear the distant beat of wings as he retreats.

"Come on, Junco, we gotta get the hell out of here!

That won't stop him for long." Aren grabs me by my arm and throws me in the passenger side of a buggy face-first. I scramble to upright myself for a few seconds, then watch him shout orders to CP as he jumps in. We speed off up the ditch, out onto the road, and then head down deeper into the Stag.

Alone.

In an open-topped buggy.

And the nightdogs howl a hungry welcome up to the sky.

Chapter Five

The buggy bumps and jerks as we travel off-road but my eyes are trained on the tallgrass that surrounds us, looking for signs of apexers. In between my private panic attacks I rewind and watch Cole's head being ripped from his body. Aren, to his credit, says nothing. And that's OK with me. I'd rather not have to keep up my end of a hostile conversation at the moment.

After what seems like hours of driving my heart begins to slow down and the rhythm of the bucking prairie lulls me into stillness and I sleep.

When I wake we're not moving. Aren's seat is empty, but I can hear him trying to get someone on the coms. The moon is gone, so it must be almost morning.

I get out of the buggy and walk over to Aren. "Anyone out there?"

He shakes his head, looks me up and down, then turns his attention back to his device as he talks. "We'll make a little camp over there for the day," he says, pointing southwest, "and hole up until the coms come back online."

I nod and climb back in the buggy and let Aren find us a camp for the day. He unpacks some gear as the sun begins to rise.

"Here, catch." He throws me a packet of food. It's a military ration, so I don't get too excited. "It's blueberry pancakes, your favorite."

I smile a little because he remembers, then open the ration and squeeze it into my mouth until the packet is flat. I wash it down with water.

Aren is still busy, but I chance a conversation anyway. "Did you see what he did, Aren?"

He looks up from his task and stares at me. I know him well enough to see the wheels spin as he replays it, but he only grunts and goes back to his work.

"I have no idea who he is. None."

This time he doesn't look up, but he does talk. "I find that hard to believe, Junco. I mean, it looks real bad the way you took off to the Stag. What were you doing?" He drags his eyes off his hands and finds my face. "And no bullshit. It's just me."

"I told you already. I had to deliver something."

"To Stag Camp, Junco? That makes no fucking sense."

"I have a"—I blow some air out my mouth and it causes my unruly hair near my chin to go flying—"family friend there. I went out there all the time with my father, Aren, so don't pretend like you know me that well."

"Not my fault you never took me home to Daddy."

His words come out jaded and I laugh. "I never took anyone home to Daddy, Aren."

His end of the conversation is now over and all I can do is watch as he gets busy laying down a sleeping bag. There is only one, and when it's all laid out he gets in, boots and all. I watch him and shiver a little as I think about how badly I want to climb in and be close to someone.

He looks at me, smiles, then pats the ground next to

him. "Come on, get in."

I smile back but shake my head. "No, thanks. I'm all bloody."

"Jasus, Junco. Just get in the bag."

I give in. Why play the game? He knows I want to sleep in there, I know I want to sleep in there. Screw it. I take off the disgusting jumpsuit and get in, boots, mud, blood and all.

I settle into his chest and he pulls me close and puts his arms around me. We're warm and it doesn't feel terrible.

"You know damn well I didn't desert you, Junco. So quit fucking saying that shit. You left me, remember?"

I think about this for a minute and then shrug. "I don't deal well with ultimatums, Aren. And you gave me one. I had a life outside of cadets, you know. But you never understood that and then you just up and left. That never made sense to me. So why?" I turn a little and try to see his face over my shoulder. "Why did you leave the RR?"

Silence.

I sigh and stay still. Waiting.

A few minutes later he gives it a shot. "A discipline action. I fucked up after your graduation. They wanted to kick me out. Make me go back home."

This sounds like a lie but I'm not really interested in making a big deal of it. "So you left the RR? That's a little excessive, don't you think?"

"Junco, I don't know what your childhood was really like since you never did talk about it, but I lived with some raging fucking assholes when I was a kid and we didn't live in Council 3 where practically everyone's got special status. My house was a shit hole. I couldn't wait to join the military and get the hell out of that place. I figured I had enough field experience to do something else, so I took my skills to the highest bidder. And frankly, I'm having a hard time swallowing this fucking holier-than-thou attitude you seem to have about it. You and I aren't that different."

I elbow him in the ribs. "Get off me," I say, disgusted. He removes his arms and turns over without saying another word and after a few minutes of silence our mutual exhaustion takes over and we fall asleep.

When I wake the sun is already setting, Aren is gone, and I'm a hot mess of sweat-caked filth. I've never felt so disgusting in my life, even when I had to spend months out in the tallgrass on maneuvers. At least then I didn't have another man's blood peeling off my body. I struggle out of the bag and look around in what's left of the daylight, then fish out a ration from the pack nearby. I squeeze pot roast into my mouth, gag, and try not to notice the film that's grown over my teeth.

Aren is down by the buggy messing with the coms.

"Are they up yet?" I yell as I walk down to him.

"Hey, beautiful, have a nice sleep?"

"Shut the hell up."

He shrugs and lets the insult slide off. "No. No coms yet."

"Why are they still down?"

"You fuck up the mission, you get penalized. Or maybe they figure it's just as easy to let us get eaten out here by the nightdogs. Who knows?"

"So this mission was to come get me. Why?"

"You'll have to ask them, Junco. I'm just the delivery boy."

"Why did Cole think I was an avian, then?"

He looks up at me and shakes his head as a pissed-off

expression spreads across his face. "Fucking Cole."

"Why, Aren?"

He shakes his head again. "Dunno, Junco. I really don't. But everyone seems to think you are. They all want you."

"All who?"

"Us, them, the avians."

I let out a deep sigh, sick of the games. "Who is us and who is them, Aren?"

He shoots me a dirty look, then comes over and pokes me in the chest, hard enough to send me back a step, and then pokes his own as well. "Us," he clarifies. Then he waves his hands up in the air and says, "Them."

I don't have the energy to point out there is no us, so I drop it. "That makes no sense, Aren. The RR wants me for what? I've been living here my whole life, I was the commander's daughter, I—"

I stop myself, unsure of what I was just going to say. Aren doesn't pick up on it but I start to have a small panic attack until he starts talking again.

"I couldn't tell you. I'm only privy to what the MR is doing and we were hired to extract you and take you back with us."

"Hired? To take me back where?" I'm starting to sound like an idiot with my questions, but screw it.

"I can't say any more, but I will say that it is somewhere safe."

"And I'm supposed to believe that?"

He just shrugs.

"Am I an avian?" I know it's not possible, but I want to hear it from him.

"As far as I know, yes."

I choke on my own spit for a minute. "You're joking, right?"

I can tell he's tired of this subject by his extra-long huff of exhaled air. "Do I look like I'm fucking around, Junco?"

My feet are moving before I even process what's happening and I walk off into the tallgrass. *Picture yourself standing on the edge of a dock...*

I shake my head.

No.

I am Junco Coot, aged nineteen. Born in the Rural Republic in 2133. My mother is Carolinia Coot, maiden name Sutter. My father was Rural Republic Commander, Johann Coot, son of Wilhem Coot. I live in Council 3, I went to sniper school when I was seventeen, I play piano, collect books and guns, and last year I was the world's mounted aerial aerobatics grand champion.

... In front of you is a mountain lake...

No. In front of me is a crapload of tallgrass filled with sleeping prairie lions.

... and behind you is a small cabin, pristine white curtains flowing in the breeze passing through the windows...

No.

No.

NO.

That shit needs to go back down now, Junco!

The sun is hanging on by a sliver when I look to the west, thankful that some of the sweat on my sticky body has dried up. The cool wind chills me as it whisks the heat from my exposed arms. If I was brave I'd just keep walking. Forget about Aren, the avian, my father, my farm, my life and everything that happened over the past forty-eight hours.

But I'm not brave. So I can do nothing but sit on a rock and stare out across the plains.

Sometime later Aren comes up and joins me.

"Shit, Junco! I was calling your name, didn't you hear me?"

"Yeah, I heard you."

"So, now you're just going to ignore me? Because I told you what I know?"

I get up furious and look him in the eyes as I poke him in the chest. "You told me what you wanted me to know, so save your bullshit for someone else."

"What do you want me to do, break my security clearance?"

"It wouldn't be the first time."

"Right back at you, Junco. You're mucking around in the same shit I am, so fuck you."

I hoof it back to the buggy and search for some water and gulp it down. I'm hungry again, but since I don't know how long we'll have to be out here, I don't take another ration. Instead I plop down in the passenger seat and prop my chin up with my hand, staring up at the sky. My old friends are still up there. But not all of them are visible since the moon is only just now rising.

The coms begin to crackle and it almost makes me jump out of my seat. "Aren!" I yell. "Aren, the coms are back!"

I hear his boots running towards me and he stops by the driver's side door and reaches in for the handset, then walks off in the dark, talking.

More secret stuff about Junco, I'm sure. I go back to my skydream and find the Big Dipper, Little Dipper, and then the North Star.

Aren returns, a look of relief on his face. Probably so happy to get the hell away from my moody ass he can't contain himself. "They're on their way. Be here in about an hour."

"Airlift, then?" I ask. But I already know that means the RR has given them permission to fly in our airspace. He doesn't confirm it either way. "So what happens to me now?"

"We take you in and that's it."

"That's it? You guys just take me in and then what? Throw me a party? Take me home? Bring my father back to life? What? What happens when you take me in?"

He doesn't answer so I decide to push my luck. "Maybe they'll dissect me?"

"Don't be an idiot."

"I'm an idiot now? Because I'm the subject of a multinational, shit, multi-species manhunt, and I'm scared about what's going to happen and where I'm going to end up?"

"You're completely overreacting."

"Am I? Oh, well, phew! For a minute there I wasn't sure. Maybe I leave right now and you don't take me in at all? How 'bout that?"

"You're not going anywhere, Junco. Just sit quietly and stop acting like a raving crazy person—"

I am out of the buggy and hoofing it before he has a chance to finish his sentence. I book it hard and I feel the calories melt off my muscles and know that I won't get far. Still, I hear him yelling at me to come back and the pebbles his feet throw up as he chases me make my day. I slip into the tallgrass and I know that I could get away, if I really want to.

Do I really want to?

I stop because I'm not sure, then pant a little as I stand on my tiptoes and poke my head up to see if he's around. I don't see anything so I walk, parting the overripe stalks of wild wheat in front of me, while still keeping an eye out.

"Had enough yet, Junco?"

I turn to find the avian less than a pace behind me and I open my mouth to scream, but nothing comes out because he's got his hand clasped over my lips.

Tight, I might add.

"I see yer friends have ya completely strung out." I blink at him, partly because he seems to want a response and partly because that's all I can do. "If I remove my hand, will ya keep quiet then? For a moment of chat?" I nod and he removes his hand, but I'm true to my word and stay quiet.

"Now, then. Shall I present yer options? Or will ya just come along quietly?"

I shrug.

"You're coming with me, regardless of what ya choose, let's just get that straight right now."

I close my eyes like I'm tired, or bored. "So, why bother me with choices?"

"The choice is whether or not ya want yer little loverboy over there to keep his head."

Shit. Now I've done it. "Please don't kill him. He's a good guy and he's just following orders."

"Good guy, eh? I think not, Junco Coot. Ya have no idea what kind of guy he is. None at all."

I grunt. "Yeah. You're probably right about that, but hey, this is coming from someone who tears people's heads off for fun."

He squints down at me, like he's insulted or something. "The man was on top of ya, ready to throw a punch."

"I didn't need your help, alien. I practically killed him with a plumber's wrench ten minutes before you decided to decapitate him and spill his filthy blood all over me." I point to my dress as exhibit A.

"So what's the problem? I finished the job."

"I didn't want him dead, I only wanted him hurt. What you did was excessive. You're like an animal or a monster."

"Now we're getting somewhere. Sure, I'm a monster. But not any more of one than you are."

"I'm not one of you," I hiss.

He ignores my comment. "I'm willing to take you right now and leave everyone else alive. The question is whether or not you accept that proposal."

My face is suddenly hot and the frustration I feel is overwhelming. The tears escape and slip down my cheeks as I slump to the ground.

He bends down with me and leans in to part my hair away from my neck, like he's going to bite me or something. I pull back, but he's got a hold of my shoulder and keeps me still.

"This posture looks like an acceptance to me, Junco, but you're quite impulsive and wild," he croons in my ear, "and I want to be sure of your decision." I can feel the words travel into my ear canal and I put up an imaginary wall and rub my hand over my ear to brush them away.

"Learning tricks, are ya? No matter, Junco, all I need is a yes and this nightmare will end. Yes, then?"

"Her answer is no, alien." Aren's timing couldn't be worse.

I quickly reach for the avian's hand that still rests on my neck, and whisper, "Yes." Then he's gone.

I stand up and whirl around to see the avian has Aren by the throat. "You promised!" Aren is choking and his hands are frantically clutching the avian's hands. I look down and see Aren's plasma rifle and scoop it up, then point it straight at the alien's head. "Stop! We had a deal!"

The avian throws Aren down on the ground and he lies there sputtering. I drop the weapon and kneel down next to him. "Shit! Aren, are you OK?"

The avian stands over us with the plasma rifle. "He's fine. Just making a big scene is all. Come on, let's go."

"Wait," Aren croaks. "Wait! I have a message for you, Tier!"

We both turn. "Who's Tier?"

"I'm Tier. What message?" Tier asks.

"My front pocket," Aren chokes. "Junco, help me up!"

I do, and he fishes the letter from his pants pocket and hands it over. The alien takes it and walks a few paces away for privacy.

"What is it, Aren?"

He shrugs. "Dunno. I can't read their language."

"Well, where the hell did you get it? Try that one."

The alien is back so Aren doesn't answer me. "Well? What the hell does it say?" He scowls and hands it over to me. All I see is gibberish.

"Apparently," Tier begins, "we have an agreement between parties."

"English, please," I snap.

"That was English."

I throw up my hands. "What does it mean?"

"Seems yer friend there needs to grant me permission ta remove ya from custody. Though it's an old document and my plans have been recently revised. So I'm not sure I need to honor it anymore."

"You're not taking her," Aren growls.

"You have no say in that, boy. None whatsoever. She has already agreed to come."

They both look over at me and my eyes move from

one to the other. Tier's tell me nothing, but Aren's speak loud and clear in their silence. "He says he won't kill you if I go."

"Goddammit, Junco, how fucking gullible can you be? Every fucking time I get you—" He stops and starts again. "Listen, Junco, he's not going to kill me. Can't kill me, OK?"

Tier laughs. "I can and I will."

"Fine," I shrug. "You want to fight over me, knock yourselves out."

Tier remains calm and looks Aren in the eyes. Aren meets his gaze and nods his head. Then the alien's face changes before my eyes and I step back and trip over a rock as I try to get away. "Aren, I'll just go—"

Aren spits on the ground and winces as he draws in a breath. "This dirty fucking avian can take his permission, his bullshit, and his ugly giant buzzard wings and get the FUCK OFF MY PLANET!"

I don't even have time to wince at his insults before Tier is on him.

Chapter Six

There is blood everywhere within seconds, but to my surprise it's not Aren's. He's got a laser knife in his hand and he's cut the avian across his chest. Tier looks down and I can see his green eyes glow with rage in the darkness.

"Stop!" I scream it as loud as I can, but they don't even hear me.

They are both in a crouched fighting position now, slowly circling each other. The blood is pouring out of Tier's chest as he speaks. "Ya have no chance against me human. None at all."

Tier actually bares his teeth and I feel my stomach clench. "Stop, you guys!"

Aren answers me this time, his eyes locked on the avian. "Junco, start running and don't stop."

"No!" I scream. "I'm not leaving you guys here to fight like children! I said I'd go, Aren, just stop! I don't want him to kill you!"

Tier is silent through this, and even though there is a lot of blood, he doesn't seem fazed or slow, or even slightly distracted. The look on his face is one of a predator about to take down a kill.

"He's not even close to killing me, Junco, he knows he can't kill me."

"W-w-what?" I stutter.

Tier answers this time. "Your loverboy here thinks he's got tricks up his sleeve, but he's wrong, Junco. I've got more tricks than he can even begin to imagine. And if you don't want to watch his head roll through the grass you'll run away like he said. I'll pick you up when we're done."

"Like hell you will," Aren snaps back.

Tier makes his move then. He's definitely not as fast on the ground as he is in the air, but his arms are almost long enough to reach out and grab Aren right where he stands. Almost. Aren ducks and catches his wing and twists it until the alien is forced to roll in the air with it or face an injury I can't stomach the thought of. He does twist and then he's free, but Aren attacks with the laser again, cutting another gash down the side of his leg.

Tier lifts off the ground like he's going to finish the job. My hands grasp around for the weapon I know is there and when I find it I hit the charge button. Aren is on the ground now and his head is bleeding. The alien hovers in the air just above him. They are talking but I'm too distracted by the charging whine of the plasma rifle to pay attention. Tier dives in for the kill, landing on top of Aren's chest. At the same time the rifle's charge button goes green and I blast the alien in the back for a full ten seconds.

He falls off to the side with a look of shock on his face.

Aren jumps to his feet and grabs my hand and we run, hard. "Is he dead?" I ask. But Aren doesn't answer me. "Is he dead, Aren?"

"Run! Just run!"

He pulls on me as I start to drop back behind him, forcing me to keep up with his pace, and we break for the buggy. When we get there he jumps in and has it started and in gear before I can even settle in my seat and we are moving across the prairie grass.

"What's happening? Is he dead, Aren?" I scream it over the raging wind that pierces my ears, but Aren is looking up in the sky and doesn't answer.

"He's coming, isn't he?" The words aren't even out of my mouth when I hear the hard beat of giant wings overhead.

Aren jams the buggy into the next gear and we go faster, but we both know that there is no way to outrun the monster circling above us.

Tier swoops down and comes straight for the buggy. "Duck!" Aren screams. I do, just as the giant talons reach out to grab me. I feel my skin open up as the sharp claws skim across my shoulders and the hot blood spills out and down my arm. The beating stops for a minute and my head goes woozy. I look over at Aren and his mouth is moving but the words don't make any sense and my world starts to blur.

I bounce as the buggy jumps the rough prairie terrain and my muscles are no longer able to compensate for the movement, causing me to slump over against the door.

Blood is flowing down my shirt and pooling around my hips. I snap back to reality a bit, just enough to realize we've stopped. Aren is dragging me out of the buggy by my arms when the monster returns and snatches me away.

Off in the distance I hear the chaos of war and feel the heat of plasma rifles as they crackle across the grassland. My senses return just enough to understand that Tier's talons are piercing my waist, his arms clasping me to his chest. We are flying.

I feel the wind across my face and try to open my eyes, but I can't. The heat of plasma fire blasts past me and it's only then that I realize we're being shot at by the soldiers who were supposed to pick Aren and me up.

A bolt of plasma hits Tier and then I am falling. It feels wonderful to be free of those claws. My bliss is interrupted as the powerful talons reach out and jerk me back into the confines of my captor and the world goes dim.

We fly until we stop, which seems soon to me, but the world is still blurry. Not as bad as it was back in the buggy, but I'm not completely coherent and I can't move my body very well. Tier drops to his knees as he lands, taking me with him. I feel the shelter of his wings as they scoop me up and I lose interest in anything else except for the warmth. I know he is talking because I feel the vibrations on my neck, but I can't hear anything. His eyes glow faintly in the darkness and I am mesmerized. It feels like we stay that way for a long time, but it could have been seconds for all I know. I have lost all sense of being.

I slip in and out of consciousness, but I do hear the soldiers off in the distance each time I come up for a gulp of reality. I can't tell exactly how far away they are, but if they are close, Tier is not worried. He never moves. I squirm until he releases my arms but not my body.

He speaks and now I can hear him. "Why do ya have to be such a troubled one, Junco?"

I'm the first to admit that I'm a fairly fucked-up person, but I'm not sure how he'd know any of that, so I say nothing.

"Why don't ya just do what yer told?" he prods.

I find my voice and croak out some words. "So, in your culture everyone does what they're told?"

"The little girls generally do, darlin'."

I manage to shake my head in frustration even though

his wings are wrapped around me. "Well, maybe this will help," I croon up to him in my throaty new voice, "I'm a human, get it? And human girls around my age are quite temperamental and emotional. You must not have had very much training in human culture if that simple fact mystifies you. I feel better now, so let go of me."

He does and is crouching down as he watches me struggle to prop myself up on my elbows. I hear the soldiers off in the distance again. "They're getting closer. Why did we stop here?"

He smiles and his eyes have a faint glow to them as he answers, "Because I poisoned ya by mistake and without the antidote you'd be dead within minutes. Healing ya was necessary for the mission to continue."

I scramble up on my hands and knees and wait there as my head clears. He makes no move to help me, but I don't ask for help. So it evens out.

When the dizziness subsides I sit back on my butt and look up at him. "So, you're not allowed to kill me? That's part of the mission?" I feel a little relieved at this revelation. At least my head won't be rolling in the grass like Cole's.

"I have no plans to kill ya yet, darlin'."

"What the fuck does that mean?"

"I'm going to be honest with ya right now, Junco. I don't care for yer filthy mouth."

Wait. What? I laugh. "You're worried about me swearing? Unbelievable. How about trying to be honest about your orders to kill me as well?"

"I told ya, I'm not gonna kill ya."

"Yet. You said yet," I growl.

"Correct, I'm not gonna kill ya yet. Perhaps I will one day. Perhaps that day will never come. But right now I'm interested in keeping ya alive."

"And that's OK with you?"

"Yes, I'm OK with not killing ya. Yet."

I get up to stomp off but he grabs my ankle and I fall to the ground face-first. "Not so fast. There are soldiers right over there, sweetheart. If ya want them to live, you'll stay quiet and still."

"Where did you learn to talk to women? Lounge lizard school for the utterly stupid?"

"So, ya want them all to die? Because that can be arranged."

I shake my head and feel bad. "No, I don't want them to die."

"Then shut yer mouth and lie still so they can move on to the next search sector."

I do lie still but they do not move on. After several minutes it's clear that they know we are here, but they don't advance. "They see our heat signatures," I say.

"Yes, that's unfortunate."

"Unfortunate for whom?" I ask, but I don't want to know the answer. Whatever happens tonight, he's made one thing clear. We are leaving and if people have to die in order to accomplish that, so be it.

Aren's amplified voice crosses the distance. "Let her go, Tier. If you let her go we'll back off and let you leave."

I hear Tier snort at the stupid offer and I feel sorry for Aren because he might be dead in a few minutes if he keeps this up.

Tier stands and pushes down on my shoulder at the same time so I stay on the ground. Unlike me, he is much taller than the tallgrass and I'm sure he makes for a very good target. But no one shoots him and that makes me think they are afraid and are waiting for him to make the first move.

He speaks instead. "You have five minutes to clear out. After that, the carnage begins. If ya advance on us, I will personally eviscerate each one of ya and leave ya for the prairie lions to devour."

After that there is silence for several seconds and I am hopeful. But that hope is shattered as a bolt from a plasma cannon fires down upon us. Tier leans down casually and covers me with his wings as the heat incinerates the grass around us. When the initial burst is over, he pushes me down to the ground and I burn my palms on the smoldering remains of vegetation. I gasp when I see his face, partly because of the soot that chars his skin, but mostly because his rage produces a bright green light that actually seeps out of his eyes. Then he is gone.

I listen to the sounds of pain around me and I know that he's killing them, just like he said. In a few hours the prairie lions will follow the stench of death and eat them, bones and all, erasing any evidence of what is occurring here tonight.

When he returns I don't even recognize him. His entire body is plastered with blood: his clothes, his hair, his face, and most of all his hands. Except they are not hands anymore, they are talons like his feet. I stare at him in horror and he follows my gaze down and retracts the razors.

I want to ask about Aren but I already know the answer and I don't think I could take hearing it out loud so I just sit there and say nothing.

He doesn't console me, apologize, or even say he warned them and they asked for it. Instead he takes flight, grabs me with his talons, lifts me up into his arms that wrap around me tight, and we fly away from the glow of fire beneath us. From the air I can see the carnage we leave behind and I have yet another horror to fill my dreams the next time I fall asleep.

Chapter Seven

We fly for a long time. I'm not sure of the direction because I can't see the sky above me. The alien blocks my view. The entire core of my body hurts from his tight grasp and my face starts to feel chapped from the wind. But at least I am warm. His body radiates heat and it exchanges easily between us.

He sets me down in the darkness and I stumble a few paces before tripping and falling over. The palms of my hands sting as I reach out to try and catch my fall, but only succeed in slamming down on the ground. I realize I'm on a rock and after I adjust to the starlight I look up and find the Milky Way. Instantly my eyes are drawn down to the beacon of hope that dominates the western horizon. Peak City has never looked so beautiful and I smile as I realize where we are.

"You ever go there?" Tier asks me casually as I stand back up, like we're just a couple of friends taking in the view.

I snort out a grunt. "I grew up twenty miles from the border, of course I go there." Peak City is the capital of the Mountain Republic. The western edge of the Rural Republic bucks up against the planet pad where the suborbitals land. Technically the pad belongs to us, as it's inside our border, but since we're such a small country and very few of our citizens will ever require a suborbital, we lease the land to the MR for a tidy sum that pays for our exceptional military.

"So it's not forbidden for you to leave yer Republic?"

"Where'd you ever get that idea?" I scowl at him. People think that just because we don't have certain modern amenities that we're backwards. It's really only the entertainment shit we renounce and it's beyond ignorant to believe that people who shun screens are backwards. We simply have better things to do than sit around watching strangers do stuff, then try to convince ourselves it's fun.

He shrugs. "You Farm Families seem to have a lot of rules."

"Yeah, we do. But we're not prisoners. If you're not Farm you can even work in the MR. Lots of people in our Council do. But if you're Farm, then," I shrug, "your job is here taking care of your land and making it productive. The city is just a nice place to visit and that's pretty much it."

"Do you resent that?"

"What kind of crap is this? Some third-degree on my political leanings?"

"From what I can tell, you seem to resent quite a bit about following rules."

"Well, you don't even know me, so how the hell would you know anyway?"

"So, all the trouble you've caused over the past few months is—what? A strange coincidence?"

"For your information I went into the Stag to see if a friend was OK," I lie. "My father just died and Dale didn't show up for the funeral. So I was—worried."

"OK. Let's just pretend that's true. What about all the other stuff?"

I look back at him. He's standing with his feet apart, arms crossed over his chest, and his wings are not quite closed tight against his body, but neither are they in any way extended. Relaxed, maybe? The wing tips sneak out from behind his body in an upturned lift, like they cross somewhere at the small of his back.

I stop myself from staring. "What other stuff?"

His head nods up and down as he grits his teeth, which makes his jaw muscles tighten. But he doesn't answer me. Instead, he turns his back and walks away. I can see his wings first-hand now, and they do cross over each other, but they also seem to have a life of their own—like the ears on a horse—rotating and lifting in reaction to external stimuli.

He stops at a dark shadow along the edge of the mountain. It's about three feet long and two feet high. There are thick roots from the tall conifers that dominate the side of the mountain branching over it, half concealing it from view. If I didn't see Tier approach it, I might never have noticed the little opening. He bends down and sticks his feet in the hole, then pushes back the woody tree roots and slips inside, leaving me alone in the darkness.

I wait for several seconds but he doesn't come back so I get to my feet and walk over to see what he's up to. I try to see in the little hole, but it's too dark. His head pops back out and I scream in surprise, covering my mouth as he looks up at me, startled. "Why are ya just standing there?"

I shrug. "What do you want me to do?"

He grabs my ankles and pulls, making me fall on my ass. Then he's dragging me under the ground into the dark hole, my dress rolls up and the rocks are scraping against my plasma-burned back. Once inside I kick him hard in the shoulder and he lets go. "Get off me, you jerk!"

He puts his face right up to mine and I feel my heart jump. "I'm tired of playing games with ya, girl. If you see me go somewhere, ya follow. Understand?"

I consider saying something nasty back to him, but his eyes are glowing again and I take that as a sign that his patience is running on empty. So I just nod.

He turns and begins to slide down the rocky hill inside the mountain and I follow, trying my best not to let loose an avalanche of stones on his head. The only light we have is from a lightstick that is the same color as his eyes. In fact, I'm not entirely sure that his eyes aren't actually providing some light as well.

When we get to the bottom of the hill we stop and then he disappears into another dark shadow in the ground, taking the lightstick with him so I'm left in complete darkness.

Again his head pops back up when I hesitate. "Jump down, Junco."

"No. I'm not jumping into some dark hole, you're crazy. If you want to take me somewhere go ahead, but you're not stuffing me down into a hole."

"Jump in the hole, Junco. Or I'll leave ya here and you'll wander around in the dark until the nightdogs get a hold of yer scent and eat ya alive."

Fuck.

I climb in after him, ignoring the stench of guano, the spiderwebs that flit against my cheeks, and the noises that echo off the walls. It isn't really a hole, more like a rooftop entrance into a larger cavern which opens up into a series of tall terraced steps that takes us further and further into the belly of the mountain. Eventually it morphs into a fairly well-defined tunnel.

The terraced steps are flat, which hints that someone shaped this passageway, but the sides of the tunnel are absolutely man-made. Even in the extremely dim light I can see the toolmarks left from when it was drilled. There must be more entrances, larger entrances, that can accommodate heavy machines.

We walk on like this for a while. It's hard to tell how long. All I know is that I am exhausted from tripping over various small objects that seem to present themselves under my feet at every opportunity. We cross a small stream, thankfully not too deep, and then I spot a faint light source up ahead. Tier grabs my hand and pulls me towards it. The width of the tunnel expands with the growing light until it empties into a spectacular wide-open cavern filled with so many different types of cave formations that it takes my breath away.

"All this time I've been living next to this place and I never knew it."

"You barely know anything, Junco." He takes my hand again and pulls me to the center of the cavern, spins me around a few times, and lets go.

"Hey, what the hell?"

"Look around."

I pivot on my heel and frown at what I see.

"You'll think twice about running off then, eh?"

I nod and find a seat at a camp table set up in the center of the room and the exhaustion takes over as I survey my new surroundings. He won't need to bind me or stick me in a hole here because there are three identical openings leading into the cavern, each one equidistant to the next. I have no idea which one we just came through.

"How long have you been here?" I ask as I take in the mounds of supplies layered around the central clearing.

He's pulling some stuff out of a container and piling it on the floor beside him. "Long enough for it to feel like home."

My mouth makes a little O shape as I spy a sleeping bag on the ground. I crawl over to it and sink into the surprisingly soft and buoyant blankets, watching him as he prepares some sort of food. "What's that?"

"Nutrition," is all he comes back with.

I yawn. "Doesn't look very good."

"Then don't eat it."

"I won't, believe me." And then my eyes close and I drift off.

The planks on the deck are warm under your feet and you're wearing a long thin white shirt, open in the front, that barely covers your body. The waves lap against the dock and you reach over and drag your fingers through the water. It folds against your wrist and slaps up the side of your arm. The drops bead against your oiled skin, pool together, then spring forth into a trickle which takes the liquid back to the source. The mountains are high and imposing and then they crowd in and consume you as the sunlight disappears...

No. That's not what happens.

I wake up and know immediately I am alone. There is a bowl of cold food sitting next to me and a note written in some gibberish. Did he really just do that? Write me a note in a language that I can't read? I toss it and smell the food as I consider how hungry I am.

Not enough to eat that shit.

I stand and stretch, taking in the room again. This time my head is much clearer, but my back is creaking from sleeping on the cold cave floor. I have no idea how long I was out but I feel pretty well-rested.

The chamber is large, about fifty feet long and maybe thirty feet at its widest point. It narrows where a massive stalactite and stalagmite meet to form a column the width of a sequoia trunk.

The roof of the cave is adorned with thousands of breathtaking stone icicles and there are large white crystals growing out of every crevice. My eyes follow the cave wall to the end and see hundreds of drapery formations hanging from the ceiling. Water flows down the curving rock and deposits into a small pool.

The floor is almost smooth, but there are soft mounds of rock which makes me think of flowing lava. This pitches the ground up and down like rolling hills as I walk.

I stand in the middle, half in awe of this cave being here in the first place, and half in awe because I am actually standing in it.

There are three wide tunnels that lead to this central room. That they are man-made I have no doubt. Whether they are enough to keep me from escaping is another story.

I study the three exits with a critical eye. They aren't all the same; they just looked that way at first because I was in a new place and I was exhausted. But now I can see subtle differences.

If you stand inside one there is a long dark column obstructing the view into the cave as you enter. I know I didn't see that as we passed through, so I knock that one off the list right away. Now there are only two, and if I take a chance, I have a fifty-fifty shot of picking the right one and walking right out of here and back to my house.

I study them a little more and walk a few paces into each one to see if there are other landmarks. The walls of one has a formation near the entrance that I remember from school. Moonmilk. I think I would have noticed that, even if I was delusional.

I walk over to the remaining cave and search for anything that might strike it off the list, but there is nothing there to make me hesitate. Then I search through Tier's supplies and find some flares, stuff some disgusting food into my boot, and grab some rope because rope is something you should probably have in a cave.

I take one last look around and then head into the dying light that semi-permeates the tunnel.

Chapter Eight

Finding my way back out to the world is child's play. I throw down the supplies and take in the view. First I look over at PC. It has a hold on me, that city. Not the kind that makes you move there. Something else. It draws me in. Makes me feel safe when I see it. Even from here, which is easily sixty miles from the ziggurat, I can see the terraces that swirl up the side of the mountain. It's not the tallest mountain in North America, but it's one of the most famous.

At night it's lit up like Vegas and I can say from personal experience that landing on the suborbital planet pad in Peak City beats Vegas as far as thrills go. Hands down. As if on cue a deafening boom announces an arrival as the suborbital plane breaks the sound barrier and comes in for a landing. My eyes follow the fluorescent pink contrail left over from atmosphere re-entry. I sort of have a thing for planet pad watching. Like stargazing, it's part of me.

I've landed on almost every planet pad on Earth and none of them have the same draw as the Peaks. Maybe everyone who lives by a pad feels that way, but somehow I doubt it. London's pad is crap—an afterthought, just like everything else in that old decaying city. Jersey and LA aren't much better. Only Vegas, with the open flat desert and the brilliance of the Strip creeping up alongside it, Tokyo, with its kamikaze landing pad floating out on the ocean five miles offshore, and Dallas, which built an entire city on top of a city to accommodate their pad, can come close to matching the landing in Peaks.

I turn my attention back to my own small world. If I stand on my tiptoes I can see faint lights through a break in the pine trees to the north. I continue my gaze northeast and see a line of tall pines that give way to a clearing that might be my ranch. It's not close enough to see anything in detail, so I'm not really sure, but it's in that general direction.

Definitely close enough to walk to.

But I hesitate.

I could go home. Very easily. But he'd just come get me again. There is no chance this hiding place with its proximity to my home is a coincidence. I could make a run for it to one of the closer neighbors, probably Mr. and Mrs. Baumer from what I can tell. But that would just be a death sentence for them. He's killed several dozen people in the past few days, what's one old couple on a cattle ranch?

I could try and look in the cavern for a radio and get in touch with my Council Elder, let him know where we are. Maybe they can mount a defense? This sounds more like a dream than a reality. Even after all these people have been killed, the RR defenses have yet to show up.

My last idea is to just stay put and do what I'm told. I laugh at that, a small chuckle that develops in my throat and bubbles up to a full-blown snicker.

And yet I do stay put. I could be halfway down the mountain by now if I wanted. In the trees, hiding and moving in silence.

Getting away.

Easily.

If—and this is a big if—Aren was telling the truth, then they all want me, including the RR. They gave the MR sky privileges, for fuck's sake.

To come get me. Because I'm not human.

Again I get the urge to laugh, but it's just not funny.

Picture yourself standing on the edge of a dock...

Fuck.

Enough already, Junco.

I stare up at the sky for a long time and find Cygnus, then up to Draco, and finally over to Cassiopeia. I wish I was a constellation, high up in the sky. And everyone would look at me in the night and marvel at how beautiful and untouchable I was. In ancient times the Gods only made you a constellation if they were mad at you, or if you were too beautiful to die. So it was either a reward or a punishment, depending on your predicament. It's funny how the very same circumstance can be eternal life for one and eternal damnation for another. It makes no sense, but it does teach a lesson in perspective.

I have a stray thought as I lie there under the Milky Way, but I push it away before it can fully form.

Maybe I just need some perspective?

Maybe I'm being brainwashed?

Or maybe I just can't think straight because of all the injuries I've sustained?

Or maybe those weird alien healing chemicals are interfering with my thought process?

It doesn't matter because the idea that wants to form slips into my head anyway. Maybe it doesn't make sense because I don't know the whole story?

Maybe I'm being lied to?

And maybe I'm lying to myself.

I hear the heavy beating of wings and know that Tier is back. He lands behind me in the small clearing and walks the few paces toward my prone body.

"What's going on?" he says as he approaches.

The question hangs between us as I tip my head back

as far as I can so I can see his upside-down face in the starlight. "Having a pity party. You're invited."

He lies down next to me. "Am I now?"

I force a smile and look at him. His eyes have just a faint green glow, but it doesn't bother me anymore, probably the brainwashing kicking in. His loose mop of black curls is a mess from flying in the wind and I wonder briefly at my own hair. I push that thought away quickly. His clothes are still stained with blood, as are my own. Funny how it doesn't even register even though some of it is Cole's.

That brainwashing is some powerful shit, I really need to cut back.

"What pity are we celebratin', then?" he asks.

I exhale deeply but stay quiet. He doesn't push, but instead waits patiently and looks up at the sky. "How many did ya see?"

I don't know how I know, but I know. "None," I reply.

"That's weak. I see one right now." Then he points and I find the shooting star at the end of his fingertip.

I look at him again, and give another smile and shake my head as the tears threaten to burst out.

"So what have ya been doin' out here?" He's prying now and his accent is a little thicker as well. Like he's reverting back to how he normally talks.

I let out another heavy sigh, but keep my silence.

"Is this yer human temperament and emotions coming out?"

I let out a small laugh and then the tears ride down my cheeks. I feel him turn towards me, propped up on his elbow, and then swipe a finger down my face to remove the ribbons of water.

"Do avians cry?" I ask, turning my head away to avoid

his gaze.

"We do," he whispers. He leans back into the grass and leaves me that way for several seconds. "We do," he says again, but this time he's talking to himself.

Then he gets up and grabs my hand. I fly up towards him like I weigh nothing and he pulls me close. "Come on," he says. "I have something that will make us both feel better."

I let him tug me back into the cave and we make the descent back to the cavern.

The walk back is uneventful and when we reach the vaulted room I plop down on the camp chair as he fools around looking through his supplies, stuffing things in a pack as he goes.

"Are we going on a trip?" I ask.

He smiles as he pokes his head up and looks over a cave formation. I smile back at him despite myself. Is it wrong to smile when so many people are dead? I definitely think it is.

"Oh, I almost forgot," he says as he walks toward me, pulling a small bag from his coat pocket. "Human food. In case you're hungry." He hands me the little white bag and I take it. I am famished. Is it wrong to be thankful for the food a killer gives you? I definitely think it is.

He goes back and begins to mess with a collection of tech and com devices that sit on a ledge as I peek inside the crumpled bag. It's a smashed chicken sandwich from Chick-Chick-Chicken in Peak City. It's pretty cold, but I stuff it into my mouth and it tastes wonderful. Between bites I manage to talk. "How did you get a chicken sandwich from the Peaks anyway?" I look down into the empty bag and secretly wish for the fries that normally go with it. I chew and wait for his answer, but the info never materializes.

When I'm finished he comes back over and sees the empty bag and smiles. "Ya were starved then?"

I nod.

He holds up the pack that's almost bursting with supplies. "I've got something in here you'll like." Then he grabs my hand and pulls me up. "Come on."

"Where are we going?" I ask. But he just grins back at me and pulls me along behind him. We enter another tunnel and begin walking down the slope, which eventually ends in a path lined with strikingly beautiful folia formations. I recall from school that means all of this was under water, probably for thousands of years, before this tunnel was made. It's not long before he stops and turns. I look at his expression and I can tell he thinks he's pretty clever, but can't imagine I will be as excited as he is when he shows me what's beyond the next corner. My doubts must be written all over my face.

"Ye of little trust, I see."

I let out a little laugh before I can stop it.

"Darlin', this will put an end to all of yer temperamental emotions, at least for a little while."

"Really? Well, whatever it is you're going to show me, it must be really fucking spectacular."

He pushes me in front of him and we walk forward into another large cavern that looks almost exactly like the one we came from. I'm about to say something rude when I see it.

"Oh, yeah. That is definitely good." I look up and laugh at his bright smile.

"There's not much a nice hot bath won't fix. Even if it's just temporary."

Sweet Jeremiah, he is so right.

The hot spring is actually a flowing stream at one end with a fairly strong trickle of water that empties into it. The basin is surrounded by flowstone rock, which allows the water to collect there before gently spilling over and continuing along through the cave system. The steam coming up from the basin makes the cave humid and this makes me think of home.

Tier is unpacking towels, clothes, and some bottles as I spy shampoo and almost moan with longing. Some prisoner I make. Right now I would totally spill every secret I have just to wash my hair.

I wait and we approach the springs together and then he throws a few lightsticks into the water so it glows green from below. I look at him, unsure what to do next. He nods.

"You don't need to tell me twice. But I have no clean clothes."

"I won't let ya walk around naked. Go ahead. Get in." And then he turns around and busies himself with the pack.

I untie my boots and my knife spills out. I slip out of the thermals and whip the dress over my head. And then I am standing in my shorts. I feel ashamed that I am about to bathe with this killer, but I'm not about to give up a bath on that principle.

I check over my shoulder to see if Tier is looking, but he's still busy with the pack, so I strip off my shorts and walk towards the pool naked. I dip my toe in and give a little gasp, then look back to check on Tier and he's laughing at me. "Get in already, will ya."

I sit on the edge of the pool, then lower myself into the steaming water and find that it's deep enough so that I sink in up to my neck. A sublime moan escapes my lips.

"Your turn."

He begins peeling off his many layers of clothes and I'm fascinated, unable to pull my eyes away. He removes his coat and shirt by unsealing the seams that run under his arm and then pulling them over his head, being careful of his wings.

I see his real shape for the first time. Wings are like another set of limbs that jut out of the clavicle. It makes his upper back bulge with the extra muscle, but aside from the wings, he looks completely human. Especially when he's got them plastered flat against his back. I study his physique like a scientist, but then my eyes travel across his body to the scars. They are white, like they've been there a long time. And they are numerous. He begins to tug on his pants and I dunk my head under to shake the filth off my hair.

I try to wait underwater until I hear him get in, but I run out of breath and surface, stealing a glance at his naked form as he enters the pool. His dark curls are covering his eyes, so my intrusion goes unnoticed until he's in up to his waist and looks directly at me. He swims over and takes my hand as my heart pounds in my chest.

Chapter Nine

He pulls me towards him and I melt at his contact even though his hands have been touching me on and off for the past two days.

"Come here," he says in a low voice.

I do.

Of course he's pulling me so if I wanted to resist I probably couldn't.

But anyway, I don't resist.

He pulls me into his chest and spins me around and I feel something cold dribble onto my head and it smells like flowers. His hands move to my scalp and begin massaging as I smile. "I could almost love you right now for doing this, you know."

"That's pretty much the point, Junco."

I don't have anything to say to that, so I keep still and quiet and his fingers dance along the length of my hair like he's massaging the shampoo into each individual strand. Finally, my entire head is frothy. He turns me around again and says, "Rinse."

I dunk under and shake my head, then pop back up. As soon as I surface he's pulling me again, and this time he leads me over to the small rushing waterfall. "Go ahead, stick your head under," he says with a smile. I do, and the shock of cold water snaps me out of my fog. I gasp for breath and rake the droplets across my lashes to clear the blurriness.

I look over at him and shake my head, but I can see a real smile underneath his pretend innocence. "Here, catch!"

I do catch and find hair conditioner in my palm. "OK, shampoo I can understand, but conditioner? You must bring all the girls down here for a midnight bath."

He laughs at that and begins to shampoo his own hair. "Right, because there are so many avian girls to choose from on Earth."

I watch him in silence for a few minutes, thinking about what he said. "How long have you really been down here?"

He dunks under to rinse out the bubbles, then bobs back up and runs his fingers through his black hair as the water trickles down his chest. "Here? About two years."

"Two years? What the hell have you been doing here for two years?"

He scowls at my cursing but answers my question. "Watching you, Junco."

"That's really creepy."

"Yeah, well. I guess it is what it is."

"Why not just leave me alone? Why do anything?"

"Because if you're avian you belong with your own kind."

"If. If I'm avian? But I've been raised human, I'm human. And I don't even have wings, so how can being avian even be a possibility?" We float there, looking at each other and his eyes slip down to my chest just below the surface of the water, making me blush and avert my eyes.

"You haven't even matured yet, Junco."

"Ouch," I say, looking up at him. "That stings. I might fight like a boy, but I'm not shaped like one."

He shakes his head, says "I'm not talking about that," and then laughs a little. I think I just made him blush.

My mouth forms a little O.

"Avians grow much like humans do, up to a point. Then we go through a second maturation process and that's when your wings form."

"You aren't born with wings?" This fascinates me. "Does anyone else know this about your race?"

"I dunno," he confesses. "Probably some of them do. The ones responsible for this... mess we're in now certainly must."

"Then why are you telling me?"

"Because in all likelihood, Junco, you are avian. At least," he pauses, "in part."

"What does that mean, in part?"

"It means that you might not be one hundred percent pure avian, but might have human blood mixed in."

"Maybe that's what I am then, part human and part avian."

"I hope not."

His words come out too quick and sting me into silence. But then I shake it off and ask the obvious. "Why?"

He leans his head back and floats there in the steam for a few seconds, thinking. "Isn't it better to be one or the other?"

"I don't know, is it?"

He laughs. "It definitely is."

"What do you want me to be?"

He smiles at me. "I want ya ta be yerself." I'm just about ready to think that's the perfect answer, but then he continues. "As long as yer one or the other."

"Oh." I can't hide my disappointment and he can't take back the words, so he moves toward me, grabs my hand, and pulls me over to the other side of the pool. "Here," he says as he takes my hand and places it on a flat rocky ledge under the water. "Sit." His smile is back, but now that I've seen the real thing, it looks superficial.

I sit and he sits next to me. Then he pulls me to his chest and wraps his arms around my stomach. His wings curve in, and cradle us both. "You want to know what I think, darlin'?"

His words come out soft and he even makes the darlin' part sound sexy, but my mind is thinking about what I am. "Sure," I say halfheartedly.

"I think yer one hundred percent avian and I think that in the end, it will be something you'll come to love about yerself."

"Yeah, maybe," is all I have to say to that. I recall the scars on his upper body and turn to look at them. "What's all this?" I ask.

He eyes track down to the scar my finger is tracing on his chest. He turns me back around and his fingertip traces a scar on the fleshy muscle midway between my neck and my shoulder, but at the same time his other hand slips to the skin just below my belly button and finds the raised horizontal line across my lower stomach. "What's all this?"

I shake off the hand on my shoulder and force his other hand up higher so it can't touch the scar. "You're in my personal space, Tier."

I feel him shrug and we move on. "So, Junco Coot. Why did ya not just walk home when ya got out of the cave earlier?"

I sigh as his hands wrap a little tighter around my middle and I try and pry them loose, but don't succeed.

"Would you have come gotten me from my home, if I did?" I ask, looking back at him. He studies my face and nods. "So, there was no point then, right?"

"And?" he prods me along.

"And—" I'm not sure, but he's waiting. "I dunno. What am I gonna do in that house by myself?"

"So, yer lookin' for company?"

"Jasus, Tier. I don't know. I'm looking for answers, I guess. Just drop it."

He moves his hand up to my neck and strokes the ugly scar on my shoulder and I feel a wave of heat rush up into my face. His hand continues, then slips over to my chin and he gently turns my face toward him and reaches down to kiss my neck. I gasp and he takes this as encouragement. His mouth reaches up to meet mine and for a moment I let him.

But then I pull away. "Don't—do that."

My words come out low and deep because I can't hide my desire, and I look into his eyes but see only sadness. He smiles again, then releases my head and I am once again facing forward.

"Do ya want me to give ya the answers yer looking for, then?" he asks.

I pull my legs up onto the rock shelf and rest my head on my knees as I hug them to my chest. Then I tilt my head enough so I can see his face behind me. "Do you have them?"

"I'm not sure. Some. Maybe."

I don't say anything to that, just sit and think.

His hand tracks to my exposed back and his fingertips trace a line down my spine into the water. I buckle at his touch.

"Does that hurt?" he asks.

"A little, why?"

"Plasma burn on yer back. When did that happen?"

"The MR. They stunned me when I was running in the tallgrass."

"Why?"

I shrug. "Who knows."

"Ya know why, so tell me. Why did they stun you, Junco?"

I look sideways at him. "Back off, OK? It's none of your fucking business."

He lets out a little burst of air and transitions into neutral territory. "How about a story, then?"

I stay silent for a moment, lost in the shiver that bursts from his dragging touch up and down my back. "What's it about?"

"The goddess, our greatest goddess, Inanna."

I look back at him, interested now, and he begins.

"We have two parental deities, the God Old Crage, and the Goddess Inanna. Old Crage is just your regular pantheon figurehead. He's pretty laid-back and he only has a few hard and fast rules for his children to follow. Nothing too extraordinary.

"But Inanna, she's something else altogether." He smiles at my smile, and then continues. "She's never satisfied, like most women." I grunt at his jab, but let it slide.

"She's already the ruler of all heaven and earth, all space and sky, and all the world's water. But there's one place where she can never go, and that's the world down below. This really ticks her off, so she conspires with her faithful servant, the magpie."

I groan at the mention of the trouble-making bird and he reads my mind. "Aye, you'll never make the right choice if ya conspire with a magpie, they're always up for trouble. But anyway, she tells the magpie that she's going to the world down below to demand that the ruler, who happens to be her sister, Eresh, submit the final realm to her and Old Crage. So she dresses in her finest attire to tempt the seven gatekeepers who guard the path to find Eresh."

His fingers are still tracing a pattern across my back and I realize with a start that he is drawing wings.

"And then off she goes.

"Inanna approaches the first gate and demands, as goddess of heaven and earth, all space and sky, and all the world's water, to be let in, but the gatekeepers demand a gift of power.

"As a token of her power she leaves her lapis rod and goes forward to the second gate. There the gatekeeper demands a token of humility, and so she strips off her gown and goes forward naked.

"At the third gate the keeper demands a gift of beauty, so she takes off her royal beads and drapes them over the skeleton of bones as she passes through.

"At the fourth gate the demand is for treasure, so she takes off her jewel-encrusted wedding ring and hands it over.

"At the fifth gate the keeper wants service, and so Inanna, goddess of heaven and earth, all space and sky, and all the world's water, bows her head and bends down to wash his feet in a tub of warm water.

"At the sixth gate she's asked to give wisdom, so she recites the prayer of protection that Old Crag uses to keep the whole world safe.

"She finally reaches the seventh gate and there the keeper is a large angry spirit who has been sent to the underworld as punishment by Old Crage. His demand is the truth.

"Inanna, who is not privy to the secret council kept by her husband, cannot provide the truth he is looking for, so she improvises and casts a spell that will reflect the world back to him in the gazing pool, and then tells him his truth is in the mirror.

"Finally, stripped of everything she has and standing naked in the unbearable heat of the sun burning the world down below, Inanna reaches her sister Eresh, sitting on her throne, and demands that her sister submit."

Tier pulls me back against his chest and begins to whisper in my ear, the magic of his words dancing across my cheek to make their way into the depths of my head, and I shiver with anticipation.

"Eresh looks at her visitor in all her nakedness and says, 'Sister, there is no reason to beg for my realm. You are my blood. And now that you have come here I think you should stay, and feel the heat of the darkness, while I shall go up and feel the glow of the light.'

"Inanna is about to disagree when Eresh takes her prisoner and traps her inside a dark trunk. Then she takes her leave of the throne room and one by one, on her way past each gate, collects Inanna's personal items so that when she comes up from the world down below she is wearing Inanna's wedding ring, her royal beads, and her dress, and has her all powerful lapis rod.

"Nins, that's the magpie's name, is tricked into thinking Eresh is Inanna by all her royal garb, and is astounded that she has made her way back and plans a great party. Later, after the party is over, Eresh is lying next to her new husband feeling satiated and glowing with excesses of food and drink.

"But Inanna, in the world down below, is plotting her return. She is well on her way to escaping the trunk, and soon, she is well on her way to escaping the Seven guards at the gates. She is the Goddess Inanna, blessed by her uncle, the god of all that is known, with more gifts than one woman would ever need.

"But her greatest gift is that of decision-maker. No other gift makes her so powerful or so feared. And her Sister, though she does possess an entire world, cannot prevent Inanna from making the decision to leave.

"Inanna crosses back over the first six gates that bind her to her sister's realm, but at the Seventh, she is instructed to provide her proxy. You see, you cannot leave the world down under unless there is someone to take your place.

"Inanna, being a goddess of love and battle—among many other things—promises a suitor to stand in for her and then she makes her way back to her home. When she sees Old Crage in bed with Eresh she is crazed with jealousy. She snatches them both up and drags Eresh back to her realm and leaves her there. To punish Old Crage, she makes him stand for her at the Seventh Gate for half the year, while her suitor will stand for the other half.

"From that day on Inanna is also given the title of Goddess of Retribution. Eventually Old Crage does get out of his commitments, but only because Inanna feels guilty and helps him trick another suitor into taking his place."

Tier stops and waits to see if I say anything. But I don't. I just lie against his chest for several minutes counting each time it moves in and out.

"Junco," he says finally, turning me to look at him. "Do ya see?"

I let out a long exhale. "Yeah, I get it. Don't be a victim."

He laughs. "Yeah, that's one way to see it. Don't let life happen ta ya, decide how it will go. We all have the power of decision, unless yer a slave." He lifts my chin up from his chest. "And yer not a slave, Junco."

I smile. "No."

And then Tier pushes me off him, stands up, gets out of the pool and walks away. "I'll get our clothes."

Chapter Ten

True to his word, he does have something for me to wear, but it's one of his outfits that was never made for humans. The soft, thick black shirt is tailored to fit a being with wings. It's really more like a vest that fits over the head and there are seals which hold it together under my arms. The thick, black, canvas-like jacket is made the same way. The pants, also black and made of the same material as the jacket, are way too long, but he cuts them with a knife, just like I did a few days ago with the jumpsuit.

Everything is over-sized in an exaggerated manner, but it feels good anyway. I have to wear my old boots because his are made for talons, and would never work for human feet, even if he had my miniature size, which he doesn't.

When we are finally dressed in the clean clothes the dreamy feeling in the hot springs pool is gone and I feel warm and fresh. He looks me up and down, then smiles and takes my hand as we walk back the way we came.

Tier halts abruptly and I slam into him in the dark. "Hey," I say in a joking tone, "what's the deal?"

He turns to face me and I see his eyes are glowing bright green. "Shhhhh," he says.

I'm quiet, more curious than worried, and stand behind him as he waits, maybe listening. Or maybe his eyes see in the dark. I'm not really sure which.

After a long several minutes, he looks back, his eyes

still bright, and tugs me forward with him. "What is it?" I whisper again. But he just squeezes my hand and stays silent as we continue to make our way in the blackness. I figure we are about halfway back to the main cavern.

My arm is jerked as Tier ducks into a small side tunnel. He pulls me in close so he can whisper in my ear. "There's a pack of nightdogs ahead."

"What?" I whisper back. "Where did they come from?" My heart beats faster with each second.

"Junco," he says so softly that I can barely hear him. "This entire mountain is a major breeding den for them. They're everywhere."

"You mean I could have been eaten alive when I left the cavern?" His eyes glow as he looks down at me, but he doesn't say anything, so I take that as a yes.

We wait there for several minutes and I can feel him straining to hear any sign that they are either still around, or are gone. He grabs for my hand, but instead of leading me out into the main tunnel, he continues down the side shaft. I have no choice but to follow him and spend a lot of time looking back over my shoulder. This is a futile gesture be-cause it is pitch black and I don't have glowing night-vision eyes.

We both hear the haunting vocalizations at the same time and the hair on the back of my neck stands on end, charged with the chill that seeps out through my skin.

We freeze and listen. The howl begins low and ever so gradually grows in pitch and intensity, until finally it is a blood-curdling chorus of screams that makes my stomach shift in terror. They are very close but I cannot tell if they are ahead in the small tunnel or behind us in the main corridor. I trust Tier to keep their location straight and just try to keep my breathing under control, but I am not having much luck. Tier squeezes my hand again and moves forward, then stops and pushes me into a crack in the wall.

"Go to the end of this crevice, it will be tight, but you'll fit, I promise. Then use the formations on the side of the rock to climb up." His green eyes look up and I follow his gaze. "There's a ledge up there. Get to it and don't move until I come get ya."

He pushes me in as I nod my head and I begin to move forward into the narrow passageway. I have both arms stretched out so I can feel for the rock formations on either side as I make my way deeper and deeper into the crevice, all the while Tier is getting farther and farther away from me.

About thirty paces in I begin to doubt him and almost turn back when the passage becomes so narrow that I have to squeeze sideways. I scrape against the rough rock and am thankful for the thick alien clothes to protect me from the ragged edges. I continue to force myself to move forward, even as the rock presses up against my chest so hard my lungs are pushed in.

There is some shuffling behind me and I stop and con-sider calling out to Tier when the screaming starts. I panic and begin forcing my body into an opening that continues to get thinner and thinner. The sound of bones breaking echoes through the caverns and I can hear the nightdogs snarling and howling. The screams are etched into my brain, but I cannot tell if they are avian or canine.

Then everything falls silent.

I wait, panting so hard that I'm afraid I will begin to hyperventilate and I will Tier to call out for me to tell me that it is safe and I can come out.

But he doesn't. Instead I hear the insane snarling of a nightdog and it grows in intensity as I realize it's charging towards me. I imagine the teeth that will tear into my body and squirm into the crevice as far as I can.

The dog attacks and grabs my coat. I hear a great rip as the fabric gives way to the razor-sharp teeth and I remember my knife, tucked securely back in my boot after I dressed in the hot spring cavern. I am wedged tight between the rocks and have no way to reach it so I force myself to squeeze even further into the crevice, hoping that the end is near and it will open up into a passage that will lead me to the rock formations on the side of the wall, and ultimately to safety.

The dog attacks again. This time it grabs my leg and I feel the skin lift up and off of my calf in a sickening squishy tear. I scream with all my breath and kick wildly where I think its face might be. After a few unsuccessful attempts I connect and the dog cries out and backs off. I suck in my stomach and squeeze my shoulder a little farther, praying to God that I'm not just making myself a nice trapped dinner meal for a pack of wild animals. My shoulder scrapes hard against the rock and even through the strong alien canvas coat I can feel the gash that opens in my skin, and then the warm spill of blood as it runs down my sleeve.

The dog makes another attempt to eat me and lunges once again, but my shoulders break through the obstruction and half of my body is free. I fall down as my leg is grabbed by the snapping jaws beyond the slim crevice and I kick hard one more time to free myself. It lets go and I scramble to my feet, feel for the rock formations, and climb as fast as I can. I lose my grip on the calcium deposits slippery with trickling water, and the first dog makes its way into the small crevice where my legs were just seconds before. I regain my grip and climb again, and when I reach the top I fall over and choke as I inhale like I'm breathing water and not air.

Both dogs are snapping below me now, but I get to my knees and begin to crawl back towards Tier. It takes me for-ever because I can't see anything and I'm afraid of falling down once I reach the edge. I hear some occasional snapping up ahead and for a moment my mind sees Tier being eaten alive. I push this gruesome thought aside and move faster and faster until I reach the edge.

I see Tier's green glowing eyes stare up at me when I peek over the edge, and my heart sinks. The area is illuminated just enough for me to pick out the eye-shine surrounding him, and I count three sets all attacking and retreating, trying to overwhelm and take the upper hand. I slip the knife from my boot, stand up as far as I can without hitting my head on the sharp stalactite formations, and jump down on top of the raging animal that has taken hold of his arm, plunging the knife into its side.

The wild dog bawls in pain as I twist the knife and puncture the lung, then remove it in one swift motion. It lets go of Tier's arm and I'm knocked down by his sudden free-dom. In a moment we have reversed positions, he is up and I am down, and the remaining two dogs come in for another attack.

One grabs Tier by his wing and I hear an anguished scream erupt from his throat that makes my skin crawl. His eyes burst with color that almost illuminates the entire passageway and I can finally get a good look at what we are facing. The scruffy mane of fur that lines the wild dog's throat protects the jugular from almost all attacks, the canine teeth are almost three inches long, and they possess the claw length and sharpness of a grizzly bear.

The light isn't enough to inhibit their attacks, but it sure scares the hell out of me. The sheer size of them causes me to scoot backwards into the side of the jagged rocks of the corridor. Tier is breathing hard and circles around behind them so that his internal light source keeps my field of vision illuminated. "Stay put there, Junco." His breathing is labored but his voice is remarkably calm. "Don't do anything else, I got this."

"Like hell you do!" I scream and then they are upon us. I hear the swoosh of wings and the another avian screech comes up from Tier's throat as his powerful talon reaches out and snatches the dog closest to him. His wings beat hard trying to give him lift to attack with both feet, but the confined space inhibits this move.

I am fixated on his futile attempt to fly inside the corridor when the other dog attacks. My knife is still in my hand and I lunge forward to meet it halfway, trying to put it off balance. It knocks me backward and I feel another tear across my calf, then the sharp clang of the knife as it falls from my hand. The animal is on top of me before I can even process the events and it pulls back before striking at my throat.

I block automatically to thwart the attack and its teeth pierce my left hand and rip. For a moment time stands still and I wonder if I still have all my fingers, and then Tier's light fades and the dog is upon me as I pass out.

I come to, probably just seconds later because the dog is right next to me and Tier has it pinned down with one of his massive talons. Then I witness the second living creature beheaded by the powerful avian claws in as many days and I shut my eyes to the hot, sticky horror that spills out of the neck and splatters across my body.

The cave goes silent.

"Junco! Hey, ya OK?"

I feel him pick me up but I'm either in shock or going blind because even though I know he is moving, my vision blurs in and out of focus. He carries me and we travel for several minutes, in which direction I have no idea because the world goes dark.

Tier is peeling off my clothes as I try to object, but his fingers touch my lips and I remain silent. Soon after he lowers me into the hot spring water once again and I feel his wings cradle me into a deep, healing sleep.

When I regain consciousness we are back in the central cavern and I am warm and dry. But I see the nightdog attacking me and I thrash around wildly and sit up. Tier bends down and gently takes my hands. "Yer OK, Junco. The dogs won't come this far into the light."

I know that. They can barely tolerate the full moon, and this cavern is lit up like the Sun. But I can't shake the feeling of the attack and I try and take a deep breath but only succeed in coughing.

"Do I still have fingers?" I finally gasp.

He smiles but doesn't answer. "Tier," I sputter and cough again. "Am I OK?"

"You're OK. Just relax." He pushes me back lies down next to me. "Just relax for a little longer, then we can talk about yer scorecard." His smile is gone but his attention makes me feel a little better.

"Are you OK?"

"Didn't I just tell ya to relax?"

"I can't help it, I need to know."

"We're both OK. Trust me, all right?"

I want to believe him, but I don't. He must see this in

my expression because he looks into my eyes, and the glimmer soothes and calms me as he begins to talk in a soft, sad, voice.

"You'll never miss them, Junco. I promise ya, you'll never even know they're gone."

And I try to say, I do trust you, Tier, but the weary darkness creeps in and overtakes all my conscious thoughts.

Chapter Eleven

I sleep until I wake, and I have no idea what day or time it is, or how long I've been tucked away in this cave, but I have an urgent need to crawl out and become one of the living again.

I wait to hear Tier's admonishing voice, but then realize I am alone. Just getting uncovered from the blankets wipes out most of my energy, but I force myself to sit up and look around. I spy some water bottles near the bank of com devices Tier has displayed on a makeshift shelf.

I pad over there in my socks and gulp a full bottle down in seconds, then reach for another. When I've had my fill I look down at my bandages and almost retch it back up. The skin wrap is high-quality and stretched tight over my hand and between my fingers so I can see the outline of what's left. Most of my pinky and ring fingers on my left hand are just gone. I wonder if the nightdog ate them or left them on the floor of the cave.

The devices on the shelf suddenly come alive with light and then I hear words in a language I don't understand fill the cavern. "Tier," I call, just in case he's nearby, but get no response. I stand up on my tiptoes to get a better look at the coms. They are little rectangle cards with smooth data displays. They show a map, much like the one I saw on that first day with Tier, and I wonder if they are trackers. Does the little beeping sound mean they've found us? I recall Tier's words a few days ago, that these people who were tracking him weren't his people. I pick one up and watch the little blinking light and listen to the foreign language. To my surprise, I can pick out a few intelligible words.

Then the talking stops and the device in my hand goes quiet, just as another one blinks and beeps, then settles back to sleep. Getting woozy standing there, I grab them all and take them over to the sleeping bag and drop them into the soft tumble of blankets. I look at them, one by one, but now they are all silent and the blinking has stopped. The one that was speaking is definitely alien tech, because I don't recognize the language. I pick that one up and tap it in various places on the screen, but it doesn't respond.

There are about five others that appear to be Mountain Republic standard issue. He must have taken these off soldiers that he killed over the past few days. This brings up ugly memories that I wish I could forget. It's difficult to merge the two versions of Tier: one as alien out to kill everybody and the other as the kind guy with wings who washes my hair and tells me stories.

All of the MR devices have a transparent "out of range" warning splashed across their screens except one. And this one does look like a tracker. I don't dare touch it, in case it activates our location. I stop cold when I realize that I just grouped Tier and me into us and the MR soldiers into them.

If Aren had still been alive would I still feel this way?

I don't have time to answer because Tier swoops into the cavern and lands next to the sleeping bag. His eyes are wild as he sees me holding the MR tech. "What did ya do?" he demands.

"Nothing, here," I say as I hand it over.

"Did ya touch it?"

I shake my head.

"Tell me exactly what happened."

"It flashed and beeped. That's it." I wait for his eyes to say he believes me, but I'm a little put back when I don't find the trust. "That one," I say, pointing to the avian device, "was talking."

He plucks it off the blanket and looks at it in earnest. "Tell me what it said, Junco."

I'm almost ready to tell him I don't know, but I realize that I do. "It gave positioning coordinates for a pick-up window. I didn't catch it all, that's all I know."

"Was it in English then?" he asks, even though we both know damn well it was not in English.

I shake my head.

"Then how do ya know what it said?"

I shrug. "I have no idea," I say as a long heavy sigh erupts. But he smiles, apparently happy about this development.

"You know because it's imprinted inside of ya. The language and culture of the avians. Just being around us draws it out."

"Is that good?"

"Better than the alternative."

I'm afraid to ask, but I do anyway. "What's the alternative?"

He doesn't answer, just stoops over to pick up the coms and carries them back to where they should have been on the wall.

"Did ya try and read the letter, then?"

I'm about to say what letter when I spy the crumpled piece of paper I tossed aside before leaving the tunnel. I look up at Tier, but he's no longer interested in our conversation, so I crawl off the sleeping bag and reach out for the ball of paper with my good hand, and begin to peel it open and smooth it out.

The writing is thick and decorative. I'm not sure if all their writing is this way, or Tier just has stunning penmanship, but I am impressed by how beautiful it looks to my amateur eye. I study each line, willing myself to understand, but I get all the way to the end of the full page document before anything clicks. It's my name, but not in English, so that's some progress. I stare at the lines that spell out Junco and I am in love with how it looks on paper. And written by Tier.

"Translate it to me, please!"

"That would defeat the purpose of the letter, Junco," he answers under his breath.

"What's that supposed to mean?" But he ignores me and goes back to inputting something into one of the devices.

I take another look at the writing and find that Tier's name also stands out to me as intelligible in the markings at the end, like a signature. My mind goes directly to the absurd and I wonder if it could be a love letter. I blush at my thoughts and glance up to see if Tier is looking at me, but he's not even close to being interested.

No, it's probably not anything like that since he wrote it before all the hot springs stuff happened.

My mind swings to the polar opposite: what if it explains things I don't want to know? This strikes me as the more real possibility.

I smooth the letter out a little more, then fold it neatly into quarters and search out a pocket in my alien canvas pants, and slip it inside. That's when it hits me. "Shit! The papers." It comes out louder than I expected and Tier glances over with a quizzical look on his face.

"Everything OK?" he asks.

I'm not sure, really, so I hesitate. I never opened the envelope. I was just taking it to Dale. Old Ben Wassing pushed it into my hands as I was rushing out of the funeral that day I hit the deer. He mumbled something about the estate and Dale. Then winked at me like a dirty old man and said it was private.

Which to me translates to secret.

"Hello?" Tier asks. This time he's got a look on his face and is starting to get up.

"My horses," I finally blurt out, not wanting to share something I'm not quite sure about just now. "My horses are alone back at the farm."

"Should I care what this means?"

His attitude ticks me off and I'm not in the mood to talk anyway. "Forget it."

Instead of going back to his business, he comes over to me instead. "Yer papers and yer horses? I don't see the connection."

Apparently someone hears everything, regardless of how he answers you. "Nothing, just some documents my father left for Dale. I really was just driving them out to him that day, ya know."

He winces his disagreement. "And the horses?"

I shrug. "Our barn manager, Michael, quit several months ago, so no one's taking care of them because I picked up the slack."

Tier looks away then, and I am just about to turn as well when he says, "I don't mean to be harsh, Junco, but yer not going to need to worry about yer horses anymore."

His directness stuns me. "What's that supposed to mean?" I ask, irritated at how little my life means to him.

"There are no horses in space, darlin'."

The whole situation hits me then, and even though I knew his objective was to take me somewhere the idea of leaving Earth never even entered my mind. I am stunned silent. And then he walks back over to his tech devices as I stand up, furious. "You're going to take me off the planet?" Just uttering the words makes me feel absurd.

He stops and turns and the look on his face tells me everything I need to know, but the words that come out in his thick accent bite just the same. "Junco, I'm a soldier and I have a mission. So, yes. I will be ripping ya from yer little horse, yer flying acrobatic tricks, and yer quaint little Council. You can huff all ya want over there," he continues, "but the simple truth is that yer imaginary life as a Farm Family daughter who lives in Council 3 of the Rural Republic, in the United Republics of Earth—is now over. The sooner ya accept that, the easier it will all be from here on out."

"You don't even know if I'm one of you. I'm not avian and I'm not leaving Earth."

"Everything has a consequence, Junco. Just remember that."

I slump back down on the sleeping bag and turn away from him. He seems satisfied with the outcome of his sharp words because I hear his footsteps as they cross the cavern to where his previous business is waiting.

But if he thinks I will just fall into his clutches without a fight and leave my whole life behind, he will make the same mistake Cole did. Underestimate me at your own risk, birdman.

Chapter Twelve

Picture yourself standing on the edge of a dock...
I'm not fucking standing on that piece of shit dock!
In front of you is a mountain lake...
I'm in a cave—
... and behind you is a small cabin...
Not.
... pristine white curtains flowing in the breeze passing through the windows...
Going.
... Down below the water you can see the scales of brightly colored fish reflecting the sunlight...
Back.

My dreams are unsettled as I sleep away my anger. In this one I am a small child and we are somewhere far away, skiing in the mountains, but not our mountains, or even the mountains of the MR because we never ski there. I'm too little to know where exactly, but I sense the people are different. I am fixing a wrinkle in my sock that is making my ski boot uncomfortable and then the three of us head off to the lifts. The dream surges ahead, and we are back down at the bottom of the mountain, on the side of a road. My breath is labored and has the stench of vomit. I feel like I will pass out. My parents are arguing and all the air rushes out of my body as I fall to the ground. They both run over, and my father is still angry. My mother pushes him and lifts me up and slips me into a large silver car. She stays angry, and they continue to argue. We end up in a cabin and then the police come and my mother is taken away and I never see her again.

I wake to the sound of Tier's voice whispering across my cheek and I put the wall up immediately to stop the gentle charm. My eyes remain closed, my breathing deep, and my body motionless. If he suspects my ruse, he doesn't show it, and I let the words he spoke sink in.

More orders.

I am inclined to stay put, as he so eloquently phrased it, but not because he told me to. Leaving the safety and light of the cavern isn't even close to being on my agenda. Teaching myself to read avian and snooping around in his personal stuff, is.

I wait for a few minutes to see if he'll come back and check to see if I'm making trouble, but I'm anxious to start my task and I spill out of the sleeping bag and sit up. He's put a bowl of 'nutrition' next to me, but I swat it away and the spoon goes reeling, clanking across the rock floor.

I think I've figured out the secret to learning the avian language thanks to Tier's offhanded comment the day before. He said that the mere exposure to avian things triggers something inside me and creates a learning experience. Well, that's my interpretation of what he said anyway, and I'm basing my planned actions on it whether it's a hundred percent correct or not.

I make my way over to the shelf that houses the tech devices. They are all on screen-lock today. It doesn't matter, I have no interest in them. I'm looking for history that I know must surely be here if this has been his home for the past two years. I figure I can multi-task as I snoop; learn the avian language and figure out what the real situation is regarding my past, present, and future without having it filtered through him first.

There is nothing in any of the various stacks I sift through first that appears useful—only food, water, clothes, and medical supplies. This last bit stops me cold for a second and I wonder if I should check my missing fingers to see what they look like. My stomach protests at the thought and I skip the medical examination, I wouldn't want to undo all the avian bandages and try to figure out how to wrap it back up. Not when I already have the use of my left hand the way it is.

I leave that bundle of stuff and make my way over to some more weathered crates and immediately hit the motherlode with a reading device. As a kid this was one of the few tech items I could have—books and reading were always encouraged. I'm not sure of the model, it doesn't look like anything I had, but it's human so I know it can't be that difficult. I try the switch but it does nothing. Maybe it's got a biometric lock? My reading tech never had biometrics, but I have a pad on my bedroom doorknob, so I search the cover looking for a place where a fingerprint might fit, or maybe a retinal scanner. Unless it is very well hidden, I don't see a security precaution.

Maybe all it needs is a battery charge? I place it on the charge pad with all the other tech devices and continue my search as I wait.

The next crate has astromaps in it. Lots and lots of astromaps. Some of them are of Earth, and some not. Places I've never seen or heard of before. One is a ship schematic.

None of them are in English, and none of them have any markings that look remotely familiar. Not a circle around a planet or star, not a symbol, nothing. I put them aside as I continue my search, but after turning over several more crates, bundles, duffel bags, and backpacks I come to the conclusion that none of this shit is of any use to me. I don't know where he conducts all his business, but apparently it isn't here in this cave.

The reading device beeps and snaps me back to attention.

I retrieve it and then thumb the little pad that looks like it might be an on switch. It blinks to life.

"Welcome, Iliana. It has been 407 days since your last access. Would you like to update now?"

Hmmm. Would I? Why not? "Yeah, OK. Do the update."

"Updating—" it says in a pleasant voice. "Update complete. Would you like to open the most recent delivery?"

I'm really snooping now, but fuck it. "Sure." I watch the screen as the sphere is accessed and have a brief moment of panic. Fuck, what if they can track this device? I am about to turn it off when I see the lock icon in the upper left corner that flashes the word secure.

A letter written in the avian language opens.

"Translating—" the pleasant voice says once again.

That was easy.

"Would you like me to read the document, Iliana?"

I laugh. "Please do!"

"Date October 1, 2151 — all communications from this device will cease. End of message."

Well that sucks. "Are there any old messages?"

"All messages have been erased, Iliana. Would you like to see your bookshelf?"

"Yeah, sure." A table of contents flashes but it's all in avian. "Why is it in avian?"

Silence from the device.

"Can you translate this?"

"This is a graphical image and cannot be translated on the screen. Would you like me to read it to you in English?"

"Yeah, do that."

"*The Seven Siblings: Excerpts from Avian Mythology —
Part One...*" The device highlights the images as it speaks and this allows me to follow along.

"Seven siblings of the aftermath
Seven wandering spirits are they
Seven siblings created by death
Seven spirits of universal sway
Six avian children of light
All are guilty of the fall
The seventh castaway in flight
Mixing blood perpetual
Making monsters that transcend
Until the seventh brings the end."

The device goes silent.

"That's it? That's the whole myth?"

"The selection is titled Excerpts, Iliana. It is not the complete myth."

"Oh. Well, what's it mean?"

"In avian mythology the Seven Siblings are punished for creating discord among the higher species of Earth. They are cast out to create genetic instability, thus shifting the gene pool towards mutation. When their punishment is over they will come back to Earth and be reborn so that the Seventh Sibling can choose which of the higher species will live."

"Will live? Why can't both of them live?"

"The prophecy says the Seventh is a mixture of both species and must choose. And the avian will be destroyed."

"That sucks. Why would they even bother reading this stupid story?"

The device doesn't have an answer for that. It must not be sentient.

I look over the myth again and find I can read some of it myself. I repeat this several times and then fish Tier's letter out of my pants and unfold it slowly. To my surprise my heart is thumping with the thought of knowing what he wrote.

It doesn't make sense at first, at least not all of it. But my mind knows. It's weird.

Is this what it's like to have programmed learning?

I shake my head. Stupid father. I never got to learn shit this quick, I had to study like an idiot.

I focus back to the letter and my brow bunches up in frustration as I put the words together. But it's not anything I want to hear. I turn back to the myth and the acid in my stomach makes me nauseas as I take in my new information.

What do I really know about this avian, anyway? Beyond the fact that he has no aversion to murder? Nothing. That's what. I know nothing about him. My entire body is suddenly hot. Why didn't I leave last night?

Jasus, Junco! You fell for the oldest fucking trick in existence. A man!

"No, fuck—calm down. I don't fall for anyone, let alone an alien."

Shit, what the fuck am I doing here? Am I in some sort of trance? Are all those healing chemicals screwing with me?

"Goddamn it—there's no problem here. I'm on top of it."

I get up and pace the floor, wondering if I should chance it in the tunnel and leave now before he comes back. I give it some serious thought, but then I look down at my hand, at my missing fingers. They don't hurt, which is just more evidence that there are drug-like factors running through my bloodstream, dulling my senses. But even more powerful than that observation is the reality of the nightdogs. I physically shudder just thinking about them and I have real doubts that I can make that walk back outside knowing this is a breeding nest. There are a few iffy spots that would have me in a panic and I don't even have my knife. It was left back in the tunnel where we were attacked.

I hear footsteps in the tunnel and know he's on his way back. *So much for taking action, Junco.* I pick up the reading device and the letter in my good hand and wait for the confrontation.

He slips into the bright light of the cavern and walks quickly over to the tech devices and supplies to rummage around, paying no attention to me at all.

So I wait.

"Can I help ya, Junco?" he asks, but does not turn or stop looking through the supplies.

"I—" I begin, but the words get lost before they come out of my mouth.

Apparently finding what he is looking for, he turns, "Ya what?" His eyes dart down to my good hand and they lock there, briefly studying the reading tech and the letter, then lift upward to meet my own gaze. "Well?" he says walking briskly towards me, the top of his wings a little higher up behind his back that they usually are. "What's on yer mind?"

I look down, switch the letter to my injured hand, and then hold each one up as he approaches me, but the words are still stuck. He looks at both, then finds my eyes once more. "Don't believe everything you read, eh?"

My whole face squints up at him in annoyance. "What does that mean?" He ignores me and instead grabs my jacket and shirt and pulls so that they slip down to reveal the bare skin of my shoulder. "What are you doing?"

When his eyes find mine, I step back a little in fear. He grabs my shoulder tightly and pulls me toward him, so close that when I tip my face up to question him, his mouth is only a few inches away. "What the hell are you doing, Tier?"

His eyes glow briefly and I am transfixed for the second it takes for him to extend his razors, slash open my upper arm, and tear into my skin. The hot blood begins to seep out before I can even understand what's happening, and by then he's already plucked out a small flexible mesh of metal. He shakes me—hard. "What is this, Junco?"

I twist and jerk until I rip myself free from his grip and my anger grows as the blood travels along the length of my arm and drips slowly out of my jacket sleeve and onto the floor. "My health tracker, you asshole!"

"A health tracker? You do realize what Republic ya live in, correct? Ya remember, the one that shuns technology?"

"We don't shun technology, you idiot! We use it when it's necessary, and when a baby is sick and requires monitoring, we monitor them. I was very sick as a child so I have a health tracker, so fucking what?"

He flicks the small piece of tech across the room, grabs me by the arm, and pulls my shirt and jacket down once more. "Get off me." I wiggle and push him back. His grip is firm and I hear my shirt rip as he forces it down to reveal my torn skin. Then he slaps a membrane over the wound and releases me with a little push.

"We're leaving right now. If there is something ya want to take with ya," he says, eyeing the letter and the reading tech, "get it now."

He turns back to his supplies and continues to pull things out of storage and shove them in the sack.

"No," I say weakly from my motionless position in the center of the room.

He turns. "No, what?"

"I'm not going with you, Tier. Whatever's coming down that tunnel that's got you freaked out, I'm not going."

He turns back to his task and ignores me.

"I'm not going, Tier. I mean it. I want to go home now."

I watch him finish packing the small sack and seal it up. And then he walks calmly toward me and the anger in his eyes escapes as light. "Yer coming, OK. I'm not asking ya. I'm telling ya."

He grabs me by the jacket once again and pulls me with him towards the tunnel I've yet to travel through. I drop my letter and reading tech as I pull away. He lets go and trains his eyes on mine. "That health tracker, Junco? It was tracking something all right, but not yer health. It was tracking you. All these years. Everything ya did. Every. Single. Thing. And ya know what we call that, in the avian world, Junco?"

I shake my head, still locking eyes with his.

"Spying. Now, let me explain to ya exactly why we're leaving, and I do mean we. Yer precious government, who by the way, has never used this tracking on any other member of the RR, sick or not, is in collusion with the Mountain Republic and every other god-forsaken pseudo-government on this continent."

My heart skips a beat, then balances out with a series of short staccato thumps that force me to take a deep breath to calm myself.

"They were coming for ya, Junco, and only yer little impulsive flicker of teenage rebellion, and my timely appearance, has saved ya from a life of poking and prodding so they can figure out just exactly how to use ya to further their agenda."

I bring my hands up to my head and close my eyes. "Tier, I don't know what you're fucking talking—"

"And another thing, that filthy little mouth ya have is really starting to piss me off."

The last few words come out as a growl and I slink back a micro-step before pushing it down.

"Ya seem to think your Republic is just and good, that ya rural people are somehow better than the rest of them, more moral with all yer rules and traditions, a little higher, a little mightier. But yer vile mouth is all the proof I need that yer just another pathetic human pretender who follows the rules when it suits ya, and disregards them when it doesn't. Have a little self-respect, Junco. If ya believe in the founding principles of the RR, at least have the self-respect to follow the rules yer parents taught ya!"

I pick up the letter and shove it into his chest and let it go. "You'd know all about following rules, wouldn't you?"

He glares down at me. "Don't even pretend like ya know me, Junco." His eyes are not kidding and his face screams back off. "You have no idea who I am beyond being a soldier, a soldier who is trying to do the right thing. So, don't look at me like I'm something I'm not."

My anger bleeds out of me. "So what I think is the right thing doesn't matter? You're just allowed to come in here and totally fuck up my life?"

"Jasus Christ, Junco. Ya fucked yer life up plenty good without my help. Get a grip, will ya! It's over!" He reaches out and thunks a finger against my head. "Think!"

What's over? I drop my guard for a moment and turn when I hear noise coming from the tunnel.

"They're here now, and we're leaving." He grabs the letter and the reading device and quickly stashes them inside the small pack and reseals it. Then he takes my hand and pulls me with him into the hazy light of the tunnel.

And we flee.

Chapter Thirteen

My thoughts of standing my ground disappear with the light and the only thing on my mind now is the darkness. And the nightdogs.

I flick my missing fingers absently as we move, and I realize, even after everything that's happened over the past few days, I'm more terrified of those animals than I am of anything else right now. Every step into the black we take makes my panic grow and I know that it will overtake me soon. I will be helpless.

In my mind I hear the snapping of my flesh and feel the cool air as the vicious animal rips off pieces of my body. I hear whimpering and it takes me a minute to realize that I'm actually crying.

Tier stops abruptly and I think it is because the dogs are up ahead. A sob escapes my mouth and the tears stream down my face. He jerks my arm and his angry whisper briefly snaps me out of it. "Shut up, Junco!"

I do. I hold it in and wait for him to pull me along again. I can hear more noise behind us now. The soldiers have found our cavern. They will follow, probably send a team into each of the two possible escape routes, and they'll use lanterns of course. The jerky light attracts the nightdogs and will bring them out in force.

This makes me hyperventilate, and Tier stops again. "What the hell is the matter with ya?"

"The dogs, Tier! They're gonna use lights to find us and the dogs will come!"

He pressed his hand over my mouth to stop the words, but his glowing eyes soften as they search my face in the dark. "I know where the dogs are, don't worry. They're not here, OK?" I just look at his eyes, but say nothing as I try to decide if this makes it better.

He removes his hand. "OK?" he asks again. I nod, and he must be able to see me because he turns and begins to pull again.

We don't travel on the main tunnel, but take a series of side passages and when I realize I would never be able to find my own way out if something happened to Tier, the panic sets in again. He catches it before I get out of hand, and pulls me close and whispers, "Yer OK."

Our pace slows after that and I don't hear any more noises from behind. Unless they have this place mapped somehow, I don't see how they will ever find us. It feels like we've been wandering forever, twisting through small passages and crawling through low tunnels until I am helplessly turned around—I don't even know which way is up. "We're lost." The words come out before I realize I'm talking and Tier stops.

"We're not lost, Junco. Just relax, will ya?"

We begin a long descent and I slip and fall so many times my hands begin to bleed from reaching out in the dark, only to find the things I'm clasping onto are sharper than the rocks below my feet. We finally end up in a place where I can hear water dripping close by.

Tier cracks a lightstick and the room is immediately illuminated with the glowing green light that reminds me of his eyes.

I search the cavern frantically, looking for any signs of the nightdogs. He catches my panic and pulls me into his wings. "It's OK. No dogs, all right?"

I nod as I press my face into his coat, but I don't trust myself to say anything. I stay there. And he lets me.

"What did ya think of the myth you read?" he asks out of nowhere.

"The Seven Siblings? How did you know I read—"

"You updated the reader, Junco. I get updates too."

"Oh. Is it fake or is it true?"

I feel a shrug. "It's a myth."

"Is it a common myth," I ask, "with the avian?"

"A bedtime story," he replies, "recited to every young clutch many times as they grow."

"Is that how you raise your young? In a clutch?"

He doesn't answer right away, and I'm just about ready to think he's gonna dodge the question when he takes a breath and begins. "It's complicated, really. We don't come from eggs, maybe you didn't know that, but we're not birds. And we don't have our young naturally, because we're—"

His sentence drops off and I wait for him to find the words.

"We're not able to have them." The explanation sounds truncated, but I really don't care about the reproductive habits of avians right now. I only want to get the fuck out of this dark cave.

When he continues I'm a little surprised.

"You know sometimes there's little grains of truth to a myth? Like the places the Greeks built and where they say the gods and goddesses appeared and did all those things?"

I nod.

"Well, there is some truth to the myth."

I step back from him as the fear leaves as quickly as it came and I look up and see his face. "Which part?"

He smiles at me, and I wonder if this was all a plot to get my mind off the dogs. "We're an engineered race, Junco. We don't reproduce naturally because, well, it can't happen that way. It's all very sterile and nothing like the families ya have here on Earth."

"Oh," I say. "That's kinda sad. I loved my family."

"Did ya, now?" he says in a low voice.

"Yes. They gave me everything and loved me back. And kept me safe, and healed me when I was sick, and trained me to take care of myself. And I really miss them." I feel my face heat up and my throat aches with the pain of my recent loss. The tears well in my eyes, but I force them to stay put, not willing to descend back into that moat right now.

"They did a wonderful job, darlin'. A truly wonderful job." He hugs me tighter and we stay that way for a while, even after it becomes weird. "There's a little more to it, Junco. Just know that I wouldn't tell ya right now if it wasn't necessary. It's necessary, OK? That ya know."

I look up at him and wait for it.

"Those Seven Siblings from that myth ya read? They're here on Earth. Right now. And I'm beginning to think you're one of them."

I halfheartedly snort out a breath. "That's stupid. You guys are all gonna feel so dumb when you figure out I'm just another human and this shit has nothing to do with me. I'm not an avian or a sibling of anyone. I'm just Junco and that's it."

"OK, well — you can believe me or not. It doesn't matter. I'm taking you with me and we'll sort that part out afterward."

I let out a small exhale and push that last statement away for later. "How are we gonna get out of the cave?"

He tilts my chin up so I'm looking at him. "I'm very glad that yer parents did such a wonderful job raising ya. And yer highly trained, Junco, to handle stressful situations. Whether ya—" he stops for a second— "whether ya realize it or not. So I'm gonna ask ya to do something now. And ya need to trust me so we can get the hell out of here and see the stars again."

"I don't think I can do it, Tier," I say matter-of-factly as I look away.

He laughs. "But ya don't even know what it is I'm asking!"

"It doesn't matter. I recognize the speech. If you need to talk me up with shit like that before telling me, then I know I'm not gonna like it."

He brings my attention back to his eyes. They aren't glowing since the lightstick is the same color, but they are serious. "It is, Junco. I won't lie to ya. It's bad. But if you trust me, I promise that you will be fine."

I shake my head and the tears I was holding back spill silently down my cheeks. "No, I can't do it anymore. I'm done."

"Aye. But you weren't done earlier in the cavern when you told me off, were ya?"

I stay quiet and make the tears stop. I wouldn't exactly call *that* one of my stellar moments of bravery, but I let it slide.

"We don't have a choice, Junco. There are only two ways out at this point. Go back, which we know we cannot do. Or go through there."

I follow his arm and he lifts it to point to a shimmering spot of light across the small room. For a moment I don't recognize it for what it is. And then it hits me and I shake my head and blurt the words out.

"No! No, no, no! I can't even swim, I swear I can't swim!"

He just laughs at me. "Of course ya can swim, Junco. Do ya take me for a fool? Ya have a pool in yer house!"

I sniffle and look up at him. "Look, if you know so much about me, then you know I only swim in that pool when they make me and it's not even close to being fun."

Shut that shit off, Junco. Now.

"Did ya hear me ask for your trust, eh?" When I don't answer he asks again. "Did ya?"

I nod.

"Either you trust me, Junco, or you will die. OK?"

I shake my head this time and look down. "I can't. That's too much, we have to find another way. We'll wait here until they go away and then we'll leave the way we came."

"No, Junco. That's never going to happen. We have about thirty minutes before they find this cavern and then they'll kill me and take you to a place you really don't want to go."

"That's not possible, they will never find this place, not after all those twists and turns we made."

"Junco, they have scenthounds. It's only a matter of time. Thirty minutes might even be pushing it."

And the sounds I've been absently logging for the better part of our trip manifest in my forward consciousness. I can hear them. The hounds. Not the screaming of the nightdogs, but the distant baying of a dog on track. And he's right. They are not that far off.

"It's time now. I have two things to tell you before we do this." He takes my hand and we walk towards the water together. He lights a stick and throws it down into the water so I can see the bottom of the pool. The water is amazingly clear and lights up beautifully. I feel myself relax a little.

"What are they? The two things?" I ask, turning back to him.

"When I tell ya, take the deepest breath you can, deeper than any breath you've ever taken before. You won't have to swim, I'll do all the swimmin' for both of us. Just keep hold of my hand, OK?"

I take a practice breath, and nod.

He removes my jacket and takes his off as well, tying the little sealed bag of stuff from the cavern to a loop on his pants. He kicks off his boots and I do the same, then he ties them to another loop. I'm going to be cold on the other side, but that's better than being drowned from heavy clothing. I stand there in my bare feet and torn shirt with the gaping sides and look up to him, already shivering with cold, or maybe fear. "What's the second thing?"

He pulls me into the cold water with him and my teeth immediately start to chatter. Then looks me straight in the eyes and I think he's going to tell me not to panic or act stupid once we're under the water. But he softens. "I need you to trust me, Junco. Can you do that?"

He pulls me close and takes my face in his hands. They are rough and calloused, but his touch is tender. My eyes are fixated on him and I almost get lost in the green. He leans down towards my lips and I feel his breath tickle my cheek and slide across to my ear. I know what he's doing but I'm in bliss and instead of putting up the wall, I imagine a flood of water sweeping up their tenderness and rushing them through raging rapids to my brain. I feel the slightest tingle against my lips and I moan. Then his mouth covers mine and I feel a rush of warmth flood through my entire body as he presses against me, his breath heavy. The kiss melts me into his arms and I whisper, "I can do that."

We hear the baying of the scenthounds as we pull apart and he tugs me further into the pool of water. "I won't be dropping any more lightsticks. If I do they'll just get through the passage all that much quicker."

I hesitate at this revelation. "Oh, come on. You're just doing this on purpose now." I shake my head at him in the dim light. "Those things are probably in there, Tier."

He laughs. "Things? Help me out here, Junco."

"Those cave river things they found a few years ago over by Ramah. They dragged a kid off when he was playing—"

"Oh, for fuck's sake, Junco. Yer afraid of fish now too? Nightdogs, prairie lions, fish—anything else I should know about?"

"Ya know what? Fuck you. I've been *chased* by prairie lions. Regularly, in fact, all growing up. Have *you* ever outrun a raging lion?"

He sighs. "Junco, on the other side we will be at the bottom of a very deep cavern with an exit straight up through the top. I'll have to fly us both out and with your extra weight it will be very difficult to make that ascent. If I leave the lightsticks as a trail, they'll catch us."

"But they can't fly, they won't be able to get past the water with anything that will help them catch us."

"They can fly, at least one of them can, anyway. And they most certainly can catch us. No lights."

I nod at that unexpected revelation. The dogs are definitely closer now.

"We have to go. On three, take that deep breath, OK? And whatever you do, don't let go of my hand."

I swallow hard, and nod. "OK."

"One. Two. Three!"

I take the deepest breath I can and go under with Tier, but something goes wrong and I sputter out half of it in a choke of bubbles. I'm just about to bob back up and take another one when I am tugged away from the surface. I let him take me and we swim down towards the lightstick. I am hoping that he will pick it up and take it with us so I can see, but he stops before we get to the bottom and slips sideways into a passageway, pulling me along with him. I scrape and bump against the hard, sharp sides and cuts open up on my bare arms. I feel strong currents of water flow past me and I realize he's using his wings to swim.

The passageway gets narrower and the darkness is absolute as we move along and my frantic heartbeat begins to increase. Soon the fast current from his wings is still and we are moving very slowly, like he is clawing his way along the rock. My chest begins constrict with the pressure that comes from being underwater and my head throbs from holding my breath. An almost undeniable urge to puff out all the carbon dioxide building up in my bloodstream takes over my thoughts, poisoning my body from the inside out. But I push the instinct down and concentrate on keeping hold of his hand.

I feel a small tingle on my back where his avian shirt is open to the water and try to ignore it, but the tingle turns into a burn and I realize something is biting me. I push it down because I can see a small glimmer of light up ahead and I concentrate on not puffing out my cheeks and releasing the foul air that is the only thing preventing me from taking a big breath of water into my lungs.

Suddenly I am jerked backwards by my pant leg and I lose my grip on Tier's hand. The light begins to fade and I let out all my bubbles in a silent underwater scream.

Water rushes into my mouth and I try against hope to prevent the inevitable inhalation of water that I know is coming. I kick at my attacker and feel it let go, then grab onto the rocks on the side of the narrow passage and begin pulling myself faster and faster back towards the light, back towards Tier, and back towards the world outside.

My lungs ache with pain and now that the expired air is no longer taking up room inside my body I struggle against the instinct to draw in the water. I see the light ahead, getting brighter and brighter, and I tell myself I am going to make it when my mouth opens and desperately draws in a false breath. The water floods my lungs and I stop swimming in shock, gasping as I choke. The world gets fuzzy and green.

Then Tier's face is in front of me and he takes my hand and pulls. I float along helplessly, knowing that I am dying and there is nothing I can do about it. Moments later, the circle of light that beckons me to safety grows larger and larger until finally I surge out of the water, gasping for air.

And that's when the nightdog attacks us.

Chapter Fourteen

The massive nightdog grabs hold of Tier's wing and they struggle. My heart beats against my chest and I try to scream, but no air will come out, only water bubbling up through my windpipe causing me to choke and go below the surface once more. My hands flail around, searching blindly for the edge of the pool, as I fight my way back up into the air that must enter into my body soon, or I know I will die. I struggle until I reach out and feel a rock, then pull myself up and over the barrier of water.

I am on the far side of the pool, and I cling there choking and coughing until Tier's strong hands grab me and pull me out, lying me on my side so I can retch up the water from my lungs.

After a few seconds I try to talk. "Where—where is the night—" I cough and sputter and can't finish my sentence.

Tier removes a heat blanket from the sealed pack and covers me and then shoves my boots on my feet but keeps his tied to the loop on his pants. "Dead, darlin'. Nothing to worry about."

"Th-th-th-there might be m-m-m-more," I manage to say through chattering teeth.

"Shhhh, no. There's only this bitch here. And she's dead. She's dead."

I stay there, shivering from both cold and adrenaline, until my eyes wander down to the floor behind him. "Y-y-y-you're bl-bl-bleeding, T-Tier!"

"Just a cut, Junco. Are you ready for the last leg of our

great escape?" he asks.

I nod.

He hovers, giant smoky black wings flapping, and I can see that the bite from the bitch has affected his flight, but he squints down the pain and his talons reach out and grab me by the waist. I gasp as one pierces my skin, and then he swings me up and stabilizes my upper body with his arms, all the while his wings frantically beating to lift us both straight up towards freedom..

It's nothing like the quick flights we've taken together before and I begin to panic as I see bubbles on the surface of the water below us. "They're coming, Tier!" I shout over the deafening sound of his powerful wing thrusts, then whisper to myself, "Holy shit, they're coming!"

The lightstick Tier used to pull me from the pool is still lying on the floor next to the dead nightdog and I can see everything. The surface becomes turbulent and I hold my breath, waiting for what will emerge. We are almost halfway now, but our progress is slow.

My eyes strain to see the water below, and then the thing breaks the surface. I gasp. "Tier," I whisper, but I know he can't hear me over his own labored breathing and thunderous undulation of his tertiary limbs. "Tier, it's..." But the words have a hard time forming because it can't be true. "It's an avian."

He doesn't answer me, so I scream it. "Did you hear me?"

Tier ignores me again, but the thing below me doesn't. "I hear you!"

Faster, I pray. Faster! But Tier's wings are starting to beat slower, and our progress creeps along. I panic for a second when it occurs to me that we might not even make it to the top, not because of the thing below, but because Tier simply won't be able to get us over the ridge of the cavern and out into the air where we can catch the wind.

"We're gonna make it, Junco, don't look down," he says as if reading my thoughts. I want to close my eyes, but they strain to see the avian in the dim green of the lightstick below. He is huge, even from this distance, and his eyes glow red, instead of green.

"Junco!" Tier screams. "Don't look at him!" I close my eyes and pray to God that we can make it out. I don't hear any wings flapping below, and we are almost to the top when I start to hope that everything will be OK. And then I feel the new current as the giant wings of the alien below force the air to part as he makes his rapid ascent.

"Holy shit, he's coming! HE'S COMING!"

I look up and the opening is right there, but our movement is like slow motion through mud, while the thing shooting up towards us is fast and quick.

We breach the rim of the underground canyon and immediately pick up the wind, allowing us to be swooped up and out over a cliff towards the vast grassland.

I turn to look around and the thing grabs me right out of Tier's arms, fumbles as Tier corrects his flight path, and then I am falling.

The ground rushes up to meet me so fast that I gasp for air, and then I am yanked from death by a pair of sharp talons around my waist. My body feels like it will snap in two as I am carried back up to the cliff where the cavern entrance is.

And then I realize who has me and I begin to scream.

"Let me go!" I swing my legs around and try to throw him off balance, but he's strong and his grip is true. Tier comes up beside him and knocks him sideways and he drops me. I fall about ten feet to the ground, roll a few times and come to a stop with my head hanging over the side of the cliff.

I scamper away in a panic as the stranger lands next to me. I turn over and lie there looking up at him.

He smiles. "Well, that was something, wasn't it?" His accent isn't avian, it's local, and his eyes aren't red, they're orange.

Tier lands in front of me, blocking my view of this new creature in a way that I find a little possessive. "Back off, Moju," he snarls.

He has a name.

Moju smiles again and steps forward. "Go fuck yourself, Tier. I'm here to talk to her."

I squint at him as I pull myself together and get up off the ground, my wet clothes covered in dirt and dry grass. "Shit," I say in my most nonchalant voice, "you don't have to throw me off a cliff to get a word in, ya know. Obviously you two know each other, so just spit it out and let's get the hell off this mountain."

"Junco," Tier snaps at me. "Go wait over there." He points to a place several yards away, as if I am a dog to order around.

"He said," I snap back, "he wanted to talk to me. So why don't you go wait over there." I motion to the same place with my head and he hands me a look that almost makes me want to pee myself.

But I don't, I suck it back in and look past him. To the new guy. "What do you want?"

This time his smile reveals dimples and his eyes twinkle. Literally twinkle. Somehow he makes it charming instead of creepy and I can't help myself, so I smile back. It's real too. And that takes me by surprise. "Who are you?"

He glares over to Tier, who shrugs like they're sharing

some private mental conversation. Moju redirects his attention back to me.

"How much has he told you about the Seven Siblings?" he asks.

"I read a poem or myth about them, that's it, really." I look sideways at Tier and he's frowning. Then back towards the new guy to see where this is going. "You want to contribute to my severely lacking body of knowledge, or you wanna just stand there glaring at Tier?"

Apparently that's funny, or cute, or whatever, because he laughs. "I'm one of the Seven Siblings, and you are too, from what that asshole over there says. So there you have it, Junco. It is what it is."

I shrug. "So what if I am. What's it to you? Aren't you working for the MR? Sent to capture us?"

"Yeah. So? They should know me better by now. Like I'm gonna bring them back my sister. What a bunch of dumbasses."

The word hangs in the air between us. Sister.

Apparently Tier has heard enough because he steps be-tween us again. "Get to the point, Moju. Or I'll knock your ass off the cliff and you'll never get another chance."

Moju steps forward and they chest-bump themselves into a standoff. They are a lot alike from my perspective. Both about the same height, although Moju might be an inch or so taller. Tier is a bit thicker in the chest and shoulders, but that's probably because he's a few years older than us.

Us.

That takes me back a minute. It's a lot harder than it seems to get this simple characterization to line up with my current situation. Who is us and who is them? Why is it so hard to figure that out?

Both avians have black hair, Tier's is longer than

Moju's, and more wavy. Moju has a more traditional military crop. And they both have a crapload of scars criss-crossing the exposed portions of their bodies.

I let out a deep sigh at their time-wasting bullshit and look up into the sky for my friends as they do the whisper fight between clenched teeth. It's a dark night, the moon must be coming up near new, and the clearness of the Milky Way astonishes me as I tilt my head upward. I make a slow spin and find each of the circumpolar landmarks: Big Dipper, Little Dipper, Polaris, Cassiopeia, and Perseus. My spin is complete when I notice the silence. They are both staring at me.

"What the hell are you two looking at?"

Tier frowns again, but Moju smiles and spills it all out. "I know where Dale is hiding, Junco. That rat-bastard, sonofabitch got away. He wasn't at the Stag camp when Tier blew it up. If it's answers you want, he's the guy that's got them. You wanna come with me to get some answers?"

Tier is growling but I just shrug, like this is the most natural thing in the world. "Sure."

He turns his back to me. "Hop on."

So I do.

Tier is still frowning as we leap off the cliff and my screams are pushed back down my throat by the impaling wind.

I hug Moju's shoulders as he sweeps me across the plains, but then, carefully, move my grip from around his neck to around his chest. His right hand reaches out and fans across the top of the dry wild wheat as we pass over. I let go of one of my hands and try to mimic his motion, but I can't quite reach. Then his body lowers, practically into the grass, and suddenly I feel them flicking against my fingertips as we move. I laugh and I can feel through his chest that he is laughing too. Probably at how easy I am to entertain.

I glance over to my left and see that Tier's annoying frown has become his default expression. I want to scowl at him for killing my happy buzz, but I smile and lift my disfigured hand into a quick wave instead. He shakes his head at me and does a quick salute with two of his fingers and smiles back.

The wind is cold as it passes over my wet clothes, but just as it was flying underneath Tier, the heat from Moju's body radiates outward and warms me.

Flying on top is far better than being clutched in the grip of razor-sharp talons, and not only for the obvious reasons. For one, I can see everything. I lay my cheek down on Moju's back and take in the southern view of rolling hills, then switch over and look north, past Tier's body, to see flatlands, which if followed long enough will lead you right into the Bread Basket.

Second, I can relax in knowing that I won't be dropped or slip through his talons. If there is one thing I excel at, it's balancing on the back of something moving very fast. I al-most feel lazy for not standing up for a few quick flips as we move through the air.

And best of all, it feels like I'm really flying and not just a passenger. If I am an avian then that means I will, at some point I suppose, have wings. I feel my heart beat a little faster as I think about what it would be like to be so in control and free from the confines of human transportation.

Wings and flying. These are the only slightly positive things that might come out of this crazy trip.

I lean down so that my lips are close to Moju's ear. "Don't freak out, I'm gonna flip over!"

He shoots me a thumbs-up, but when I look over at

Tier, his scowl is back. I hold up one finger to him, the universal give-me-a-minute signal, then flip my body over so that I'm lying on my back. Tier is instantly next to me, holding on to my arm, and I look over and laugh at the look on his face. Moju lets out a roar that makes my heart skip, and then I look up.

It is amazing. The stars flying by from the back of a bird. Only God knows what this feels like. Well, God and me. As if reading my mind Tier flips himself over too, his powerful wings let him soar into the wind with little difficulty, even when upside down, and then we are flying together. Time stops for me and all I can see is us. He flips back to maintain his thrust and resumes his position off to Moju's left side.

I find my favorite constellations once more and then flip back over to press my cheek into Moju's back and slip my hands under his wings and feel his powerful muscles. There are two distinct sets, those which power the wings and those which power the arms, and from this vantage point I can almost see them working together in my mind. He is extraordinary, capable, commanding, and mighty and I instantly love him, whether he turns out to be my brother or not.

We fly this way for a little while and then I feel Moju's body drop into a more vertical position so he can land. I gauge the distance to the ground, match it to his slowing speed, and jump off—rolling forward into the grass and then popping back up to fling my arms in the air like I'm waiting for the dismount applause.

The guys land next to me and Tier is clapping. They are both smiling and this makes my heart happy for some reason.

"Gah! You didn't have to jump off, Juncs!" Moju is beaming down at me. His face has a bit of a wind burn to it, but I can feel the energy pent up inside him. Carrying me for a few dozen miles has not even begun to tap his reserves.

I shrug. "I'm a show-off."

He grabs me and pulls me in so he can rough me up a little and I feel it. I feel the connection. It swells within me and I hold on to it, like something precious.

Tier breaks the spell. "So, where the hell is Dale? He's hiding in the woods?"

We are on the edge of a clearing where the long grass tapers in to meet a pine forest that rolls up into a steep cliff. There is an old house on top with a crazy slanted roof and I know where we are.

"He's up there?" I ask, pointing up to the house.

Tier screws up his face. "He's not up there. That place has been abandoned for a hundred years."

He's right. I know that because that old house is a fairly common party spot for RR cadets, but I'm not sure that he should know that. It makes him feel local.

"Nah," Moju says. "We're gonna spend the day here so we don't have to fuck with the security until after we rest. He's about three miles southeast still, Juncs. We can't just bust in there, he's not totally unprepared."

Tier lets out a long breath and I can see the argument coming. "If yer taking us to where I think yer taking us..."

Moju cuts him off. "Tier, will you shut the fuck up already? You know exactly where we're going, so stop with the bullshit."

Tier just stares him down. "So we're gonna sleep where? Here?" he says, pointing to the ground. "You want Junco to sleep in the pine needles?"

I open my mouth to say something but Moju beats me to it. "She's a fucking field soldier, Tier. I'm sure she's slept outside before."

"Yeah," I nod, "I'm a soldier. I've slept outside billions of times."

Tier turns to look at me. "Are ya now? A soldier, I mean?" His look is far more serious than is warranted for this stupid conversation.

"Tier, you know—"

He puts a hand up and cuts Moju off. "Are ya sure about that, Junco?"

"Of course. I was on scrubs maneuvers all summer."

He smiles at me then, as if relieved. "Well, I guess we're sleeping on the ground then."

We truck up the north side of the hill to find a flat area that can still provide us cover from any aerial reconnaissance and lie down, Tier on one side of me and Moju on the other. Tier is not a big talker, but Moju is because he's asking me a million questions about my life. I answer each one patiently until Tier has had enough and growls for us to go to sleep like a couple of kids. We laugh at him and cover our mouths and generally act like children. Tier is lying flat out on his stomach, his hands tucked under his forehead like a pillow, looking at me. But when Moju pulls me into his wings for sleep, he turns his back and I feel shunned for being happy.

Chapter Fifteen

... and up above in the sky you see the eagles as they soar, free from terrestrial boundaries...

Finally, something that's actually true.

But I'm still not going back.

So get the fuck out of my dreams...

... because they are a restless garble of incoherent imagery that make no sense. I'm walking the streets of some dirty Old E-Bloc city one minute, then competing as an aerialist in the next. Twisting and turning in the air like a bird flying into the wind. My feet are bare except for the footwrap tape which binds along the ball and heel. The white powdery rosin makes them sticky as they search for the sweet spot that exists on the back of every horse at full gallop. There is no sound except for the tick-tick of a clock in the background. Even in my dream I realize this means time's a-wastin'. At first I'm frantic, but after a while the ticking fades into the background and finally, after what seems like an endless barrage of me slinking about in dark clothes, in even darker cities, it fades so far into the background that I can only hear it if I strain myself.

I come to the end of a dark tunnel and there is a man waiting for me there. I know who he is before he even turns around. Mr. trigger-happy commander from the motor pool. I absently wonder if he ever got the chance to shoot CP in the head, but then he speaks. This is the first sound in the whole dream besides the clock, so I lean in to pay attention. But all he squeaks out is one ominous statement. "It's all lies, Junco. Better come back to reality quick."

My eyes fly open and I reach over for Moju, but he's gone. Tier opens his wings so I can move. When I realize what just happened I'm angry. "You were in my dreams again, weren't you?" In the fading daylight I can see his face screw up as he gets ready to deny it, but I turn my back to him and push his wings off me to let the cool autumn air in.

He sighs. "Whatever happens in yer dreams, Junco, it has nothing ta do with me."

I let the anger from my dream fade away and we both stay silent for a few seconds. "Where did Moju go?"

"Top of the hill, ta find the landmark for the entrance."

"Entrance to what?" I feel like an over-sleeping mountain man, completely out of the loop after what should have been a short rest.

He props himself up on his elbow and turns me back to get my attention before answering. "The tunnel where Dale is hiding."

I lie there looking at him. His eyes are just plain green now, no glow. Nothing to make him look different. And his wings are drawn back tight against his back, the tips cupped over his shoulders. He almost looks like a human.

He studies me back and it makes me smile and blush.

"Can I ask ya something?"

I look up into his eyes as they search me for some elusive answer. "Go for it."

"How is it that ya know him for mere minutes and ya already have the look of complete trust in yer eyes?"

"Who? Moju?" I shrug. "I dunno. He just feels genuine."

"But me? I'm just lying about everything, right?"

A huff escapes my lips. "I never said that."

"Ya didn't have to. Ya tried to kill me."

He's got a point there. I feel a little reality panic coming on and begin to babble. "You came out of nowhere, Tier. I'd never even seen an avian in person before you. When he came up that tunnel I was already in the rabbit hole, ya know? I've just acclimated to strange stuff since that night on the hill. It's not that I don't trust you. Didn't I say I did before we went for that little swim back there in the caves?"

"Sure," he says, but I can tell he's not sure at all and the silence hangs. Besides, I roll back the memory and I know damn well I never actually said I trusted him. I said *I could do what he asked.* He probably remembers it correctly too.

"OK, you want to know the difference between you and Moju?" I ask. "As far as I can tell, he doesn't want anything from me. There, I said it. You want to take me to your leader, or *whatever.* Away from my home and my life. And I've got to tell ya, I'm not really interested in leaving my planet. Call me crazy, but I'm a little attached to it."

"How could you be? That's the part I don't understand."

I turn my head away. "Wow, you really are an alien. You have no clue at all." I turn back to see his expression, but it's blank. Nothing. "What kind of childhood did you have anyway? Oh, yeah, I forgot... you guys don't have families. I guess that explains things. I may not know very much about Moju, but from what I can tell at least he understands love."

Tier sneers at me. "*Love?* You think that monster understands love? You mean like yer pal Aren? That traitor ya think is such a good guy? Shit, Junco, you really have some great intuition going there, a regular Mystic

Martin. Do ya pick all yer friends this way? Hell, no wonder we're in this fucking mess."

His anger tells me that I've crossed the line somewhere, but I'm not really clear on where that line was drawn, so I'm irritated. "Whatever."

He turns then, muttering under his breath. "What's that?" I ask.

He doesn't turn back, but he repeats the words anyway. "I said, yer just so lost ya can't even see what's right in front of ya."

I discard this comment completely. "I have no idea what you're talking about, Tier."

"Then ya better pay closer attention to those dreams, darlin'. Yer having them for a reason."

He starts to get up. I tug on his arm and he stops, but doesn't look me in the face. "Wait. We're not done yet."

He lies back down and looks up at the pine trees as he speaks. "I'm tryin' ta help ya, Junco. That's all. Just help ya. And all ya do is fight me." He turns to me then. His face is blank but his eyes want to say more.

"The thing is, Tier," I smile a little to settle him, make him listen, "things have just been off since you came into the picture. I mean, everything was fine up until I wrecked the Goat and saw you on the hill and you dragged me down this stupid rabbit hole."

His lip goes up in a snarl. "Me? I'm the one who dragged you down the rabbit hole?" He huffs out some air and shakes his head.

"See, this is what I mean. You seem to be under the impression that I am the problem here. And that makes no sense to me. If I've done something to you, why don't you just tell me what it is?"

"Here, how about this, Junco. Have I ever done anything to you? Anything?"

"You killed Aren."

"He was not who you think, Junco. You don't know what I know."

I sigh. Do I want to know what he knows about Aren? No. Not right now. "You poisoned me with your claws."

"That," he huffs, "was an accident. And I healed ya right afterward. A small scare, no damage whatsoever."

"You abducted me."

"Really? You made yer escape quite quickly from my recollection. I found ya outside in a jumbled mess, remember? You could have left. I never tied ya up, I never threatened ya, I never did anything. So the truth is, yer here of your own volition. I never abducted ya."

I feel my heart quicken because he's right about that. I could've left lots of times.

"Besides, *Junco*," he drawls out my name and I tuck down a grin, "you shot at me twice, chopped me in the throat, kicked me in the jaw, and stunned me with a plasma rifle for an extended period of time."

I sit up and laugh. "It was on stun!" I knock myself in the head with the palm of my hand. "I did not understand how you could have survived ten full seconds of plasma fire." I look down at his face and then control my laugh because he is not amused.

I lie back down and change the subject quickly. "Well, you threw a boot at me. Could've hit me in the head. It was touch and go there for a second."

He smiles and then it turns into a laugh as he shakes his head, but this time I hold mine back. "And you slashed open my arm and pulled out my fucking health tracker. You're lucky I don't really need it anymore, otherwise I'd be pissed off. Plus, I have a huge gash that will probably be a scar."

"So you'd prefer to be in the custody of people who would keep ya against yer will?"

I click my tongue in frustration. "Says you!"

"Yeah, says me. And let's just take a look at the *gash* I left, OK?" His eyes meet mine as he leans his upper body over my chest to check the wound on the arm farthest from him. He looks down and gives me a smug grin and pulls gently on the corner of the membrane that he slapped over it before we fled the cavern. I can't help myself and I crank my head to the side so I can watch. He peels it back a fraction at a time, like he's trying to take care not to pull on my skin, but it doesn't hurt at all. The membrane comes off and he tosses it in the pine needles.

"See for yerself." And he leans down on me as he holds my arm up.

There's not even a scab where his razors slashed my skin open. There's dried blood, but as for the slash, there's not a red mark, not a discoloration, or any outward appearance that he ever touched my arm.

"Wow, that is some good shit you got on that membrane." I smirk up at him and wink before he groans about my swearing. He smiles and leans back, removing the weight of his body off mine, but his upper body is still positioned over the top of me. His face dips for a minute, like he's gonna kiss me and my heart literally skips a beat.

I swear he feels it.

"Do I make ya nervous, Junco?" he asks in a low voice.

His lips have my full attention but I manage to answer. "Not exactly nervous, no." His face dips a little closer and I look up to his eyes. They are his normal green color, but with little sparks of glow in them. "What does that mean?" I ask. "When they glow like that?"

He shrugs before answering. "It can mean a lot of

things. Fright. Excitement. Anticipation."

"What does it mean now?"

He laughs a little. "All of the above."

"What could you possibly be afraid of now?"

His eyes search mine. "Another rejection," he says softly.

I just look at him and then he begins to move away but I grab his arm. "Where are you going?"

He takes his hand and brushes some hair out of my eyes, a tender gesture that makes my body tingle. "We've got time for this later, lots of time."

I grab his arm again. "What if we didn't? Have more time for this later, I mean?"

"What are ya trying to tell me, Junco?"

My eyes get lost in the green depths and I whisper, "Just kiss me, Tier."

He's all business now as he takes my face into his hands and his thumbs caress the skin near the corners of my mouth. I stare into his eyes as he moves towards my lips. When he's a breath away I close them, and then his mouth is on mine, our tongues searching. It's slow, and heated, and perfect. He breathes me in and slides his hand down my face and slips it behind my ear to draw me closer. It's the best moment in my current memory and I hold my breath.

Tier pulls back for a moment and I open my eyes to look at him. "Breathe out, Junco. All the best parts are in the exhale."

I let it out and he takes me in again.

I feel Tier's body move as he takes a half-hearted kick in the back. "Get a fucking room, you two," Moju snarls in disgust. "That's my sister, you asshole."

I begin to pull away but Tier takes his time and finishes our moment. And then he is on his feet and holding out his hand. I take it and he pulls me up without effort. I can't tell if it's because I'm such a small person to begin with, or because I'm floating on air. Either way, it doesn't matter. I can barely breathe and it takes me a minute to recognize the aftereffects of happiness.

Chapter Sixteen

"I don't know," I say.

My resolve to find Dale and get answers is fading fast as I look down into the dirty hole Tier and Moju are asking me to climb into. "It's pretty dark in there."

Moju is swinging a lightstick by a lanyard in his hand. "Hence the flares, Juncs. It's fine. Plus, we have night-vision."

"Yeah, but I don't."

Tier looks down at me. "No, but you have us," he says simply.

I look up at both of them now. "And you're sure he's down there?" It seems unlikely that he'd be down in a hole in the ground.

Moju answers, "Juncs, I heard them say he was there. He's working with the MR."

Tier pipes in then. "Junco, it's not what it looks like on the outside. Underneath it's another world, believe me."

"How do you know?" I ask, wondering just how much he's holding back now.

"Yeah, Tier. How the hell do you know that?" Moju clearly knows Tier's part in all this, but wants to put him on the spot.

I look from one set of glowing eyes to another and give in. "Oh, fuck it. Keep your damn secrets." I motion to one of them to go first, and Tier takes up the lead, with me in the middle, and Moju last.

Underground the earth smell fills my nose and makes me want to vomit. It reminds me of mushrooms and personally, eating fungus is a sure sign you're either starving or are being force-fed as punishment.

We create a pattern as we descend. Tier's boots clang on the metal rungs which line the side of the tunnel. Then mine. Then Moju's softer thunk of bare flesh on the rung above my head. It takes forever and I count three hundred and twelve rungs before we stop. I don't even want to think about climbing back up.

Tier grabs my ankle and I almost scream. "Stay put here, Junco. I'm serious, no funny business."

He drops down and I can hear his wings as they catch air. I can't see anything, but a tiny splash (a long way from where I'm standing, it seems to me) signals that he's on the ground. I hear his wings again, then the sound fades and is gone. Moju lets out a long sigh but to his credit he doesn't ask me to move, or go down, or even complain that Tier is taking too long.

We just wait.

I am just about to whine about my arms being tired of holding on to the rungs when I hear Tier's wings. He grabs the rung below me. "OK, I don't see anything. Junco, I'll hover below you. Let go and drop, I'll catch you in the air. Then Moju can come out."

I want to say two things in reply. One, obviously, is how sure should I be that he will catch me before I splat in the puddle far below. The other is what does he mean he didn't see anything? Thing? Not anyone. But anything. This worries me. I let that slide too, because to be honest, the truth isn't all it's cracked up to be. Ignorance can be bliss. What you don't know can't hurt you. And the ever popular, if I knew then what I know now, I'd never have done it.

"Tell me when," I say instead.

He says "When," and I drop. His arms grab me a split-second later and he holds me tight as we descend to the ground.

Moju lands beside me and breaks the lightstick and the tunnel glows green as he drops it to the ground. I catch Tier staring down the tunnel before he notices me and smiles. That's when I know this whole thing is not going to end well. He's worried.

The tunnel is massive. It's at least five stories to the ceiling and a hundred feet from side to side. The ceiling is curved, like a suborbital hangar, and the cracked and deteriorated walls are made of concrete. Various-sized debris piles line the floor for as far as I can see in the dim glow and bits of rebar are sticking out here and there as puddles of liquid ripple when small rodents scurry into the shadows. "What is this place?"

Moju answers, "US Military nuclear weapons transport tunnel. There's an entire highway underground and this is just one little off-ramp in the middle of nowhere. They were shut down more than a hundred years ago during the Succession Revolutions. Like Tier said, it's another world down here." Moju's jovial disposition is gone now.

"How do you know this?" I ask.

He looks at me and throws his hands up. "I know a lot of shit I shouldn't, Juncs. Comes with the job."

Tier is speaking before I can ask what job. "Get on Moju's back, Junco," he says as he takes my hand. "We'll need to fly from here."

I swallow and he squeezes my hand in a show of support. "It's no big deal, really. But it's better to fly."

I decide to trust him and hop on Moju's back. We fly slow and cautious and this is yet one more red flag telling me to stop and go back.

But I can't.

Like it or not, Dale is a player in the game of Junco. And I know that Tier wants me to see him. To talk to him. Otherwise he wouldn't have let me come down here. My destiny is tied to this foul-smelling subterranean tunnel and if I go back now I'll be as clueless as I was before.

I'm not going back.

Moju slows down and we land so he can light up a stick and look around while Tier remains above us, keeping an eye on the darkness. I don't offer to climb down off his back and thankfully, he doesn't ask me to either. Moju throws another lightstick and I watch it tumble end over end until it splashes down in a puddle slick with sheen. He cracks another one and throws in in the opposite direction and only then do I fully understand the size and scope of the place we are in.

We are standing in the middle of the nuclear weapon freeway. It is massive, easily a quarter mile across, but I know that distance without reference is deceiving, so it's probably closer to half a mile wide. The height of the ceiling is the same as the off-ramp, but this one seems to be reinforced with layer upon layer of steel beams. At least it doesn't seem likely that it will come crashing down on us.

"Which way?" Moju asks.

Tier is still staring off into the blackness as I look over at him. "Moju, I thought you were the one who knew where Dale was?"

I feel Moju shrug beneath me. "Tier has always been in charge down here. He knows it better than I do."

Tier gives me a not-now look, so I drop it.

I hear scuttling off to the right and turn in surprise.

"Up now, Moju," Tier commands. We fly up and hover in the center of the tunnel, their wings straining to hold the position. I look down as dozens of small creatures crowd against the barrier which separates the green glow from the pitch black. They seem hesitant to come into the light.

"When ya live in the darkness long enough even this bit of light is blinding," Tier says, as if reading my mind.

"What are they?" I ask.

Moju shrugs, but Tier answers, "Nothing we need to worry about. Yet. Come on, it's this way."

He picks a direction, whether it is east or west, north or south, I have no idea, and we fly along once again. My stomach grows more and more unsettled with each wingbeat. There are lots of things in the dark, things bigger and meaner than the small creatures that shied away from the green glow. Things that hiss and drag large limbs behind them as we pass.

Neither of the guys react or fill me in, so I just keep my mouth shut. If there's one thing I remember from cadets it's to do the job you're trained for, and if you're not trained for the job at hand, shut up and stay the fuck out of the way.

We stop again but Moju doesn't crack a lightstick this time. I can feel his arms moving, and I get the feeling the guys are using hand signals that only they can see in the darkness, but they don't include me. Clearly talking is forbidden, so I stay silent once again.

I feel Moju reach into a pocket and pull something out and extend his hand. I can only imagine that Tier takes whatever it is and then Moju flies us backward. Tier joins us in a few seconds and then I hear a small crack and we all move forward together and land. I hear a whoosh of air as Tier strains to pull on something and then a crack of light floods the dark highway just long enough for us to slip through a massive vault-like door and quickly shut it behind us.

Things scrape against the other side of the door once it is closed and every hair on my body stands up on end. Moju shrugs me off and I slide down on the tiled floor of the hallway and look back at the door with some trepidation.

Tier and Moju are whispering to each other now. "Hey, guys? There's something on the other side." My voice must surprise them because they both look at me like I have two heads. "There are things out there," I say.

"They can't get in here, Junco." Tier explains by explaining nothing.

"Yeah, but what are they?"

He shakes his head at me again.

Now, I don't know him all that well, I mean—it's only been a few days since our first encounter on the hill, but I've seen him in quite the array of stressful situations, so I feel I can correctly infer what this head-shaking means. And it means those creatures will do terrible things to us given the chance.

So I drop it. Because ignorance is bliss and what you don't know can't hurt you and all that good shit. If I'm going to be eaten alive by some hissing freak in the dark, I'd rather not dwell on it.

Really.

Moju takes my hand and we follow Tier down the hallway. The fluorescent lights above, the ones that work, anyway, flicker and the strobe effect makes me feel like puking. "Where's the power coming from?"

Moju shrugs but Tier, once again the purveyor of everything giant nuclear tunnels under the RR, answers, "They have solar panels and a small wind farm over by Ramah. Ever seen it?"

Tier oozes little tiny bits of local knowledge that he shouldn't really have if he's just a visitor here. "I thought all that crap was shut down decades ago?"

"It was," he continues. "Officially anyway. The wind still blows and the sun still shines."

"Are we under Ramah right now?"

"Yup."

That means we aren't really that far from my farm. Ramah is only about thirty miles from us. This blows me away because in my mind we are on another planet.

"I thought you guys said this place has a security system?"

"It does," Tier answers.

"So where is it?"

Moju laughs and turns back to me as he continues to walk. "We just passed them, Juncs."

"And more up ahead," Tier adds.

"So how do we get back out now that those things are on the other side of the door back there?"

This time all I get is silence.

I stew in that silence for a while as we continue to walk the long empty corridor. It's littered with papers and debris, discarded folders, computer bits, and what looks like various charred robotic parts. The left-overs of some long ago shoot-out? I can only hope, but my best guess is that the technology lying around is not antique and neither was the battle.

The only sound in the passageway, besides the light step of our feet, is the slow drip of water that seeps out from cracks in the ceiling. The hallway branches off every now and then, but we continue on the straight and narrow until we reach the last hallway and then we take a right. A few dozen paces on Tier stops by another door. This one has an active biometric pad and Moju makes no move to grab a charge and blow through it. Instead, Tier presses his hand up to the pad and I hear the lock sequence from within. My brow furrows and I stare at the back of his head, willing him to look back at me. But he doesn't, just turns the long steel handle and pulls the door open with a whoosh.

Moju pushes me against the wall as a series of beeps confronts Tier's request for entrance, so I can't see what he does, but the beeping stops and Moju pushes me to the other side of him as we walk through, trying to block my view of the source of the beeps. I slip around him and let out a gasp. Granted I haven't seen a lot of high-tech robotry in my life in the RR, but this thing scares the shit out of me.

It's about as tall as me for one, and the eight legs protruding from its spherical body begin to click on the hard tile floor as it spots my curiosity. There's a biometric pad on the thing's chest and some compound sensors that ring its head. It makes a new noise as Tier steps back between Moju and me, and then goes quiet.

No one says anything, so I don't either.

Then Tier pushes Moju forward and we begin to walk away from the sentry. Tier follows and quietly passes us before we get to the next door. We repeat this action twice more and when we pass through the third door and close it behind us, there is no sentry in the hallway.

Tier looks me straight in the eye as he whispers, "Good job, Junco. Keep quiet and still and follow Moju."

And then he slips through a door down the hallway and leaves us standing there.

Chapter Seventeen

I look up at Moju but he shakes his head at me, so I do as I'm told and keep quiet and still. At first all I can hear is some distant buzzing of electrical equipment, and a wheeled chair rolling across a hard floor. Then some commotion and a few subdued swear words.

It is definitely Dale's voice.

Tier clears his throat.

"What the hell, Tier?"

The question hangs in the air, but Tier says nothing. I can hear his boots across the floor now, so he must be off stealth mode. They fade into the distance, getting farther and farther away from us. Still Tier says nothing.

"I told you we're done. This intrusion won't be ignored." His voice starts loud and then fades slightly, like he turned his back on Tier.

"Mistake number one," Moju whispers. I only have time to nod in agreement before I hear the thump of a body being thrown to the ground and gurgling noises coming out in short bursts.

Moju makes his move and I follow him into the lab, but there is no time to even look around before I see a robotic sentry blast Tier with some sort of pulse weapon. He flies backwards and hits a wall before slumping down into a pile on the pristine white tile floor.

Moju runs off to the left while I stand there in a panic as the thing turns its attention to me. Then I see it lock on, ready to fire and I snap back to reality. I throw my body upwards into a flip I've done a thousand times on the back of a galloping horse, but never used trying to escape a crazed piece of machinery.

The pulse passes beneath me and I grasp a light fixture and fling myself, monkey-style, from one to the next until I am on the other side of the sentry, swinging from both hands. It's searching the far side of the room for me when I hear Dale's voice command.

"Stand down! Stand down!"

The thing stops so I drop to the floor and walk over to Tier. He's back on his feet now and looking really angry. "You OK?" I ask.

His lips form a snarl as he pushes me out of the way and strides back towards Dale. But Dale doesn't back down, instead he meets Tier head-on. "What the fuck are you doing bringing her here?"

Tier pushes him, but only as a gesture of dominance, not to hurt him. The sentry perks up but retains its last command. I look around for Moju, but he's MIA. That's when I see what's in the room with me. "Oh my God, what the fuck is going on here?" I look at Tier and Dale and they both stop to follow my accusatory finger.

Which is pointing at a massive life-support machine that dominates the center of the room. The circular base protrudes out in a bulge that takes it all the way up to the ceiling. There are eight symmetrical arms which spread out like tentacles and each arm is home to half a dozen capsules with a transparent casing that allows a red glow to permeate into the lab.

But that's not the disturbing part.

It's the things inside them that make me stoop over and vomit, right there on the shiny sterile floor.

Tier steps aside and waves a hand at Dale. "Go ahead. Tell her what's going on here."

Dale looks at me as I upright myself and spit, but says nothing. Really, what can you say to someone who just discovered that you have dozens of copies of her body, in various stages of development, growing in vats filled with red goo.

"Junco, it's not—"

"What it looks like?" I finish for him, then swipe a hand across my mouth to remove the spittle from my lips. "Are you fucking kidding me? You're cloning me!" I scream the last part and I can feel rage bubbling up inside of me as I race towards him and deliver a roundhouse kick to his cheek. My field boot connects with a sickening whack, and he goes scrambling down to the floor, blood spurting out of his mouth. The sentry is back in business. It fires at me, but I flip and then run towards it and flip over to the other side once again.

It learned its lesson from last time and doesn't even pivot, just switches sensors and fires at me again, but I'm a flipping expert. Literally. I can flip all fucking day long. Once again I end up swinging from a light fixture.

"Stand down!" Dale says again, this time with much less enthusiasm.

"Don't do me any favors, you creepy piece of shit!" I snarl as I drop in front of him and kick him as he tries to get back up.

"Don't push your luck, little girl."

I've known this man my whole life but today he is a stranger. I'm about to remove his teeth with my boot when Tier takes my arm and pulls me back.

"We came for a reason, Dale—hand over the cubes. *Now!*" He doesn't scream the word so much as growl it, but I step back a few paces. For the first time since I met him I get the feeling that I have no idea what an angry

Tier actually looks like. Like I've only seen the sugar-coated version and nothing more.

Dale pulls himself together as he stands, straightens his glasses, and passes a hand over his messed-up gray hair, trying in vain to make it lie flat against his skull. He spits blood out onto the tiles at his feet, and then looks at me, ignoring Tier's demand altogether.

I know right then, he's a fucking dead man.

"You're just another clone, Junco. Nothing more and nothing less. You have no claim to that body, that brain, those skills, or anything else that's part of you. We created you and you're not even"—he looks up at Tier—"a legal citizen of this planet. What you did last week was—"

Tier backhands him so hard he falls to the floor again. The sentry's sensors blink like crazy as it tries to discern if it should disobey orders, but holds steady.

Tier grabs him by the shirt collar, pulls him to his feet and walks him back towards the lab bench filled with computers running model simulations, pipettes, and various sizes and shapes of glassware. "The cubes. Now. Or I'll cut yer stomach open and make ya knit a sweater with yer own intestines."

"You don't want her, Tier. She's not—"

Tier backhands him again and Dale shuts up.

I walk away, leaving Tier to get what he needs in whatever way he feels necessary. I am drawn back to the vats of clones and look at each one as I pass by them. I stop at a little girl. Me at age five or so. Her hair sways in the goo, back and forth across her face. I don't even look back when I hear Tier hissing at Dale about whatever. It's his business, I can only deal with one thing at a time right now. My carbon copies.

I move on to the next one, and the next, and the next. Watching the girls grow older before my eyes. As I come around to complete the circle I see an exact replica of me today and I want to smash her face in.

Who am I? Am I real? Am I just another copy? Did I crawl out of these vats? When did I crawl out? A few weeks ago? The day I ran away? Are there girls just like me lurking somewhere? Here?

I glance around the room with trepidation as some glassware behind me goes crashing to the ground. I hear muffled groans from Dale, but I don't even turn to see what Tier's doing.

There are lots of doors, lots of hidden crannies, come to think of it. And where the hell did Moju go? I take a deep breath and let it out slowly to calm my thumping heart, then turn back to Tier.

I can't tell if he's actually making progress, but the place is a mess. Papers are still in mid-air, falling in a floaty back-and-forth motion to the ground. Glass shards are all over the tiles and the previously tidy bench is now a catastrophe.

I walk up next to Tier and Dale turns his hatred towards me, then spits blood on my boots. "As you can see, Junco, you're entirely replaceable. The next girl was already dispatched."

I shrink back, a microscopic amount, but Dale catches it and laughs.

"Don't listen to him, Junco. Do ya see an empty vat over there?"

"No, they're all full."

"Case closed. We're gonna kill them all on the way out. Yer the original." He has a knife in his hand and it's pushed up to the sensitive skin just below Dale's left ear. I watch him stick it further into the skin so that a trickle of blood escapes and runs down his neck and into his shirt. Then Tier looks at me. "Yer the original and that's how it's gonna stay."

Dale laughs. "Don't be stupid, Junco, he's only here to save his own ass. That's why he wants the evidence."

Tier lets him speak his mind this time, but I put a hand up. "Save it Dale. I could give a shit why he's here, what he's done, or who he's done it for." Then I look up at Tier. "I'm ready to go."

He smiles. "Just waiting on Moju."

Dale's posture straightens at Moju's name, but Tier answers his unasked question before he can get a word out. "That's right, asshole. The two of ya just can't seem to get enough of each other, can ya?"

The power goes out and Tier laughs. "Goodbye, Junco's clones." The giant central artificial life system that powers the vats goes dark and whines as it drains the last few electrons through the circuits. The hum of living turns to the silence of death and we stand there in the dark.

Dale's rage bubbles over. "I will kill you for this, Tier. You'll be looking over your shoulder for the rest of your life, you miserable fucking piece of shit."

Moju appears and throws down a lightstick for my benefit. He's still breathing heavy from running and being loaded down with the plasma rifles. He throws a rifle to Tier and one to me. We both catch them in mid-air, a fraction of a second apart, as Dale wiggles free. Moju shoots a pulse in his back and he falls forward, smacking his face on the stone-cold tile.

The sentry wakes up and a siren blares into my ears, followed by a blinking red strobe light. It wails, drowning out the heavy moans coming out of Dale.

Tier blasts the sentry on full pulse for several seconds, long enough to make it stop and think up an alternate plan.

Moju looks at me, then Tier. "Take her out. I'm right behind you."

Tier and I both run towards the door and I don't stop when I hear the grotesque slash of razors on flesh, or even the thunk of what I know is Dale's head as it splats against something hard.

We pass through the open door and into the hallway, backtracking to the exit. I hear Moju's bare feet slap the ground behind us and then the massive explosion throws us forward and we slam into the floor, then slide into the wall and stay still.

Moju recovers first, grabs me at the same time that Tier makes it to his feet, and we haul ass down the corridor, towards all the sleeping sentries waiting for us to try and get past them.

Chapter Eighteen

The heat from the explosion beats against my back as Moju drags me down the hallway. I slip and fall, but his hands are there and we're running again before I can even register my misstep. Tier stops at the first corner and we almost collide with him. He is still and quiet, but there is nothing to hint at what awaits us if we turn into the next hallway and the wailing alarms block out any hope of hearing movement. He makes a signal to Moju, and then flattens his head against the wall before peeking around.

Lasers swipe past his face and I can see several strands of hair catch fire just from the proximity. He pulls back and swats the fire out while giving Moju another signal. Moju pushes me behind him and they both move forward firing.

The exchange is quick and then Moju has my hand again and we are running towards the first door. Tier presses his palm against the biometrics panel, but the door is dead.

"Blast the bolt on three," Tier yells.

Moju nods and in three seconds they fire. The bolt melts with the intense heat and I move back to avoid getting a proximity burn. Laser fire comes from behind me and I turn and squeeze the trigger at my attacker. There are several smaller bots scurrying down the hallway and I pick them off one at a time, leaving the hallway a blazing mess. Then Moju grabs my hand and we squeeze through the blasted door and run again.

This time the sentry isn't waiting around by the door, it's hauling ass to meet us. The laser pulses flash past me and I hear Moju holler out as one grazes his shoulder. Tier blasts the sentry with continuous fire while I pulse at its top sensors, essentially blinding it. It explodes and we duck behind a corner to avoid the full effects of the blast.

I grab Moju's hand and pull him along. I look back and see his shoulder is still smoldering and he winces in pain as we pass the blazing mess of what's left of the second sentry. Tier tries the biometrics again, but it's the same as the last one, which is all bad luck for us.

Tier and I fire straight at the bot, while Moju picks off the stray bots that are now clattering up behind us in force. I look back and see there are dozens of them now. I watch as Moju fires and makes them explode, but then I see what happens to their remains. They self-reassemble into more bots. Some are larger, some are smaller, but it doesn't matter. They cannot be totally eliminated. I turn my attention back to the sentry door which has a large hole through the middle.

Tier grabs me and pushes me forward. "Go through firing, Junco—I'll get Moju!"

I do. My plasma charge is already a quarter empty but I blast that shit on continuous stream as I squeeze through the burned-out door, sharp edges catching my shirt, making it smolder as I pass.

The sentry is directing all of its primary lasers at me, which is bad enough, but then the top of its head pops up and a rocket launcher emerges. "Tier, get in here quick." There's no answer and I steal a look behind me to see Moju struggling to get through the door without setting himself on fire. They are both a lot bigger than me. Tier pulls him back out, but Moju rolls several canisters towards me as he disappears from my view.

Grenades.

I pick one up, pull the pin, then lob it down the hallway just as the sentry sends a rocket flaming past me and through the door.

I duck as the double explosions rock the tunnel, and part of the ceiling comes crashing down, hitting me on the back.

My ears are ringing as I try to stand. The dust has obscured everything from view and my heart thumps with adrenaline as I frantically search the massive hole that was the second door just a few seconds ago.

"Tier!" I scream, but I can barely hear my voice over the ringing.

I run to what's left of the door and pick my way past the debris, swatting away the dust and coughing as the minute particles stream down my throat to clog my lungs.

I see Tier getting to his feet and I pick my way through the rubble until I'm a few paces past the door. Moju is underneath, protected from much of the blast. Tier has burns all over his body but he still pulls Moju to his feet and yells something in his face. To my injured ears it sounds like "Move yer fucking feet, warrior!"

Moju stand there, bent over and coughing for a minute, then to my surprise, he straightens up and salutes.

They both turn and start running towards me and we pass through the hole together. I look back apprehensively to see if there are more bots reassembling behind us, but the cloud of dust is too thick to see through.

We run towards the final security door that will lead us back out into the ruined passageway, then finally back to the main highway. We reach the door and Moju hands Tier a grenade and he pulls the pin and throws it, yanking me back behind a corner. The blast heat almost knocks me over, even though most of it shoots right past us. I can feel my body reaching its limit and for the first time I wonder if I will live through this.

We wait a few seconds, then Tier grabs my hand, I grab Moju's, and we drag each other down the hallway and through the blast hole. We stumble, slower now, down the remaining hallway and stop when we reach the door that leads to the outer tunnel highway.

I can hear the scratching on the other side, even with the residual ringing in my ears. My stomach clenches as I think about the creatures that are now waiting for us. I hold it down for as long as I can, but I turn and start to heave. I don't even remember the last time I ate, so there's nothing, and I mean nothing, left in my stomach.

"Now what?" I ask, wiping my hand across my face.

Tier throws down his rifle, takes a deep breath and looks at Moju. "My charge is out, give me all the grenades."

Moju leans heavily against the wall, fishes around in his pockets, and pulls out three canisters and hands them over to Tier.

And that's when I hear the clicking from the hallway behind us. "Shit! They're back!"

From the hazy cloud of thick dust a massive amalgamation of bot parts appears. I scream and both Moju and I train our rifles on the thing that comes towards us. We blast it back a few paces and it's forced to reassemble. I steal a look at Tier and he's already pulling the pin on the first grenade and running back towards me yelling, "Fire in the hole!"

Moju dives for the corner as Tier grabs me and yanks me to the floor. The blast renews the ringing in my ears and I'm disoriented as I struggle to my feet. Tier pulls me up and then we are running again.

Moju is bringing up the rear and firing hard at the reassembled thing behind us. But it's made a weapon and it fires, causing a projectile to skim past Moju's thigh. He falls and I break free of Tier to go back and get him. I fire a continuous stream of plasma at the amalgabot for several seconds, then grab Moju and yank him up and pull him back towards Tier. Moju aims his rifle at the creatures that are now filing through the hole as Tier pulls the pin on the second grenade and tosses it out on to the highway.

We hit the deck again, just as the explosion blasts body parts in all directions and now I know my hearing is fucked forever.

Moju pulls me up and we half limp, half run towards Tier who waves us through the smoking hole and out in to the main tunnel. Before I even know what's happening Moju is in the air and his talons have me by the waist. The razors puncture into my flesh as he grabs me with his hands, but I can't even feel it. Then Tier is out in the hallway and the remaining creatures are all over him. Moju swings around and I fire my rifle at the creatures, hoping to God that the stream doesn't hit Tier.

Tier breaks the grip of one that has him by the shirt and takes flight.

I am just about to breathe a sigh of relief when the MR tanks roll through the cloud of dust clogging the far end of the highway and suddenly there are hundreds of soldiers piling out of vehicles.

Tier yells something as he points down the tunnel and Moju and I take off, flying back towards the hole we came down. I hear a final explosion and then Tier is below me and Moju screams, "Ride with Tier, I can't carry you, Junco!"

And then I am falling through the air.

I land on Tier's back and his hands rise up to steady me. The soldiers, wounded but not down, are still firing at us as we make our escape. I flip over and frantically fire the stream of plasma particles back towards the advancing army until my rifle is out and I hurl it into the air.

The army disappears in the distance and by the time we get to the lightstick that marks the off-ramp we came in by, there is nothing but the clattering of small bots scuttling over the greasy water below us.

I watch as Moju dives down to pick up the sticks and throw them far down the dark highway. We fly slower now and I can hear both Tier and Moju breathing heavy with effort. We get to the last lightstick that marks the exit and I watch Moju pick it up, then toss it to me. "Stick it in your pocket, Junco."

I do, and then Tier flies me up to the hole that leads outside. "Start climbing, and no matter what—don't fucking stop."

I grab the rung and pull myself up into the tunnel.

They don't follow me and I want to turn and ask what's going on, but then I think about the three hundred-plus rungs that I must climb before I can make it out and I do what I'm told.

I climb and I don't fucking stop.

I'm on rung one hundred and thirty-three when I hear the plasma crack below and I almost panic and lose my grip. Then Tier is behind me, urging me to go faster, but my legs are shaking and I'm all out of breath.

"I can't, Tier, I can't climb anymore." I whimper.

He comes right up on me and grabs the rung above my head. "Let me in front, Junco, then wrap yourself around me and I'll take us both up."

The fire from below is getting closer, but I do as I'm told and then I am on his back and his hands are pulling us up the hole faster and faster. It seems like an eternity, but we break free and are out in the open air. I cry with relief and look back for Moju, but he's not there.

And then I scream in anguish as Tier flies us though the tallgrass, away from whatever is left of my brother below ground.

Chapter Nineteen

We fly for a long time, and we fly fast. Most of it I have my face buried in his back, but then I look up to see where we are. He lands us in a field of tallgrass on the edge of the pine trees and I drop to my knees in exhaustion when my feet hit the ground, then fall over and lie on my back. He drops with me and we stay quiet for several minutes.

"He's not dead, Junco."

"How do you know?" I scream.

He leans over and cups his hand over my mouth. "Shut up! Ya want to get us caught after all that?"

I turn over and refuse to cry.

"It was part of the plan. His plan."

"Well," I say evenly, "no one asked me what I thought of the fucking plan."

He leans over and pulls me around so that I'm looking at him. "I know, I'm sorry. But it was his decision. So I could get ya out of there alive."

"How do you know he's not dead?"

He laughs at this and I'm instantly pissed. "Junco, he works for them. They're not gonna kill him. He's the only thing they have that's worth a shit."

I can't say I'm surprised. I already knew this, really. But hearing it out loud right now makes it difficult for some reason.

Tier watches my face and then continues, "He does shit like this all the time. They let him out and he takes off and creates chaos. The MR had to know what was down there, Junco. Moju found his lab a few months ago and did the same thing to his doubles, so how convenient is that? They let him hear shit so he'll go do their dirty work for them. They wanted Dale's lab destroyed because they already have what they need in their own labs. They're only collaborating with the RR because they didn't have the skills to go it alone, but do not assume they are on the same side."

"What the fuck are they doing down there? Why do they have clones of me?"

He throws up his hands. "You tell me, Junco. Why do they clone you? I don't know what game you're playing with me, and really, I don't care at this point. But I'm sick of this bullshit I-have-no-idea routine you keep pulling."

"You're sick—? That's hilarious, how the hell did you know where the clones were then? And how the hell did you have the biometrics to get past those sentries?"

He jumps to his feet and then grabs my hand and pulls me up without asking.

"So, you're not going to answer me? You're just gonna pretend that you're not hip-high in shit with everything that's going on in my life?"

He pulls me towards him and shakes his head. "Another talk for another time, Junco."

I push him away. "Fuck you then." And I start walking into the pine trees.

"Where are you going?"

I ignore him completely.

"Yer gonna get lost out here in the dark."

I stop and turn, my lip curled up in rage. "Really? I'm going to get lost, am I? That's funny, considering that I grew up in the tallgrass and I can tell you how to get to seven different farms right from this spot. I'm not lost,

Tier." I sneer his name as it comes out of my mouth. "And I might be afraid of the dark, but that's what the stars are for."

He laughs a little at that and it makes my face go hot.

"Something funny?"

"Yer afraid of the dark too? Let's see, fish, nightdogs, prairie lions, and the dark. That's some list ya got there, Junco."

My whole upper body heats up. "If someone dumped you out in the middle of the tallgrass at night when you were eight and told you the apexers were gonna eat you alive if you couldn't fend them off with a sword, you'd probably be afraid of all that shit too. *Asshole.*"

His mood stays light as I turn and walk away. "Well, damn. You must be one hell of a sword fighter."

I halt again and turn back to him. "That's cute, is it? Leaving small children out in the night to be eaten? For your information I couldn't even lift the sword, Tier. I was eight. And if I'm this size at nineteen, how fucking big do you think I was at eight? I didn't fight them off, you idiot. I climbed up a pine tree, ripping out three fingernails in the process, and then jumped limb from limb until I ran out of branches. I stayed in that last tree for *three days* before they finally came and got me."

Jasus, Junco. Lock that shit down—now.

He shuts up after that and just walks with me. After another quarter mile I find the overgrown footpath that leads up the mountain. Tier follows in silence.

It takes a lot longer to get there than I remember, but finally the lake comes into view and I can make out the little fishing cabin set just off to the side and under the protective cover of the pines in the approaching dawn.

My eyes pause at the dock...

Picture yourself standing on the edge of a dock. In front of you is a mountain lake and behind you is a small cabin...

But this is not the dock I want so badly it hurts.

"Whose place is this?" Tier asks.

"Mine."

The door is unlocked, so I go right in, find the candles and matches and draw the curtains so the light won't be noticed by anyone passing nearby. Not that anyone would, this is my land now and it's private property. But habits, right?

Tier flops himself down in a chair in the small living room and watches me closely, but does not interfere.

I lie down on the couch opposite Tier's chair and it takes me about ten seconds to be oblivious to the world.

I wake to a painful rumble announcing my hunger and I try to remember when I ate last. I look around the cabin and spy some avian nutrition packets on the kitchen table but pump some water from the kitchen sink and drink instead.

When my stomach is bloated with liquid I go find Tier. We only have one bedroom in the cabin, so it's not like I have to look far. Besides, his boots are hastily discarded in the hallway and his charred clothes are strewn about like a trail of breadcrumbs.

I think of my own smelly clothes, which are covered in black soot and burn holes and smell like blast chemicals, and I regret sleeping in them. I push the door open and stare at the naked form lying face down on the bed, completely uncovered except for his wings which are spread across his back like a blanket. His body is almost sideways, like he fell into bed accidentally, and his face is stuffed into the pillow, muffling the snores trying to escape his mouth.

I shake myself out of it and leave, closing the door behind me and pass the food packets on the table—life is too short to eat shitty food—and pull some fishing gear out of the front closet.

I've been fishing here with my dad since I was two, and I know exactly where the fish tend to bite, even in the late afternoon. I wade into the shallow lake water up to my hips, tie a fly and cast out.

Fishing isn't just about catching fish, that's just what you get at the end if you're good at it.

Fishing is about the journey, and the journey is typically the thoughts you have as you go through the motions. Fishing, my dad always said, is a thinking man's sport.

I watch the sun dropping into the trees in the west and my thoughts sink to sadness. I roll the past few days around in my head as I seek out a taker for my fly, false-casting back and forth in an open loop to let the line go out further into the lake. I do this for the better part of an hour, and I'm losing hope quick as the sun sets when I get a taker. I pull the bass out and its normally olive-gold scales are dark green in the fading light. He'll have to do.

I gather up all my gear and turn to go back to the house when I see Tier staring at me from the back porch. He's sitting on the deck shirtless, legs hanging over, his arms and chin resting on the bottom railing.

He waves. I stop walking and just look at him for a moment, wondering if I should keep my distance in case I decide to bow out of this shit, or if I should wave back. I hold up the fish instead, and he smiles.

He waits for me on the porch. "Hey," he says, a little question mark at the end. Like he's trying to figure out if I'm still mad.

"I'm not in the mood to talk to you right now, Tier. I'm hungry and stink like chemicals, fish, and shit. So just leave me alone." The screen door smacks the wooden frame as I leave him outside, and I take the fish to the kitchen and begin prepping it.

The cabin is for hunting and my dad would have important buddies up here with him over the years to track deer and shoot ducks. After my mom took off he never really left me alone, so I was a permanent fixture on these trips as well.

But beyond that, the cabin is our safe house too. If you just stumbled onto it somehow and came inside it would provide you with shelter and water, but not much else. But if you knew where to look you'd find everything you need to survive here for at least six months.

I slide the pocket door that reveals the empty pantry and bounce my boot on the floorboards until one pops up in the corner. Then I slip my fingers beneath the board and find the latch, pull it, and hear the click as the mechanism releases the lock on the hidden door.

The empty shelves on the far wall move on recessed rollers to reveal a reinforced trap door that when open leads down to a lead-lined concrete cellar filled floor to ceiling with six-gallon buckets of survival gear, dry goods and freeze-dried meat. I unscrew the resealable lids and rummage around for a mylar bag labeled rice. It's enough to feed thirty people and I only need a cup, but who gives a shit. There's like five hundred pounds more where that came from.

Dinner takes about thirty minutes start to finish. Then I go find Tier.

I can see him through the screen door, right where I left him. Still sitting on the deck, legs hanging over, head and arms pushed through the railing. It's cool outside now that the sun's gone, but he doesn't look cold. I kick the door and he glances sideways over his shoulder at me.

"Dinner's ready."

He smiles but doesn't get up right away. Instead he brings his hands up to his forehead like he's got a headache, and lets out a deep breath.

"You gonna eat or what?"

He gets up and joins me inside without a word.

I follow him into the kitchen and go to the cupboard. "You want a bowl or a plate?"

He just stares at me for a few seconds, then finds his voice. "Plate, I guess."

"Sit, I'll bring it to you."

I watch him take a seat near the window and I shake my head as I pile on the food and then slide his over and sit down. "You look like you've never sat at a table to eat a real meal before."

"I have," he says quietly, "but it's been a really long time."

"Oh."

What do you sat to that?

We eat in silence.

Chapter Twenty

"I'm taking a bath," I announce after eating and staring out the window at the lake for several minutes from the couch.

"Wait." He's lounging in the living room chair sideways, feet dangling off one end, and he grabs my arm as I pass by. "There's hot water?"

"There will be after I turn the on the water heater." He just stares at me, blinking. "We have a generator," I say. He smiles and nods, and I'm angry at his assumptions so I sneer at him and continue to walk towards the bedroom. "I can practically read your thoughts, Tier. And they're not flattering."

"What are ya talkin' about?"

"Your disparaging view of us Rural people. Like we're backwards freaks and hot water is something we give up for God." I slam the door behind me and fire up the generator in the bathroom. The cabin is pretty simple, but hot water was something my mom insisted on since camping makes people filthy and stinky. This is one of my more solid memories of her and my heart aches when reality hits me about how alone I am in the world.

The tub takes a while to fill since it is old and deep, so I peel off my disgusting clothes and lie on the bed to wait. The rustic room with the wood-paneled walls and comfy old sagging bed looks exactly like I remember, except for Tier's shit that has somehow made its way in here. He's got several of the tech devices lined up on the small table my mother used as a vanity, and I spy the letter and reading device on a chair.

I get up to get them when the tracking tech lights up and begins beeping. I hear the thud of footsteps as Tier realizes it's active and charges towards the door. I'm standing there, naked as the day I was born, when he barges in.

He stops short when he sees me. His eyes look me up and down and I raise my eyebrows at him severely, and all the while the device is beeping like crazy. I stand where I am and then he slinks past me, grabs the tech, and leaves the room, closing the door behind him. Saying nothing.

I grab the reader and letter and take it into the bathroom where the tub is just full enough for me to get in and not feel like I'm sitting in a puddle. There are some old bubbles in the cupboard under the sink and I empty the container under the running water. They froth up like marshmallows and I step in, making sure not the get the letter and reading device wet.

I look at the letter and read it again, just to make sure I completely understand what it is he's trying to say.

Dear Junco,

If you think about what makes a man it comes back to duty, honor, character, and courage. I'd like to think I have all four, but I'm sure by the time all this is over you'll disagree. I'm sorry about that. If I had all the time in the world, I'd let you come around on your own. But I don't. So you'll just have to trust me. I'm sorry, Junco. Duty calls your honor and courage reveals your character.

Capt. Raubtier
Aves 039
Presidential Guard

It makes me want to throw up, not because I actually understand the full meaning of his words, but because I understand the underlying sentiment. Whatever his feelings for me, they don't matter. He's got orders, he's got his duty, he's got more important things than me to worry about.

I look at the signature to try and make sense of it. Raubtier is his full name, apparently. It sounds familiar to me, but I can't immediately place it. Aves must be their own word for avian, which is also interesting since it is the word scientists use to classify birds in Earth taxonomy. Presidential Guard sounds important, so it's pretty clear he's got rank. I crumple the letter up and throw it on the floor across the room and then turn my attention to the reading device.

It babbles at me for a few minutes, basically asking the same stupid questions as before and I throw it across the room to join the letter, then sink down into the bubbles to soak the confusion away.

I'm not sure how long I've been in the tub when I hear Tier's knock on the door. It's locked, so when he tries the knob, it just clicks back and forth.

"Junco, open up."

I slip down in to the water to wet my hair again. It's tepid and the bubbles lie flat and sparse across the water.

"Junco!" He pounds harder now.

I ignore him and stand up in the water and pull the plug. He must hear me moving around because soon after his footsteps thud across the hardwood floors and finally fade.

The towel is large, but not luxurious in any way, and it wraps around me almost twice before I can tuck the corner in to hold it in place. I swipe the steam off the mirror and look at myself. The last time I did this I looked horrific, and soon after Tier sent a man's head spiraling up into the night as I watched helpless.

Why am I so unsettled?

I'm mad at him but I can't put my finger on the reason. I could say it is because Moju is gone. And yeah, that's probably a good portion of it. But that's not the only thing. If he's telling the truth then Moju did it so I could escape. Me fucking it all up by going back to help him and getting captured in the process would just make everyone's situation suck.

I'm more mad at myself, I think.

And a better question is why am I still hanging out with him?

A successful completion of his mission requires me to leave my planet. That's just crazy talk. It's never gonna happen. So why am I here?

Maybe the last time I asked myself this I could explain it away because of the healing endorphins, if that's what they were, but not now. That stuff has to be out of my system by now.

I hear Tier's heavy footsteps once again and lose my patience when he knocks. "Knock on that door one more time, Captain, and I'll make you sorry you ever met me."

He doesn't reply.

I swipe at the steam on the mirror once more, look myself in the eyes, and ask myself a final question. "What are you gonna do about all this, Junco?"

I wait until the tub has drained, then start the hot water again for Tier, and finally leave the bathroom. He's sitting on the bed waiting for me.

"I started the water for you. It's all yours now."

I walk over to the trunk at the foot of the bed and open it and begin searching for clothes that might fit me.

They are all camos for hunting, but who cares. I find a white tank, a pair of snow-patterned fatigues, and a matching jacket and toss them all on the bed. Then I rummage around for a pair of socks and some old field boots and finally close the lid.

Tier is still sitting on the bed looking at me.

"If you're not gonna take a bath, get the hell out so I can dress."

He walks into the bathroom and closes the door without saying a word.

After I dress I take a seat outside on the grass, my back resting up against the large flat redrock that my dad put in the ground for stargazing when I was a kid. My well-worn fatigues should be a little snug since I haven't been out here in several years, but they aren't. I've probably lost ten pounds over the course of this affair. They are soft and comfortable though, and it makes me feel almost normal. I look up to see which of my friends are putting in an appearance and find all the ones I can currently see in the November sky, plus map out the ones I can't see and guesstimate when they might appear, if at all.

Tier is next to me before I hear the sharp slap of the old wooden screen door close behind him. "Got room for me out here, Junco?" he asks with hesitation.

The rock is long enough to fit a family of stargazers, so what am I going to say? "Sure."

He sits down next to me and leans back against the rock. I can smell soap on him and look over to find him shirtless and make a little grunt of disapproval. "It's a little cold to go without a shirt, don't you think?"

"Ya, but I didn't want to cut up your da's shirts without askin'. Wings, right?" He points to his back.

"Oh." It comes out pretty weak. "Well, you can cut one up, that's OK. It's not like he's going to be needing them." I look back up at the sky and pretend to search for familiar stars.

"So which one would ya be, then?"

"Huh?"

"The constellations," he says, pointing up. "Yer forever looking up there. Like ya wish you could fly away. How about Sirius?"

I laugh. A real outburst. "You're really lame, ya know that?" He just stares at me. "Well, not Sirius, that's not even a constellation," I say playing along. "Everyone names their dogs after Sirius anyway. Proper Farm girls should not aspire to be Sirius."

"Shouldn't they?" He leans forward and all I see of him are his black wings, the tips of which are curling along the ground they are so long. They are magnificent, even in the dark. I want to reach out and touch them, but I don't.

"Besides," I say, looking upward, "Canis Major isn't even visible this time of year. I usually choose from the ones I can see."

"Aye, but Sirius is also the star for Isis, who's a later version of Inanna."

I look at him and tilt my head. "Really?"

He nods. "On your world anyway. But Inanna herself is Venus, right? The morning and evening star. Which one then? If ya could be immortalized in the sky?"

I shrug. "Cetus?"

"The sea beast?" He cringes at me. "Now that is telling, Junco. Truly. Yer not a beast."

176

I think about it for a minute as Tier leans back against the rock. I can feel his warm arm touch me as he drops his head into my space. His dark hair tumbles down over his eyes, which have just a hint of glow to them, and he whispers, "And don't pick Draco either," with a wink.

I smile, and he smiles back. "No, not Draco. No matter what myth you read, Draco is always killed."

"Good point. But Cetus isn't much better. All the heroes of our sky tonight will kill him too. How about the Little Bear?"

"Hmmm," I say, thinking about it, "nah, little is only good if you're a kid. If I was Cepheus I'd be the king."

"True, enough. Ya, I can see ya as a Cepheus. I'd call ya Cephi. It's easier to say." I look up at him and he breathes out.

I laugh then, and my guard drops. This is how you got here, Junco. He's charming and funny. He has giant beautiful wings and a gorgeous body. And he knows just what to say and do.

"So yer settled then? It's the King for you?" he asks.

I look back up at the sky, thinking.

"Andromeda?" he prods.

I scowl. "No way."

"No, not the beauty waiting for her rescue?"

"Absolutely not. She comes off as helpless. Besides, she has all those children later on." As it comes out I have a tinge of regret, but I can't place the reason.

He laughs at that. "How about the vain Cassiopeia?"

"Her mother?" I scoff and shake my head. "I know who you'd be, though." I say as I look up at his face.

He smiles down at me. "Who?"

177

"Aquila, the eagle. The bird of prey."

He scoots closer to me then and reaches over to take my hand. "That would make me the property of Jupiter, though. And I'm no god's property."

"Then maybe you're Perseus? The hero who flies in on the winged horse."

"Ah, but if anyone's flying on the back of a horse then that would be you, Junco."

"But I'm a girl. So I can't be Perseus."

"Nah, you're not Perseus at all," he says and puts his arm around me and pulls me close. "If I were to choose, I'd make ya Cygnus, the swan."

I can feel my face go red, but it's dark, so hopefully he can't tell. "Why's that?"

"Because when you come home with me you're going to turn into a beautiful bird."

"How do you know that?" I ask, almost breathless as I take him in.

"Because, Junco, as much as ya might want to deny it, I know you're one of the Seven Siblings. And I'm calling ya back."

I look back up to the sky and point over to the east where parts of Taurus are just beginning to appear above the horizon. He follows my finger. "Ay. That's them. You call them the Pleiades, the Seven Sisters, but we call them the Siblings."

"I'm not sure I like your myth," I say. Mostly because I have nothing else to add at the moment and I don't want there to be silence.

"Nah, that was just some weird translation in that reader. Kinda hard to really appreciate the stories behind it. But there's another version of the Seven Siblings and how we got here. One that you'll like better, I think."

"What's it about?" I ask, interested despite myself.

"What all good stories are about, Junco. Forbidden love." He smiles me and then gets to his feet and extends his hand out to help me up. I give him my hand and he lifts me up in one gentle motion, just like that first night out on the hill in the Stag.

"Come on, let's go in and I'll tell you the other story," he says as he tugs me towards the cabin.

But I stop. "Wait a minute, Tier. You never told me who you are. In the sky," I say, pointing upward.

His smile is gentle. "That's easy, darlin', I'm Orion, the hunter." We walk together towards the little cabin but I can't help but wonder, if he's Orion then who's he hunting?

Chapter Twenty-One

Inside the candles are out and the place is dark. I am just about to take a seat on the couch when I feel his light grip on my upper arm. "Not the couch, Junco. It was a mistake to let you sleep there alone last time. If someone would have found us, you'd be their prisoner right now." I follow him into the bedroom and lie down on the bed and pull a blanket over me. He slides in as well, and then turns me around and pulls me close, my back against his bare chest, and his left hand goes to caress my neck while his right hand rests on my belly.

I shiver at how close we are and at how he makes me feel. He must interpret this as a chill, because he pulls me even closer.

"Warm enough?" he asks.

I nod, but don't speak.

"This version is a proper story," he begins in a hushed voice that travels across my cheek, seeking out my ear. I know this is one of his charming tricks, but he feels so good, I don't want to stop him. "And these players are in the time of Old Crage, who, in case you haven't figured it out, is an ancient god. Like Jupiter."

I nod, and he continues.

"But the story is completely different and it's all about how Man and Birds, avians, like me, lived on Earth together thousands of years ago. Before the separation the Men and the Birds had no problems at all. They farmed the land, and raised the sheep and cattle, and traded and lived together for all of history. The only thing they didn't do is marry one another because Old Crage forbade the mixing of the higher species. But there was one Man, named Erane, and one Bird, named Irin, who were friends from childhood. And they did everything together.

"Never was there a time when someone saw Erane that they did not also see Irin because they lived in the same village, on the same dirt road, and even in cottages that stood next to each other. They were both born on the same day and shared every childhood experience together. As they grew older and began to mature, their differences became apparent. Birds aren't born with wings; it is only after they mature during metamorphosis that they develop from the form of a man to the form of a bird. As children you cannot tell one from another.

"But the time came for Irin's change and she was told that Erane could not see or hear about anything that happens during the morph. Irin was devastated because she'd never had to do anything alone ever before. She cried and pleaded that Erane be allowed to come with her. But the answer was always no.

"Irin kept up her pleading and when it came to be the night before morph, she threatened to run away. Her parents got upset and went to talk to Erane's family, asking if maybe the rules could be broken just this one time, for the sake of poor Irin who was helpless without Erne's company.

"Erane's family confessed that he too had threatened to run away if the two were separated and so the families went to seek the advice of the Council. The Council was worried, but not about the children or the families. They knew that Old Crage's rule about mixing the species was taken very seriously by Old Crage himself and if he ever found out that the children were making such threats, he would punish them. But since the time was upon them for Irin's transformation, there was nothing they could do but allow Erane to attend to her during her time of change. And this is how Erane became the only Man to ever know the secrets of the morph.

"And he was very careful and attentive to her as she grew her beautiful wings and fledged into a stunning avian female. She was so beautiful that he fell to his knees and proposed marriage. Irin was so overcome by his emotion that she accepted and they planned for a great wedding and feast to celebrate their love.

"On the day of the big celebration Old Crage was sitting on his throne in the sky when a magpie appeared to deliver a message. The message told of the marriage between Irin and Erane and Old Crage became so enraged he killed the messenger and flew down to the Earth and stood in the middle of the ceremony threatening to destroy the world if the two marry.

"But the community was tired of Old Crage's rules about staying separate. Isn't love enough, they asked? Isn't it better to let them love one another in all ways than to keep them apart?

"Old Crage didn't want to hear anything from the community so he gagged them to make them mute. And then he approached the bride and groom and asked if they would disobey him.

"Erane was the first to speak and he said, 'Old Crage, we love you. We love that you protect our world and we respect you and your views, but this community of Men and Birds has decided to become one. We ask, why should we not marry when we already live together, farm together, and pray together. This marriage will bind the Men and Birds together forever and this is how we wish it. We no longer accept your rules of segregation.'

"Old Crage held his temper very well, at least until he could ask Irin if she felt the same way. She did. Then Old Crage turned to the community of Men and Birds, lifted the mute spell, and once again asked if this was the consensus of everyone. And one by one each and every Man and Bird agreed with the marrying couple.

"When they had all said their peace, Old Crage turned back to Erane and Irin and said, 'You disobey my one and only law. And you break, by your own will, the covenant of peace. From this day forward you will never live in harmony again.' He banished the men to be bound to the Earth while casting out the Birds to the heavens, never to return until their transgressions had been cleared.

"Old Crage was far more unhappy with the Birds because they were his celestial race and so he also put a curse on them, corrupting their genetic essence. Slowly, over the punishment period, the genetic code of the Birds would deteriorate. But he didn't stop there, he also put a time limit on their free time as children, and any Bird who wasn't morphed and fledged out by the time they were twenty years old would die.

"And then he cursed the village for their disobedience, and made the Seven Siblings to watch and follow the punishment cycle. And the Seventh Sibling, the impure being that was neither man nor Bird but a mixture of both, will choose which race was to blame for the disobedience of Erane and Irin so that the final punishment can be handed down."

I force myself to ask the question even though everything inside is screaming not to. "What's the final punishment?"

"When the Seventh Sibling chooses the guilty species, they will be wiped out. Total annihilation."

Holy shit I hate mythology.

I am still for a long time after he finishes, and so is he. Then finally I find something to say. "Was that supposed to make me feel better?"

He sighs deeply, but I can feel his calming breath pull back from my cheek. "No, Junco. That was a way to let you know that there are consequences if you choose not to come with me. And sometimes," he pauses for a second, "forbidden things have to stay forbidden. It's just a story, less true than the version you read earlier even, a story."

I push his arms off me and roll over so that I am on my stomach and he can't see my face. "You know what, Tier, I think I'll take the answers you have now, if that's OK with you."

"Ya sure about that, Junco? You really want the truth?"

I turn my head to see his face, my cheek squished against the soft bed. "No, not really."

He smiles and rakes the hair away from my eyes and then huffs out a small breath. "Yer so strange, girl. I've never met someone so unsure of herself, yet so capable at the same time. How did ya get this way?"

I just look at him. "Get this way?"

He nods.

I shrug. "I have no idea."

He sinks down next to me, his face creeping closer to mine until we are so close I feel the heat radiate off his skin. "But ya do, Junco. Ya know exactly how ya got this way, ya just don't want to face the truth. I can tell ya what I know, but yer not gonna like hearing what I have to say." He swallows and then shrugs his shoulders.

"I feel the spaces inside. The missing places that shouldn't be there, shouldn't even be possible. I'm not sure I want them back, but it's catching up with me, Tier, I can feel it. If you want me to go with you, then tell me."

He pulls back, surprised. "And if I tell you, you'll come home with me?"

"Yes."

His eyes narrow in disbelief. "What if you don't like what I tell you? Then what?"

"Is there really any chance that you're gonna let me stay here?"

He turns away from me, then sits up and swings his legs over the side of the bed. I can hear his talons click on the wood floor as he leans down, stretching out his back muscles, and making the skin between his wings taut as he puts his head in his hands.

I sit up on my knees and reach out before I can stop myself. My fingers touch the thin membrane between his wings that make our backs so different. I feel him shiver, but he doesn't turn and he doesn't stop me, so I continue up to his wing and trace the outline of the bone that runs along the top until I get to the arch over his right shoulder. My fingers fall a little and I skim along the feathers.

I take one between my fingertips and rub it softly and he turns, forcing me to let go. We stare at each other, our eyes locking, and then I see his gaze drift down to my mouth. I involuntarily let out a breath, and he lifts his eyes up to mine, then wraps his hand around my neck and pulls me towards him.

I keep my eyes trained on his as he pulls me closer and closer. Then I feel his lips brush softly across my own and I breathe out. He pulls back a little and tries to talk, but his voice is barely a soft whisper. "I'll tell ya everything I know, Junco. But yer not gonna like me after."

He begins to move forward but it's me who pulls back a little this time. "Tier," I say in a low voice I barely recognize. "Please, I need to know."

He moves in towards me. I feel his lips pressing on my own and my eyes lose his gaze as they close. His tongue explores my mouth as his hands explore my back. He eases me back onto the bed and continues to kiss me gently on the mouth, on the neck, and then down to my chest. I stop him there and he lifts me up a little and pulls me into him, wrapping his wing and arm around me at the same time. Then he flips me on my belly so my face is pressed against his soft feathers and lifts up the back of my shirt to expose my skin. "My turn," he says.

His fingertips caress my shoulder blades and trace down my spine, I squirm and arch my back at his touch, then let out a little breath of air as he brings his fingers back up to my shoulders and drags them gently over to the nape of my neck. The touch of his lips makes me cry out softly. I don't want him to stop, but he does, and I can feel him trying to catch his breath as I do the same.

Chapter Twenty-Two

"If ya want the truth, darlin'," he says into my back so I can barely hear him, "I'll give it ta ya. But your world will never be the same again. So, I'll ask ya one more time, Junco, is this what you want to hear? Because I'd much rather tell you things that would make you love me instead."

"Is the truth that bad, Tier?" I turn a little so I can see his face.

He doesn't say anything for several long seconds and I'm about to repeat myself when he finally meets my gaze and nods. "It absolutely is."

"I need to hear it," I whisper.

"The world as you knew it a week ago is gone. This is a fact, just as it is a fact that I killed every last person in the Stag Camp."

"But why did you kill them?"

"Junco, whatever you think you know about Dale and those other men out there in the camp, it's either all wrong, or mostly wrong. What ya saw yesterday in the tunnels barely scratches the surface."

I swallow as he continues. "Dale was a part of the RR defenses." He feels me stir, and stops mid-sentence to head me off. "Look, Junco, I realize you've been told somethin' different, —but ya said you wanted the truth. Do ya still want it, then?"

I nod and stay silent.

"And not just any unit, either. Dale was part of a very advanced network of scientists who, contrary to how the rest of the RR lived their day-to-day lives, lived in a high-tech world of weapons, biotechnology, and bioengineering. He used alien genetics to make horrible creatures. Not just avian genetics, but the other races on Earth as well.

"Yer right about one thing though, I do have a pretty low opinion of the people in the RR, if only because I know their leaders and what they've done. How they lie to ya, all of ya, and how they keep ya subservient with their moral rules. But most of all, because ya let them do it.

"But let's just back up a little and start a few decades ago. You, Junco, are part of an avian clutch of seven, we know that for certain. And we now know that you came from genuine aves stock. From an immature aves called Gyr who went missing when he was sent to Earth. Way back before you were ever born. This was the very first hosting we did with our military class back in the Band where we live. He was in his sixteenth year and we sent him to the MR where he would be considered an adult. His reports were regular for about a year. He was making friends and was fitting in nicely. Then one day his report didn't come in and then the next report didn't come in, and finally, after several weeks of no word, we sent down another immature avian to check on him. He was gone. Simply disappeared.

"Life went on, other aliens made contact with Earth, and eventually a few years later we did as well. No one ever found out what happened to Gyr. And no one really thought about it either. Until a non-avian alien asked us for help in breaking out his brother from a camp out in a place several hundred miles from Peak City.

"I'll cut a long story short and tell you that we agreed, thinking maybe Gyr was there as well, and what we found was far worse than anyone ever though was possible on a civilized planet."

"Was I there?" I whisper.

"Yes, Junco. You were there. As were hundreds of other things that they'd created through their bioengineering projects. Most of which were monsters, literal inhuman monsters straight out of fairy tales and nightmares, created with an amalgam of DNA from all races as well as animals. Those things down in the tunnels we saw? Just the leftovers that have taken root, just the memory of the atrocities we found at first. And we killed them all."

He says it in such a matter-of-fact manner that I can't think straight for several seconds.

"But the avian children were kept separate, away from everything that was going on in the larger experimental area. As our team was gathering them up for relocation back to the rendezvous point, the RR defenses showed up and retaliated with massive force and they were forced to leave ya all behind. You were just babies then.

"It wasn't until years later that we found out what happened to ya, that you were all farmed out to different sectors of the United Republics, and that the experiments had never really stopped."

He pauses then. "Ya still with me, Junco?"

I sigh. "Yeah."

"The RR kept you, Junco, only you. They gave ya to a local couple who couldn't have children, and gave them the privilege of Farm Family status. From what I can tell, they treated ya right for a while. But I don't know that for sure, so stop me if I get it wrong. I don't know everything, Junco. Not much at all, in fact. But enough to tell you this story."

I look back at him. "How do you really know I'm that girl? The avian child? You weren't there, you're not that much older than me, so you were a small child back then too." I see the disappointment in his eyes as the words are coming out of my mouth, but I don't care.

"Before ya seven were taken back by the RR, the avians grabbed DNA samples from each child. I ran yer sample myself that night on the hill. You're one of them."

I just lie there, not quite sure if I should be sad, angry, or defiant.

"When I killed the others at the Stag Camp, that night ya hit the deer, I found more of these same creatures."

"What happened to them?"

He just shook his head.

I turn over and show him my back. "What else?"

"Your parents—"

"Stop. That's enough, OK. I get it. My parents were good people, Tier. My father loved me and I had everything a kid could ever ask for."

"And did that love include visits to your Uncle Dale's compound of genetic mutants over the years, eh?"

"There were never any monsters out at the Stag, I think I would have remembered that."

"Not if they didn't want ya to, Junco."

"OK, fine. My parents were monsters, too. Got it."

"Do ya want to know what happened to the others, then?"

"What others?"

"Your siblings?"

I stay silent, but I guess the question was rhetorical, because he turns me back around and answers anyway. "So obviously ya know Moju. But what ya don't know is how he grew up. The MR kept him in a cage for the first thirteen years. They morphed him early, at fourteen, and when he came out of it they taught him every which way he could torture and kill. You know what that name means, Junco? Moju?"

I look up at him now, my mouth drawn down and my eyes squinting.

"It literally refers to a sick and twisted psychosexual predator. He gave himself that name, Junco. A little telling, eh?"

"That's bullshit. He was perfectly rational and normal when I talked to him."

"He remembers ya, Junco, even if ya don't remember him. They didn't give him the drugs to dampen down his nightmares. You were right about one thing though. I was just pissed that you figured it out so quick." He stops and looks at me for a second. "If he appears normal to ya, it's only because he loves ya and wants to spare ya the pain of knowing who he is and what he's done. But make no mistake, he's a psychotic sonofabitch. If he'd of come out of that tunnel he would have promised ya all kinds of things to keep ya on Earth. Every lie your heart wants to hear right now. Everything you want me to say, but I won't. And then—"

"Then what? He'd change into a psychopath and tear my arms off in the night?"

"Lying to ya, to get ya to stay would be the equivalent scenario. If you don't complete the morph before yer twenty, you'll die all on your own. Our genetics are made so that they need this renewal, Junco. Maybe it's not a punishment like the story says, but it is real. And not morphing has consequences."

"And you?" I ask defiantly. "Are you a psychopathic killer as well?"

"Me? Yes. Me too. I've killed more people than I can count. And I don't shed a tear for any of them. Even your father."

I shoot up out of bed. "What did you say?"

But he just stares at me.

"WHAT DID YOU SAY?" I scream.

"It's true. It was me who took his last breath, but only to put him out of his misery."

"Misery! What misery?" I scream again, and then he clamps his hand over my mouth.

"Shhhh."

"Don't you tell me to be—"

But his hand presses tighter and cuts off my words. "That's enough." His words burn with anger as they came out and so I force myself to settle down.

"I asked ya if you wanted the truth before this started, and ya said yes. I, on the other hand, urged you to reconsider." He lifts his hand and I fling myself away from him and sit up on the bed, wanting to get up and walk out, but not sure if I should push it and piss him off any more.

"You said if I stayed with Aren I'd end up like my father. You made me believe that *he* had something to do with it! And now"—I half turn my face towards him—"I find out you're the asshole who ruined my life."

He puts a hand up and squeezes the flesh above the bridge of his nose, like I am giving him a headache. "I'm not done, Junco. Do ya want to hear the rest of the truth? Or should we just leave it at that and you can go and throw yer hissy fit?"

"There's more? Who else did you kill? My first goldfish? My dog? Any of my avian siblings?"

"Yer father begged me to kill him, Junco. It was a merciful act—"

"FUCK YOU!" I scream as I get up to flee the bedroom.

Chapter Twenty-Three

I don't get but a few paces before he yanks me back by the arm. "Let go of me, Tier," I say between gritted teeth. He just looks at me and shakes his head.

"No, darlin', you asked for the truth and if I let you go now, you only have half the story."

"I don't want to know any more, OK? So don't bother."

He shakes his head again. "Sorry, Junco. You're gonna get it this part whether you like it or not. So get back in here and *sit down*." His command makes me jump a little, but I try to pull my arm from his grip anyway. He resists and pulls again. I look up at his face and see the anger in his eyes and give in. "Fine, talk," I say as I sit down on the bed.

He sits next to me and I move away from him, like I'm in third grade and he's got the cooties. I feel a little juvenile at my reaction, but not for long because his words begin to spill out once more and I'm forced to hear it through to the end.

"Yer father, Junco, was absolutely in on the cover-up of who ya were and where ya came from. I've looked at this from every angle, and there is no way to deny it. Yer da took you to the Stag twice a year. I found the medical records to match that schedule when I was there last week. They—" He stops here and I'm afraid to say anything, so I just sit quietly. Finally the silence drags on too long and I have to look up to see if he will continue.

"They what?" I ask.

He just shakes his head and looks down at the ground.

"What? Just fucking say it!"

"They changed ya. That's all I know right now, they changed ya—somehow and for some reason."

I lie back on the bed and feel the tears come quickly. "What did they do to me?"

When he finally speaks, his voice is soft, barely a whisper. "I don't know for sure, Junco. Made ya more"—he stops for a moment—"avian, I think. Took yer human parts away."

My head spins and I have to close my eyes and press my fists into my eye-sockets to make it stop.

"I'm not sorry for killing your da, like I said, he asked me to finish it. But I am sorry this is your fucked-up life. Ya don't deserve it."

I don't have anything to add so I lie there with my silent tears streaming down my cheeks.

"Where did yer father die, Junco?"

I screw up my face, thinking for several minutes. I'm trying, I'm looking, but I can't find that memory anywhere.

"Convenient, isn't it?"

I grunt. "What's convenient? Quit fucking with me and just say it, Tier."

"It was in a church, do ya remember that?"

I am back in the dream the first night I met Tier, out on the hill in the Stag. I'm a figure in a stained-glass window. I let out a deep breath. "A church?"

He nods his head. "There was a meeting, some secrets were leaked about what was going on in the Stag. They were making plans for ya, Junco."

He looks down to see if I am following what he's saying. My face must look confused, because then he breaks it down into smaller bits for me. "Yer da was gonna sell ya, Junco."

The laugh comes out too quick and even to me, it sounds forced. "OK."

He shrugs. "It's the truth."

"And then you magically show up and kill him? What? To save me?" I let out a snort. "That's bullshit."

"No, Junco. I had no intention of saving ya. Like I said, I only put him out of his misery. Do ya remember any of this?"

"No," I lie, "not one bit."

"I was watching you for a long time already, when that night came for yer da to die. But there were some"— he hesitates and I know he's choosing his words carefully—"unusual developments—leading up to that night. Yer da was called to the church in Ramah. I watched the whole meeting through a third-story stained-glass window, so I didn't catch all of it, but enough." He looks down at me. "I saw enough. The killer tortured yer da until he passed out from the pain."

He stops and looks up at the ceiling before he finds his voice again. "I killed seventeen people that night. Including your da. But I let the torturer go."

"What?" I turn to look at him. "Why?"

He looks me straight in the face but he doesn't answer that question. "I'm sorry for a lot of things, Junco, but I'm not sorry for taking a single life in that church."

My mind is racing, trying to put it all together. The thought that's been nagging at me, eating away at me, finally surfaces. "They have more clones of me, don't they?" It isn't exactly a question, but more something I needed to say out loud to make it real.

"Aye, you can bet on it. And they had a lot of plans for ya—plans you weren't necessarily on board with."

We sit there for a long time and eventually he climbs back into bed next to me, but he doesn't pull me close and I don't move towards him either. My mind is jumbled with the new information and I frantically rack my brain to try and remember something, anything that will corroborate this story outside of that dream. But there is nothing there.

I fake sleep after a while. Finally, just after dawn, Tier gets up and takes a tech device to the other room.

I get up too. But not to check on him or see what he's doing.

I open the window, slip out in silence, and run like hell through the woods.

I expect to be caught by him within the first few minutes, but I run on and on and on. Up the hill, over the patch of medium grass which outlined the place I called the meadow when I was a kid, into the conifers, and towards the only people I know to go to.

My feet falter and I trip more than once as my heart pounds with adrenaline. My breath comes out in long hard gasps as I make my way through the forest. Finally I have to stop. I bend over and grab my chest with one hand and lean my other against a thickly barked pine. I feel the sticky resin on my fingertips as I try to get myself under control.

In my mind, Tier is the liar. Not my father, not my Council, not my country.

Tier.

I feel it in my heart. I know it.

I look around and see shadows from the trees and all I think of are those dark wings and long talons waiting to take me back to the nightmare.

And so I run again.

Because to stay, to accept everything he told me without question, would be betrayal.

Treason.

Maybe there is some secret program that creates inhuman monsters from the genetics of children. Maybe I am an avian. Maybe my father willingly allowed me to be subjected to experimentation and cloning and was about to sell me.

Maybe.

I may be sheltered from most of the horrible things in the world living in the RR, and I may be naive in certain ways. But I am not stupid. And it would be the epitome of stupid to willingly allow everything—my life, my family, and every rule I've ever lived by—to be wiped out by one good-looking guy with wings who tells me they are false.

My legs burn as I climb a steep hill that will take me into the outlying area of the Baumer farm and when I get to the top, I stop.

The view is incredible and I can see everything. Including the large mass of soldiers who are at my house in the distance.

Of course they are at my house! They are looking for me, I'm an RR citizen who was kidnapped by an alien. I've been missing for, hell, I have no idea. My days are so mixed up. A week, I think. I'm a prominent Farm Family daughter, World Grand Champion Mounted Aerialist. I'm probably on the front page of every newscreen on the planet.

I strain my eyes to make out details at my property and I see plenty of military vehicles, but I also see many farm trucks as well and I breathe a sigh of relief. The military isn't there to kidnap and hold me as a state secret. If they were, then my neighbors wouldn't be allowed to just pull in the farm and park their trucks.

They're waiting for me to come home.

The tears stream down my face as I accept that thought as truth and I feel a flood of stress flow out of me. These people love me. I'm not a freak, I'm not an alien.

I'm just Junco.

They're worried about me.

I get back under the cover of the pine needles and make my way down the hill to the modest farmstead below, wiping the tears from my face, and taking a moment to catch my breath and find some calm.

I am just about to the edge of the clearing, where the crunchy carpet of needles meets the grass that will take me to the Baumer's driveway, when the doubt creeps in.

I stop.

And look up into the trees and make out a shadow standing on a branch.

It's Tier.

My heart skips, literally skips and flutters so bad I think I will die on the spot from a heart attack, and I cannot breathe.

He smiles. "Go ahead, Junco. Go see for yourself. Tell them everything I said. Don't leave out one word."

I bend over to try and calm myself as the hyperventilation takes over. I don't hear him come down, but he's next to me, putting his hand on my back, bending over to try and see my face, saying nothing.

In between my sharp gasps for air I manage to speak. "I'm. Not. Coming."

"I know, Junco."

But I can't stop talking now. "You're lying. I—"

I what? I can't finish my sentence. So I just drop to the forest floor and sit, and try to regain some control over my body. He drops down next to me and leans back against the tree trunk, letting me stay that way for a long time. But even after that, nothing makes sense.

I am playing with the long-dead pine needles on the ground when he finally speaks. "If ya have these doubts, Junco, then go. I want ya ta come on yer own, I want to make it a choice. I don't want to steal ya away, I really don't."

I sniff loudly, desperately trying to control my running nose, and then get to my feet. "But you will if you have to? Is that what you're saying underneath those nice words?"

He stays silent.

I wipe my hand across my nose and find my voice. "I'm going home. If you want to stop me, then go ahead, but I'm not walking away from my life just because you tell me some far-fetched story about monsters." And I turn and step out in the grass.

He doesn't snatch me up or call out to me. As far as I can tell he doesn't even get up off the forest floor. So I just keep walking forward until I reach the driveway, then follow it up to the house.

The Baumer place is a very traditional farmhouse complete with a large covered front porch. When I reach it, I stop and turn back to look into the trees for a moment. Tier is still there, standing now, just on the edge of the shadows that fall around the branches. For the first time I realize that we're wearing matching hunting gear.

Snow camo pants and jacket with a white t-shirt. He crosses his arms and waits for me to make the final decision. I turn my head and climb the porch stairs and force myself to knock on the door.

Mrs. Baumer answers and when she sees me she begins to cry, taking me by the shoulders and asking me questions. I look back at the woods once more, but he's gone, and then her husband appears and the old couple ushers me over the threshold and into the familiar farmhouse.

Chapter Twenty-Four

Mrs. Baumer has me in the tiny downstairs bathroom with the door closed and she's talking a mile a minute, but I just stand there and let her wash my face, even around my puffy eyes, and it stings when the soap touches each and every cut and bruise. I can hear Mr. Baumer in the kitchen down the hallway, talking to someone on a com tech.

Mrs. Baumer's flushed face is right in front of me then, like she's waiting for an answer, but I never heard the question. "What?" I ask.

She softens up when she hears my voice. "Your fingers, Junco. What happened to your fingers?"

I forgot all about my missing fingers to be quite honest. And right now, I really don't want to be reminded.

"Did he chop them off, dear?"

I look at her for a minute, my brow in a furrow I'm sure, then try and imagine Tier chopping off my fingers, but that's something I can't see in my mind's eye at all. "No," I finally say. "A nightdog ate them."

She gasps and begins tearing off the bandages that I had also forgotten all about. I look down and they are filthy with dirt and grime and dried blood. How could I have forgotten about my missing fingers?

She keeps pulling, looking up at my face to see if she is hurting me, but she isn't. And I don't stop her. So she continues. "What kind of bandage is this?" she asks, more to herself than to me. But I answer anyway.

"Avian. It's an avian membrane."

It takes forever to unwrap the long tissue-thin swathe of synthetic textile and the air tickles with cold as it rushes in to fill the space. She continues to peel the bandage off, again looking up to see if she is hurting me. But she's not. By the time she removes the last layer and my fingers come into view I am less surprised that they are healed than I would have been if they were mangled. Mrs. Baumer lets out a curt "Hmph," and then throws the bandages in the trash.

I bring my fingers up to my face to see them better. They were bitten off at the first joint from the bottom, so there is really nothing left of them. The skin is white and smooth, like any newly formed scar, and I find that I have very little control over what they do and when they do it. If I wiggle them, they don't really move, but I still feel the missing parts that should be attached.

Mrs. Baumer has left the bathroom while I was preoccupied with my new disability, and now I can hear her talking to Mr. Baumer down the hall. They're arguing about whether or not to let the military come get me. Mr. Baumer says no, and if they try he will shoot them before they get to the porch. I smile at that.

Mrs. Baumer is trying to talk some sense into him when I enter the kitchen and they stop talking. Mr. Baumer is still holding the com tech and he leans in and whispers, "I'll call you back."

"Junco, please sit down here, dear." He pulls a chair from the kitchen table for me to sit in. I do as I'm told. "They want to come get you, but I told them no. We'll drive you home ourselves when you're ready. Is that OK?" His eyes smile down at me and this gives me some courage.

"Mr. Baumer, I need to ask you some questions." His happy face slides into sadness and he ushers Mrs. Baumer out, handing her a rifle from the kitchen counter and telling her to go keep watch for the military men. If she sees them, she's to nick -em in the knees when they come down the walkway. The kitchen door swings behind her as she leaves and Mr. Baumer stands there for a few seconds just looking at me.

"What is it, Junco?" he finally says.

"I don't even know where to start."

"Try the beginning, dear."

"This isn't about where I've been or what I've been doing, or even who had me."

"No?" he replies, pulling up a chair next to me at the table.

"I've been with the avian, I'm sure everyone knows that already. He's—"

"He's what, dear?"

"He told me some things," I say, looking over at him to gauge his reaction. "Things I don't want to believe to be true." Sweat is dripping down his face and he reaches in and produces a handkerchief from his pocket to wipe his brow. "And since you were a Council Elder for, hell, I have no idea, most of my life..." His eyebrows go up at my cursing, but he stays silent. "I figure you'd be the best one to ask."

"Ask, Junco," he says with the most serious face I've ever seen. And then his hand reaches over and takes mine, the one with the missing fingers. If he notices them, he doesn't show it, so I assume Mrs. Baumer didn't get around to telling him about how they became snack food. I sit there and struggle with the right question before choosing my words carefully. "Are you, or were you, involved in the secrets that surround my origins?"

His mouth draws into a flat line across his face and he nods.

"Am I human or avian?"

At this he simply shrugs. "I don't know, Junco. I knew you were adopted but they have been telling me some wild stories over the past few days."

"Stories like what?" I ask.

"Stuff I refuse to believe," he says simply.

I can relate. I can't believe them either.

"I think we should take you home now. There are quite a few people there who want to talk to you. I'm sure they can answer your questions."

He gets up but my good hand reaches out to take his arm. "Mr. Baumer, were my parents good people?"

He sits back down. "Junco, I knew your dad from the day he was born. And your mother and our smallest daughter were best friends for years before your father proposed. Your parents loved you, and that's all I can say about the rumors that are floating around right now. They loved you. They were good, from what I knew of them. That's all I can say."

"Did they both come from Farm Families?"

He laughs at this one. "Yes, they both came from Farm Families."

Finally, a confirmed lie from Tier. I feel a small bit of satisfaction to have proved this point wrong and since Mr. Baumer seems to be waiting for my next question, I ask another. "Did you know my father's friend Dale?"

He looks me straight in the eye again. "I didn't, Junco. I can't vouch for him or answer to any of the things they are saying about the Stag right now. I'm sorry."

"OK," I say, and begin to get up.

But he stops me with a gentle hand. "I did think it was weird that your father took you out there all these years. The Stag is no place for children."

My heart feels like it's being clenched with a fist.

Maybe all the things Tier told me aren't true. Like maybe there aren't any monsters, and maybe I'm not an avian, or maybe I'm not going to die if I don't go with him to grow wings before I'm twenty, but some of what he told me about my life is true.

I can feel it.

We walk outside together and find Mrs. Baumer sitting on the porch swing with her rifle. She takes me by what's left of my bad hand and leads me to their farm truck. I climb in and slide over on the long seat bench and they each get in so I am sandwiched between them. We roll along the gravel drive slowly as we make our way towards my farm, but the only thing I'm wondering is whether or not Tier is watching me from above.

My house couldn't be more different than the Baumers' little farmhouse. It is a third-quarter modern geometric, built last century, and is really nothing more than a hollow square with all the rooms along the perimeter, while the courtyard encompasses the entire middle interior. Not all geometric courtyards have domes, but ours does, housing the pool and a lush tropical landscape that oozes with humidity, regardless of the season or temperature outside.

Out of habit I count the horses in the paddocks as the house comes into view from the back road and I know from the number that they are all out on pasture. Good. While there's not much grass left, it's better than them being cooped up in their stalls starving for the last week.

Our barn is also a modern geometric based on the same design. It sits about a hundred yards back from the house. The stalls run the entire perimeter, while the interior, which is only a partial dome, houses the main arena. A breezeway separates the arena from the stall doors and when we pass it from the back, I can see all the way through to the other side.

I study the house and surrounding grounds as we approach and I feel the excesses of my sheltered existence for the first time. If you compare our house to the Baumers' little farmhouse, there is a clear discrepancy of wealth, yet Mr. Baumer was a Council Elder for decades.

I had never thought about how much money we did or didn't have before. Or whether or not I had more than others. But I can't get Tier's words out of my head. My parents were rewarded with wealth for their active participation. My excitement for discovering that they were not rewarded with the title of Farm Family is gone now. Obviously they got their title genetically, but that doesn't explain the wealth. My grandparents' homes were more along the line of the Baumers' little farmhouse. In fact, there were only a handful of Families that deviated from that template, and none of them had a house as different as ours. Someone built it, but it wasn't my father and mother because the house was almost seventy years old. So they acquired it along the way somehow.

The activity at my house is indescribable chaos as we ramble slowly up the long driveway. There are people that are neither military nor neighbors and friends and this confuses me until Mr. Baumer says, "Who let the media in, for Jeremiah's sake?"

They swarm the old truck, pushing at each other to get a look at me, their hands high in the air to try and get an overview shot, but Mr. Baumer, to his credit, keeps on driving. I'm almost afraid he's going to run them over, but they jump out of the way as soon as they figure out he has no intention of stopping.

When we do finally reach the house and stop they swarm again, and then the RR Defenses are there, surrounding the truck and pushing them back. Mrs. Baumer leans over. "Are you ready, Junco?"

I shrug, and she takes that as a yes and opens the door. A soldier helps her out, and then I scoot out her door as well. They are yelling my name and pushing at the RR soldiers. Someone fires a shot in the air and everyone screams and then whoever is in charge is shouting for them to get back. Another soldier grabs my upper arm firmly and pulls me away and when I look back at Mrs. Baumer, she's already been pushed back into the truck and then they are rolling again.

Chapter Twenty-Five

The Defense soldier is talking to me, but nothing is getting through. I just follow him into my house and when he shuts the door everything goes quiet. This seems to be his cue to stop and explain things.

"Miss Coot, I am very sorry for all this intrusion into your home. I am Lieutenant Stockton, RR Defenses, and I am ordered to take you to the commanding officer immediately."

I nod up at him and he leads me to the door of my father's office, knocks, twice, then opens the door and gestures me in.

Aren is sitting in my father's chair, his head in his hands, looking like complete shit. Stockton closes the door and we are alone.

"I thought you were dead?" I say.

He lets out a deep sigh. "Ditto, Junco. We've been looking for you everywhere." He gets up and comes over to me and hugs me. I hug him back out of politeness, but I'm not sure what's going on yet, so I pull back.

He looks me up and down. "Did he hurt you?"

It takes a minute to sink in. "Did he hurt me? No. But a nightdog ate my fingers." I hold them up matter-of-factly and he just stares at me, then takes them in his hand to examine them, as if he's a doctor and he can glean important information just by looking at them.

"How did you survive?" I ask. "I thought he killed you? He kind of led me to believe that everyone was dead back there in the Stag. I certainly didn't see any survivors when we flew away."

Aren takes me by the shoulders and steers me towards my father's big chair and pushes me until I sit. Then he takes a seat on the desk and puts his head in his hands again.

"How are you the commanding officer here, Aren? Why are there MR soldiers outside?"

He rubs the stubble on his chin, but doesn't answer.

"Are you going to just sit there? Or will you answer my questions?"

Now he meets my gaze, but still no words come out.

I get up and walk towards the door. "Fine, I'm going to my room. I've been played with enough for the past week, I don't have the time or interest in playing with you today. So, when you're ready to tell me what the fuck is going on, you let me know. OK?"

"Wait," he says before I can reach the door. "Just a minute. Hold on, OK? Just give me a second to try and put all the pieces together."

I turn back to him with a sneer. "Let me help you, how about that? I'm some freak bird alien. Oh no, wait— I'm not a bird, did you know that avians aren't birds? Well, they're—I mean we're not. I'm an alien, my parents are monsters who took me in for some sort of genetic experiment twice a year, the RR is as corrupt as all hell, and you're in on all of it. How's that for putting the fucking pieces together?"

His brow furrows a little. "Junco, I swear I don't know if any of that is true, not one word of it. But I've heard things that are beginning to be repeated so many times they're getting hard to dismiss."

"What things have you heard?"

"You, your parents, and the Stag. It was some massive cover-up with the United Republics, and I just want to make this very clear, right now. I am not involved in any of that. None of it."

"So which part are you involved in?"

He lets out a deep sigh. "I'm just the delivery guy."

"And my brother?"

He shakes his head at me. "What brother?"

"The avian the MR held hostage all these years?"

"Shit. Shit. Shit. Shit. I know of him, Junco. Of him. I want to be clear here, I don't know anything else. Nothing."

"And you're the commander here? Not likely, Aren."

He comes toward me where I'm standing in the middle of the room and looks down into my eyes. "Now you see where I'm at?"

I shake my head no. Because no, not really. I don't.

"They're using me, Junco." It comes out strong, but I can see the fear on his face. "I'm going down here."

"If you're not really in charge, then who is?"

"Colonel Slag, Junco. That goddamn RR bastard's been after you forever. He rolled in to the MR a little over a week ago, had the superiors all up in a wad, put me in charge, and told me to bring you back and kill the avian."

"What do they want with me?" I ask coldly.

"I don't know, I swear."

"Why do they want to kill Tier?"

"Because he was sent here to kill *you*."

I laugh. "Kill me? Well he's got a funny way of killing me, since I'm still alive and he let me walk away."

"So he tested you and you're not the Seventh Sibling?"

I shake my head. "What are you talking about now?"

"He was sent here to kill you, Junco, I saw the orders myself. You're not one of the Six, you're the—"

"The what?" I ask, unable to let him keep going for fear of what he will say.

"You're the Seventh, not the pure avian like the last girl they took."

My head spins and I suddenly realize I'm going to faint when Aren grabs me and pulls me over to my father's couch. I sit back and wait it out. "What last girl?" I finally manage.

"Oh, shit. I'm sorry, Junco, I thought he told you that. You know about the other guy, the other avian. I just figured you knew about her too."

"I'm going to be sick," I say as I run towards the bathroom connected to the office. I slam the door behind me, lift the seat on the head and dry-heave my guts out. Then I sit back on the cold tile floor and listen dispassionately to Aren barking orders at people on the other side of the door.

A little while later he knocks, tries the knob, and when it turns he pushes forward, but my body is leaning up against the door and it opens only a few inches.

"Junco?" I can hear the hesitation in his voice.

"What," I answer. Flat. Emotionless.

"Lemme in."

I scoot away from the door and he opens it the rest of the way, then yanks me to my feet without speaking.

"No," I protest as I fling my arms around so he will drop his hands. "I don't want to see anyone yet."

"Fine, but you're not going to mope on the bathroom floor all day. Get up and come out here with me."

I follow him out to my father's office and plop down into the deep couch, resting my head on the armrest. "Tell me everything you know," I demand.

And to my surprise, he does.

It comes spilling out like he's been waiting his whole life to talk to me. For part of it I sit motionless, waiting to hear the terrible truth, and other parts I let the tears escape. It's not quite the same story that Tier told me, but close enough to establish that most of what he said is either true, or significantly close to true.

A soldier interrupts us at one point, and I recognize him as CP from the makeshift field-camp oh so long ago. He's smiling when he first looks at me, but then his face drops when he sees my expression. When Aren turns away to sign the papers he brought, he silently mouths something encouraging. I turn away before he's done and watch as Aren hands the pen back. CP turns to leave, then stops, and looks back at us. "Sir? The men wanted me to ask if there are blinds that can be drawn on the windows, so the media can't see in?"

Aren pushes him out the door, mumbling something at him. But as soon as the door is closed he turns back to me. "Can we block the windows, Junco? It really is annoying being so exposed since the house is literally made of glass. I don't know how you could sleep in a house that has no shades. Especially since—"

"HOUSE?" I ask the ceiling.

"Welcome home, Junco, I've missed you dearly, my friend."

I breathe out quickly, then gasp for more air. "Thank you. Can you please opaque the windows?" The room is instantly dark as the light shining through the wall of windows facing the courtyard blacks out. "And turn on evening lights, too?" The lights pop on and the courtyard is glowing with soft artificial illumination as I watch the astonished expression on Aren's face. "Thanks, HOUSE."

"You're welcome, Junco. I hope you are feeling OK. I detect some anxiety in your voice."

"Unfortunately, I'm not. But thanks for your concern. I appreciate it."

"I'm sorry, Junco. Please let me know if there is anything I can do for you."

I nod and she's silent.

Aren is still looking at me in disbelief. "What now?" I ask.

"You have a sentient house?"

"For security," I say.

"You have a sentient house?" he asks again, like I didn't hear him correctly the first time.

"Yes, Aren, I have a sentient house. What?" I ask when he begins to shake his head and mumble under his breath. "What?"

"You Farm Families are such blood-sucking hypocrites!"

Now it is my turn to be stunned. "What the hell are you talking about, Aren?"

"You're a Farm Family, in the Rural Republic, Junco. Surely you aren't so far removed from our society that you think a sentient house is an acceptable form of tech?"

"It's a security system, Aren. Lots of people have security systems in the RR."

"Yeah, it's called a dog." He says it with such contempt I'm taken aback for a minute. "Is this how all of you live? With a heated pool in the courtyard, a tropical rain forest as your personal garden, songbirds singing on every branch, and some artificial intelligence thrown in for good measure?"

"Are we really having this conversation?" I ask, completely pissed off.

"Do you want to know how I grew up, Junco? We had no indoor plumbing, no central heating in the winter, no air conditioning, no hot showers, no cars, no trucks, and certainly not enough sense to know that our parents were completely nuts for making us live like this until I moved out and discovered the entire civilized fucking world took toilets for granted."

"You really want to play this game? I didn't ask to be born into this family, and guess what? It turns out I wasn't born into this family. I didn't ask for this life. And if you want to trade, I'll be happy to go out to wherever the hell you're from and stick it out while you bask in the artificial sunshine next to our pool and then learn that you're not even human!"

The lights dim and HOUSE's voice booms out from the ceiling. "Lockdown will be initiated in fifteen seconds. Lockdown will be initiated in fifteen seconds."

"Give her the signal, Junco," Aren growls.

"I'm fine, HOUSE, signal protocol 3zsk256478."

"Security action aborted," my house replies. Then it adds, "Junco, you should ask these people to leave for your own safety. Would you like me to make them leave?"

Aren puts his head in his hands and takes a seat on the couch to calm down.

"No. He's fine. We're just really stressed out right now."

"Would you like me to call your dad and tell him to come home, Junco?"

I never explained his death. In fact, I can't even remember if I talked to anyone during the time between his death and my excursion out to Stag. I let the words escape, half because I can't stop myself even if I wanted to and half because for the smallest moment I want so badly to believe that this is all a nightmare. "Do you have a number for him, HOUSE? I really want to talk to him. Can you find him for me, please?"

Aren comes over and puts his arm around me. "Don't do this, Junco. Stop. Make her stop."

But she answers before I can. "I'm sorry, Junco. I have no number for your dad right now. If you tell me where he is I can look him up in the data systems."

I wipe my hand across my face, push the shit back down, lock it in, and look Aren in the eyes. My response slides out without a hint of emotion. "He's rotting in hell, HOUSE. Try there first."

Chapter Twenty-Six

I'm back in the bathroom, but this time Aren leaves me alone in there for so long that I actually fall asleep on the rug in front of the sink. When he finally knocks I sit up so fast my head spins.

"Look, Junco," Aren says through the door, "we need to come up with a plan here. Come out of there and deal with this."

I come out and plop back down onto the couch.

"Things are spiraling out of control outside. The media is here, I mean media from all over the world, Junco. You might have been a minor curiosity before you were taken by an avian, but right now you're the biggest story on the planet. We need to get rid of them, and then we need to come up with a way to defuse what's happening here."

"Well, maybe you should start by telling me what is happening here."

He walks over to my father's chair and sits down, then spins it so he's looking out at the spotlights lighting up the lush tropical landscape of the courtyard. "I think we're all about to be killed."

"By who?" I snort.

He spins back to face me. "Take your pick?" he says, and shrugs. "Maybe the aliens, the RR Council, the United Republic Secretaries, Council 3, the Mountain Republic, hell, maybe it will be your neighbors and friends. Who knows? All I know is that from my viewpoint, the shit is stacked, Junco. Fucking shoulder high."

He spins back to the tropical view of the courtyard so all I see is his military haircut peeking out from the top of the massive leather chair. "I'm dead, that's all I know," he continues. "They gave me this assignment for one reason and one reason only and that's so they have someone to blame it on."

Oh shit, now he's paranoid. "Blame *what* on?"

He spins back again. "The attack! Don't you pay attention to anything?"

"What attack?" I growl. My patience has run out and I feel the heat rise in my face as I look at him.

"The fucking avians, Junco! They're everywhere out there. We can sense their shielding, they have more ships out there than we have reporters!"

"OK," I say, trying my best to remain calm so HOUSE doesn't initiate the security protocol again, "when I said tell me everything you know, that meant everything you know, you asshole. You never mentioned avians attacking!"

He lets out a deep breath and continues to spin between the courtyard view and the office and it's really pissing me off. "I've got it. You make a statement to the media, right? You let them in on a few choice details, this creates interest in your story, your face is all over the newscreens, and then they can't come in and take you. How about that?"

"What kind of statement?" I ask with hopeful hesitation.

"You know, just bits and pieces to make your story compelling, like the nightdog eating your fingers. Flash your stubs to the cameras, then add in your daring escape, and say you're very happy to be home."

I sniff loudly. "I don't know."

"Trust me, Junco. They aren't leaving until they hear from you. You have to go out there and say something."

"And when they leave, so what? How does that stop us from being killed by the Council or the avians, or whoever else wants to sweep all this under the carpet?"

He bites his thumbnail as he continues to swivel in my father's chair, and I'm just about to scream at him when he answers, "Call a meeting. Of the council." He looks up at me, smiling. "No, you say you already asked for a meeting with the Council tomorrow, and they accepted."

"But they haven't."

"Sweet Jeremiah, Junco, how the fuck do you make a living at covert ops? You're playing them. You say that they agreed to meet with you tomorrow, then everyone waits to see what happens. Meanwhile, no one can attack us tonight, and we'll have a little more time to figure this out."

"I don't make a living at covert ops, by the way." He sneers at me and shakes his head. "But letting that comment slide, what the fuck do I say to them in the meeting?"

This time he doesn't spin, or bite his nail. He just sits for a few minutes, eyes darting back and forth. "I'm not sure yet. Give me the night to think about it."

"Well, I'm not going out there to make a statement looking like this. I need to go to my room and get cleaned up."

He puts his hands out and shakes his head, an expression that from my end reads, so what the fuck should I do about it?

"Come with me, Aren. I don't want to be alone."

This makes him smile, the scared little girl needs the big strong man to protect her.

Whatever. I let him have his moment.

Just keep talking. Keep drowning out the voices in my head so I can damp them back down into submission. *Otherwise I'll be picturing myself standing on the edge of a fucking dock. In front of me is a fucking mountain lake and behind me is a small fucking cabin...*

I watch Aren's face as he looks around my room.

"What?" I growl.

"Well, no offense, Junco, but it looks like a princess threw up in here."

He's right. This cannot be my room. I haven't been six for a very long time, but my name is on the door and my fingerprints trigger the biometrics on the doorknob.

So.

Apparently it is.

"Shut up and take a fucking seat on the flying carpet while I take a shower."

He eyes the bench covered in a genuine Persian carpet suspended from the ceiling by cables, and for a minute I wait to see if he actually tries to climb on, but he plops down in the white fuzzy beanbag chair. Then he grabs a photo album from the little end table next to him and thumbs through it.

I was right about him being chatty because I can hear him talking to me all through my shower. I just have no idea what he's saying because I'm too busy standing under the blasting hot water to care. At one point he even comes into the bathroom to ask about a photo of me on a pony, but I just shoo him out and tell him to wait.

I take my time washing and conditioning my filthy hair and lathering myself with sweet pea soap, then comb it out in the steamy mirror. I peel off a few avian membranes on my calf that I didn't notice during my last bath and check every last bruise, burn, and cut on my body before wrapping myself up in my thick cotton bathrobe.

When I come out he's sitting on the end of my purple canopy bed, his camo fatigues clashing badly with the unicorn pattern on the quilt, and his combat boots are resting on the white bed rail so he can prop a photo album in his lap.

"Junco," he says, looking anything but properly embarrassed. Hell, I'm embarrassed for him. "Are all these pictures of you?"

I wrap my hair in a towel and then take a seat next to him on the bed and grab the album. I'm about two and my very first pony, Magpie, is galloping on the long line. She's a slick and shiny black-and-white pinto Shetland. I'm wearing a pink unitard with a white tutu and ballet shoes. My auburn hair is up in a tight bun, and my face clearly exhibits happiness that no two year old should be able to fake. I have one foot planted firmly on her back and another sticking out behind, my hands splayed out in front of me with "pretty fingers" to make it look official.

"Yeah," I say, but in my mind I see the little girl in the clone tank and begin to wonder. "They always said I was born on a horse."

He flips the pages again and points to me at about six. This time I'm doing a handstand on Esmeralda. "Yes, again. They're all me."

I think.

"Can we use these for the presser?" I just look at him, so he clarifies, "Can I pass out copies to the media, so they can post them in the sphere?"

"Why would we do that?"

"It makes you look, well—sort of innocent and vulnerable. Child-like."

I'm about to ask if that's the look we're going for when he stands up and grabs one of my more recent trophies. "What's this one from?"

"Worlds, from last year. That picture is out there already. Probably."

"How about this one?" He points to another trophy, not as bright as the last.

"That was Worlds, when I was thirteen." I stop and look up at him. "Right after I met you at cadets, don't you remember?" I talked about it incessantly that year because I didn't want to go. The contest was in Sydney and for some reason thinking of Sydney makes me sick. Aren just smiles and we go on like that for a while, he points and I clarify, then he chooses it or puts it back. When we're done he's got about eight awards and pictures to display and then he leaves me to get dressed.

But I'm not ready to get dressed now that I've got my whole life out in front of me. I look over the images and marvel at how young I was when I started. The Magpie picture was the earliest one at around two, but I must have been training for some time if I already had balance and could stand on one foot as she galloped in the circle. If I was adopted, and clearly I was since everyone has the same story, my parents got a hold of me young. And not only that, they had big plans for me. It's not like they stuck me in a corner and waited for their orders to bring me back to the Stag. No, they put me on a horse and started training me in aerial acrobatics.

Why? Why bother?

A soldier knocks on the door and announces that the media is ready when I am, so I break off my thoughts and spend a good amount of time trying to find something in my closet that isn't fifteen years out of date or that makes me look six.

I finally settle on a pair of khaki slacks and a brown t-shirt with our farm logo on it. Then I run a brush through my hair and choose some slightly muddy barn boots over the ballet flats that some other Junco seems to be fixated with.

I take a deep breath, grab my brown canvas farm jacket and open the door. There are several soldiers waiting for me and they take me by the arm and lead to me to the front of the house where I can sense the sizable crowd that has gathered in my front yard to hear about my ordeal.

A flashing thought occurs to me as I walk towards the massive double front doors. Maybe I should have actually prepared something to say?

As soon as I step through the doors Aren is there and he takes my hand and leads me up to the makeshift podium. The crowd is loud at first, but when they see me, a hush falls over my packed front yard and they wait. Aren and I reach the podium together and he lets go of my hand, but I snatch it back and then turn to him and smile. He smiles back, and nods his head ever so slightly to give me encouragement.

My eyes sweep over the mass of people lit up in the flood of our outdoor security lights and I calculate the number in my head real fast. Maybe a hundred and fifty people are crammed onto the lawn, their faces upturned, and the questions waiting on their tongues.

I clear my throat, ready to speak, but I suddenly have no idea where to start. I glance down at a conservatively-dressed young reporter with long blonde hair, she doesn't look much older than me. She meets my eyes, then her gaze darts down at the notes on her membrane and she ever so quietly begins to speak. "Junco, can you tell us why you were in the Stag last week?"

And then she smiles.

"I... well, my father—" I stop and hesitate, but the young reporter nods at me and so I continue. "Maybe you don't know this, but my father di— was killed a couple weeks ago in a terrible... incident. And on the day of the funeral I—"

I what? Went a little crazy?

"I noticed that a family friend was missing from the ceremony. So I went to the Stag to see this friend. Well, a man I thought was a family friend. But I never made it there. I hit a deer about halfway to the camp and crashed my truck. It was then that the avian found me. And healed me from my numerous injuries."

I look at the young reporter and she prods me again. "Why did he take you, Junco?"

"He took me..." I have every intention of answering her but as my gaze passes over the crowd I see him. The RR officer I saw holding a gun to CP's head at that makeshift camp in the Stag. Several reporters notice the direction of my eyes and look back to find what I'm looking at. He doesn't move or make a single gesture or motion. Aren sees him too, and gives my hand a tight squeeze, and when I look over at him, he nods to keep going.

I clear my throat and begin again. "He took me because many years ago the United Republics stole some avian genetics to make clones or mutants, or something like that. To use for bio-engineering experiments." The crowd gasps, and the RR commander turns and walks away from the crowd.

The questions are flying now, and I put up a hand to make them stop. I wait for it to get as quiet as I dare and I continue. "He, the avian, took me to kill me because I'm one of those experiments." The chatter of shock erupts again and I scan the crowd to see who will walk away now and that's when I see Tier. Standing in the back, leaning up against the ruddy bark of our tallest Ponderosa pine tree. He crosses his arms and shakes his head at me before disappearing. Once again the crowed follows my eyes to find my target, but they see nothing and the whispering gets louder.

Aren squeezes again, and leans in to tell me that I should wrap it up. "And so," I belt it out to try and get everyone's attention, "and so that is why I have invited the Rural Republic High Council to meet with me tomorrow at 6 PM. And they have so graciously agreed to this meeting so that we can set things right. So that no other children are caught in the lies and deceit that have ripped my life apart over the last week."

"Junco," the young reporter shouts, "what about the avian? Where is he? Will he take you away?"

I look back at the tree where Tier was standing moments before, just in case he's still hanging around and I can't see him. "I have no plans beyond tomorrow."

They erupt in chatter as they rush their reports out in the sphere and I say thank you, but no one hears. And then Aren is leading me back to my father's office and before I can blink, I'm sitting on the couch.

CP closes the door behind us and Aren is pacing the floor, his hands behind his head. "Shit! I can't believe you said that!" He says it a little too enthusiastically.

"What do you mean? Did I say too much?"

He kneels down in front of me and takes my hands. "Not at all, Junco, you were brilliant! Did you see the

Colonel storm off? He was pissed!" Aren jumps back up and resumes his pacing. "Everyone saw him. I bet it's all over the world by now! Shit!"

"I don't get it. Is that good or bad?"

"Oh, well, that depends who you are tonight. If you're me and you, I personally think this is great. Fucking perfect! They can't touch us now."

"Did you see Tier out there, by the tree?"

Aren stops now and stares down at me. "He was here?"

"Yeah, he was leaning on that big Ponderosa in the back and then he just vanished right in front of my eyes."

"Fucking avians. They have some kind of shielding that makes them appear invisible, and I'm not talking about how we can make things look invisible, with the shimmer of light that gives you away, either. It's damn near perfect."

"So, is that good or bad? I mean, if you're you and me?"

But he doesn't answer, only continues his pacing.

"HOUSE," I ask as I look up to the ceiling.

"Yes, Junco?"

"Are there alien ships outside?"

"Yes, Junco."

Aren has a look of stunned shock on his face. "She can see them?"

"Can you see them, HOUSE?"

"No, Junco. But I know they are here."

"How do you know?" I ask.

"They announced their presence with your security clearance this afternoon."

Chapter Twenty-Seven

The barn is quiet and the smell of horses and alfalfa hay fills my nostrils. These smells have never bothered me. I was a horse lover from day one and there isn't a single thing about them that turns me off. Not the slobber as you slip the bit in, not mucking out the stalls, cleaning sweat-caked saddles, picking feet, pulling manes, the nasty stench of worming medicine, being bit, kicked or thrown. Everything about them is good.

Darby is my number one. A giant dapple-gray warmblood with a temperament so cool she's a cold front blowing through a still summer prairie. She nickers at me when I approach and slide the stall door open. I click my tongue and she exits and trots to the arena and begins a brisk walk around the perimeter. I swing the pipe gate closed and let out a genuine smile as I look down the breezeway.

The Goat is parked near the back entrance to the barn where Aren had the tow truck drop it off. I rummage through the back seat and surface with a pair of filthy thermals and a large white t-shirt. Also dirty. Then I spy the envelope with Dale's name on it peeking out from under the passenger seat and open it up. I flip through the various official documents and let out a big sigh and set it back down on the seat. It waited this long, it can wait a little bit more. Besides, I can't get my clean clothes off fast enough.

There are no boots since I took the extra pair back when I changed out of my funeral shoes, but I won't need them. I slam the door and jump back in surprise.

"Why must you sneak up on people?"

"I didn't want to interrupt you," Tier says.

"I bet. Did you get a good enough look or should I strip for you again?"

"I've seen it all several times now, Junco. But if you want to strip again, I certainly won't stop you." It might have been a joke under other circumstances, but the way it comes out makes it feel—a little sad.

I turn away and walk towards the tack room so he can't see the confusion creeping across my face. I flip the light on and search for some tape, then hop up on the counter and begin to wrap the balls of my feet. "So, what do you want?"

"Well," he says as he fiddles with a bridle hanging from the rack on the wall, "I have some news."

My right foot is finished and I start working on the left one. "And?" He continues to fiddle. "Tier, I'm tired of the games, all right? If you have something to say, then just spit it out." I finish the left foot and hop down. "And to be quite honest I'm just about ready to pretend none of this ever happened." I step into the rosin box and shuffle my feet around, taking care to coat the tape. "Because none of it makes any sense. I don't even know if you're telling the truth about my father, although why you'd want to lie to me about *that*, I don't understand. But right now I don't understand anything. It's been a very long fucked-up day and I just want to relax."

I flip the light off and head back out to the arena. Darby is still walking but when I click my tongue, she begins to trot. I slide under the pipe gate and walk onto the thick loamy dirt and position myself in the center of the arena before clicking for her to tighten up into a regulation circle. Tier takes a seat on the small wooden bleachers on the long side of the arena and I run alongside Darby, grab her mane, and swing up onto her back with little effort.

"You gonna be a spectator tonight, Tier? Or you gonna talk?"

"It can wait," he calls.

I tap at her girth with my toe and she eases into a controlled lope. She's so easy to ride, so smooth and natural that I automatically relax with her and the rhythm fills my core and drops to my seat as I sink into it. I let the tension drain away and then pop up to a stand and watch as Tier does the same. "You've never spied on me in here, or what?"

My back is to him, but when I come around the perimeter, he's in the arena with me, standing in the center pivoting as I circle.

"It makes me very nervous to watch."

I smile and flip backwards in the air, landing onto the sweet spot in the bow of Darby's back. Tier's face is contorted into a look of shock and I laugh and do it again.

"I always thought they made ya do this. I never knew you actually liked it."

I click and bend my knees so I can absorb the increased pace as Darby extends her canter to a gallop, then do a double, this time landing on one foot. "This is heaven." I drop back down onto her back and touch her with my toe twice and she collects. We make several revolutions and I feel my shoulders and neck loosen up. "Have you ever ridden a horse, Tier?" My breath is heavy now and the wind we make hisses loudly in my ears so I don't hear his answer. I tap and Darby changes gears like the professional she is, slows, slows, slows. And we are walking again. I make subtle squeezes with my lower leg and take her over to Tier, breathing hard. "Get on."

His mouth pulls a little at one corner before looking up to me. "No. I don't think it's a good idea."

"Why not?"

"A few hours ago you were running away from me as fast as you could, now yer suddenly OK with everything?"

"No," I say quickly, "I'm not OK with anything. It's time to forget. Now get your ass over here and jump on the fucking horse."

He doesn't smile with his mouth, but I can see it in his eyes.

And then he is behind me. Even Darby is surprised because she stretches her long neck around to see what's going on. I touch her belly with my toe and we walk out of the barn and into the night.

Tier's hands slip around my waist as he pulls me back a little into his jacket. I lean into his warmth because the night air is cold. We walk and I point out things in the back paddocks, name the horses that didn't wander into their stalls to sleep, and then direct Darby up a path into the woods. After several minutes of climbing we leave the woods and enter a meadow dominated by a large red sandstone outcrop.

"I've seen ya up here lots of times." Tier says.

I jump off Darby and climb the rock that reaches out towards the mountains to the west, my taped feet finding each foothold without much effort. This has been my thinking spot since I was a kid.

Tier flies up and lands next to me.

"You had something to tell me?" I ask as I turn to look at him.

He just shrugs.

"Maybe I should start, then?" I hug myself to ward off the shaking that comes with the cold now that I'm not next to him.

He takes off his jacket and drapes it over my shoulders, then walks back to the opposite end of the rock and takes a seat, leaning back against another rock that runs perpendicular to the one we're standing on. I slip my arms into the jacket and pull it tight around me as much as I can with the cuts he made to accommodate his wings. I follow him over, but I don't sit. I just stand there, legs apart, arms hugging my body. There is no good way to have this conversation.

"So how many of the other Seven do you have, besides Moju?"

His eyes narrow as he stares up at me. "We don't have Moju, Junco. No one has Moju. Even when he is in custody, he is wild. But we do have another girl back in the Band, where our habitats orbit."

"So you didn't think this information was relevant to me?"

He doesn't even blink. "We've had her for years. She grew up in the Eastern Utopia and she came along no problem. And ya know why, Junco? Ya know why she came along so easily?" He pauses to see if I'll take a stab at it, but I stay silent. "Because no one fed her a constant dinner of lies her entire life and when we came to get her she didn't have to take a few weeks to figure out who she was. She wanted to get the hell out of that place. Fucking Communists are all crazy, even her dumb ass knew that."

I don't grab the bait. "And she's one of the Six, the avian children of light? Not me, though." I know I've caught him off guard this time because he looks away.

"I'm the Seventh castaway in flight. The one who brings the end."

He shakes his head. "It can be fixed." I open my mouth to say something nasty, but he interrupts. "Do you understand what I mean?"

I shake my head. "No, Tier. I have no idea what you mean."

"Why am I not surprised?" He holds up a small silver cube and rolls it back and forth between his fingertips. I know what it is without asking. His smile leaks out slowly but once it's out, it's bright.

"How do you know it's the right one? He could've given you anything."

His smile disappears. "Ya think I'm an amateur, Junco? Shit. Let me tell ya a little about what I do—" He stops and takes a deep breath and then continues. "Never mind. I took everything he had. And I've checked each and every one. This one," he rolls it around again and I see a glint of starshine reflecting off the sides, "is all you. I have your complete genome, biomarkers, DNA aggregates, hypo-adrenal biog, personality adjustments, and programmed muscle memory."

I just stare at him. I don't really know what I'd expected to be on the data cubes he took from Dale, but it certainly wasn't my personal human augmentation profile. "What the hell are you talking about?"

He gets up and walks towards me, then past me out to the tip of the monolith where he stops. "Christ, I'm so fucking tired of having these clueless conversations with ya."

I stay where I am but I am pissed. "Really?" The word seethes out of me. "Then why don't you just tell me the rest of it then? And not some half-ass fairy tale either."

He turns around and shakes his head. "It's not mine to tell, Junco. It's yours. I have very little to do with any of this"—he extends his hands out to either side in a wide sweeping gesture—"bullshit you're going through right now. Ya want the truth of what I'm doing here? I'm Perseus, Junco. I'm the only thing standing between you and death. Or you and slavery. Take yer pick."

I just stare at him.

"Ya know why I was sent to kill ya? Because I fucked up and this job was supposed to be my way out of some very bad shit. So let this sink in real deep before you go making demands or accusing me of being less than helpful with your personal dilemmas. I have disobeyed orders for you, Junco."

"Well, congrat-u-fucking-lations. Should I pat you on the back now because you found your spine? Maybe I should just kill *you* instead?"

"Well, at least ya'd be doing what comes natural, then, right?"

"Says the lion to the wolf."

He doesn't respond. Instead he sits down on the ledge and swings his feet off the overhang, staring out towards the mountains which have a tinge of orangey-pink reflected from the approaching sunrise behind us.

I stand there for a while watching his back. Thinking. "You don't want to be the messenger, fine. Whatever. I'll see you later then." I turn to climb back down the rock and then he speaks.

"I'm leaving tomorrow night." He looks east at the approaching dawn and amends his statement. "Tonight, I mean."

"Is that why the ships are all over my house?"

He screws up his face. "If there were avian ships here, Junco, we'd already be on our way back to the Band.

We don't fuck about with ships in the atmosphere unless we're doing something."

"But my HOUSE says you have ships."

"Your HOUSE is wrong."

"She's an AI, Tier."

"Then she's corrupted."

I let that sink in for several silent minutes.

"Anyway, time's up, Junco. If you want a good piece of advice I'll give it ta ya, no charge."

"What's that, then?" I say, turning.

He gets up and walks over towards me. Looking up at him I can see that he's sincere.

"Run. If yer gonna stay here for the rest of what will be a very short life, Junco, my best advice is to run like hell. You've got everyone pretty fucking confused with this memory loss bullshit, you might as well take advantage of it."

A small half-hearted laugh escapes my lips. "I don't lose memories, Tier. It's impossible. I have perfect recall."

Now it's his turn to laugh. "Is that right? Shit, Junco, you've forgotten more things in the last few months than most people will in a lifetime. So cut the bullshit and face the facts."

I look away from his accusations before I speak. "You don't even *have* the facts, Tier. So do not lecture me. I don't lose memories. I just—push them down. So I can keep on living with myself, with what I do, and what I am." I lift my eyes and turn to look at him sideways as my voice hardens. "If I don't recall them at times, it's because I have a damn good reason. And I'm not running anywhere. I'm tired of running."

He stares down at me with sadness and I feel my temper rise.

"Keep your pity, OK? I'm not sorry for any of it, so don't fool yourself."

It's his turn to laugh. "Ah. OK, then. How about this? I won't fool myself if you don't. I mean, yeah, I can see it now. Yer little memory tricks work great, right? That's why yer barely able to sleep without dreaming some horrific nightmare time after time. Take my advice and listen to the inner whispers, Junco. They're speakin' ta ya."

I let out a half-hearted grunt. "I don't think you really want me to do that, Tier."

"And why's that, darlin'?"

"Because the voices in my head only ever tell me to do one thing, and that's kill people. In very interesting ways."

He laughs. "Shit, Junco, you were right about one thing. Yer certainly no Andromeda."

I look up at him now, but there is no smile on my face. "And you're no Perseus, either."

His smile fades and then he is serious. "Junco, if it's a hero ya want, just say the word. Come with me and it all goes away."

"And then what? They'll kill me and you know it."

"No, Junco." He holds the cube up between his fingers again. "The answers are all in here. If it can be written, it can be rewritten. That's what we do. We don't have babies, remember? We make them. Just like someone made you."

I hesitate and he turns away from me again.

"Don't make me force ya, Junco. I don't want to force ya." He stops and turns back to gauge my reaction to his words, but keeps silent.

"Then tell me what you know about the dock. Tell me."

He shakes his head and whispers some curse words under his breath. "This part, Junco, is all you. I have nothing ta do with any of that. Nothing." He turns and starts walking away.

I close the few paces between us and grab his arm. "Wait. Do you know what it is? Where it is?"

He lets out a little noise that might be a half-hearted attempt at a laugh, but devolves into a sigh. "Don't make me tell ya this shit, Junco. I told ya the first part and that was bad enough. You already know all this." He taps my head gently. "It's already up there, remember?"

I stare up at him and he averts his eyes. "Maybe it is. But I can't count on myself to bring it back in time, Tier. Time's up, right? Time's up." I pull on him like a small child until he looks at me, but then he just closes his eyes. "Please." He shakes his head, but I claw at his clothes and beg, "Please. I'll do whatever you say if you just make that part fit back together."

"You said that last time, remember?" He looks down at me now, nothing but sadness written on his face. His fingers play with something in his pocket and it makes a small clinking sound. He pulls out his hand and opens his palm, revealing several dozen tiny cubes like the one he was twirling in his fingers earlier. He picks through them, sorts them, puts some back in his pocket and then there are only four left. Four tiny little silver cubes.

I look up at him and take a deep breath. "What are they?"

"One is yer profile." He points to it. "One is Charlie's profile." He points to another but my head spins and he grabs me before I can fall down.

Chapter Twenty-Eight

Charlie.

"... the planks on the deck are warm under your feet and you're wearing a long thin white shirt, open in the front, that barely covers your body. The waves lap against the dock and you reach over and drag your fingers through the water. It folds against your wrist and slaps up the side of your arm. The drops bead against your oiled skin, pool together, then spring forth into a trickle which takes the liquid back to the source. The mountains are high and cast just the right amount of shadow to protect the nesting colony of eagles against the heat of the summer."

"Are you sure this will work?"

"Picture yourself standing on the edge of a dock, Junco. In front of you is a mountain lake and behind you is a small cabin, pristine white curtains flowing in the breeze passing through the windows. Down below the water you can see the scales of brightly colored fish reflecting the sunlight..."

He stops.

"It works, Junco. Just picture yourself standing on the edge of a dock. It's not a big deal, this is kid stuff."

"Kid stuff where you come from, maybe." But I'm teasing and he knows it. "Why can't we just stay here in the real world, Charlie?"

"Silly, Junco." His voice on the coms sounds farther away than he really is. "You know why."

I know why.

"So, just put those little buds in your ears, they're marked so you know which one goes where..."

"I see it. OK, they're in."

"... And listen to my voice. When you get there, just enjoy it until I come in with you. If you ever want to leave you just say OFF, and you'll be back in your room. OK?"

I nod, but then remember we're on coms. *"Yeah. I got it."*

"Picture yourself standing on the edge of a dock, Junco. In front of you is a mountain lake and behind you is a small cabin, pristine white curtains flowing in the breeze passing through the windows. Down below the water you can see the scales of brightly colored fish reflecting the sunlight..."

The sun is so warm I close my eyes and stare at it, letting the bright orange seep through my eyelids. Charlie comes up next to me and takes my hand.

"I told you it was fabulous."

I open my eyes and look at him. He's tall and muscular, with golden skin that reflects light off the tiny hairs on his arms. *"I can't believe you made this!"*

"Where do you think it is, Junco?"

I look down at the green-blue water and then behind me towards the cabin. It's not my cabin, but it's close. I smile at him. *"Good times in there, right?"*

He laughs. *"Now he can't accuse you of seeing me. Technically we're not together. So you don't have to worry about disobeying his order and you don't have to lie."*

I feel a little sick at the thought and I take a deep breath, but nothing happens. Oh, yeah, I'm in a virtual. Projections don't breathe. For a minute I have a little panic attack, but Charlie's hand takes mine and leads me back to the cabin. Inside all the walls are whitewashed, unlike the dark wood of our hunting cabin. The floors are painted a light blue, and the furniture is all white. He leads me over to the couch and plops down, then draws me into his lap and plays with my hair.

"You like it?"

I nod.

"What's wrong then?"

"I have to tell you something, Charlie. I have to tell you—"
But he's gone. Just blipped out of the scene.
"EXIT," I say.
Nothing.
"EXIT!"
Nothing.
"EXIT! EXIT! OFF!"

I'm back in a room and someone is banging on the door. I run up a ladder and fly across the room to open it. A hand reaches out and slaps me across the face. I fall to the ground and my father looms over me. "I'm very angry with you, Junco. Bring her to my office."

The soldier reaches down and picks me up after he leaves. "What were you doing?"

"It's a virtual reality." Tier shakes me. "Junco, it's just a virtual."

I swim back up from the vision in my head and open my eyes. "We made a virtual."

He smiles, then nods. "Not all that common for a couple of RR kids, right?"

"He was MR. From Peak City."

Tier nods.

"We were in love."

He nods again. I look up at him but he points down to his open palm, at the two remaining cubes.

I stare at them and begin to pick up the memories.

The soldier without a face takes my arm and pulls me along. I dig in to the rug with my heels, but he pulls and the rug slips along with me.

"Stop, don't. No!"

But he pulls again and I fall down, face-forward. He picks me up and another soldier opens my father's office door as we approach. Inside he drops me on the couch.

My father is on the coms and then he holds it out for me. "It's for you," he says.

I get up, my whole body shaking like I am out in the freezing cold, and reach out and take the coms. My father stares at me, and waits.

"Hello?"

"Junco!"

"Charlie? Charlie, what's going on?"

The crack of plasma echoes in my ears and then I hear a voice. "Project terminated, sir."

I throw the coms down and it smacks against the hardwood floors. The back of my father's hand finds my face and I join the ruined piece of tech on the floor just as the world goes black.

"He killed him." A sob escapes as the pain twists my heart and I break. "He killed him."

Tier hugs me and pulls me to the ground with him, but says nothing. I try my best to keep the tears in, but they don't flow down in little ribbons this time, they pour out in rivers along with the memories.

The bruises on my face are yellow-green as I stare in the mirror of my father's office bathroom. I reach up and touch the shadows around my eyes and wince. The color is fading, but the pain isn't. Someone bangs on the door and so I take the sample and open it. The lab tech whisks it away from me and my father points to the couch. I stare out the window after I take a seat. It's dark outside. The lab tech confirms what I already know and I scream. My father grabs my arm and delivers the ionizer to my nose.

I break away coughing. "What did you just do? You fucking bastard! What did you just do?"

The cramping begins almost immediately and he has someone drag me to my room where I am dumped into the shower to wash away the blood.

My body writhes in pain for hours, expelling the baby from my womb, and I can only think of one thing: how my pain will be nothing compared to what I'll do to him once this is over.

"I'm the one who tortured him."

Tier nods against me. "Now ya see why I didn't kill the torturer, eh?"

I stalk the men with my scope from behind the branches high up in a nearby pine tree as they patrol around my house, their faces burned onto my retinas. They laugh and joke, smoke and swear, and generally revel in the safety of their positions. And I know them. Lived with them on the scrub for weeks on end. Played cards with them, tracked animals, did PT, and ate with them.

And in the end, it meant nothing. I meant nothing. Together they delivered me to my father's punishment and left me to writhe in pain as I endured the aftereffects. I consider dragging out their punishment, like they did for me, but that would draw too much attention. Instead I ready the rifle, check conditions, and send off two silent shots into the night. One into each head. I collapse the rifle, pack it up, climb down, and walk back home.

The next day I'm in my father's office and he's screaming at me. His face is red and his hands tremble as he grabs me by the shirt. I ignore him and look casually out the window at a yellow songbird that is hopping from branch to branch in the courtyard.

I almost laugh at my punishment. Sold to the highest bidder. What a joke. But I don't, I feign an apology, talk him up about honor and family, and then take the smack that he delivers across my mouth, before finally starting to sniffle so he thinks I give a shit.

He has me delivered back to my room.

The last mistake he will ever make is not killing me in his office.

I stay silent, remembering the blood in the shower. "No one came to check on me."

"I don't know this part, Junco. I never knew why ya did it other than Charlie ended up dead."

I want to cry. So bad. But I've already done that. I cried about it for months, and there is nothing left to feel. "I was pregnant, Tier—"

"Aw, fuck."

"And he dosed me with an ionspray—"

"Fuck!"

"And had some soldiers drag me into my shower and leave me there until it was over. No one even came to check on me." The last few words come out in a low whisper and I feel the pain creeping back in like I am still there experiencing it. And then it is replaced by the anger. Another voice is also in my head. A familiar voice.

Project terminated, sir.

I feel Tier's chest launch sporadically a few times and I realize he's trying to hold it together too. I lie down, my head on his legs, and after a long while my breathing slows. His hand goes under my shirt and rubs my back with his fingertips.

"No one even came to check on me," I say again. "I thought I was going to die." I sniff and wipe my hand across my face, trying to get control of my nose. The fingertips trace a pattern on my back, lulling me into a slow state of acceptance and calm. *I'm your hero*, his fingers spell. *I'm your hero, I'm your hero, I'm your hero, I'm your hero.*

"I'm going to kill them all." His voice is low and steady, but to me that is even more frightening than when he's visibly pissed.

"I never even got to tell Charlie about the baby."

Tier straightens and pulls me up so he can reach into his pocket. He sorts through the tiny little cubes once more and comes up with two. "These two, Junco, are your virtual. There are two constructs here. One is you and one is Charlie."

I take the little cubes and clench them in my fist. "Thank you."

"If you want, I can give ya some time in there."

I swallow hard and look at him. I've never seen this expression on his face before. It's a mixture of hate, anger, and sadness. "Is that a good idea? Given the fact what I really need is a few years of psychotherapy?"

"It's all related, Junco. You, Charlie, the virtual, the memory loss. All of it."

"There's more to it than that," I say, shaking my head. "I don't want to go back. It's a bad place now."

He stays silent for a while. "Junco, did they kill him while you were in the virtual?" The revulsion in his voice is almost palpable. "Because that really would explain why yer having such trouble letting go."

I mull it over and sniff loudly. "No, he pulled him out first. Pulled us out. And then he had me listen to it over a com. It's dark in there."

"You should go back in. His cube was pretty badly damaged, but I had Layla clean it up. Just go in and make things right, and then leave on yer own accord—"

"Who's Layla?"

He smiles down at me. "My science contact here on Earth." He laughs. "Really now? Did I have ya fooled? Did ya really think I was the brain behind all this bioengineering going on?"

I shrug.

He fishes around in his pockets and pulls out some virtual buds and brings them toward my ears.

"No, I said." I push his hands away. "I don't want to go back in."

"Look, Junco, it has to be done. You're so fucked up it isn't even funny. I can't take ya back like this. She won't help me do it if we can't clean you up a bit."

"Now what are you talking about?" I want to feel angry but I just can't muster up enough emotion to give a shit.

"The morph, Junco. Layla says she can rewrite it. It's already there, she says, just turned off. Ya can't go in like this, Junco. The repressed bits will follow ya and come out the other side. It's not good. We have to clean this up."

I look up at him and shake my head. "Tier, I'm not ready to go back with you—I have things to finish here."

"You *will* come home with me, Junco. Because I'm not leaving ya here ta fight these bastards alone."

I stare up at the sky for a few moments, thinking about these words, and then he continues.

"Anyway," he says, changing the subject back to the buds in his hands, "if ya want, you can go back in, then initiate the exit. But, Junco..." He takes my face in his hands. "You can stay as long as ya want. It's not set in real-time. An hour in there is like a minute out here." He checks the buds and brings them towards my ears.

I push his hands away again. "I'm not going in. I said it's fucking dark in there."

He lays my head back down on his legs and his fingertips trace his pattern across my forehead until I calm down. Then he pulls out his com and loads our constructs and gently slides the buds in place. I hear soft music.

And then the familiar sequence begins, but this time it is Tier's voice telling me what to do.

Chapter Twenty-Nine

Picture yourself standing on the edge of a dock. In front of you is a mountain lake and behind you is a small cabin, pristine white curtains flowing in the breeze passing through the windows. Down below the water you can see the scales of brightly colored fish reflecting the sunlight...

... and then I am there.

I can feel the heat on my body and I lie down on the dock and soak it up, listening to the various calls of the nesting eagles on the side of the mountain. It's a nice touch, I think. I love eagles. He put them there for me.

I feel him behind me but I can't bring myself to look. He's dead. That's not really him, just his construct.

He sits down next to me and pulls his knees to his chest as I steal a look. His body is golden tan and he's wearing swim shorts and a white cotton shirt, open in the front like mine, and it flaps in the breeze coming off the lake.

"God," he says, "it's so perfect here, isn't it?" He smiles as he looks down on me and I smile back and reach for him. He takes my hand and pulls me up and puts an arm around me. We sit there and watch the sun try to set. It hangs there, just above the highest summit, like it always does, and then slowly begins to drop behind the mountain.

Charlie turns to me and smiles. "God, I miss you so much."

My face creases and I hold back the tears. "It's gonna get dark now, Charlie! We have to go!"

"Shh."

"No! We have to get out of here! Look," I point up to the last bit of sun fading behind the mountain, "it's almost gone! We have to go now!"

He smiles. "Don't sweat it, OK?"

"Oh God!" The sun is gone and the darkness swoops in, the howling of the nightdogs begins and I pull away.

But his strong arms reach out and pull me back down. "Wait, let me show you what to do."

"I have to get out!"

"No, Junco. You don't—look!"

He's pointing to the sky, so I look up.

"The stars, Junco. They're just tiny dots of sunlight. All you have to do in the dark is find the stars and you'll be fine."

He's right. Starshine is sunshine. I exhale a few short breathes and try to pull myself together. "I'm so sorry for what he did."

"Shh."

"I don't want to go on without you, Charlie."

He hugs me tighter now. "Don't be silly, Junco. There's no point in you doing something stupid. When you leave here, just know that I'm still around, OK?" He leans down and kisses me on the lips. "Your father can rot in hell, because we'll always be together, babe."

I wipe my nose and nod. "We'll always be together."

"Ready?"

I nod.

"Picture yourself on the side of the mountain, sitting on a great big red rock with Tier. The sun is rising in the east and an early winter storm is rolling in from the west over the mountains. Storm's coming, Junco. Better get ready—"

I open my eyes and Tier looks down at me and winces. Then he hugs me and we sit there for a while. *I'm your hero, I'm your hero, I'm your hero, I'm your hero.*

"So," he says, breaking our silence after a few minutes, "what will ya do now?" I hesitate and he shoots me a look. "Ya can't even be thinking about staying, really?"

I shrug. "I have some unfinished business."

"Aye," he says with a soft breath of air. "Me as well. And then?"

I get up and so does he. "What's gonna happen if I leave with you?" I search his eyes for something, but I don't know what. "What if I don't change? They'll kill me, Tier. I'm the one who brings the end, remember?"

"Junco." His tone is not as soft as it was just a few seconds ago. "Ya just have to trust me. Do ya trust me?"

I hesitate and I see his face change from frustration to anger and then he turns away. "I want to trust you." He turns back and watches me this time as I struggle to find the right words. "But I don't know anything about you. Nothing. I don't know anything about your world, what it looks like, what the people are like, your customs. And your food looks gross." He takes my hand and pulls me back down.

"All ya ever had to do is ask, Junco."

"I asked about the scars, you just ignored me."

"Ya want to know where I got those scars?"

I nod.

He looks up at the sky. The stars are almost all invisible now, and the sunrise behind us has blanketed the top one-third of the western mountains a hazy pink. It takes a few more minutes before he begins. "It's a long story, and there's a lot more to it than what I'm gonna say now. But one day, Junco, we'll have time. And I'll tell ya anything ya want to know."

I nod.

"Our world is not like Earth. We are a large population confined in a limited space, compounded by a longevity that ya can't even begin to understand yet." He takes a deep breath and his fingers are absently playing with my hair. "I said we don't have families, but that's not the whole truth. We have something else. And yer born into it, like a family, but it's an occupation."

He looks down at me now and I smile.

"I'm in a special military cluster, the Aves cluster. Was born into it. And that's why I am who I am and why I do what I do. Our training involves being sent out to Earth as children." He looks down again. "Before we morph, right? No wings. We're just like human children. So I was sent down here when I was five and the goal was to stay ten years, go back, fledge, and get on with my adult assignments. But it didn't happen that way."

"What happened?"

"An angry, alcoholic foster parent. Not anything atypical for where I was staying. Of course, I didn't realize that at the time, and being who I am—I was less than accepting of some crazy drunk controlling me with his delusions of superiority and violence."

"Who are you?"

He smiles. "I'm a pretty high rank where I come from, Juncs. Was born with the potential and gifted the things required to give me this rank. I had a bit of an ego back then, so—"

"And they, your parents, did that to you? Beat you and made those scars?"

He nods. "So I killed him when I was twelve. Not the female. She was beaten just as bad as I was." Then he shrugs.

"And is this what you did wrong that you have to make up for by killing me?"

He laughs. "Nah. No one cared about that, and that was, hell, a dozen years ago now. They just called me home and I fledged out early and went on full assignment. But I killed some other people too." His voice lowers and gets a little more serious. "Those they did care about. But those fuckers had it coming."

That hangs out there for a while and I remember Aren's words from what seems like so long ago. *Since you went AWOL yesterday and were tracked to a certain alien who killed more than two dozen scientists out at the Camp, not to mention a whole shitload of corporate executives from all over the United Republics...*

The silence drags on a little longer before I ask my next question. "So what's in it for you, Tier? If you bring me back?"

Some air blows out past his lips and he thinks for a moment before answering. "Redemption, Junco. Isn't that what we all search for? Just a little bit of redemption for past mistakes. I see ya and think, she doesn't have to have that life. Doesn't have to stand for it. And I want—"

I wait but he stays silent. "What?"

"I just want you to have yer chance, Junco. And yeah, it's risky what I'm asking ya to do. It is, but I've already started it. Made decisions that can't be undone."

"So, you're basically telling me that you're a big fuck-up?"

He looks down at me and I'm smiling. "Yeah, Junco. That's about right. I'm just one giant fuck-up."

I lean my head into his chest. "I can relate."

We stay that way for several more minutes, just breathing. Being. And then I break the peace. "I know you're worried about me asking you how you had the biometrics to get in the tunnels."

He takes a deep breath and my head on his chest goes up as he inhales, then down when he lets it out. "I am."

I sit up and look at him. "I know you don't want to tell me. Maybe you'll never tell me."

Maybe the truth isn't all it's cracked up to be. Ignorance is bliss and all that good shit. I turn away, half ashamed at myself for not having the strength to push him on this. But there's something to be said for second chances and if he's willing to make a sacrifice for me, then who am I to judge how he got here?

I turn back to look him in the eyes. "And it's OK, ya know? I won't ask again. If you ever want to tell me," I shrug, "well, then I'm here."

He lets out a little bit of air through his nose that substitutes for a laugh and answers in a whisper, "Now why would ya give me a pass on something like that, Junco?"

I mull it over for a few minutes.

"You ever hear of synchronicity, Tier? It's like— when two things, or acts, or situations—*whatever*. When two things happen that you think have no meaning or connection suddenly line up and come together to create something meaningful."

I look up at him and see that he's listening, and I smile. I'm the storyteller for once.

"And whatever it was you've been doing with yourself here on Earth, it made this outcome possible. This moment, right here on this rock. Sitting here with me.

"It's like being old and looking back on your life and seeing all the mistakes. Some really bad ones, right? And you think, damn, if only I never did—whatever. If I had only done something different, didn't hurt that person with my actions or words, didn't let that person take advantage of me, or I made this decision instead of that one—then life would be different.

"But every choice leads to your end. Regardless of whether it was good or bad. And yeah, if your end sucks real bad, then maybe different decisions would have made life better.

"But even if at the end there are more bad things than good, if you changed those decisions then all of the good would be gone too. So, if you're looking back thinking, fuck, I should have done things different, you have to ask yourself, am I willing to give up even one moment of good that came from the bad, just for the possibility? Because if you do, then this moment is gone. It never happens.

"And I know that I'm not qualified to grant you absolution. But I do anyway, no confession required."

I look up but he won't meet my eyes, he just stares off at the horizon, then shakes his head. "I could almost love you right now for saying that, ya know."

I laugh. "That's pretty much the point, Tier."

His gaze wanders over across the horizon where the dark and heavy clouds are surging over the mountains off in the west. The reflected sunrise has turned them all the colors of Jupiter and they roll with the threat of a winter storm.

"I've been watching ya for a while, Junco. Trying my hardest to figure out what's going on here, whether or not yer a clone, or a Six or a Seven, based on yer actions." He looks down at me now and cracks a half-hearted smile. "And it wasn't easy, I'll tell ya that. I watched you do so many things. Celebrate the good stuff, cry about the bad, go out on maneuvers with yer team, meet Charlie, fall in love and be loved back"—he hesitates slightly, then continues—"kill, very effectively I might add. And then lose everything. And still—no matter what bad things happened to ya—ya always got up the next day and did it all again. Yer not a quitter. I have often wondered where ya get the strength, how ya have such determination. I'm barely four years older than ya and I feel like I've lived a hundred lifetimes of misery. And when I wake up each morning I don't want to keep doing it, Junco. When I wake I ask myself, *how much longer before they will just let me die?*" His chest expands suddenly and I sit up a little more to see his face. "I have that thought more than I'd like to admit."

I lean back into his chest. "But that's just me on the outside, Tier. If you saw what's really inside me—it's nothing but screams and lies."

He sucks in a deep breath and we sit for a while in silence.

"When I was coming back from the Stag that night—and let me just clarify—I wasn't following ya, I was trying to wrap things up out there because they called me back. My time with you was over, my commander wrote ya off and gave the order for me to complete the mission—and that was exactly what I was doing.

"But then I saw yer Goat barreling up the hill as I was flying home and I thought to myself, this is it. She's finally lost her mind for real. She's not coming back from this one. And then ya hit that deer."

My thoughts drift back to the accident. It seems like years since that happened.

"I flew down there just to see if maybe you'd be dead and I'd be let off the hook. But, shit. All ya did was suck it up, haul yerself out of that pile of shit ya drive, and look for a solution. No crying, no whining. Nothing but action from you, Juncs. And I made the decision. Finally." He stops and looks at me. "It felt like relief, making that choice."

I lie still, my heart beating against his. "Why?"

He lets out a grunt. "Because they've fucked ya up so bad, they lied ta ya, they taught ya things a fully-fledged aves warrior never learns and then they paraded ya around the world killing people. They took everything away to break ya. And still ya get up. Sling yer fucking arm up in a belt, hike up a hill and take stock. And then of all things, ya try and kill me outright, not once but twice. Without even batting an eye."

"I'm sorry about that, Tier. I was a little wild that night—"

"No, that's not what I mean. I mean, whether or not ya realize it—yer fearless, Junco. I offer ta help ya, and ya tell me, I've got two legs so yer on yer own, buddy."

He laughs. "You've got more survival instinct in ya than anyone I've ever met. And I thought to myself, just think how great she'd be if someone just loved her and didn't play with her head. How fucking much she'd have to offer the world. Us. If she could just make one or two decisions based on the truth instead of the lies. She's worthy. That's what I thought. She's worthy—it's just that no one sees her potential."

I feel my throat tighten up and try and swallow back the tears. His hand reaches down and lifts my chin and makes me look at him. "I fucked up bad with Dale, Junco."

I shake my head. "Stop, Tier. I don't need to know."

"No. I let him use my genetics for his experiments in exchange for information. Information I used to kill a lot of important people."

His hand lets go of me and my chin drops back down to his chest as I breathe in deeply.

"I'm not gonna lie to ya. I don't have it in me to string ya along like that, taking advantage of yer trust. Whatever ya do, whatever choice ya make, make it knowing at least this much about me. And if we have the opportunity to make good stuff happen in the future, stuff that makes us thankful we made all those mistakes just to get to our end, then I want them to happen because we went into it understanding the beginning."

My heart beats wildly and my chest suddenly heaves in and out with the struggle to hold it all in. I lean against him, counting as his breathing makes my face rise and fall. I take my time getting it under control and when I'm ready the words come out as a whisper. "I could almost love you right now for saying that, ya know."

He finally lets out a small, stunted laugh and traces the pattern on my forehead with his finger. "I'm on yer side, Junco."

I breathe that in and enjoy it for several long moments. And I smile. "You know what?"

"What?"

"This is the first time I can think of that the truth didn't hurt."

He leans down and gives me a crooked smile. "Funny how that works, right? People are always lying so they don't hurt each other. But it's the lies that kill ya in the end. The truth gives ya strength to go on."

Yeah, I think. Maybe it does.

Chapter Thirty

It's well past dawn when I make it back to the barn to collect the envelope on the Goat's front seat, then back to the house. CP approaches me as I enter and I flip him the bird and continue walking to my room. I go inside and find a marker and then open the door and write on the outside in big letters: *If you wake me up, I'll make you regret it.*

Someone from my past gave me some good advice about making threats. They said, quote, threats are better served up cold, quick, and clear, unquote. It's true, too. I don't fuck about in the threat department.

I go back in my room, slamming the door behind me.

But it's wrong.

It's all wrong.

This is not my room, I can feel it. I mean, it's all my stuff. I have memories of all this stuff. Of sleeping in the bed, pretending to be a genie on the magic carpet, and plastering my room with princesses cut out of magazines and books. But that was not last week, which apparently was the last time I was here at home. Sleeping in this ridiculous bed.

I flip the light on in the closet and look at it.

It took me forever to find that horrible outfit for the press statement because almost everything in my closet is either a nightmare of ruffles that was in fashion two decades ago or stuff I'd only let a horse see me in.

On one side of the walk-in is a double row of nothing but pink, purple, and orange. On the opposite side are the greens and blues. *Yes, Junco, your closet is color-coded.* And there is not one shred of camo.

My heart begins to thump as I wonder if I really am a clone who was dropped into this life not too long ago. I take a deep sigh and fall on my knees into a pile of clothes. I look at the stuff under the hanging garments and then I see something that strikes a familiar chord.

An old black field boot. Much smaller than my current size.

I reach for it and pull, but it snags on something in the corner. My curiosity gets the best of me and I shuffle under the clothes and start flinging random socks, shorts, and a slew of mittens out behind me.

And then I see the shoelace. Caught under one of the floorboards.

I pull everything out, I mean shit is really flying out behind me, and then I can see what's got the old shoelace in its clutches.

It's a hidden door in the floor.

Now we're talking.

I stand and push my foot on the floorboard in various places, like I do with the secret pantry in the cabin, and sure enough, a board pops up. I lean down and swipe my fingers under the board and grin as the mechanism clicks and the entire cut-out lifts up on a chain and rests back against the far wall.

I crack a smile. I know that whatever is in this hidden room, it is the real me, and my pulse goes wild as I climb down the ladder.

My toe taps the hard concrete floor and I feel around on the wall for a light sensor. When it flicks on I gasp with delight.

Now this is more like it.

The chrome and glass bed frame is sleek and modern, close to the floor, and the mattress is piled high with several black down comforters, more pillows that I could ever need, and it's a complete mess.

Which totally confirms that this is my room.

There is an entire wall of built-ins filled with books on one wall. On the opposite wall are more built-ins. But these hold weapons. Lots of weapons. Plasma rifles of all shapes and sizes, ion-blasters, EM pulse rails, a few projectile pistols, swords, several bokkens, steel knives, and laser knives. It simply takes my breath away.

On the far end of the room is a holomat, which is an elaborate piece of tech for an RR kid, but I'm not really just your ordinary RR kid, am I?

No. I'm Junco. The commander's daughter. A trained RR sniper. The fucking Seventh Sibling and a whole lot more.

The holomat allows you to program in mixed martial arts moves and watch them play out in 3D. You can even make adjustments on the fly to see how things work. It's a great way to come up with new moves or counter-moves and the memories of me using this device for training flood into my forward consciousness in a deluge.

I go to the closet next and find my real wardrobe. It's not color-coded and like the bed, it's not neat. In fact, most of the clothes are on the floor and not one scrap of them is pink. I have black, army green, gunmetal gray, black, desert sand, woody brown, and black. There are no pumps or sandals in sight and I breathe a huge sigh of satisfaction when I see the box of cigars sticking out of an open drawer.

I shake one out of its box, touch it to the striker, and puff like there's no tomorrow. Then laugh. Maybe there won't be a tomorrow. The air filters kick in to process the smoke and I blow some rings.

I am home.

I peel off my clothes and slip a fresh tank top on, then turn the sensor off and lie in the dark, watching the red embers of my cigar light and dim the room until the ash gets long. I flick it into the ashtray lying in the middle of my belly and think up so many ways to kill all these motherfuckers in my house I almost get giddy. The voice on the phone comes back to me. *Project terminated, sir.* It's a voice I know well.

Sun Tzu said all warfare is based on deception. Which seems to contradict Tier's take on the truth, but really they are not connected. War is war. And anything goes. The object of war is to win. Period. Nothing else matters, and if it does, you're not at war.

But personal requires a little more finessing because by definition it encompasses emotions, and that's the messy stuff that gets in the way of war. If you make war personal, you're fucked. War was never meant to be emotional and only detached objectivity gets you through. That's just the facts and anyone who wants to win had better face them fast.

I stew in that for a while and enjoy the comfort that comes with being in my own bed, surrounded by my own stuff, and secure enough to be OK with who I am for the moment. That can change, certainly it will change, but for now, I am just Junco.

Sun Tzu also said desperate soldiers lose their fear and I can relate. Not a drip of it leaks out of me. I'm the scariest bitch on the block. I puff the cigar down to the nub, stub it out and flop back into the soft pillows.

And I dream. And the dream is all mine too.
I'm not standing on the edge of a dock.
I am no one's project.
I am no one's redemption.
I am not anything.
I am just Junco.
And I am at war.

Just as I get to the part of my dream where it makes
no logical sense I hear someone banging on my bedroom
door. I roll off the bed and fall to the floor, shaking my
head as I try to remember where I am.

The banging comes again, only louder this time, and
then my reflexes kick into gear and I'm climbing, then
rushing towards the door to pull it open.

"This better be good." It's CP. For some reason this
little squirmy guy grates on my nerves. "Can't you read?" I
say, pointing to the big black letters scrawled across my
door.

He looks at my legs and I realize I'm in my bed
shorts. He jerks his eyes back up to my face. "It's noon,
Junco. Aren wants you in his office."

"*His* office? Hmmm. The last time I checked he
didn't have an office in my house, so where exactly would
I find said office?"

"Uh, sorry. Your father's office."

I slam the door in his face.

I go back down to my real room and stand in my
closet.

I'm in love.

I step into a pair of old ripped jeans and pull a
faded black hoodie over my head. There is an array of

field boots to choose from and I pick the oldest, most thrashed pair I can find. None of this stuff triggers any more of my misplaced memories, but if I had any doubts that this room was mine they disappear when the boots mold to my feet.

I twist my hair into a pony and head to Aren's office. Just thinking those words makes me want to strangle him, but I push it down and smile as I pass the MR soldiers who smugly roam my house at will.

The doors fly open and I enter. He's about to yell at the intrusion and then stops himself at the last minute. "That's all for now, CP."

CP leaves and pulls the double doors closed behind him.

"Junco, did you have a nice sleep?" His smile is huge, but his eyes are narrow as he assesses my mood.

I smile back at him, forcing it all the way up to my peepers. "Lovely. I haven't slept that well in... well, since the last time I slept in my own bed."

Ignoring me, he gets up and walks around the desk. "I have decided that we'll ask the Council for reparations for what they did to you. This will include—"

I put my hand up and he stops. "I'm not interested in any reparations. Just the truth."

He comes over and takes me by the arm and leads me over to the couch as he talks. It takes every ounce of self-control not to pull away from his touch. "I know this will sound crazy, and maybe you won't agree to it, but—"

There's a knock at the door and CP enters again. "Sorry, sir. There's a message from—" He stops and looks in my direction.

"From who, CP? Spit it out."

"It's private, sir." He thrusts a piece of tech at Aren who puts his hand up like he's warding off bad spirits.

"I'll be back in a minute, Junco."

I plop on the couch. "Take your time." He ignores me as he leaves and I shoot CP a dirty look before he can shut me out with the doors.

"Junco," HOUSE says, "please enter your father's safe room."

Do I not deserve a single moment that is not clouded with confusion and the phrase, what are you talking about?

"Junco," HOUSE repeats, "please enter your father's safe room."

"I heard you the first time. But it would be nice to know—"

As if on cue the massive bookcase on the east wall pops open on a hidden hinge, leaving a crack of darkness. The door swings in as I push and I step into the darkness. HOUSE closes the door behind me and the world is black and silent. Then small lights appear along the floor, illuminating a path that takes me down below the house. Apparently my father and I have similar tastes in which level we prefer our secret rooms.

"HOUSE? You still there?" No answer. Since it's called a safe room I figure it's safe, so I walk slowly forward, following the dim path laid out before me. The lights stop at another door and I try the handle, find it unlocked, and open it.

Inside is a room about the size of my private bedroom. One wall is lined with screens, obviously hooked to security cameras I don't recall having. I can see every room, except my real room, every hallway, and every outside space within fifty feet of the house. In each one people are going about their normal business.

"Finally, I get you alone. Jasus H. Fuck, Coot. You're done this time, I swear. I'm not putting up with this bullshit one more fucking minute, you understand?"

I turn to see a man sitting in a large executive-type office chair at the far end of the room. His face is cast in shadow, but I can tell he's military, about middle age, and his hands are fiddling with a stack of papers. The Colonel. My heart beats faster and he picks up on it.

"Damn right you know what this is," he says as he gets up and walks over to me, thrusting the papers into my hands. "You've been on the run for what? A week?"

I shrug. I did actually lose count.

"I told you after that last little side-job of yours that this shit was over, and now this? Two fucked-up decisions in as many weeks doesn't get you far. Now. You wanna tell me why you've been traipsing around with these avians like you're old friends or something?"

"I would love to tell you, sir," I say. Can't go wrong with sir. "But—"

"But nothing, you sorry excuse for a soldier. And you will address me as Colonel Slag, who the hell do you think you are?" He's screaming now, and I absently look up, wondering if the room is soundproof.

"Don't look away from me, you rat's ass piece of shit! I said, explain to me why you were traipsing around with an alien on my time?"

"Sir, Colonel Slag, he kidnapped me, sir." It comes out before I can stop it.

"Did he now? Oh, that's rich. Because I have screen of you flying on his back, *shooting at the rescue team* in the tunnels under Ramah. Care to explain how he could have possibly kidnapped you that time?"

I wince and scratch my neck absently as I think, but he's already moved on.

"... caused me a lot of headaches, Coot."

He stops and my eyebrows go up as I stare at him.

He stares back. "What are you supposed to say for yourself when shit like this happens, Coot?"

I can't think of anything, so I just shrug.

He walks back to his chair and sits down. "You're officially retired, Coot." Then he tosses me a pen and I catch it in the palm of my three-fingered hand. Two, if you don't count the thumb. He scowls at my recent disability.

"Sign the papers, your discharge is on there."

I quickly begin signing, page after page. And then I get to the discharge papers and there's a small silver cube taped to the upper left corner. I look up at him, expectantly, and track his eyes to the cube, then back to my face.

"Sign the paper, Coot. Or your final days in the military will be spent scrubbing your own latrines." And then he shuts up and stares at me, to see if I have anything to add.

I shift my weight and sign, then hand them back and he does the same.

While he signs I look around the room and see photos of this guy, Slag, and my father in many of them. There are a few of me as well. In all of them I'm in a junior cadet uniform, none of me over the age of fourteen or fifteen. I spy several cameras and realize we're being recorded.

Then it all slips into place.

He finishes up and then opens a drawer, grabs a tech device, slams a drawer closed and throws me the reader. "There's a digitized copy of everything on the discharge paper. Make sure you read the terms. Oh, and one more thing, here—" He digs in his pockets and fishes something out, then throws me a slender blue rod that turns end over end as it flies through the air towards me. "It's been disabled, Coot. So your mission days are over. Consider yourself lucky I don't have you strung up on treason charges."

I catch the rod and my hand knows just what to do with it. I slip it under my shirt and press it to the scar just under my belly button. I feel the magnetic strip under my skin activate and yank it off in horror, shoving it in my pocket.

I look at Slag again, and he sends me a severe scowl. And then something else. It's slight, barely noticeable, but my eyes catch it just before I'm about to turn. A nod towards the back of the room.

I walk past him and see a dark hallway. I follow it to the end and push through a door which leads me into a storage room. I climb the stairs and come out in the kitchen, then walk back to my room and close the trap door behind me as I descend.

I have no idea what just happened, but I do know one thing.

Slag is a friendly.

Chapter Thirty-One

The reader is one I used as a kid, but since data cubes have been standardized for the better part of three decades, my cube slides in easily after removing the one that is already in there. I pocket the old cube and turn the device over to flip it on. I expect it to need a charge, but it doesn't.

It pops to life, registers the cube, and a screen flashes.

It's a video. The face staring back at me from the still shot is someone I barely remember, but my heart aches at the sight of her anyway. She's holding a newscreen, and the video camera zooms in on the date.

The events she describes on the feed are almost too horrible to imagine. But I find a memory for all of them. Starting with my first assassination assignment at age six. Six. Who does that to their kid? She moves on to political matters but I can't pick up all the nuances of what she's saying. I get the gist of it, though.

War.

Revenge.

Death.

Atrocities.

Twenty minutes later I switch the reader off, pop out the cube, and almost stuff it into my pocket along with the ones Tier gave me, but I pull back at the last minute. Her final words stick with me and roll around in my brain. *There is a big difference between patience and inertia.*

Maybe. But also a very fine line. I throw the cube across the room. Fuck her, she's on her own.

I lie on the bed for what seems like hours, but when I glance over at the clock it's not even 2:00 yet. I remember the blue rod Slag threw at me and fish it out of my pocket. The energy it contains electrifies me as I hold it in my palm for several seconds, then slip it under my shirt where the long white scar runs lengthwise under my bellybutton. How many times did Tier place his hands there over the past week? I can't even count them. He knew it was missing. What else does he know?

I can feel it charging on the plate under the thin membrane of skin and maybe ninety seconds or so later it's complete. I reach under my shirt and pull it back out to take a closer look. It is definitely some kind of stone, magnetic since it sticks to the charge plate, and so shiny I can see my own distorted face peering back at me. One end is thicker than the other and I instinctively know that the tapered end holds a biometric for my thumbprints, while the rest of the rod is tracked to my palm. I roll it from hand to hand to see if it registers both. It does.

And then I flick my thumb over a small raised imperfection in the stone and the loop of the enhanced plasma SEAR knife materializes.

Disabled?

OK.

The SEAR, an acronym for SEcondary Alloantigen Repressor, was outlawed last century. Besides making a wickedly fucked-up slice in anything from steel to human flesh, it also completely scrambles your DNA.

In scientific terms a slice from a SEAR triggers an autoimmune response once the plasma loop touches the skin, which subsequently shuts down protein synthesis for collagen production. The unfortunate victim dies a slow and horrific death, even if they manage to survive the initial wound.

In simple terms, if it cuts you, it kills you. No matter what.

The safest way to use a SEAR knife is to have it biologically coded to your genetic profile so that the immune response cannot be triggered in the first place. There is no way for me to be sure that this is the actual case for my SEAR knife, so using it is almost as big a risk to me as my enemy. The effects are irreversible, hence the ban. Someone decided that the SEAR was not a weapon that could be legally owned by civilians safely.

Good thing I'm not a civilian, then.

Well, technically I am.

But surely, it won't really count until the paperwork is processed. Who knows how long that could take.

A few hours ago I'd be left wondering how my stomach managed to hold a docking pad for an illegal weapon, but after watching my mother spill out the details of my fucked-up childhood on screen, life makes a hell of a lot more sense than it used to.

I have the urge to test my weapon out on some pink ruffles upstairs in my other closet, but SEAR knives leave a tell-tale smell behind. It's not something you can filter easily and I'd like to keep the element of surprise. All warfare is based on deception, right?

I have a thousand questions for Slag, but if he was worried enough about surveillance in the secret room to go through that ruse, then it's better to stay away.

For moment I think of Tier's hands again, going to my belly. And I thought he was trying to be sexy. Nope. He's just checking to see if I'm armed with contraband.

I flip the knife off and stuff it back under my shirt and think of Charlie. I don't recall if I ever got to go to the funeral and this thought makes me wonder about his family. What do they know? Do they know how he died? That he was killed for loving the wrong girl?

I get up and tear my room apart looking for some kind of com device. Anything that has the sphere on it or can send a message. But after several minutes of searching there is nothing but a pile of crap on the floor to show for it. I was never one of those kids who rebelled against the tech rules of the RR. I never secretly wished for mind access to the sphere or coms, none of that shit impressed me.

But today, I'd give two more fingers to have a sphere access implant for five minutes because the need to see Charlie's parents, talk to them, fills my heart and I feel my face go hot as I struggle with the tears.

I get up and climb back up to the princess room and leave, pulling the door closed behind me. Out on the front porch I crane my neck to see past a cluster of pines. The western sky announces its intentions with a dense fog that seeps in and wraps its arms around the reporters on the other side of the gate. They crowd against the iron fence waiting patiently for the council members they know are coming.

Back in my room I search the various debris piles for the discarded cube, grab a thick packet from a boot in my closet, and take the stack of papers addressed to Dale from the Goat, then pause at the line of weapons before me. Something small but intimidating. I grab a TZi .357, load it, then slide the holster on my belt and let the gun slip in. Back upstairs at my childhood desk I put together the three packages, then grab my barn coat and walk back outside.

The fog has invaded the front yard and the snow is falling in light flakes that begin to stick to the ground. No one gives me a second look as I bounce down the porch steps and ease into the dreary afternoon. I make my way down the driveway and then halfway to the gatehouse I leave the road and finish the rest of the walk under the scant cover of the pine trees. I watch from behind a tree trunk as the two guards crammed into the small building point and comment at something below my line of sight.

I wait until both sets of eyes are diverted, then slip past the gatehouse and make my way to the iron barrier that separates me from the world. A couple of reporters see me and they bustle to life as my eyes search the crowd. I spot her just as my view is obstructed by the mass of bodies hurling questions at me. My left arm slips through the bars and I point with my remaining fingers in her direction. The bodies part and then I get a better look.

The young blonde reporter is smoking a cigarette and chatting up one of the hovercopter pilots when my gaze catches her interest. I motion for her to come here. To her credit, she doesn't hesitate much. She takes another drag on her cigarette, then lets it fall to the ground just as her expensive boot crushes it walking toward me.

The guards are out now, asking me questions, but I ignore them and punch in the code to open the gate. The reporter hesitates, but I wave her forward, still ignoring the guards. When she is through I close the gate back up and lead her over to the gatehouse.

"What's going on, Junco?" she says.

"I just need a private word, is that OK with you?"

She nods.

I smile and open the gatehouse door but the guards step in and one grabs my shoulder. "Junco, you need to go back to the house now." I elbow him in the face, take out the TZi and point it at his head.

"One smart move by your buddy over there and I blow it straight off, got it?" He nods and I look at his partner. "You OK with this, then?" He nods too. Then over to the reporter. "How about you?"

She raises an eyebrow, puffs up her lips a little, and simply shrugs. "Whatever you say."

My smile creeps out. "Good, then open the gatehouse door and go in and leave the door open."

She does and when she's out of sight I back up towards the door and push my hostage aside and slip in behind her. Her face is not showing as much fear as it should, but I let it slide for now. Plenty of time for that later.

"What's going—"

"Shut up and listen. I've got a proposition for you..."

"Selia," she offers.

"... Selia, but it's a one-time deal and"—I peek out the front window and watch the guards running back towards the house—"since I only have about thirty seconds to sell you on it, let's not waste any of them, 'K?"

She nods. Good girl.

I shake out the three envelopes on the small desk and then pick up the first one. "This is a bribe. Part of it is for you and the rest is for whichever pilot you can convince to fly you out of here in the next five minutes." I slap it down on the desk and let the weight of it impress her. Her eyes linger on the thickness longer than I dared hope, so I consider her sufficiently impressed and move on.

"This," I hold up the second envelope, "is none of your fucking business. But I need a way to get it to some people and in case you haven't noticed, I'm not going anywhere anytime soon. I don't know where these people live, I just have the name of one dead MR soldier."

She looks at the envelope and reads the name and her eyes light up. "Yeah, that guy who was killed during a training mission a few months back, right?"

"If you say so, Selia. Like I said, this isn't for you. It's for his parents. This is the favor I need. Will you deliver it to them?"

"When?"

"Now."

"You mean leave this story and run an errand for you? I don't think so, Junco. I mean—"

I wave the third envelope in front of her face and cut her off. "This, Selia, is your story. Not the bullshit that's gonna happen here tonight." I shake my head. "Every asshole with a fingercam is gonna stream that shit live." I wave the envelope again. "But this is so fucking new I only found out about it thirty minutes ago. And I'm gonna give it to you."

She looks at the envelope and hesitates.

I look back out the window and I can see movement behind the curtain of fog. "Five seconds, Selia, take it or leave it. I have dozens of other people I can ask."

She folds like the bipod on a sniper rifle after the kill shot. "OK, I'll do it."

I stuff the three envelopes in her coat. "Listen carefully, OK? Your first objective is to get out to that cute pilot you were talking to and give him half of this cash to get you in the air, because the shit is gonna fly as soon as Aren gets out here."

"Yeah, sure. Got it."

"Your second objective is to get that information to Charlie's parents, next of kin, whatever they are. Someone who loved him, do I make myself clear?"

"OK."

"And third, this envelope contains my story." My life summed up in a twenty-minute screen-feed, I don't add. "Tell everyone you can because tonight I'll either be dead or out of the loop for a while."

I look back out the window, missing Selia's last nod of acceptance, and even from twenty yards away I can see the rage swelling up on Aren's face.

"I'll make a scene, you get away without drawing attention." My hand slams down on the gate release and it begins to open. "Stay behind me until they swarm, then get the fuck out of here. Oh, and Selia?"

She stops and looks back at me.

"If you cross me I'll hunt you down like a nightdog looking for a bitch on hump day and kill you in a way that will definitely make the news, understand?" She swallows hard and nods. "And don't count on me dying tonight, either. I'm no long-shot."

"I'll do it just like you asked."

The fear she should have had from the start is finally there and I feel satisfied as I push open the guardhouse door and move into the bulging crowd. "Who's next? Who wants an interview?"

The mob goes crazy as Selia slips to the edge of the crowd and makes her way out to the road. I watch her pilot buddy lean in to hear what she's saying. Then the bodies are all around me and the red lights of fingercams blink in my face, obstructing my view.

"Junco!" Aren grabs me and pulls me back so hard I fall to the ground. The reporters go wild and I look up at

278

Aren's raging face and smile. Someone fires a shot in the air and the guards push the reporters back as the gate begins to close.

Aren reaches down and jerks me to my feet, then bends over so his lips are practically in my ear. "What the fuck do you think you're doing?"

I pull my arm hard and he loses his grip on me. "Who the fuck do you think you are, Aren? This is my house and I can open that fucking gate any time I feel like it."

He looks up at the blinking red lights that are now outside the gate and less abruptly turns me around, pushing me towards the house and taking my arm once again. "Junco, this is a military operation now and you are under orders."

"Wrong," I say, stopping in the driveway and violently shrugging off his death grip a second time. "I'm retired, Aren. Or haven't you heard? Slag had me sign the discharge papers this afternoon. I'm not under anyone's orders. Un-fucking-fit for duty."

The anger in his eyes manifests in a disturbing twitch of his lip. "That's the first reasonable thing you've said in months, Junco."

How would he know? I haven't seen him in years before that day out on the scrub. "Yeah? Well, maybe I'd be a little more reasonable if my father hadn't had my boyfriend killed and then dose me with an ionspray to off our unborn baby."

He yanks my arm fiercely, pulling me towards the house again. "Keep your fucking voice down."

"Why? So no one finds out that we're all a bunch of sociopathic killers in here?"

"Speak for yourself, Junco. I left years ago."

"Is that right? Well, maybe you can explain why I just got a video message from my mother that says you've been working with her?"

His face hardens and he leans in again. "Junco, you have no idea how much I will hurt you if you cause trouble here today. You understand?"

"No, Aren. I really don't understand. Yesterday you said you were being set up by Slag. Now I find out you're playing for yet another team? That's quite an accomplishment. Really. Not many people can manage to betray two different countries before they're twenty-two years—"

"That's enough. I'm not even sure what you're talking about, but I do know one thing, we're not talking about it now. We're settling this shit with the Council tonight and that's all I'm interested in." He grabs my arm once again and I can feel the bruise forming in real time. "And you're going to that meeting and you will not act insane, you will be rational and agreeable. Do you understand me?"

"Or what, Aren? Or what? Maybe you haven't noticed, but I don't respond well to threats. Now," I ease up on the hardass bit and throw a card down, "if you want to talk a little business, well, then maybe I can find it in me to bob my head up and down a few times when they look in my general direction. I'll have to think about it."

He laughs. "This is about money with you? Seriously, Junco?"

"What else is there, Aren?"

"Power."

"Yeah, that too. So, when you go into that meeting and broker your little deal, you better find a way to cut me in on both accounts." I wait and see if it works. I have no idea what kind of deal he has planned, but clearly there *is* a deal.

"Don't even pretend like you know what's going on here, Junco," he laughs, "because I know better. Your father didn't tell you anything unless he had to, I'm one hundred percent positive of that."

"I got a message from my *mother*, Aren. And it said you're working with those rebel Subjectives up in the Northern Territories."

His expression shows confusion, and I may not be an expert in reading people, but I'm fairly sure this is real. I hesitate for a second, doubting myself.

He looks down at me and the good buddy routine from the scrub is gone now, "Junco, you better shut your fucking mouth and stay out of the way or I swear, this night will not end well for you."

I get the feeling that we're not yet on the same page, but there's something there. Might not have hit it on the head, but I came close. "More threats?"

"You want something from me? Or not? Say what you mean because I don't have time for games."

My smile is back. "Hey, I'm a free agent now, right? Sell my skills to the highest bidder, sound familiar?"

His confusion continues and this almost makes me stop. My inner cynic is screaming that there's a problem with my theory on what's going on here, but there's no time to backtrack and think it over. I'm past that now, it's move forward or give up.

I move forward.

"I want a rank within the MR equal to yours, Aren. Shit, you're not real clever, are you?"

I see the satisfaction spread out from the corners of his mouth as his lips turn up in a slight smile before he checks it. I might not have all the little details worked out perfectly, but this hits home with him and that's all that matters. "How do I know if I can trust you?"

"Aren," I sneer at him with contempt now, "I tortured my own father, helped an avian kill a state scientist, and assassinated several high-value targets on direct orders of Rural Republic Command, all of which is on record somewhere in that house."

The whine of a hovercopter fills the late afternoon and I grin, making it as bright as I possibly can. "Give me some credit. We're both hip-high in the same shit, remember? But I'm sick of you ordering me around, I'll play nice if you do, but you gotta get the fuck off my back and leave me alone." I shrug off his death grip on my arm one last time and walk away, waiting to see if he plays his card.

But he holds it.

Like Sun Tzu says, all warfare is based on deception. That shit rings true no matter what century you're in.

Chapter Thirty-Two

Back under the princess room I let out a deep sigh and laugh a little. Then abruptly stop because it makes me feel a little crazy.

Junco, he's all in, don't underestimate him.

Yeah, yeah.

I shrug off the internal warning and go look in the closet to find an appropriate outfit for the council meeting. In the end I choose garments that look like I have a hard time taking them off for laundering.

Favorites.

The t-shirt is a faded olive green with a few small rips in the seam near the left shoulder. It's a few sizes too big and states proudly, *Snipers do it from behind.* Must have stolen this one out on maneuvers. I slip it on and tuck it in, leaving a gap in the front for access to my SEAR. I pull on a pair of forest camo-patterned fatigues and the same old field boots I just took off. I slip on the double-arm shoulder holsters and then fill them with the electromag 9Mv Boltblaster and the TZi .357. A sage-green flight jacket that has definitely served me well, if the ripped lining and pockets full of stale cigars are any indication, covers it all up.

The princess room mirror projects my outfit for scrutiny and I nod to myself, check the sparkling tiara clock on the bedside table, then lie down on the unicorn bed and put my hands behind my head to relax. I have no intention of showing up on time. Aren needs me now, so let him come get me.

I cycle back to my mother's message for lack of other things to think about. She was always beautiful, in a traditional rural kind of way, and we share a lot of the same facial characteristics even though I now realize that isn't physically possible. We both have the same heart-shaped face, though she has a pair of perfect dimples in her cheeks when she smiles, while I have none of that cutesy shit going for me at all. The dimples never materialized in the video, she never smiled, but I assume they are still there. Not typically something that disappears over time.

Her hair in my memory is medium length, more blonde than brown, and ends naturally in a slight upturned flip. Again with the cuteness. In the video she made last week, the day of my father's funeral to be exact, her hair is more gray than blond, severely short, and her previously bright blue eyes have dulled down to a slate color reminiscent of some of the guns I have on the rack downstairs.

My own hair is more brown than red and my eyes are nothing but an angry swirl of brown, black, and green. I've been told they're the perfect shade of hazel. As if hazel was even a color. It's not. It's just a term used for eyes when people can't describe them with one word.

In the video her mouth was drawn tight in a line that perfectly mimicked the emptiness of a distant horizon. Not at all like the mouth I remember as a child. I have full lips and upturned corners that require a little extra attention to make them even out, let alone frown. This feature makes me out to be more approachable than is professionally comfortable. The flat line of indifference is a better way to go in my opinion. Lowers expectations of chumminess upon first impression.

Her outfit was the only thing that connected us. Crisp military-issue uniform of an advanced rank, planed out flat from the steam press. I can be crisp when I want to and I have the service uniform in the closet to prove it. But I haven't worn it lately. Not even to the funeral.

I take a deep breath and play the message back in my head. Even though a lot of it was *about* me, the message wasn't really *for* me. A propaganda piece for the benefit of her political party. The Subjectives' benefit, I correct myself. Her people these days, apparently. The ones she really works for. I suppose that's debatable though, since she comes right out and states on the video that she's double-gunning for the MR as well.

Nice.

Scattered loyalties are awesome, especially when they're all fake.

The Subjectives are just the most recent cult of personality taking root up north in the wilds above the Front Range and extending up into the Tetons in the old American state of Wyoming. That area is unincorporated and has been since the Succession Wars ended back in '98. As far as I can remember, no one's given the place a second thought since then.

I suppose the world will have a whole new outlook on the philosophy of Subjectivity come morning. Hope they've got bunkers dug out in those tits, because if my mother is telling the truth, then this whole area will be up in flames real soon and I envision a steady stream of retaliation hellfire up in Subjective Land come morning.

Slag must be in on it since he was the one who delivered the cube to me, but why even bother informing me at all? Why not just get that shit out to the media herself? Makes no sense. Maybe she figures since I killed the bastard who had her deported I was also interested in joining her little make-shift military. Maybe she thinks that she can lure me up there to take part in whatever fucked-up plan they have going?

She's wrong.

And not just for the obvious reasons, like abandoning me when I was little. This whole military thing is getting real old, real fast and I'm just not sure I'm into it anymore. After tonight I can see a nice long reprieve from killing and drama. A vacation somewhere maybe, that's what I need. That floating metropolis they have out in the middle of the Atlantic sounds pretty fucking nice right about now.

Nope. I'm not interested in her wars, regardless of who she's got on board with her. And to be honest I'm a little put off that she had to drag me into it at all. Now Selia's gonna broadcast it all over the fucking world and I'll forever be connected to her outrageous acts. Just so I can get a simple little message to the family of the man I loved. Hell, we'll probably both make it into the history books. *Double agent Carolinia Coot and sociopathic Rural Republic sniper daughter, Junco Coot, implicated in the Mountain Republic invasion of 2152.*

Unexpectedly, I let out a laugh. What a crazy bitch. At least I know I come by it honestly.

Sort of.

At any rate, it's out of my hands. I did what she asked and got a message out to Charlie's family in the process. What Selia does with it from here is her problem. Personally, if I were Selia, I'd burn those papers and melt that cube down in a bonfire the first chance I got. But something tells me Selia is a go-getter.

The knock on the door finally arrives and I instinctively check the tiara clock. 6:01. Once again, the laugh just comes out. Aren is either restless or fastidious about punctuality. I lean on the first one and swing my feet out of the bed, straighten my guns a little, then walk to the door and pull it open.

I half expected CP to be the one to walk me to the conference room, but it's not him. The strange soldier greets me and smiles. "Commander sent me, Junco. They're all there and waiting."

I thank him and walk towards the conference room. There is a disturbing amount of activity around the house and, as I peek out the windows, on the grounds as well. A serious bit of build-up has happened in the past few hours. The guards knock and open the double doors of the conference room for me as I approach and when I step in I realize I've interrupted. They are all standing, facing this way and that, hands in the air, as if to make a point. But their talking stops abruptly.

I take a deep breath and survey the room and Aren practically scrambles over to me to break the silence.

"Junco, you've arrived. I'm sure you know everyone here, right?"

I look at each person individually, all the elders I've known my whole life, and Slag. My eyes stop there and Aren takes the cue. "You remember Slag, right, Junco?"

I stare up in Aren's eyes and realize he's lost. Has no idea who I am or what memories are available right now.

Slag nods as he eyes my inappropriate choice of clothing, but doesn't give off a vibe either way. Aren pulls the chair at the bottom of the table open for me to take a seat, but I ignore him and push it out of the way so I can stand near the edge. I don't look at him, but I don't have to see his face to feel his rage.

It doesn't matter.

I snap off the names of each of the remaining elders in my head as my gaze quickly travels around the large glass and chrome table. How these five fuck-ups managed to escape the wrath of Tier that night in the church, I'll probably never know.

Oran Alger is a big guy, built like a pillaging Viking with a blazing head of red hair, complemented by a beard that is an even more shocking orange. Substantial arms poke out of his massive body and he's wearing coveralls. At least I'm not the only one underdressed.

Tarik Darzi is the only bachelor in the history of the Council, and that's the way he'll stay because he's as gay as a songbird in the spring. I think the Council was surprised when he was elected last term because he's one of only half a dozen people who have ever decided to emigrate to the Rural Republic in my lifetime. We are naturally suspicious of strangers and even though I really do love my country, it's not a place you'd ever want to emigrate to.

Abe Cavello is a dentist who works in the MR. People wanted to throw his ass out the last election, but his father was a Council Elder for a long time so money changed hands and that was that.

Hogan Bosco is just an ordinary farmer who grows wheat and soybeans in the southwestern part of Council 3. He's loaded but refuses to farm with a tractor so every spring he's out there in his field walking behind his horses for fourteen hours a day. He's known to go a little crazy before planting season is over. My father sold him horses regularly so he's been at our house lots of times.

And finally Old Sam whose brother was the actual one elected, but died the second week in office. Sam took over and no one stopped him. I admit I never thought that was weird until now.

Five men of the community, an MR field commander, a RR Colonel, and me. Just a wild girl who can shoot straight under pressure.

Slag is standing in the back corner, behind Aren. His arms are crossed in front of his chest and he has a bemused look on his face that I don't actually care for. It implies I'm the entertainment.

"All right, gentlemen, let's start the show, shall we?"

They mutter and one or two object, but it's Aren who stands up. "Junco," he says, trying to placate me with fabricated congeniality, "I've already explained to the Council what's going to happen and why you're here so—"

I see Slag wince out of the corner of my eye. "Aren, you have no idea why I'm here, so sit down and shut up."

"Who the hell—"

I jump up on the table in a single two-footed hop, my field boots crashing against the thick glass, and growl at him. "Shut the fuck up, Aren!" I slip the SEAR out from my shirt and switch it on in one fluid movement, then look at them all one more time, beginning with Aren.

"Let's cut the bullshit and presume you all know what this is and what I plan to do with it, OK?"

Their mouths are open in surprise, but each nods in agreement.

"Now, I don't know what Aren's just told you, but let's also assume that too, is complete bullshit."

Once again they nod. I check out Aren and he's about to open his mouth when I shake my head at him.

"Shhh, Aren. I'm not interested." My gaze shifts to the Elders. "What I am interested in, gentlemen, is the truth about one certain night two weeks ago in which each of you," I glance back to Slag and point to him with my weapon, "with the possible exception of you, witnessed me take this little SEAR knife," I wave it around casually in the air, "and do some very horrific things."

I wait for them to digest the situation and glance back to Aren, who is enraged, but as far as I can tell, still holding it down. For now. I throw him a smile, and this sets him back in his chair a little, but makes Slag furrow his brow.

I walk back to the end of the table where Abe is sitting. "Did you see me in the church the night I cut my father and sentenced him to death?"

He nods. I look at the next in line, and raise my eyebrows. "Don't make me repeat the question, Hogan, yes or no?" He mumbles out a yes. I continue down the table and elicit a yes, or something close to it, from each of them. "Great, we're on track here." I glance back at Aren and the sweat is pouring off his face. "How about you, Aren? Did you see me in the church that night?"

Every head in the room shifts to him and he stands up abruptly, knocking the large conference chair back into the window facing the courtyard. "Junco, I'm going to ask you to leave the room right now or I will be forced to disable you, probably resulting in your death."

"Aren, if you have nothing to add, shut up and sit down. I'm not in the mood." He resists and I walk towards him and catch his eye with the bright glow of the SEAR.

I stare at him until he grabs the chair and complies, his finger busy fiddling with something on the arm rest.

"Now we get to my question, my Honorable Elders, the only thing I want from you. And when I get it and I'm satisfied that it is the truth, you can leave here and we can put this all behind us. Because I don't want to know what you know about my so-called childhood." Most of these guys probably don't have any idea, but Sam is older than them and he shifts uncomfortably in his seat.

I stare directly at Sam as the rest of them squirm. "And I don't want to know about all the times you turned your head when they took me away to the Stag."

All of them visibly relax with my revelation and I feel a dry heave coming up in my stomach. I push it back down with everything else that's trying to come up.

I look over at Slag now, meeting his gaze, but I continue speaking to the men around the table. "Because I don't need you to tell me those things. I already know the answers. And gentlemen, I am here to tell you that a time will come when you'll stand in judgment for your silence and reap your reward."

They don't look at me, but I continue, "And who knows, that night might be tonight. But it's out of my control."

Abe the dentist, the last guy to my right, speaks up. "I'm sorry, Junco."

I look down at him and nod. "Then Abe, how about you be the first, then, huh? Just answer my question. No matter who told you to stay silent. Even, Abe"—I stop here and stare into his eyes—"if it was *me* who told you to keep quiet. Understand?"

He nods. I look up at Aren and I see panic in his eyes, but I continue. "When you saw me torture my father, Abe—who did my father promise me to in order to get me out of the RR?" He swallows hard and the sweat is pouring down his face. "You can say it, Abe, go ahead." He looks across the table to the other Elders, then his gaze travels down the line of men and stops at one. He lifts his hand and points.

Chapter Thirty-Three

"You fucking psycho bitch!" Aren shouts. "We had a fucking deal, Junco! You wanted to do this, that insane memory bullshit is twisting the truth *again*! This whole thing was your idea!"

I walk towards him, my boots thumping hard on the glass table top. Aren pushes back from the table, but Slag is behind him so the chair pins him in. "Aren."

"You signed on, Junco! You signed on! We had a deal. You, your father, and me. This was always the plan, Junco, just *listen*!"

I stare down at him. "Tell me why I wanted my father dead, Aren."

He calms down a bit and his voice comes out in a low growl. "You signed on, Junco. It was all your idea."

"No, Aren. I don't think so."

"You wanted out of the RR and I said I'd take you. Your father wanted it, I wanted it, and you wanted it. You were done killing, Junco. And the MR said they'd take you. You wanted this."

"Even if I did, Aren, then I was insane at the time because I cannot even imagine a life like the one you're describing. Now, back to the question, why did I want my father to die?"

He stares at me, evil and hatred projecting out of him like the stench of a three-day dead mule deer out on the prairie.

"I already know you killed Charlie, Aren. You fucking coward. And I know you think I didn't recognize your voice on the phone the night he died. But the thing about my training that you assholes never understood is that while I might hide from the memories at times, they never go away. I can pick that shit back up. Any. Time. I. Want."

He moves his hand slightly on the arm of the chair and I shake my head. "Move one more fraction, Aren, and I chop your fucking head off."

He stops.

"Junco." The voice comes from Oran and I turn. "We—"

"LOCKDOWN!" The voice is mine, but the words don't come from my mouth. Aren has a small device up to his throat but drops it on the floor as he grabs my ankles and pulls, causing me to crash hard against the glass table. My head slams backward and I hear it crack. The air rushes in as the gash opens up and I feel the heat spill out and pool around me.

HOUSE has mapped the room in a laser grid to track every square inch of movement. "THIS IS A HOUSE LOCKDOWN PROTOCOL. YOU ARE BEING TRACKED. ANY MOVEMENT WILL RESULT IN DEATH. DO NOT MOVE, ANY MOVEMENT WILL RESULT IN DEATH."

Sam panics, pushes back from the table, and the lasers slice his body into thousands of pieces.

Aren stands up and from my position on the table I can see that the laser lines on his back are black. He's immune to the protocol because HOUSE is programmed to sequester the body that makes the LOCKDOWN command. This is a secret back door application that Aren should not know. I train my eyes on my own body and it practically glows bright green with targets.

Obviously I am not immune.

He sees my gaze and interrupts my thoughts. "That's right, Junco," he says, "I'm in control of the HOUSE now and your command has been overridden."

Now it is his turn to jump on the table and he struts down to the end and kicks Abe in the face. I listen to the body behind me slump, and then the rapid falling of a thousand body parts and they thunk on the tile floor. The action is so smooth and instantaneous that Abe's scream is caught in his throat. I can hear it exit his body as a puff of air.

"I knew you'd sell me out first, you fucking kiss-ass," Aren growls. "Anyone else have something to say?" Aren walks back to my prone body. He reaches down, casts a shadow of protection over my hand, and lifts the SEAR out.

It immediately shuts down. There isn't a chance of him using it against me, but it probably makes him feel superior. And then his finger flicks over the small imperfection and the arc of plasma is back. He sees the surprise in my eyes and laughs. "Ya know Junco, you're not bad to hang out with sometimes, but you are seriously the dumbest girl I've ever fucked." He stares into my eyes. "That's right, baby, palm imprints are not as secure as you might think."

He walks back down the table holding the SEAR up like a trophy. "Who wants to see Junco die by her own instrument?" No one answers, of course, and this pisses Aren off and he walks back over to me. "Nothing to say, Junco?" I stare straight ahead, as still as I can be. "You're really taking all the fun out of this, baby."

My eyes are drying up as I struggle to keep them from blinking. He bends down and I see him cast a shadow over my arms as he stares down at me. "Junco Coot, there is nothing special whatsoever about you, honey. Not your skills, not your freaky genetics, certainly not your looks, but your ability to believe, Junco. Now *that* is impressive. You're so fucking gullible." He laughs and I watch the shadow crawl up to my chin as he looks around at his prisoners.

I move my eyebrows up slightly to try and ease my discomfort from not blinking and he catches my movement. "Oh, poor thing! She can't blink! Who feels sorry for Junco? Oran?" Oran, his Viking heritage probably kicking in, grunts loudly at Aren, but he remains still because he remains alive.

Aren looks back down at me and I see the shadow cast over my bottom lip. I force myself to remain still. "Oran says I should let you blink, Junco. How about we make a deal? I'll let you blink and you let me fuck you before I deliver you to your next master?" He laughs, but his hand draws near my face, ready to cast a shadow over my eyes and let me blink. I feel the shadow more than see it and wait... over my bottom lip, my top lip, the edge of my nose—

"LULLABY!" I scream—the room goes completely black. I buckle my back and send him flying forward, face-first on the glass—the SEAR slips from his hand, powers down, and slides across the table and out of reach of both of us. I buckle again and flip up on my feet, turning, shadows in a panic all around me as we all try to get out of the room.

"Run, Junco!" Slag screams as I scramble across the table, leap over the shadow in front of me and aim my feet for the double doors as I fly sideways through the air.

It bursts open and I fall in a heap in the hallway, regain my footing, and book it, slipping on the slaughtered remains of any soldier stupid enough to move after the house went on lockdown.

I lose my balance and as I fall my hand slides into the slick pile of flesh and blood. Through a faint glow coming from the window I see Aren emerge from the conference room, powered-up SEAR in hand.

I clamber back to my feet and reach for the .357, emptying my magazine into the wall of confused MR soldiers near the front door. They dive sideways, and I burst through, out into the encroaching darkness and snowfall.

Outside is chaos and before anyone can figure out what's going on I run down the driveway and stop. I scream loud enough for the reporters at the gate, and probably the Sheffields down the street, to hear. "Come on, you worthless, traitorous piece of shit! Let's see what you've got out here." I hold the .357 up and sight it on Aren's chest as he walks casually down the stairs.

Far off down the driveway the reporters are scuffling over the walls to get their shot for the sphere. Aren's long legs cover the distance towards me surprisingly fast and I pray for a moment that I haven't underestimated him. I force the bravado one more time. "You can even use my own weapon, what do you say?"

He stops a few paces from me, the SEAR snaps as the snowflakes hit it, and he lets out a low laugh. "That's hardly fair, is it? You have a projectile weapon, while I'm all dressed up and ready to go for close combat."

He takes another step. My mind calculates the distance and it's not enough for the kind of effect I need out of the Boltblaster. "Sucks to be you, I guess," I say, slightly out of breath.

And another step, almost there. "You play a good bluff, Junco. I counted the shots back there, baby. The mag is empty."

I knew you would, ya bastard. "Then come and take it from me, Aren."

He rushes me and delivers a hard knock to my throat before I can get the Boltblaster from my holster. I go down. He's on top of me, hands around my neck in seconds. I immediately lock my legs around him in a tight guard, then drop it to the floor, slip my boot into his hip and push him off. I force his head down and send my knee into his teeth.

He drops back slightly stunned, and I reach for the bolt and fire. The two charged slugs exit the double barrel carrying the 9Mv charge. One grazes the inside of his leg, but the other slams into his thigh and he goes down, shaking like a junkie who missed his last fix. It'll have to do.

Another soldier grabs me from behind in a choke hold. I fire the Bolt, aiming at anything behind me, but it misfires. I toss it and bend my knees, back into him, drop my shoulder on the choke side, and flip him over. His eyes look up at me and then my boot stomps down on his face.

Three more appear. One attempts another choke while his companions each take a wrist. I fling my arms wildly and one guy loses his hold on my wrist. I flip the choker over my back and his body breaks the hold his other buddy has on my other wrist. I slide my feet back and wait for the next guy. He shakes his head at me.

I'm about to call him out when I hear the whine of a plasma rifle against my left ear. The static charge coming off the barrel sends the loose hairs around my face flying out in an electromagnetic field arc.

"Move again, Junco, I'm begging you. Because just thinking about killing you is making me hard, you stupid fucking bitch."

He yanks on my right shoulder and I slip in the snow and fall to the ground, slamming my back into the icy concrete. My lungs expel every breath of air inside me and I gasp trying to replace it.

Aren leans down and his eyes narrow into angry slits. The blood pours out of his split lip and drips onto my cheek and I wince. He pulls back his arm and slams his fist into my face, breaking my nose with a loud crack. The blood clogs in the back of my throat, cutting off most of my oxygen supply, and forces me to roll over on my side, coughing.

Several pairs of hands pull me up and hold me. Unable to follow the movement, my legs drag until one guy elbows me in the ribs and orders me to stand. I shuffle my feet until the soles of my boots find ground. Someone searches my pockets but comes up empty.

I hear the sharp crack of a suborbital entering the atmosphere and I smile, then spit a clot of blood onto Aren's shoes and wait for the next blow to find my face.

But he's lost interest in punching me. I'm yanked to the ground by various hands from behind and Aren steps over my body, his lips curled up in a snarl that says I crossed a line.

He drops to his knees, straddling me, as the soldiers painfully pin my shoulders to the frigid snow. His eyes shine in the faint light as he holds up the SEAR, fingers the arc down to a short stub, and inserts it into the skin just under my right ear.

Then slowly, ever so slowly, he drags it down my jawbone towards my chin.

I scream as small tendrils of flesh-saturated smoke rise up from my face, filling the air with the stench of burning tissue. The soldiers push my cheek into the snow and force me to hold still for the torture.

My mind shuts down and the world blinks out of existence.

Chapter Thirty-Four

Picture yourself standing on the edge of a dock...

Oh, I am so fucking there.

But I'm not standing, I'm lying down. I reach over and swipe my hand through the water and pull back a little at the glacial nature of the lake. The golden rays of the sun are raining down on me, but they make my whole body shiver. I try to open my eyes but Charlie whispers in my ear. "Stay down, Junco. It's not time to get up yet. Stay down."

I hear a small whimper and it takes me a minute to realize it came from my mouth. I try to answer but my jaw won't move. My hand makes a move up towards my face, but Charlie's voice is in my head again. "Not yet, babe. Keep still."

The whimper grows stronger and a cry erupts before I can stop it. "Shhhh, I'll tell you when." My hand falls back down to the dock and bumps into something cold and hard. "Grab it, Junco. But stay still."

My two remaining fingers close and my thumb passes over the familiar stone, marveling at how smooth it feels. It catches on a small notch and the tingle of an electric field travels up my arm.

"Stay still," Charlie repeats, "target is at 12:00, aim high. When you see the light, on your feet." The voice in my head goes quiet, but then I hear the faint whisper in my ear. "I love you, Junco."

I love you too, Charlie. I try to say it out loud but my mouth only lets a stifled moan escape.

I feel the kick of a boot in my ribs and I'm back on the ground, lying in front of my house as the wet snowflakes stick to my body. I hear a series of distant explosions and crack a reluctant eye open just in time to watch the faces of a half-dozen soldiers look north in wonder. My eyelid tires, falling back down as Aren barks orders to his men.

I am busy soaking up the vibrations from the scattering of boots around me when the sun explodes and Charlie's voice is back. "Now, Junco!"

My muscles, trained over and over in the same patterns, year after year, recall their conditioning and dig for the programmed memory of what to do.

The adrenal biogs shunt the epinephrine to my thighs and core, and then combine it all into one single synergistic act as I kick my knees back to my head, throw my body upwards, plant my feet on the ground, and extend the SEAR loop out to its full length of three feet.

Aren is standing at my 12:00—time slows down to a crawl and my world becomes silent—then my controlled breathing fills in the emptiness and I relax in a ready stance.

Aren's face turns towards me, his hand over his eyes, still recovering from the blaze of light flashed from above and I know I can kill him several times over if I want to.

But I don't.

Just once will do.

I balance and deliver a jumping spinning hook kick that makes his head snap, then follow through with the SEAR, dragging it across his brain stem and out the other side. I recover quick enough to watch his head fall to the ground and spoil the pristine white snow. A river of scarlet runs out and my eyes follow it with unabashed detachment.

The few soldiers remaining around me still have their mouths open as I wield the SEAR like a katana, approach the nearest one, and slice his chest open in a kesa move that continues into his buddy's hip and exits without a snag at his knee in a single downward swoop.

Their bodies leak fluids and tissue as they slink to the ground.

I turn and find my front yard in total chaos and the real world is shunted back into my forward consciousness as time speeds up again.

An alien ship is hovering overhead as I gather the facts of the scene before me. Bodies everywhere, some avian, most human. Plasma charge fills the air and lights up the darkness that threatens to suffocate the atmosphere below the massive ship. I look over towards the front porch and see Slag battling it out with a MR soldier and I break into a run, ignoring the agony as my face throbs with each boot fall.

The scream stops me in my tracks as I look up and then the black wings enshroud me into a cocoon of darkness as they push me to the ground.

My heart aches as I reach for him, but the face that stares down at me is unfamiliar. "Stay down, girl. No trouble from you now, I'm only following orders."

I let myself slump down onto my belly, almost beaten, and breathe heavy as I stifle down the pain, fatigue, and sobs, listening to the slaughter happening around me.

Minutes pass like this and then I feel the avian on top of me lift himself and straighten up. I hear Tier's voice and I push myself up onto my knees, grab the avian's outstretched hand, and allow him to stand me up.

Tier and Slag are screaming at each other near the porch. Tier pushes him and he falls backwards onto the steps and Slag puts his hands up as the massive avian descends on top of him.

"Stop!" I scream it and then break into a wail from the pain that escapes from the wound that has sliced my jaw open. "Stop!"

Tier straightens and turns.

Slag's face, full of pain like my own, seeks out my eyes, and I can see him breathe a sigh of relief as I approach slowly. I take one shaky step after another, trying my best to lock shit down.

"Please stop, Tier." It's barely more than a whisper.

He lifts his head back and lets loose a sound that would make any demon in hell proud. I sink to the ground and cover my ears as the wave passes through the air, down into my ear canals, and reverberates though my entire body. All around me the avians mimic his roar and it becomes a deafening chorus of anger and hatred. When it stops I stay on my knees and the nightdogs beyond the borders of the farm answer the call of the birdmen with their own blood-curdling wails.

When I look up he's at my side and I get a chance to see first-hand what an angry Tier really looks like. He is in uniform, like the rest of his people. Black armor covers every exposed part of his body, except for his unsettled black wings and his head. The wings are upright in a position I've never seen before—high above his shoulders and spread out slightly to make him appear bigger than he actually is. An offensive posture, a predator on the attack.

His face contorts into a look of pure hatred, lips curling up like a wild animal exposing teeth that are longer and sharper than they should be. His eyes are glowing so bright the light reflects off the snow. He watches me carefully as I study him and then walks away, out towards the center of the driveway, keeping his back to me. I retract the half-forgotten SEAR and stuff it under my shirt. Then crawl the rest of the way to the front steps, locking down the sobs.

I reach Slag and slump down next to him. Waiting, like the avians, to see what Tier will do next.

When Tier finally begins talking he is quiet and calm.

"And you have the audacity to use the word *humanity* to mean acts of concern and the alleviation of suffering."

He's not looking at me, so at first I'm not sure who his hate is directed towards. And then I see them. The reporters who scrambled over the gate hoping for a story tonight. One by one they peek out from behind the cluster of pine trees on the far side of the driveway.

"Humans did THIS!" he roars and the sound wave of pain comes back before I can shut it off. After a second or two it subsides and when I look up he's pointing at me, but his eyes remain locked on the cams as fingertips scramble to zoom in on me.

My face contorts as I try and push down the years of psychological damage that desperately want out. My chest heaves and it takes every ounce of inner strength not to hide my face.

Tier paces back and forth in front of the reporters, each finger winking red with the cams. His audience. "And ya call the avian *monsters?*" It's barely a whisper this time.

He turns and walks away and runs his fingers through his hair, gripping, as if trying to make sense of something.

Overhead the ship suddenly powers up and dozens of blue waterfalls stream down, creating a grid of light across the driveway. I watch as the avian pick up their dead and wounded and walk towards the lights and step inside. Tier stands in place, quiet and still.

One by one the avian are shunted upward into the ship and as they disappear, so does each occupied blue stream. I straighten up a little as I realize there is just one blue light left.

And just one avian left.

Tier's head hangs as he waits. Then takes one hesitant step towards me, lifting his eyes up to meet mine. And finally, he speaks directly to me.

"Junco."

I feel my lips quiver with sadness as I look at him and the tears start to spread across my cheeks. I get to my feet.

Tier lifts his head. "Darlin', let me ask you one more time. Have I hurt ya?"

I shake my head. "No, Tier."

"Have I been honest with ya?"

I nod and wipe the back of my hand across my face. "Yes."

"And has anyone here, to the best of yer memory, done the same?"

I follow his gaze to Slag, who drops his eyes.

I shake my head. "No. They haven't."

Tier nods then and looks back at the reporters who have crept up onto the driveway and are barely a few yards from where he stands. He looks at them straight on. "Do ya trust me, darlin'?"

I take a step towards him when Slag speaks. "Junco, wait."

Tier's head snaps back around and covers the distance between us in flight. The reporters scramble to stay with him and he lands in front of me.

I turn back to look at Slag.

"Junco, you don't have to go with him. I can make it right. You can morph here, I can make it right."

Tier's hands are wrapped around his throat before I can even blink and I hear a collective gasp from the reporters as they fall back.

"Let me clarify what happened here tonight, *Slag*." He drawls out his name in pure disgust. "The girl said stop and I stopped. Otherwise you'd be a bloodstain in the snow like everyone else, understand?"

I take a deep breath, but this time I sit it out and say nothing.

Slag gasps and Tier throws him back into the porch stairs where he coughs, but still continues his speech. "Junco, do you want to leave with him?"

I look back at Slag, then at Tier and let out a sigh as I bring my hand up to the wound on my jaw that has coagulated into a thick crust of blood. The reporters crowd in as I turn back to answer.

"I think," I start, but hesitate to find the right words as the memories come flooding back to me in a rush, and have to begin again. "I think that we might have been friends under different circumstances, Slag. If I wasn't—" I breathe out and Tier shakes his head at me, but I put up a hand and continue. "If I wasn't just another military experiment turned political pawn."

I look down at Slag and his eyes are glassy, but there's only one thing left to say to him. "Maybe you're a good guy, Slag. But somehow I doubt it. And maybe you did help me at the end, in your own way. But that's not enough. When I needed a hero, Slag, needed to be saved, you always had the means. And you turned your head with all the rest."

The reporters are right in front of us now, and I have to give them credit. Tier and I are definitely apexers, yet the vultures think they are safe among their brethren predators.

I glance away for a second, again sliding my fingers down my wound. "Now that I've got myself a little more in control, I think"—I feel them all, even Tier, lean in to hear my words—"I should have just let him kill you and been done with it."

My eyes drop down to his face and he draws his mouth into a line that shows no emotion. "I mean, at least he," I point to Tier, "is sorry for what you guys did to me. And he had no part in any of it."

Tier walks out towards the solitary blue stream of light and turns, then extends his hand. "Junco, if I could, I'd stand here for the rest of my life waiting on ya to be ready. Ya know that, darlin'. I'd wait for you ta choose. I would. Ya have ta know that."

I nod my head and smile.

"But it's not up to me anymore and I'm calling ya back. You need to come with me right now."

I walk out towards him and then stop and look back at the reporters one last time, straight into the blinking lights. "My mother has initiated an invasion of the Mountain Republic on behalf of the Subjectives. And I hope they kill every motherfucker who ever had a part in what they did to us down here. But make no mistake"—my eyes burn into the blinking fingertips—"if she can't quite get them all, I'll be happy to come back and finish the job."

My hand reaches out and I give him the words he's been looking for all along. "I trust you, Tier."

And then our fingertips touch.

I am swept into his arms under the warmth of his wings, and we ascend the shower of blue light together.

Chapter Thirty-Five

Imagine you feel completely safe for the first time in your life. Inside a shower of blue light that fills you up with happiness. And you rise, reaching out for your future, with complete trust in the one who carries you towards it.

That's me.

Now.

Tier hugs me close and we climb the scattered molecules of air until they drop into the depths. Then it is just us. I gasp as I try to pull oxygen into my lungs but it burns. And then Tier's mouth delivers a kiss of precious life and I let go, into blackness.

Somewhere, someone is carrying me. The jerky motion of my body and the pattern of curt boot steps on a metal surface echo in my brain and tells me we are moving quickly. All around me there are voices yelling, panicked. A mask covers my mouth and nose and then my lungs expand out in a burst as they fill with oxygen.

I come up swinging.

And coughing.

Hands restraining me.

Voices all around me.

"Not gonna happen, Tier—"

"— like shit, you sure—"

"— done it this time—"

"— don't know what it's—"

"— off! Now!"

But only one voice matters and I catch all of it.

"Junco, I've got you."

My head rolls back and my eyes open to the world that bobs around me. I can't make any sense of where I am until I spy the metal grates that serve as a spacecraft ceiling. I try to smile and say thank you, but the darkness looks pretty sweet so I let my eyelids fall and follow the call that beckons me.

Finally, my world is truly silent.

The voices come back eventually, but fewer.

Two.

I only recognize one.

"... telling ya it looks worse than it is, Layla."

"You think so?" The voice has a slightly different accent from Tier's. "Let's see," —I hear the sound of tapping on a screen as she talks—"more bruises and talon punctures than you can personally count, a hunk missing from her calf, a repaired rotator cuff, broken nose, a hairline fracture in the occipital lobe, some avian neurotoxin metabolites in her blood, a ten-centimeter gash down the side of her head, possible irreparable inner-ear damage, a ten-centimeter SEAR wound down the side of her jaw, plasma burn on her back, *two fucking fingers missing?*"

"Calm down, OK. Most of those are old, she's already healing—"

"Calm down? You've got to be fucking kidding me! These are only the recent injuries, Tier! She's one long battle scar from head to toe!"

In my head I wonder if he yells at her for swearing, too. Somehow I don't think so. A sound escapes my mouth and the screaming stops.

"She's waking up," the Layla voice says.

"See? I told ya. Junco, can you hear me?"

I cough.

"Junco, can you open your eyes?" A flash makes me squint and I force my lids up. The light flickers at them and reflexes take over, closing them tight. The light disappears and I try again. Layla's face is way down in my personal space and my arm instinctively comes up and pushes her back.

A laugh from Tier. "Told you, Layla. She's fine."

Layla looks to be a little older than Tier, which puts her at least half a dozen years older than me. She's got long black hair pulled back in a pony and is wearing what is apparently the universal uniform of doctors and scientists. The long white coat. Her dark wings are pushed up a little bit, the tips hovering just above her shoulders and the ends jutting outward past her waist. In Tier, I recognize this as an expression of unease, but who knows what it means for her. She steps back and crosses her arms in front of her, a severe scowl on her face. I cough again, then turn my head towards Tier and manage to croak out some words. "What happened?"

"Low oxygen on the ascent, Juncs. No big deal, right? Yer fine now."

"Tier, don't sell her that shit! She's not fine! She's also dehydrated and malnourished. Borderline starving, in fact!"

"Junco, when's the last time you ate, darlin'?"

I crinkle up my face and think. "Dunno."

Layla nods her head at this, vindicated. "She can't go under like this, Tier. She'll fucking die."

313

"Well, then goddamn it, Layla, fucking feed the girl! Hook her up with a line and push some fucking nutrients in her! We've got fifteen minutes to get her under and it *will* happen or so fucking help me God I will kill the fucking pilot and take us back to fucking Earth!"

I've never heard Tier string together so many profanities in one breath and even Layla takes a step back. She shakes her head at me and turns away, busy getting things to pump up my condition.

"Junco, did ya eat when you went home?"

I shake my head.

"Have ya eaten since the dinner we had?"

I shake my head.

"The fuck's the matter with ya, Junco? Why didn't ya eat?"

"Well, there was kind of a lot going on, Tier. It just never became urgent."

Layla's back with a line and a bag. She pushes the needle in my arm without asking and starts a drip. She looks down at my shirt. "What's that mean anyway? Snipers do it from behind?"

"Don't answer her, Junco, she's being an asshole."

"You mean I'm sticking my ass out for you two, don't you?"

He shoots her a look that would scare the shit out of me, but she sends one right back that is even more terrifying and I break a smile. "I like you, Layla," I say with a small laugh.

Her scowl melts and she smiles. "Everyone likes me, Junco. It's my natural charm." Then she reaches down and squeezes my arm.

My hand goes up to my jaw and I feel for the crusted blood, but it has been cleaned and a smooth membrane has been placed on the wound. Layla's eyes follow my motion.

"Was it coded for you, Junco?"

"I'm not sure. Probably."

Tier takes a deep breath. "I've seen the aftereffects of a non-coded SEAR wound, Layla. It begins immediately. She's coded. It's built into her." He slides my shirt up and then slides the rim of my pants down to reveal the SEAR knife on my stomach. "See?"

"What the hell is that?" She pulls back a little. "Is that the SEAR? Docked on her body?"

"Meet the United Republics' most discreet biological weapon."

Layla stares a lot longer than is polite and I pull my shirt down and push Tier's hand away.

"I'll have to recode her collagen gene to make sure. No sense taking chances."

She leaves to do that, I figure.

"What's really going on, Tier?"

He smiles, but it's thin. "Yer going into morph as soon as Layla gives the word, Junco. It'll take a few weeks to get to the Band, until then I'm still in charge of ya and they can't stop it. By the time we get there you'll almost be half through. They won't mess with ya until yer ready to come out. Then..."

I take a deep breath as he pauses.

"Then we'll have to wait and see. Junco, it might be a little rough at first, but I promise ya"—he places his hands gently on each side of my face—"it will be OK and they will not kill ya. So don't even think that is a possibility. It's too far along even now. They won't kill ya."

I nod, but he's talking himself up now. He can't say that for certain. I turn away and then feel guilty for my doubts. He put his neck out so I decide to trust him. Let him worry about it. Someone other than me, for once.

Layla yells from across the room. "Get her prepped, Tier. I hear boots shuffling outside."

His fingers begin unlacing my boots and he slips them off, dragging my socks along for the ride. Then reaches down and takes my hand and pulls me up on the bed until I am steady. He yanks the tucked-in shirt a little so the ends are all free and lifts it off over my head and lets me fall back slowly to the pillows. "Sorry, no clothes in the tank, Junco."

I stop his hands at my pants. "I can do it, Tier." I unbuckle and start squirming out of them. He grabs the legs and pulls, then grabs a sheet from the next bed and drapes it over me as I slip off my shorts.

A door chime diverts his attention as I fix the sheet around me, suddenly cold and shy of my body. He's at the door before I can even register that he's moving and I see it open a crack, then wider as another avian guy is allowed in. They talk in low whispers and every few words their eyes look over at me.

Layla is back with a tray of vials that she expertly attaches to the drip and pushes into the line. "You'll feel a little funny now, Junco. It won't last long, this is just the code we're gonna use to get things started."

"What will it do?"

She looks at me sideways. "Turn ya into one of us, hopefully."

"Is that a difficult thing to do?"

She laughs. "Impossible, for any other human. But for you, it should work. It's like they've been preparing you for this your whole life—hedging their bets, maybe. Almost all the sequences are already there, just turned off—if that makes sense."

I shrug and look back over at Tier and the other guy. His face registers now. He's the one who covered me during the fight on Earth. That thought shocks me, to think that we're not even on Earth right now. My sight starts to get a little dizzy, but other than that I don't notice anything weird. "Now, what happens?"

It gets a little heated over by the door and both Layla and I exchange looks. "Let's get you in the tank, Junco."

She helps me out of bed and walks me and my IV drip over to a cylinder tube that looks a little too much like the clone vats in Dale's lab for my comfort level. The goo inside is green, not red, but still.

She takes the sheet from me and holds it up like a little screen to shield me from the guys and nods her head at the tank. I shake my head back at her. "I don't know, Layla."

She smiles, but I can tell by her backwards glances that she's getting nervous. "Junco, I get it. It's weird. Shit, even avians have trouble accepting the morph sometimes, so I don't expect this to go easy for you. But"—she glances back at the door—"Ashur is telling Tier that they are planning on storming in here to stop this, so if you want to live, get your fucking ass in the tank."

I step in.

It's warm, and that makes it a little easier as I slink down into the goo. Layla bunches the sheet up and throws it across the room to get it out of the way.

"Good, now for the hard part." Her hands reach down and grab some tubing that is hanging off the machine. "Unfortunately, Junco, this is going down your throat."

She waits, probably to see if I will overreact, but my attention is diverted as Tier comes back, leaving the other guy standing at the door.

He forces his smile this time. "We ready then?"

Layla and I both answer at the same time, but we say vastly different things. The three of us stare at each other in silence for a few seconds. Then the tubing is coming at my face and I put my hands up to stop it.

Tier leans in and pushes my hands back down to my sides, thrusting his arms into the goo up to his shoulders. "Tier, I'm not—"

"Junco, we're doing this, there's no discussion, no out clause. It's happening."

"But—"

Layla stuffs the tube in my mouth and I begin to gag. She switches the machine on and it comes alive on my tongue, small fingers reaching out and crawling down my throat, spewing out goop in my windpipe as I feel it travel into my chest. I panic and begin thrashing, but Tier's arms hold me steady. I calm down a little as I realize I can still breathe and Tier smiles. A real one.

Their hands are on me, pushing a mask over my face and forcing my body under the green goo that covers my eyes and glues them shut. I lie still for several moments. Feel the grip ease up. And then I burst up and fight to pull the tube out.

I give it my best shot, but I go down anyway.

What can I say? If I have to go down, well, then I'll go down the only way I know how.

Fighting.

Turn the page to read the first few chapters of Fledge, Book Two of the I Am Just Junco series.

If you enjoyed this book please take the time to leave a review on Amazon.com, tweet about it, tell your Facebook friends, or recommend it on Goodreads.
It only takes a second and it helps indie authors like myself to spread the word.

FLEDGE
PROLOGUE

A bead of sweat tickles me as it slides down my ribcage, clings tight as it rounds the curve of my back, and finally drops to settle on the towel underneath my body. I squirm a little to shake the feeling and cool air rushes in where there was once only heat. I flip over on the towel and put my hands under my forehead and try to go back to sleep.

"You're gonna burn, Junco."

"Mmmmhmmmm. Maybe."

I jump a little as the cold squirt of lotion drops onto my back and rough hands begin massaging it into my skin. I pick my head up a little and mumble, "Thank you."

He laughs. "Believe me, it is my pleasure."

He moves his hands to the back of my legs and I laugh and kick him away. "Tickles, Charlie." He increases the pressure to make the tickle stop and I relax back into the small dent my body has made in the sand over the past hour. When he's done he sits back in the beach chair next to me and is silent. I peek up at him with one eye, squinting at the sun. "Quit it. It hasn't changed. Just ignore it."

He looks down at me and nods, but the words tell another story. "What do you think he's saying?"

I let out a huff and turn back around so I can look out towards the lake where the apparition floats, just a few feet off the end of the dock. "Who cares?" I look back up at Charlie, but he's still staring. "We can't hear him, so who cares, Charlie."

"Junco, if he didn't have something to tell you, he wouldn't be here at all."

I lay my head back down and mumble, "Not interested. Not one bit."

Charlie gives up and slides down next to me on the towel, slipping his arm around my body and kissing the back of my neck until I arch my back and giggle. "Let's go inside," he breathes in my ear. "He's giving me the creeps."

I smile and then I laugh. "He's a hologram, Chuck. He can't see anything. Shit, he can't even get the talking part straight. Just ignore him. He'll go away. Eventually."

But he ignores my plea. Instead, he grabs my hand and pulls me to my feet. Then swings me over his shoulder and starts running towards the cabin. My body jerks and bounces with each stride and I laugh so hard it hurts. "Oh, God! Stop! Stop!" I beg, but he just swings me over and plops me on the ground, then grabs my hand again and pulls me inside.

I fall down on the rumpled blankets and laugh as he crawls towards me from the foot of the bed. "No tickling!" I warn.

But he just takes my wrists and holds them over my head and leans down onto me. "No tickling? Since when?"

I laugh and squirm. "I'm serious." But he knows I'm not.

He gathers both of my little wrists into one hand and then slips the other under my back to unclasp my bikini top and covers my mouth with gentle kisses. "I love you, Junco," he breathes as he lets go of my wrists.

My hands go to his back and I draw my fingertips up towards his neck, making him buckle this time. They continue up into his blond hair and I pull his face towards me. I open my eyes and he's staring at me. "It's almost time to go, you know. That's why he's out there."

I shake my head as I search his brown eyes. "No, Charlie. I'm not going back. Ever."

He lets out a puff of air. "Silly, Junco. You can't live in a virtual when you still have a body. You have to go out so you can come back again."

My head is shaking before he is finished. "No."

His lips reach down to my neck and touch me softly. He leans into my ear. "Babe, I'll always be here. They can't ever take this away."

I feel the tears well up in my eyes and he lifts his head to study my face. "Shhh, not now, Junco. Now I just want to love you." His hands remove the loose top and then slide down my thigh and I moan and grab him tight and I thank God for every second we have together, every breath that escapes, and when the release comes I am bathed in the rays of total and complete happiness.

I wake later, when the moon is out and the wind has picked up enough to make the sheer curtains in the window blow in towards the bed. Charlie is gone and I am alone on the cool white sheets. I swing my legs over and dress in a large white shirt and some old denim shorts and make my way out of the bedroom. The moon is so bright that the ripple on the lake reflects the glow indoors through the picture window. I stand near the small kitchen and watch Charlie out on the deck, sitting down in front of the apparition of Tier.

My heart aches for him and for me, because he's right. Tier is here for one reason and one reason only. To announce the end of— whatever this is. My throat tightens up and I swallow hard to fight back the sadness. I walk out onto the deck, making just enough noise to let Charlie know I am out here, but he doesn't turn back to find me and the sinking feeling drops a little further into my stomach.

I walk down the steps slowly and then step into the soft sand that was never present at the lake cabin this virtual was based on. My toes sink in and I walk towards the dock and step on. Still, Charlie remains fixated on the holo hovering out over the water.

I can feel the vibrations on the deck as my feet touch down, and as I move out over the water the planks have a little more give than they do near the shore. Still, Charlie remains fixed.

I am halfway to the end when I hear the voice and I stop. It's Tier's voice. When he first appeared it was like the holo was stuck in a repeating pattern. No sound would play and we sat in front of it, just like Charlie sits tonight, and tried to read his lips. Tried to think of what he might be saying. Added in our own words, laughing at the absurdity of what we came up with. And finally, we just gave up and ignored him.

I cover the rest of the ground and take a seat on the edge of the dock. Charlie takes my hand and I lay my head down on his shoulder.

By then I already know what Tier's message is. He repeats the same two sentences, over and over again.

Trust no one, Junco. Show no weakness.

Trust no one, Junco. Show no weakness.

Trust no one, Junco. Show no weakness.

Trust no one, Junco. Show no weakness.

And I come out of it just like I went down. Swinging for the dumb fuck who just ripped me out of the happiest time of my life.

Chapter One

I burst out of the tank and the desperate gasp for air is like a prairie devil sucking up a farmhouse. My fists latch on to anything that will prevent me from going back under as waves of thick goo slosh around my body. Only the whine of plasma charge snaps me out of it and I allow a multitude of hands to grasp my arms and keep me still as the voice booms next to my head.

"Don't make me regret letting you live, Junco."

I cough and somewhere deep inside my vomit reflex is triggered. Shit comes up, clogging my airway and making me struggle against the firm hands. Since my eyes are still glued shut, I have no idea what comes out.

They pull me up out of the tank—completely out of the tank—so that I'm in mid-air for a few seconds, and then my feet hit the cold tile floor. My legs know what to do, but it's not happening. They drag me and I count six pairs of boots as we travel. Damn. Six fucking avians for me. I'm about to feel special when I'm dumped on the floor. A door snaps shut and I know I am alone.

A hydraulic click makes me twitch as my heart pounds in my chest. I take a deep breath and Tier's words come back to me. Trust no one. Show no weakness. I count to five to calm myself, breathing in and out, up and down, and then scoot on the floor until I bump into a wall. My hands flail out, finding a rail, then I pull myself up and force my legs to stand. My whole body shakes with fear, atrophy and cold, but the legs hold and I straighten my back, let go of the railing, and lift my chin.

And wait as the thick, sticky tank goo crusts in the ventilated room. My body feels lighter than normal and I realize that gravity must be less than one-G.

It helps.

A fine mist sprays out in all directions and I lift my arms up to let it coat me all over. It is only then, when my muscles are asked to respond, that I realize what's happened.

The smile comes out and I laugh, soft at first, then wildly, hysterical, and I turn my face upward to the drizzle as my lids are freed from their prison. Hot water blasts the soap off my body and I finally open my eyes.

I expel the fear.

I've been reborn.

The water drenches me and then I step back to wipe my eyes and look around, holding the handrail for support. It's a shower room, obviously. Small, but I can see through the clear surround that there are close to a hundred of them all lined up. Mine is the only one in use at the moment. I look through the glass to try and see if anyone is around, but the large room outside the stall appears empty.

My attention returns to my shower and I lather my new body with gel provided by a wall dispenser. When my hands touch my chest and upper back I gasp with the changes. My upper body is pure muscle. The smile creeps along my face as I imagine the new power this will bring to my old skills. I turn my head to try and see my wings but all I get is a glimpse of the tips as they roll over to cup my shoulders.

The water cuts off and the hot air blasts me in all directions, making my long hair fly up and whip around my face. Several minutes later the door opens with a click and my hair falls flat as the wind ceases.

I scan the room and count more than two dozen possible surveillance points, then step out and look down the long row of empty showers and start walking. At the end I find a small pile of clothes inside a cubby. One small square filled among hundreds that are empty.

I take the clothes and walk over towards a flat piece of furniture that sits low to the ground. I've worn Tier's shirts back on Earth, so I know it goes over my head. I fuss with the bodice, noticing that the missing fingers on my left hand are still missing (oh well, one can hope) and then the remaining digits automatically track to the SEAR wound that runs the length of my jaw on the left side. I drag a fingertip down the raised line of scar tissue and allow my mind to jerk back to the memory.

And then let it go.

It is what it is.

My attention returns to my girls, which need to be smashed down into the cups of the upper body garment. Tier's shirt never had cups and they feel heavier than I remember, so it's a struggle to get them to cooperate before sealing up the sides.

In the end it fits like it was tailored specifically for me.

The pants are made of the same black material as the top, synthetic, thick as light armor, and soft. They slip on easily up to my hips and it's only then that I notice my SEAR dock under my belly button is completely covered by skin. I touch it and the dock opens, revealing the small blue wand within.

I admit, I have to hold back my revulsion.

"Do not remove the weapon, Junco." The voice on the speaker is emotionless and direct.

I completely ignore it and slip the SEAR knife into my hand. My thumb flicks over the small imperfection near the tapered end and it comes to life with a buzz. Another smile graces my face. I flick it off and dock it, then look up and find what may be the closest surveillance point. "You went through all this just to kill me in the waiting room? I don't think so. It's mine and I'll take it out whenever I want."

I button my pants and move on to the socks and boots.

This time I'm stumped. My feet are no longer feet and I stare at them in awe. Or maybe confusion, I'm not quite sure. Four toes and they are extraordinarily long. All point forward, but the two outer toes seem to have a mind of their own and can point sideways and almost backwards, if I wiggle them enough. I get up and walk around a little, looking down as I try out the new digits. They move and adjust as I change my pace. The talons clack on the hard tile and I imagine what it would feel like to clutch things. I wrangle them back into the forward position and tug on the socks and boots.

When I'm finished a door opens and I walk through.

The space is empty except for a mirror long enough to allow hundreds of avians to gawk at their new bodies at the same time. I stand there, stunned at what I see. I flex my back muscles and the wings respond. One stretches out to its full length and then retracts and folds, cupping back over my shoulder. I squeeze the muscles a little and I feel them collapse completely against my back. It makes me look human for a moment and I grin back at my reflection.

My wings are not black. I get close to the mirror and try to see my back. They are a strange color—not white, not cream, not tan, not brown, not gray—a mottled mixture of all these hues. I squint at my eyes in the mirror, moving my head back and forth to get a clear look at them, expecting to see orange like Moju's or green like Tier's. But they haven't changed at all and a grunt of disgust leaks out of my mouth.

"Well, that fucking sucks. Not only do I still have hazel eyes, but you fuckers gave me hazel wings too." I look up, but get no answer. Then I whisper under my breath, "That is so fucked up."

I'm done looking, satisfied with the novelty of my new body, but the next door does not open. I think of how I should act so that I don't show weakness and decide on boredom. I lean my wings against the wall and then slide my back down until I'm sitting on the floor. I tilt my head back and close my eyes and my mother's voice is in my head. *Patience and inertia are not the same thing.*

She's right after all. So I wait. And think about where Tier is. Hell, where I am for that matter. Are we in the Band? I'm not really even sure where the Band is, but Tier talked about it before we left Earth a few times. And then my thoughts slip back to Earth—to Selia. Did she get the message out? To Slag—what did he do after we left? To Moju. My hearts aches for him and I let a little frown cross my face before I catch it.

This seems to be the magic signal that I am calm and ready to be rational, because the door opens and a man walks in.

He doesn't look avian. For a moment I wonder if I ever left Earth. But I feel the weight of the wings and the lightness of the less-than-G gravity and let that go. It doesn't matter where I am—I am no longer human.

He's not a friendly-looking man with his height and muscular bulk, not to mention the down-turned mouth and intense stare. His suit is black, tailored, and screaming money. His hair is fair and this too is different. So far all the avians I've ever met had black hair. Except me of course. My hair is still the same ugly auburn brown. His complexion is fair as well and his smile as he approaches me is forced.

I look up at him for a moment, then get to my feet and wait.

"I'm Lucan, Junco. Your new commander." His voice is deep and calm. Almost soothing.

"You don't look like a commander," I say, raising my eyebrows at him. For one, he's not that old. Maybe early thirties. And for two, he's wearing a fucking suit. I don't get it.

He gives me an indulgent smile, like I'm a toddler. "You've never seen an avian commander, so how would you know what one looks like?"

I watch his deep blue eyes as he talks, find the power there and make myself behave. "You're right. It's a pleasure to meet you, Commander Lucan. Should I salute? Shake? You'll have to forgive me, I am almost one hundred percent ignorant of your culture."

Another indulgent smile as he extends his hand. "We can do it your way, if you like."

I take his hand and shake it politely. "I would not like, actually. I would prefer to know how I am expected to act."

He retracts his hand. "We'll get to that in time. But for now I'd like to know how you came to be on my habitat when I gave a direct order to kill you two months ago."

I smile. "Oh, that's easy," I say, still grinning up at him, "I was invited, of course."

"Ah, yes, your invitation. Would you like to know where Tier is?"

"Not especially, no."

His brow furrows at my answer and I tuck down a smile. I can play too, buddy. Let's dance.

"Well, Junco, that surprises me. I think he would very much like to know where you are."

My stomach churns, but I shake my head. "No, I don't think so, Commander Lucan."

"And why's that, Junco?"

I shrug and turn my back to him and walk a few paces, testing out my wings and feeling my new talons move and be restrained inside my boot. God, no wonder Moju was barefoot. It's kind of annoying.

"I'm nothing to him. He's nothing to me. Why would we care what the other is doing?" I turn back and wait. *Patience is not inertia, Junco.* "He brought me back because I can be used and I came because, well—I'm sure you probably realize why staying on Earth wasn't a real option for me."

He smiles again. I don't. My face will crack if I have to keep up this fake shit much longer. He turns sideways towards the door and waves his arm, signaling for me to pass through ahead of him.

I do and I am met by six avian guards with their plasma rifles pointed at my head. I listen to their footsteps and decide they are the same guys who just saw me naked and covered in goo not too long ago and shoot them a smile.

They keep their aim true and ignore me.

Lucan and I walk side by side down a long hallway wide enough to drive a few tanks through back on Earth. My gaze stays straight ahead and I do not gawk up or around, but instead listen to our footfalls echo as we travel. The guards match our pace and they surround me in a semi-circle, walking sideways to target me.

I look at Lucan's face and he feels my gaze and directs his eyes down in expectation. "I think it's possible you've misjudged me, Commander. I'm just one small girl. Do you really think you need six heavily armed men plus yourself to control the situation? If so, you will seriously inflate my ego."

He sighs and I know the charade is over. "Junco, we know exactly who you are, what you do, and what you're capable of—so you will excuse my enthusiasm for protection until we can all come together on the same page. I ordered you to keep that weapon of yours," he hesitates as he points to my stomach and I squint up at him, "sheathed. Yet you insisted on removing it."

"Commander Lucan, that weapon is biologically attached to me. Taking it out and giving it a quick check was like wiggling my new toes. A simple reflex to make sure everything is working." I reach for it and the rifles emit an electric field so strong it pushes me backwards. "Cool it, guys. I'd be happy to hand it over if it makes you feel better."

"Hands off, Junco. You will not use that weapon here, do you understand?" I don't meet his gaze and I don't agree to his terms, so he continues, "I would take it, but it cannot stay away from you for long, we tried while you were under. It was—not ideal."

I shrug. "I lived without it for weeks on Earth."

"This isn't Earth."

Yeah, I think I'm getting that, thanks. "Well, you know, I can't help that the thing is attached to me. It wasn't like anyone asked if I wanted a biological weapon grafted onto my body, ya know."

He stops in the hallway and waves the men off a bit. Without the echo of boots the only sounds are the environmental units pumping out conditioned air. The guards step back but the rifles are still on alert. "Junco, I'm not playing games. This sweet-talking you gave Tier will not work on me. So save your breath."

I laugh out loud this time, I can't help it. He gives it a good shot, but he's unsure what to make of me and it shows. "Commander, I don't know who you've been talking to, but it certainly wasn't Tier if you think the reason I am alive and fucking up your habitat is because of my wily ways with men. Tier and I had no conversations about what he was and was not doing beyond a handful of words the very last time we talked."

Lucan's composure is back and his lip curls up slightly as he speaks. "Is that so? Well, Tier must be mistaken then, because he said something quite different."

I don't even miss a beat. "You're a liar. He never said anything other than what I just stated because that was the truth. And if you know so much about me, then you know that death carries very little meaning at the moment. You can try and kill me if you want—I don't give a shit. I have nothing to lose. You're no different than the assholes I left back on Earth and if you really want to know what I'm doing on your habitat, you better ask yourself. We both know I'm here because you want me for something."

I watch the guard behind Lucan raise his eyebrows at me and smile, then redirect my eyes back to Lucan's face and wait for his reply.

He turns and continues to walk and I catch up and walk by his side. We travel in the echo of our footsteps once again and then he stops at a door, palms his hand over the biometrics and it slides open. He waves me in and I step through, but he stays where he is.

"Goodbye for now, Miss Coot." The door closes.

Chapter Two

I turn and find Layla gaping at me from the far side of the room. I look up and around and she smiles and waves the thought away. "No cameras allowed here, Junco. I'm so glad to see you!" She walks over to me and hugs me to her chest.

I return her hug and push her back. "What did they do to Tier?"

She winces at his name and shakes her head. Her mouth drops downward as she speaks. "He's fucked, Junco. On trial for treason."

I stare out at the room for a moment, stunned. Treason. That is the worst. I shake it off and study the room. It's a cross between a lab, a clinic, and a hotel. It screams Junco's new vivarium. I pull a chair from the table and sit across from Layla as she waits patiently for me to settle. The chairs are strange, with only a thin backrest, but as soon as I lean back I understand why. It supports my spine without crimping or impinging on my new wings. I slouch a bit, even though the straight back makes it difficult, and feel very tired and sad. Since Tier's warning instructed me to trust no one, I have to presume that Layla will deliver reports on my moods and behavior and force a neutral expression as I wait for her to give me some sort of explanation.

She smiles and then lets out a long breath. "When we discussed everything that could happen when we brought you back, Junco, treason never even entered the realm of possibilities. But"—she hesitates—"here we are."

"What were the possibilities?" I ask as I avert my eyes and study the furniture. In the living area there is a bed, a desk, a large screen on the wall, and a bedside table. I see a door that might lead to a bathroom. That takes up about a quarter of the space.

About half is devoted to medical and lab equipment—centrifuges of various shapes and sizes, some molecular cloning machines, glassware of course, a bench lined with bottles of chemicals, buffers, pipettes, books, a plate reader, cell sorter, a few medium sized coolers, a hood for tissue culture, four microscopes, a gleaming stainless steel minus-80 freezer for samples, and lots of other stuff that looks like it belongs in a research facility. Let's just call it a well-stocked, scratch that, a well-funded lab.

The other corner has a counter that holds canisters filled with paper goods, 2x2 gauze, cotton-tipped applicators, shit like that. There is also a built-in sink and glass front cupboards that hold enough drug canisters to treat a small town back in the RR.

"Demotion, mostly. We thought maybe if we were really fucked they'd kick us out of the Aves. We spent quite a few hours talking about what we'd do if they did."

My brow furrows and I try and put it together. "Are you and Tier—together?"

Her smile is crooked. "No, Junco. I'm on his team, his scientist. We've been together, hell, since he came out of Fledge really. Not counting that stint I did on Lacerion for post-training in moleculars."

"Sorry, I feel a little lost here, ya know. I have no idea who he is, only that I agreed to let him bring me here. We never discussed anything that might happen afterward, so—"

"We figured you'd be like a bonus—one of the Seven that we thought was lost but wasn't. We were pretty sure it was gonna work fine, Junco. It's not like we were just yanking ya on that end. And it did, right? Look at ya! So pretty."

Her sudden pickup of Tier's speech patterns makes me swallow the sadness once again. "I don't like the color, to be honest."

"Really?"

She looks a little hurt and I wonder if she made me this way on purpose, but it's too late now and I just shrug. "I like the black wings. These," I say, peeking back at their almost yellow paleness, "feel like a target."

"Oh, well. Sorry. I think they're beautiful. And I bet everyone else does too. You'll see. Anyway, the whole purpose of being on Earth was to get the Seven and bring them back. We knew you were the Seventh," her fingers do little air quotes, "and the Seventh Sibling is not well-liked around here in theory. But we discussed this for days before we came to the decision, Junco. I'm pure because someone made me that way. Ditto for everyone else. So, if someone altered you as you grew up, and they did—we know this—then how can you not be pure? Just because your alterations took place after birth, why should that make any difference?"

I look away at her question because I don't want to think about anything right now, least of all my avian biological status. "So, what went wrong?"

"After we put you under we let the others come in, but you were undergoing the morph, so you had special protected status. It's a vulnerable position. Being unconscious for weeks on end, helpless and under the control of your medical staff. They couldn't do anything to you then. They just had to wait it out."

I don't want to ask the question, in case someone is listening or Layla is taking notes on my questions, but I do anyway. "And Tier?"

She shrugs. "He's ranking officer, so they couldn't do anything to him either, unless they wanted to mutiny, which they didn't. But, well, everyone has a boss. And Lucan was beyond pissed when we arrived in the Band. They arrested Tier immediately."

"The charges," I ask, still avoiding her eyes, "are treason?"

She nods and gives me a half-hearted crooked smile when I finally look over at her.

"Because he didn't kill me."

This time she doesn't acknowledge me, just releases a deep breath.

"Anything else? Charges, I mean?"

"Something to do with breaking a treaty. And the old stuff, the unauthorized murder charges. He was on— like a probation—and they revoked it for this last charge."

I nod and get up and walk across the room to the bed. "This for me?"

She nods but doesn't rise.

"And all this?" I say, pointing to the medical equipment.

"Tests. Not today though, it's late and I'm sure you're still tired. And," she hesitates, "maybe it will help to know that these feelings you're having right now, the sadness and lethargy? It's normal, Junco. We all get this way after morph. It's an endocrine reaction, the changes really fuck you up. So whatever you're feeling right now, just give it a few days, OK?"

I sit on the bed and start unlacing my boots.

"We'll have to have guards in here with you at all times, just for a little while, though."

I shake my head without looking up and write her off for good now.

"Ashur is taking the night shifts and Braun is taking days."

I remove the boots and the socks and finger the blister that has formed on my right foot after the short walk from the showers and I wonder for the first time how I will hold up in this new environment.

Layla stands up and walks towards the door, then turns back. "It'll be better tomorrow. We'll do the tests and then you can leave here. You'll see."

I lie down on the bed and turn my back to her.

"See you tomorrow. Ashur's outside, you remember him? From the battle at your house?"

I ignore her.

"OK, well, I'll send him in on my way out."

"Layla?" I ask without turning to look at her.

"Yes, Junco?"

"Why aren't *you* on trial for treason?"

"I'm his subordinate, Junco. He's my captain. I could no more deny his order to save you than anyone else on the ship."

I close my eyes and never even hear the other avian enter because I simply shut down and go looking for the dock.

But it's gone.

So I settle for nightmares. They come easy. History repeating.

I toss and turn in the bed as my nose wrinkles with a familiar but out-of-place smell. It fades and my dream takes me to my bedroom where I lie on the bed in my shorts and puff on a cigar, happy with who I am.

Wait.

That wasn't a dream, that was real.

Where am I?

"Junco?"

The strange voice triggers my reflexes. The SEAR comes out from under my shirt and I'm standing on the bed in attack mode before I can even process all my actions.

The large avian is bent down in a defensive stance, his plasma weapon pointing up at my head. "Junco! Put it down, now!"

"Fuck!" I let out a long sigh and retract the SEAR and slip it back into the dock. "What the fuck?"

He watches me step off the bed and stand on the other side of the room, but he does not lower his weapon.

"Ashur?"

He nods.

"Put your fucking weapon away or we're gonna tangle."

"You cannot take that knife out, Junco. Ever. If you do, you're going to get hurt."

I shake my head at him. "It's docked. What more do you want? Put your weapon down, Ashur—or we will fight."

He stands upright and slides his weapon in the holster that hangs at his hip. My eyes trace the familiar smell that woke me and I lean to look past the formidable avian. A smoldering cigar is sitting in an ashtray on the table. "You did that on purpose."

He gives me a crooked smile. "I know you like them. And I was bored. Can you think of a better way to be woken up?"

I just stand there, kinda pissed. "Well, yeah, actually. There are about a thousand better ways of being woken up than having some strange guy in my room smoking a cigar that reminds me of home. Thanks."

Ashur walks over to me and takes my arm and leads me over to the table where he was sitting before I went commando on him. He points to the chair and slides a cigar over. "Here, have one. Relax a little, shit. You're so jumpy."

I don't have it in me to protest and the little gray box that holds the cigar is calling my name. I slide it out, press it to the striker, and puff. "Thanks."

He takes his seat and I do the same, then we both puff in silence as we watch the screen on the far wall. The sound is off, but it's the news so the captions at the bottom of the feed tell all you need to know. I guess some things never change, no matter what world you're on.

"What time is it?"

"2 AM Standard, why? Got plans?" His lips attempt to smile around his stogie.

"What time did I fall asleep?" I say as my attention goes back to the screen.

"Eight or so."

I nod. "Oh."

"Done sleeping then?"

I look back at him. He could be Tier's brother, that's how similar they are. "Probably."

"Want some breakfast?"

"No." Just the thought of food makes me want to heave.

He takes his cigar out of his mouth. "What do you mean, no? You haven't eaten in almost two months."

"Obviously that's not true or I would be dead. I'm definitely not hungry."

He's still holding his cigar in his hand, not puffing. "I've already been warned about your eating habits, Junco. I'm in charge of making you eat breakfast, so we're having some."

I screw up my face at him. "I can't think of a single person who would even know what my eating habits are, Ashur. So spare me."

"Both Layla and Tier mentioned your lack of enthusiasm for food."

I snort out a laugh. "And how they hell would they know?"

"They said you were severely undernourished when we took you, that's how."

"Which means nothing. You guys got to see the tail end of what a very bad week does to my appetite, so what? I wouldn't base anything off what I did that week, let alone assume I have an eating disorder."

"Good, then we'll have eggs for breakfast."

"Knock yourself out, Ashur." Just stop fucking talking to me, I don't add.

He gives me a look of superiority, like he won the argument or something, then pushes back his chair and exits the room through the door I thought was the bathroom last night.

I stub out the cigar and go back to bed watching the newscreen. It's all in English but it shows a lot of stuff that makes no sense. Winged people fighting each other. Killing each other actually, in what looks to be an advertisement for an upcoming arena fight of some kind. Some more winged people having a party. Some people with no wings in what looks to be a government session. Some personal interviews. I just sit there in disbelief. I didn't watch the screens much at home, only when on the road, but it's all a little too familiar. I traveled hundreds of millions of miles, I'm on a totally different planet, habitat, whatever, and still the news is filled with the same shit. Violence, parties, and politics. The irony isn't lost.

Ashur returns a few minutes later with eggs and toast and beckons me to the table. At least it's real food and not that shit Tier tried to feed me in the cave. It doesn't look horrible, but my head shakes out a no as he slides the plate in front of me. I keep the disgusted look as I meet his eyes. "If you make me eat that I'll throw up."

He shrugs and takes his seat, shoving food in his mouth before he even settles. "It's good, real eggs and everything. Tier said you only eat fresh food, so lucky us, right?" He shoots me a smile.

"Tier would have no idea, Ashur. He saw me eat a total of three meals."

"He's the resident Junco expert, like it or not, what he says goes. Might as well enjoy the food, Fledge food is like military field rations."

I force myself to eat three bites and push the plate away.

"Ya know, you don't have to make everything so difficult, Junco. You can have it made here, if you want."

"And what would I have to do in order to have it made?"

"Follow the program," he meets my gaze, "and just do what you're told for once."

"For once? You're an asshole." I let out a deep sigh, get up, and go flop down on the bed and bury my face in the pillows. "I'm sorry I came here."

I hear him set his fork down and push back from the table and look up to see what he's doing. His head is in his hands. A gesture that reminds me of Tier when he was thinking out at the cabin, right before he told me that he killed my father.

"Ya know something, Junco, we're probably all sorry you came here. Except one person, maybe. And that's Tier. So for fuck's sake, try and do what you're told for his benefit. The guy's sitting in prison for saving you and"—he lifts his head and stares at me with bloodshot eyes—"and if I had it my way, Junco, I would have killed you myself in order to save him from that."

He stands up and walks to the door. "If you need something, I'll be outside until Layla comes."

Good job, Junco. Making friends already.

Chapter Three

Layla is busy getting the equipment ready as I watch from the table. "Ashur's mad at me." It slips out because I can't stop thinking about what he said.

Layla talks to me under her breath between curse words directed at the control panel. "Well, Junco, Ashur is not the sanest guy in the Cluster. He's always been a little touched, don't take it personal."

"He said he should have killed me to save Tier."

She looks up this time. "What?"

I shrug with my hands. "That's what he said." I watch her face as she processes this, expecting her to say something, but she doesn't. She just looks back at the machine, apparently in agreement with the guy who's a little bit touched.

I change the subject because the thought of both of them wanting me dead to save their friend is a little too unsettling. "So what does this test do anyway?"

She curses for a few more seconds before answering. "We gotta map you again. I took some images while you were under, but it was hard to see everything. This way we'll have a good baseline at what we're looking at."

"What are we looking at?" I ask.

She stops this time and gives me her full attention. "Sorry, Junco—I forgot that you haven't seen it yet." My heart thumps as I wait for the reveal. "I've never seen anything like it before, but—"

"But?"

345

"You've got a lot of technology inside you. Like everywhere. In fact," she's just warming up, I can tell, "your entire nervous system is controlled by circuits that reside outside of your brain and peripherals. Like in your hands—there's a whole pad of circuits in the palms of your hands. And that SEAR dock?" She stops to shake her head. "I have no idea what that is."

I let out a grunt. "That's awesome."

She ignores me and goes back to the machine. Thirty minutes later I'm naked and standing behind the transparent shield that will allow Layla to see inside me.

She describes the process, how it will feel, and how long it will take but my mind is on Ashur. I feel the need to set this right for some reason. He was the only person Tier allowed in the room with us right before they stuck me in morph and he was the person who shielded me from the battle that happened in my driveway. I don't have to trust him, but I don't have to make him hate me either. And some small part of me secretly wants him to leak out more information about Tier. I wonder if Tier even knows I'm out of morph?

I stand as still as I can as the lights begin to pass over my body. When it's over I get dressed and flop back on the bed to wait for the confirmation that I am a freak. When she resurfaces and calls me over to her I can sense her hesitation.

"See this?" she says, pointing to a large white splotch superimposed at the base of my spine in the full-scale image of my body.

I nod.

"That's your endocrine biog."

"OK, that's not so weird, is it? I mean, Tier said my biog protocols were on that cube."

"Right. No, you're right. The biog isn't weird, hell, I have one too. But…" She stops and looks at me. "Junco, this thing controls your whole body. Your glands don't make the hormones, this thing does."

I shrug, not seeing the big deal. "Anything else?"

"Well, actually yes. See these?" She points to more white blotches on the image, one at each joint of my bones, and more throughout my body.

"Yeah, and?"

"Most of these are in the same place as your lymph nodes, or where the lymph nodes would be."

"Layla, get to the point, OK. I'm not an anatomy expert and I don't feel like digging down to find the memories from school."

"OK, well, you don't process your blood in the same way as most people. It gets shunted through these other things, and then these"—she points to the many white lines running up and down my legs, arms, and trunk area—"take it to the muscles," she points, "the lungs," more pointing, "and then finally back to the heart where it interacts with this"—she screws up her face and raises her eyebrows—"master circuit."

I just stare at her blankly.

"Junco, you're half machine."

I grunt. Of course I am. And why wouldn't I be? My body was altered since I was a toddler, I should have seen this one coming. "You're fucking crazy," I say instead.

She shrugs and snaps the image off the viewer and takes it back into the lab. I follow and watch as she rolls it up and stuffs it into a tube.

"What are you doing?"

She scowls at me. "I have to take this to Lucan right away. Braun will stay with you until I come back."

And before I can protest or demand to know what that will mean to me, she's gone and a guard enters to take her place.

He's tall, like Tier and Ashur, but not as dark and more muscular. Both his wings and his hair are more brown than black and I recognize him as the smiler from yesterday's hallway showdown with Lucan. He looks thrilled to be invited in, so I try not to make an enemy.

"Wanna sit?" I ask pointing to the table.

"I'm Braun," he says as he takes a seat.

"Junco."

"Yeah, I know. Was with you when you were picked up from Earth."

"Oh." I stop, trying to see if I recall him, but I have no memory of anyone but Tier, Layla, and Ashur.

"That was pretty funny the way you talked shit to Lucan yesterday." He laughs. "I bet it's been a long time since anyone's talked to him like that."

"Oh," I say again. "He hates me, doesn't he?"

The avian smiles and his eyes glow a little orange. "Lucan hates everyone. He's an Archer." A shrug. "No sense of humor, those guys. So what have you been doing in here all day?"

I walk over to the screen and pretend to watch the news. "Tests."

"Did you pass?"

I look back at him, trying to decide if he's serious or not. If pushed, I'd peg him as a guy who doesn't get serious unless he's forced, but he looks sincere. "No, I don't think so."

"Wanna tell me about it?"

"No, not especially."

"Wanna play cards then? Pass the time?"

"I don't know your games, so—"

He pulls a deck out of his jacket. "You're a soldier, Junco, all soldiers can play poker."

I laugh. "Oh, well, OK."

Braun is the first normal guy I've met in a long time. We get along and there's no arguing and he doesn't pretend to be better than me or even seem bothered that I have the SEAR tucked under my shirt. We play using 2x2 gauze as chips and it only takes a few minutes and I'm laughing. He's got a nice sense of humor and when he asks me if I'm hungry he doesn't lecture me when I say no. But he does leave to get some food and when he brings it back to the table I am hungry and it's not bad.

We've been playing for hours and I owe Braun six thousand rills, whatever that is, when Ashur enters. Braun smiles and stands up, counting his cotton wipes to double-check his winnings. "I cheated her out of enough paper products to buy a new house, Ash." And then he laughs. "See you tomorrow, Junco, I'll bring beer for the next game."

Ashur just raises his eyebrows. "Braun, don't—"

"Ah, shut up, man. And get off her back, she's stressed. Make her happy, why don't you?" Then he looks at me. "We'll have fun tomorrow, Juncs." And then he walks to the door, his weapon slapping his thigh with each step as he leaves.

I'm still smiling when I look over at Ashur and force myself to dial it back down.

"You'll want to stay away from that one, Junco."

"Why?"

He shakes his head. "He's trouble."

"Oh, I see. He's trouble, yet I'm the prisoner, Tier's on trial for treason, and you wish you could kill me. Well, thanks for clearing all that up." The tension is back and I miss Braun already. I walk over to the bed and flop down.

My desire to make things right with Ashur is gone with the return of my sour mood.

He walks into the lab and takes a minute before coming back in the living area and sitting down at the table. His back slouches and his long legs sprawl out in front of him. "I spoke to Tier today."

My heart skips, but I don't answer him.

"He asked about you."

I turn my back to him and let out a big sigh.

"Do you want me to tell him anything if I see him again?"

"No."

"Do you care to explain that, Junco? I mean, the guy is on trial for you, the least you can do is send a message to say hi."

I turn back. "You know something, I'm beginning to wonder how well you actually know him. The Tier I know does not want to hear from me right now, Ashur. And you're lying if you tell me he's sent a message, because I know for a fact he wouldn't do that. So stop with the bullshit, OK?"

He shakes his head and turns his attention to the screen. We don't speak another word to each other. I don't set anything right. And Ashur makes no attempt to make me happy. I lie there for a long time before falling asleep.

I wake in the middle of the night again. My sleep is way out of whack. Ashur is still slumped in his chair, one arm crossed over his chest, his fingers playing with his shirt on the opposite shoulder while watching the screen.

He's got a cigar box in his other hand and he taps it gently on the table until he notices me looking at him.

"Cigar?" He extends his hand out and I lean over and take the little gray box, shake out the stogie, and light it up.

"Thank you."

He hands me an ashtray and I prop myself up in bed and set it on my stomach. He's watching a screen about a girl who is being chased by some psycho murderer on an abandoned habitat. Despite myself, I get into the drama. I can see the draw of mindless entertainment, even though I can count on one hand the number of screens I've seen all the way through in my lifetime.

We sit in silence until the credits roll and then he speaks. "I'm sorry for saying that shit, Junco. I don't want to kill you. And we all like you, we don't wish you never came home."

I stare at him until he looks me in the eyes. "You need to butt out of my life when it comes to Tier, Ashur. It's over. He sent me a message"—I hesitate—"and like I said, he never told you to tell me anything, did he?"

He shakes his head. "No. He didn't. But it doesn't make sense, I watched him put you under in the morph, and you two weren't fighting."

"It doesn't matter, does it? It's over."

We sit in silence and watch the screen as another show comes on. "I've seen this one," Ashur says when it starts. "It's not bad."

We watch it and chat some. After a little bit I fall back asleep and when I wake in the morning he's gone.

Layla and Lucan are standing over me, talking in avian. I squint up at them and try to string the words together. "I'm right here, you know."

Both sets of eyebrows go up.

"Yeah, I understand too, so that shit you just talked about me is not going over well." I push up and extract myself from the bed to go take a shower and when I'm finished, I find a closet full of clothes. It has five identical outfits to the one I was just wearing.

And one that makes me smile.

I tug on the camo fatigues and button them up. They are looser than they were when I put them on last and I make a mental note to try and eat more. Then I wrestle the shirt over my back and stretch and rip at the arm holes of the sniper shirt until I can jam my wings and arms through. I realize I look ridiculous, but I don't care. My old field boots are in there too, but there's no way they will fit on my new hulking feet. Besides, I'm feeling Moju's affinity for going barefoot.

When I walk out of the bathroom Lucan and Braun are at the table talking and Layla is in the lab clanking glassware around.

Braun laughs. "Snipers do it from behind? They saved that for you?"

"I knew you'd appreciate my shirt, Braun." His eyes dance as he laughs again and I catch myself wondering how long I'll have to wait until we can play cards.

Lucan interrupts my daydream. "Layla, Braun. Junco and I need some private time, please."

Braun winks at me as he passes. "Beer's in the fridge, Juncs." I absently wonder if I'm old enough to drink on this habitat or if Lucan will frown on that, but he stays seated and points to the chair Braun just vacated.

"Layla has some interesting developments from the tests yesterday. Do you know what it means?"

I shake my head, but keep silent.

"You're not human."

He waits for my reaction, but I hold it in.

"You're not avian."

Nothing.

"You're not machine."

I laugh now. "OK. So what am I?"

"All three, apparently. It's highly unusual."

I squint, but do not avert my eyes. "Will you kill me now?"

It's his turn to stay silent. We stare, willing the other to speak. I have nothing to say so I am patient until he gives in. "That will be entirely up to you, Junco."

"How's that work, then?"

"We have a strict, structured society here. A lot of people must share space in the hundreds of habitats we have scattered throughout the Band, but habitats are not easily made and resources are precious. Do you understand this?"

"Yeah, of course."

"When we create the clutches of children we do so with the entire population in mind. We try to make them into their genetic ideals but not all of them will be able to reach their full potential. Which is why after they go through the morph they must go through Fledge. Do you know what Fledge is, Junco?"

I shake my head.

"It's a test of sorts. To see which individuals can fulfill the potential bestowed upon them. Everyone you've met so far has succeeded in Fledge. Proved themselves worthy."

Tier's words on the rock on Earth come back to me, *She's worthy. That's what I thought. She's worthy—it's just that no one recognizes it yet.*

"And there is a very simple test to determine if you're worthy or not." He stops and waits for me this time.

"Which is?"

"In this case it is a series of fights. That's what Fledge is. A series of fights to the death."

"So you want me to kill people in order to prove myself."

He nods. "Your clutchmate, Esta, went through Fledge a few years ago. So she earned her place. And if you want to stay here, you must do the same."

I shrug. "OK."

"You may not use the weapon."

"Lucan," I snarl his name, "seriously, if you think the most dangerous thing about me is that stupid weapon, you are grossly mistaken."

"There is one more thing."

"And that is?" I ask, looking at him sideways.

He hesitates and I notice the slightest crack of a smile beneath his facade. "You must testify against Tier."

"No problem." I catch his shock like a firefly in a jar and tuck down my satisfaction.

He physically moves backward. "And you will tell the truth."

"I always tell the truth, Lucan."

He regains his composure. "Very well. I will set it up."

"You do that," I say to his back as he exits the room.

You do that, Lucan. And I'll do the same.

End of Book Shit

Things you should know:

My editor rocks. If there are a few typos in here, it's all me.

If you liked the book—please leave me a review. :) I'm an Indie, I seriously need them. No matter how many reviews my books have, I still need them. It only takes a minute and you'll be helping me get some attention as well as helping other readers find books they might like.

I write romances too. So if you like love stories, try my Rook and Ronin series.

Finally—thank you! I appreciate you taking the time to read my stories and I hope they entertain you and maybe even make you think a little.

ABOUT THE AUTHOR

JA Huss is the USA Today best-selling author of the Rook and Ronin series, the epic science fiction I Am Just Junco series, and hundreds of kid-friendly science books in subjects such as biology, physics, anatomy and physiology, astronomy, and forensics. She has an undergraduate degree in equine science and a master's degree in forensic toxicology. She has never taken a creative writing class and she hopes she never will.